BETWEEN

DUTY

AND

DEVOTION

BY

M. J. BRETT

To Clara —
Best wishes
Margaret J. Brittschneider

Blue Harmony ♫ **Press**

Blue Harmony  Press

528 Southern Cross Drive
Colorado Springs, CO 80906
EbrettMBour@aol.com

First Printing, October 2006

Copyright by M. J. Brett

Cover Photography by Ron Hosie

Printed in the United States of America

Without limiting the rights under copyright reserved above, no part of this novel may be reproduced, stored in or introduced into a retrieval system, or transmitted, in any form, or by any means (electronic, mechanical, photocopying, recording, or otherwise), without the prior written permission of the copyright owner.

This is a work of fiction. Names, characters, and incidents either are the product of the author's imagination or are used fictitiously. Events have been rearranged and/or compressed in time, and characters have been combined and fictionalized. Except for public figures or musical artists of the era, any other resemblance is purely coincidental.

Acknowledgements

An author has an idea, or in this case, curiosity and questions, and must work these through to a finished project. Though the writing itself is a solitary endeavor, many people help clarify details or talk out ideas. By way of research, several friends freely offered private letters, diaries, journals, and even divorce papers. Taken altogether, they helped create the fictional and unconventional love story of good people who never meant to hurt each other, but who did anyway. Sometimes the best efforts fail when subjected to unusual pressure and human emotion. These are not real individuals, but a composite of all those whose marital lifestyle has caused them pain.

Special thanks go to my husband, Eric, and to our family who have encouraged me in storytelling, and to taskmasters from my two critique groups, Sue, Cindi, Marcella, Joan, Irmgard, and another Sue, who kept me on target. The "real Neil" (actually a composite of five officers) offered precise details for the Epilog. Thanks to Ron Hosie for a photo cover that brought out both the patriotism and the responsibility of our Army Officers, and to patient friends from Cheyenne Mountain Newcomers, Curves, and Department of Defense Overseas teachers whom I've cornered constantly for help with a title. That seems to be the hardest part.

Special credit is due military friends who helped me track down factual events and technical data, from training information to acronyms, and to those who wanted readers to understand both the deception and devotion that exists, and the role duty plays in any relationship.

Dedication

Some years are tougher than others, and 2006 has seen the loss of many loved ones. My heart goes out to their families and friends. This novel of love and loss is dedicated to all of them:

My 94-year old mother, Mary Jean Brant,
My dear smiling Irish friend, Col. Alvin F. (Big Al) Murphy,
My dear history-loving friend, BG Gerald C. (Jed) Brown,
Fellow military wives Jeri Bronham and Carol Trapp,
Fellow DoDDS teachers John Peterson and Babe Reisinger,
Enzian Club members Art Johnson and Vic Myers
Skyway member Ann Merrigan,
Swimming buddy Sharon Gibson,
CMNC friends Hildegard Still and Pat Kimak

All loved life, offered lives of dedication and service to others, and will be sorely missed. *Any* time to lose them would have been way too soon.

Rest in peace, dear ones

Prologue – 2005

The couple sat quietly on the back veranda, slowly rocking and staring at the outgoing tide as though it could answer all their questions.

A solitary loon bobbed on the current, occasionally ducking beneath the waves to search for fish, while an osprey sailed majestically overhead, no doubt looking for his evening meal before nightfall. No sound intruded on the pair's solitude except the lapping of waves on the rocky coastline below and the rockers' soft creak on hundred year-old floorboards--a steady, reassuring sound that promised some things lasted.

"What really happened to us?" she asked, her voice barely audible.

"I wish I knew. All I ever wanted was to be with you. You're the only woman I've ever known who only wanted to please me."

"And that always seemed to get me in trouble, didn't it?"

Her low chuckle moved him, as always. The man reached out and took her hand across the narrow void between their chairs. "Yet, here I am, holding your hand again, and remembering all the joy you brought into my life…when I still had one. Now, I'm wondering how much of it I have left. I'm glad you came…one more time."

"You knew I'd come, soon as I heard. It's been…too long."

The Maine breeze wafting off Penobscot Bay blew wisps of his newly graying hair over his forehead. Unconsciously, he brushed them back. His hand shook, she noticed, and his face was bloated and puffy, probably from the medication.

She couldn't draw her eyes away from his face. She struggled to conceal her heartbreak that his condition had so deteriorated since last they were together. That had been under such different circumstances. *It's hard to be with him now. It would have been harder not to be.* Her thoughts brought tears, and she wiped them away with her palm, hoping he wouldn't see.

The man rose to his full height, pulled her to her feet and kissed her, softly and deeply. "Don't cry," he whispered, as she buried her head on his chest. "This is just the way it worked out. We're together for now, and even a few moments alone feels good."

It felt so natural to be in his arms--as though they'd never been apart. She could feel his long-remembered body against hers and closed her eyes.

"The old fire is still there, isn't it?" he said. "I can feel your heart beating…a sign…a comfort. This devotion for each other never really goes away."

She looked up at him with a sardonic smile. "I suppose we shouldn't be feeling this now, in our sixties. Aren't we supposed to be sedate and cool by now?"

"I'd have to be dead before I'd regret feeling like this again."

His mischievous grin warmed her pained heart. Relaxing against him, she said, "I understand now why this is your favorite spot in the world. I can feel the peace, just watching the sea--or maybe it's being here like this--with you."

Standing with their arms around each other, swaying a bit with the breeze in spite of the pain in his irradiated hip joints, the peaceful feeling extended longer than either realized. They watched the last errant folds of twilight sink into the black sea, neither wanting to break the communion of their spirits--or the touch of their bodies.

"Look at the stars--there's the Big Dipper." He leaned her back against him as he pointed out each constellation, one arm wrapped around the front of her shoulders.

"Do you remember the first time you pointed out stars to me?"

"In our attic in the Alps? One of the highlights of my entire life!" After a few moments searching the night sky, each remembering silently, he turned her to him again to kiss "…for old time's sake," he said.

"And this is all we'll ever have, isn't it? A chance to kiss good-bye, again."

"A pity. We dreamed of so much more. But this will have to be enough to last me until…." He didn't finish the sentence.

"We must be the poster children for bad timing," she whispered.

"It would be comic if it weren't so tragic. Timing appears to really be, as the saying goes, 'everything.' It has certainly had its way with us."

"Even now, I don't understand it." She leaned her face back to look into his eyes, reaching up to caress his cheek. "Do you? We never meant to hurt each other, or anyone else. And everything seemed so…so right…so meant to be…." Her voice rasped into a sob. "I wish…before it all ends, I'd like to at least understand…where we lost the dream…."

With a soft touch to her temple, he pulled her head again to his chest and rocked her back and forth in his arms. "I don't know, my dear. I wish I did. I would have preferred to spare you…." His sigh was laced with sad resignation. "Somewhere we missed a communication, I guess. The most difficult decision of a lifetime, regret from the choice, my fear-paralyzed inaction at a moment of truth--I'm not sure. It's painful to remember…."

They fell into silence and the lapping of the waves finished his sentence.

1

1973	The young blonde hurried across Ft. Myer
Commissary parking lot pushing an overloaded cart of groceries.
Though not pretty in the soft, feminine sense, Faye Sedgwick
might have been considered lovely in a classic, tailored way, had
she smiled. Instead, she focused doggedly on the task at hand,
there being no time or inclination for such frivolity.

Running at her side and trying to keep up was a gangly six-
year-old eager to help stack groceries in the back seat.

"Now, Katy, don't go putting the flour on top of the eggs
again," the woman snapped. "Watch what you're doing!"

The little girl flinched, jumping backward and locking her
hands together behind her.

"Get in the car. Now! Don't dawdle. Your father will be
home soon, and I have to heat up lunch. You know I have a
meeting this afternoon."

The child climbed into the front seat and leaned her head
against the soft upholstery, tears visible on her eyelashes.

Faye started the car and pulled out onto the street, ignoring
the tears. *I shouldn't have yelled at the child like that. The problem
isn't really her. I'm not even sure what it is.* Impatiently, she added
out loud, "You need to understand that I have to hurry."

Katy was still silent, opening her eyes wide and blowing
upward in the way she had learned would rid her eyes of offending
tears. Suddenly she asked the question Faye had been dreading.
"Are you mad at me and Daddy again, Mommy?"

Faye jerked her head around to face the child with eyes
narrowed. "Why do you say such a thing? Did he tell you that? I
happen to love you and your daddy very much."

"You yelled at him at breakfast, and you act mad now."
Katy said the words in soft tones, as though saying them out loud
would make them sound worse. She shifted toward the door.

"Nonsense!" said her mother, almost spitting out the word.
"Your father and I are married forever and ever. Things have never

been better. You saw the nice photo on the cover of the base newspaper with the three of us coming out of the chapel last Easter Sunday. You were so cute in your yellow dress. You saw the headline—'The Model Military Family.' You saw it," she repeated more forcefully when Katy silently glanced at her from the corner of her eyes. *I hate that expression on the child. What could be going on in her head when she looks at me that way?*

"Yeah, I saw it lots of times. You hung it on the wall."

"Yes, I did! I want everyone to see it." *If it's up where we all can see it, constant exposure will make it true.* "And say 'yes ma'am,' not 'yeah.'" Faye corrected the child. "It's just that Mommy hates to clean quarters and move each time your father's stupid military orders come. You know that, right?"

Katy nodded, still gripping the seat at her sides as though she were afraid something would knock her out of the car. She obviously made a deliberate choice, folded her hands in her lap and said, "Tell me about 'forever and ever,' Mommy."

The child knows how to make me change the subject, doesn't she? She asks so often for that story. As they drove down the manicured parkway, past the parade ground, and toward their home on officers' row, Faye began the story that held her life together for probably the hundredth time. "Once upon a time, a cadet at West Point looked for just the right girl to be his wife so he would someday wear the stars of a general. His roommate knew Mommy's friend, and the two of them set up a blind date."

It was my very first date. I don't see why those stupid high school boys ignored me. I was terrified that first time....

"It was love at first sight," she announced firmly to dispel the memory and spin her cliché. "When graduation came, the new second lieutenants all got married at the chapel under crossed swords, and Mommy and Daddy did too. We promised that we would be together forever and ever. It was a magical ceremony, and now we are living happily ever after."

Faye tried to force her fairy tale in line with reality, but she couldn't quite get them connected. She deliberately chose the fantasy.

The child again interrupted her thoughts. "You forgot to tell about what your mama told you."

Faye heaved an exasperated sigh. *Why do kids ask for a story they've already memorized, and then try to catch you in some omission?* "My mama always told me, 'Faye, girl, you're much too shy. You need to smile more and catch yourself a fine young man and have lots of babies. That's what life and duty are all about. And that's the only way you'll ever be a grown-up married lady.'"

Faye took a deep breath and continued. "My mama was so happy when I met your father. She said, 'See, I told you that you wouldn't have security until you married. Now you'll do your duty for a nice military officer who'll provide you with enough money to get through life. He'll go places, and you'll help him get there'." *Too bad she didn't tell me that 'doing my duty' meant performing an act I detest. But that's one of the dirty little secrets we women keep. After all, I've done it when he's pleaded. He owes me.*

"Now, Katy, you remember this story. Speak up and smile, so a nice man will notice you and provide for you forever and ever, too. Right?" She forced her bright smile on the child.

"Yes, Mommy." The little girl raised her eyebrows. "What does duty mean?"

Faye looked at the child to see where this conversation was going. *Damn! Again that inscrutable look.*

Faye turned her attention to the steering wheel, slipping with an unmistakable bump over the curb into the driveway. "It's something you have to do, whether you want to or not, because everyone expects it of you--like picking up your toys. Like moving every time the government tells us to--like your daddy going to Vietnam." She shut down the motor and faced the child. "In our family, we always do the duty expected of us."

And I've always done mine. I'm the one who must protect our position, yet he could still leave me a penniless widow because he takes care of his Army troops at all costs, even in war. I wish he'd fail for a change. If he keeps getting promoted, he'll never get out of that military uniform, except if he dies.

The two emerged from the car and began transferring

grocery sacks to the porch. A tall, sturdily built officer of perhaps thirty-one emerged from the house. He stood ramrod straight, with his short haircut and craggy face enhancing his military bearing.

"Daddy!" Katy sprang up the steps and jumped into his arms. Neil Sedgwick laughed as he swung the child to his shoulders and pretended to be an airplane.

Faye tightened her grip on the sacks, angry that Katy's giggles pleased him so.

"The least you can do is come help me with the groceries," she said. "I haven't got all day. I got some exceptional bargains. Spent nary a penny extra."

Neil slowed the spin enough to face his wife. "That sounds more like something your mother would say. You don't always need to hunt for bargains, Faye. We have enough money for whatever you want. We aren't destitute, for crying out loud."

"You work far too much for the Army," Faye accused.

"And that puts me in a bit of a double bind, doesn't it, since you very much like the things my working long hours brings you." He sighed. "Katy needs some of my time, too, Faye. Just leave the groceries and go on inside. I'll bring them in a couple of minutes." He returned his attention to the giggling little girl.

"We have that appointment after lunch, Neil. I must do this now, with or without you!" She continued to lift bags, deliberately turning her back toward her husband and gritting her teeth.

The man sighed, swung Katy to her feet, and bent to meet her eyes. "Let's get Mommy's groceries now, so you and I can go for a walk in the woods soon as we get back from the meeting."

The child sprang forward, eagerly carrying too many items and dropping them. Faye saw Neil bend to retrieve each article, adding it to his own substantial load. By the time he had made three trips, Faye was slamming plates on the table, hoping he would notice her tightly sealed lips and recognize her anger.

"Here, let me do that," Neil said, calmly taking the silverware from her hands and handing Katy the spoons. They finished setting the table together. Faye noted that Katy never offered to help her unless she was told.

Faye leaned against the sink, forcing her back to a rigid position. *I hate it when I lose control, and I hate him when he is so patient and calm. Marriage sure isn't like my mama promised.*

Neil sent Katy upstairs to wash her hands for lunch. Only then did he approach Faye, "What time is the appointment?"

"One o'clock." She vigorously stirred the leftover spaghetti sauce on the stove.

"It might have been better if we saw a civilian counselor, so our problems wouldn't be on military record. But, as usual, you've made the appointment without talking to me about it. What does the minister want to talk about today?"

"He said the session is private. You know how marriage counselors are." Faye carefully kept her back turned. "He wants you to understand me so we'll be happier."

"Are you unhappy?"

"Occasionally." She shrugged, biting her lip.

"Me too." He murmured almost under his breath, "It might be nice if you tried to understand me sometimes, too. But what is some counselor going to do about that?"

"Now you behave nicely in front of the chaplain," remonstrated Faye.

"And what's wrong with being honest, Faye, if we really want to get to the root of our problems and find solutions?"

"What would he think of us then? Don't tell him anything embarrassing." Faye worried about their public image.

Knowing it was no use arguing, Neil sighed and helped Katy into her chair.

I'll do nothing to make Neil leave me penniless, thought Faye. *He must stay with me forever and ever. What other choice do I have? Whether it's like I thought it would be, or not, it's all I've got.* With her mama in mind, she smiled sweetly up at him.

With white linens and sparkling crystal goblets in contrast to heated up leftovers, the husband and wife went through the motions of "the Model Military Family"--at least through lunch.

2

1973   "Wait up, Spence," Neil had called earlier that day, hailing his friend on his way out of the Commander's meeting. The sandy-haired young Army Captain had waited near the curb.

"Congratulations," said Spence. "I saw your name on the Promotion List for major, and 'below the zone,' yet."

"Thanks. I feel really lucky."

"Hey, you should be more excited. Our whole lives revolve around making that next promotion. They don't select many people ahead of candidates in the primary zone," said Spence. "Only twelve this year in the whole Army. Your combat bridge-building techniques probably got you in. Advanced promotion now will put you on the fast track toward making general some day."

Neil shook his head with a sardonic grin. "There are also many subsequent opportunities to fall *off* that fast track."

"Yes, but below the zone is good. If any of us don't make the next regular promotion, or are passed over, we're discharged. So it's 'go up or go out,' Buddy."

Neil could detect no trace of envy in Spence's assessment, but his own confidence wasn't up to the challenge. "You know, when I told Faye I was in the zone of consideration for promotion, she said, 'You'll never make it!' as though she knew something I didn't." Neil caught himself almost mimicking Faye's strident voice and immediately stopped, embarrassed, trying instead to make it seem a joke. *She always squelches my hopes—never encourages me. She acts like she wants me to fail.*

"Some confidence Faye has, then." Spence tsk-tsked playfully, waving his finger in the air. "When I'm up for anything, my wife just smiles and says, 'Go for it, Spence,' though she knows I haven't a snowball's chance in Hell." He stuffed his notes from the commander's briefing in the side pocket of his fatigues. "Want to stop for a sandwich at the Officer's Club?"

"Can't today, Spence. Have an appointment this afternoon.

Next time."
    "Something for Katy?" asked his friend.
    "Nothing serious. Just routine." He felt guilty saying it.
    "Okay--rain check. My regards to Faye." Spence waved
and moved to his own car.
    Neil stood still a moment, watching him go. *Gosh, now I'm
lying to my friends.* He had a momentary siege of hatred for
himself, for Faye, for the gods that caused them to lose the infant
boy last year, for the military system that could scramble the career
he loved should it be known his marriage was in trouble, for the
damned 'forever and ever' nonsense with which Faye filled his
child's brain. He was a realist who knew his marriage had been
dead a long time, but he was so conventional and dutiful that he
couldn't give it a decent burial.

###

    "What do you feel is your goal in life?" intoned Army
Chaplain, Leo Stewart, as Neil sat an hour after lunch in the sun-
drenched counselor's office. Neil assumed Faye had made the
appointment with this man thinking he would understand her side
of the 'temporary misunderstanding,' as she continued to call it,
even after years of friction.
    The office was hot. Though Neil had changed out of his
heavy fatigues, the lightweight slacks and shirt he had donned did
not lessen the swelter. *Or am I so uncomfortable because I'm
probably here for personal criticism even beyond Faye's?*
    "Doing my job well, I guess," he answered slowly,
measuring the minister's tone. *This guy will think I sound like a
recruiting poster if I tell him the truth—that I want to make a
difference for the Army. Better not say anything he'd think corny.*
"Not letting my soldiers down, raising a happy child, lifelong
learning and, someplace in there, I'd like to be happy." He worried
he might sound pompous.
    "What makes you unhappy now?"
    Neil thought for a moment. *Can I say what bothers me?*

Not here--not now. What I say could make matters worse. Do I even know what the problem is? "Faye and I haven't talked in a normal tone of voice for years--and it's been worse since...." The unusual crack in his voice betrayed an emotion he couldn't touch whenever he thought of the premature little boy struggling to breathe. He forced himself to continue. "I hate being screamed at, and I hate Katy seeing it happen, yet it happens all the time."

Faye shrieked with fire in her eyes. "You! You! You're blaming this on me? You're too busy with your soldiers or too involved with Katy to comfort me." She rose to face him, waving her hands frenetically. "This loss has been harder on me than you. It's far harder for a mother to lose a child than for a father. I'm the one needing comfort."

"It's a hell of a lot easier to be at work than to come home to you," Neil responded with equal force. "At least *there*, I know I'm needed. I feel alone when I come home. I needed you to comfort me too, because, contrary to your opinion, the baby's death destroyed me, as well. But you go to bed at eight and pretend to be asleep when I come to bed. When am I supposed to comfort you? We haven't...been ...together since years before this happened. You've never ...touched me in all these years."

"For you, it's *always* sex, isn't it?"

"For you, it *never* is."

Their voices had risen until the counselor held up his hands and shouted, "Enough." When startled looks replaced the angry ones, the minister motioned them to sit back down and listen. "I know this last year has been rough for you both."

"They've all been rough," said Neil. He felt discouraged.

"Faye, have you been avoiding your husband by going to bed early?"

"I work in the house all day, and he comes home and wants to talk about his troops or some engineering bridge and stupid stuff like that. Why would I want to listen to all that nonsense? Of course, I go to bed early to read or watch television."

Neil's voice rose again, his normally mild temperament taking on a grittier edge. "Nonsense? Is that how you view what I do for us--for our country? Besides, you always manage to take time from all that housework to play bridge and chit chat with your girlfriends for hours. And you only read silly romance magazines."

"How dare you criticize my girlfriends! I'm good enough to take a casserole when someone is sick. I should think you'd be proud of how needed I am in the community—how I uphold our image. My television and my magazines are all that give me pleasure!" She brought her handkerchief up to blot her eyes and looked sadly at the minister. "Neil can't see that I'm doing what is socially appropriate to his rank and status? All my friends know that Neil does well with his career because of me."

"I suppose gossiping with all the women on post seems the mark of good leadership to you," Neil said with a tired voice. "But don't you see that you never speak civilly to Katy or to me? You never want to do anything fun or go anyplace with us."

He turned to face the minister. "I'd like to be able to discuss my work intellectually with my wife, but I can't. She's learned nothing new since we married. I can't interest her in lectures, concerts, sports, books, trips--anything. I ask her to read an engineering article I've written, and she ignores me. I've grown, and she hasn't. That's a big part of the problem."

"That's not true. I'm the mature one. I had the child."

Neil took a deep breath, girding himself for the anger he knew would come. *I'm sick of pussyfooting around, so here goes.* "We fell into marriage right out of West Point, marching down the aisle like the other good little cadets, as though that was the expected thing to do after graduation night. We were okay a while—I hoped we could love each other, and she could be sweet at times. But after Katy was born, she pushed me away, called me 'oversexed,' wouldn't let me near her, and didn't want me around. She's only sweet when she wants something."

Faye sputtered, but before either of the other two could respond, Neil hurried on, trying to make Chaplain Stewart understand. "She didn't even seem happy when I came home from two tours in Vietnam more or less in one piece. She seems angry all the time and won't discuss why. I'm a stranger in my own home. Faye has never wanted to be a companion or a wife."

The counselor narrowed his eyes at Neil while turning to see Faye's expression.

Neil realized he'd said too much—way too much. He looked at Faye to see her reaction. *There she goes with that sweetsy little martyr face again, and I can see Leo is taken in by it. I hate this! I said what was wrong and now they look at me like I'm a freak for having feelings.* He turned his face to the window--his attention to those walking outside. He'd rather be having fun with Katy. The child and his challenging job were the only lights in life. *I want—no, I need, a companion I can love--who can love me--who will share the fun of military social life and travel opportunities.*

The minister turned to Faye. "Do you see your marriage the same way as Neil?"

"Of course not," Faye said firmly, wiping an imaginary tear from her eye. "We were both *very* much in love when we got married, and we *are* happy." She tossed words angrily at Neil. "I don't know what he has to be upset about. I did everything expected of me. I fixed his meals, ironed his shirts, worried about the finances, was nice to his unit officers, had a child…two children…" Faye's voice regained its stern tone. "I've always done my duty by Neil, and I expect him to do his duty by me. I want to be secure and independent financially, and immune from his talk about divorce. I refuse to consider parting. We're in this forever and ever." Her chin jutted forward. "There's never been a divorce in either of our families, and I do *not* intend to be the first one."

Neil sighed and turned to observe a sparrow outside the window. The little fellow was resilient, bobbing with each windy bounce of the branch to which he clung. *Yeah, we were oh, so happy. I was shy--never had a date. My roommate took pity on my celibacy and set Faye up as my blind date for a cadet dance. She acted like I was the greatest guy she'd ever known. I guess I was, since I learned later that she'd never had a date, either.*

Neil lost himself in the moment, trying to remember something good about their relationship. *She hung on my every word once, and allowed me to have my first sexual experience as though it were part of her plan--just so far and no farther. Naturally I was intrigued. I was in hormone hell and she was the first girl who seemed interested in me. I soon found her interest was only an act to get what she wanted--a wedding ring.*

"There was a point at which she acted as though she liked me," he said to the minister. "The minute I met her parents, though, her mother rushed into wedding plans, as if she had been expecting it to happen. *Of course* we married. It was expected, and we were probably both afraid we'd never find anyone else!"

Inexperience begets inexperience. A stupid mistake by two naïve people and now it's a life sentence. She cried our first time together, and it was never any good for me, though God knows I tried! Inexperience again, I suppose. She imposed so damn many limits that having sex was like negotiating a minefield. Perhaps I hurt her, though she never said so. Having sex is 'doing her duty?' That's disgusting! What does she think my duty is to her? "What's the use of talking about all this now?" Neil said aloud, looking out the window. The brave little bird was gone.

The minister adjusted his spectacles over his nose and tried to drag Neil's attention back to the matter at hand. "No matter why you married, no one is speaking of divorce. Divorce is not an option in our religion, and you've been good churchgoers. We need this to be a permanent union in God's sight. We must find a way to put this marriage back together." Leo pondered, one hand holding his chin. "You both were happy when Katy was born, and devastated when you lost the baby boy. Have you considered having another child as the glue to cement this holy union?"

Neil urged his mind back to the conversation. *Did he just say what I thought he said? Holy union? Made in Hell, I'd say. God, I should have been listening better.*

Faye smiled. "Oh, Reverend Stewart, what a wonderful idea." She reached out and took Neil's reluctant hand. "Neil, the pastor is right. I truly don't want you to leave me. I'll do anything you like to be a better mother." Her instant, saccharine smile somehow offended Neil.

"Faye," he answered in his most patient voice, "you've

always been a good mother. That fact is not in question." He hesitated a bit too long.

"Then it's all decided, dear. Another baby will be just what we need."

She smiled in such a coy, appealing way, Neil felt himself weaken. Somehow, they were on their way home, and Faye was beaming. Apparently, Neil had shaken hands with the chaplain, found the car keys, and was now wondering if he'd missed something vital.

Later, after dinner, Katy's bath and the father-daughter ritual of tuck in, story, and prayers, Neil entered their bedroom to find Faye still awake--for a change. She lay on the bed in a blue negligee. *Where on earth did she get that? Normally, it's a t-shirt and pajama bottoms.* He moved toward the bed, not sure if he would be rebuffed as usual if he approached her. But it had been a long dry spell, and he was horny as hell. He knew the best he could hope for was a missionary reaction, with many 'don't touch here' or 'don't touch there' interferences, but even that would be better than nothing--nothing.

Afterward, a clinging Faye wouldn't stop babbling into his ear about a baby being just the thing to glue their model family together. He wasn't sure how one thing was related to the other.

Long after midnight, Neil sat on the edge of the bed, squishing his bare toes on a small Persian carpet--the one luxury he'd persuaded Faye to buy at a bazaar. *It's ironic that a soft carpet is more comforting than my marriage.* He ran the days' events over in his mind. *Glue! Forever and ever? Model family?*

Suddenly he knew the end of it. He'd done what Faye saw as his duty, to provide her with another child. And now he was trapped, once again. He would never have the life's companion he craved—someone to love--and Faye had no desire to ever *be* that someone. As Faye slept peacefully, her mouth resembled a satisfied smirk. *She'll continue to demand my life be lived her way.* Neil leaned his elbows on his knees, put his head in his hands, and saw his dreams decapitated. Obligation took their place.

3

1973   The color guard captain held out a carefully folded American flag to her reluctant hands. *Did his action somehow make Gary's death official?* Sara Sutton fought the surreal urge to reject the flag--to run away. She could picture her flight between the gravestones, because if she touched that flag, Gary would really be dead. But, feeling the eyes of her children upon her and the young captain waiting patiently, she sighed and embraced the inevitable. Nodding her thanks, she gently touched its folds and gathered the flag into her arms.

Neighbors poured into the cottage where she had spent her married life, bringing food, hugging her, and telling her inane things about Gary's "peace" and his "being in Heaven now." *Is there a Heaven? What kind of God would take away my best friend, my husband and lover, the father of our children, in such a cruel and useless way?*

"Thank you, Mr. Jacobs. The flowers are lovely. Gary would have loved them." *Had she actually spoken the words? They seemed to come from a far distant place, as though the thoughts belonged to someone else--someone she didn't know.*

"The casserole will certainly come in handy, Mrs. Feldman, thank you so much."

How could a just God allow a drunken driver to careen into Gary's motorcycle and mow him down on the street? She found herself sobbing again, gasping for breath, remembering that he'd only bought the Yamaha to save money after his four years in the Army while they'd both finished college and become teachers. But he'd continued to ride it longer than he had intended, long after they could have afforded a second car. And it had killed him.

Even after three months of widowhood, nothing was any easier. As she walked aimlessly around the back yard, Sara was drawn to the roses and camellias Gary had planted there. He had studied horticulture during their junior high years from an amazing teacher who instilled a lifetime love for plants. Their yard boasted the only orange tree in the neighborhood that also produced lemons, thanks to Gary's experimental grafting. And he had cultivated more than fifty hybrid camellias, his special favorite. Almost every day after teaching, he would work a twilight hour in the garden, and come lay a perfect camellia on her pillow when she eagerly joined him there. *I miss him so*, she thought longingly.

She touched a withered, dead plant--the third that died in a week. She had called the local garden center to ask what she could do to save her husband's camellias. The owner had come to look and said there was no earthly reason for them to die. "They should be fine," he'd said. *Nothing earthly...*

Sara knelt on the ground near yet another sick-looking plant, oblivious to the grass staining her soft blue dress and the wind blowing her dark curly hair. She noticed the myriad holes dug in the back lawn by their Bassett hound and smiled, remembering how Gary had finally given up scolding Cleo and formally christened the back yard a "miniature golf course." He'd even produced golf clubs for the kids of the neighborhood. It was a good memory, but even good memories brought pain and longing.

Their youngest daughter, bubbly Lynette, walked up to put her arms around her mother. "Are you sad again, Mom?"

Sara wiped her eyes and rose to hug the twelve-year old. "I'm trying hard not to be, but more and more of your Dad's camellias are dying, and I can't seem to save them. I thought we could keep them as a little part of all he did for us."

"Maybe Daddy needs the flowers with him in Heaven. They're all dying so they can go there to be with him."

The mother had no words for such childlike logic. They decided to kiss the dying camellia, hoping Gary would know the kisses came from them when the plant reached Heaven.

By the time slim, businesslike Lisa, only a year older than her sister, got home from school, Lynette and her mom were giddily running around the yard, kissing every camellia bush, and laughing together. Lisa shook her head, mystified, and called Cleo into the kitchen to be fed.

"Our school play is Friday and Saturday, Mom," said Lisa over dinner. "Which night would you and Grandma like to go?"

"Hm?"

"The play, Mom. The play."

"Which play is that, dear?"

"Duh, Mom! Only the one we've been working on for weeks--<u>Spoon River Anthology</u>. Don't you remember? You helped me learn my lines. All those satirical dead people talking."

"I'm sorry. I forgot. Pick whichever day you prefer. Your Grandma and I have no particular place to go." She absent-mindedly turned over a pork chop with her fork.

The girls looked at each other helplessly. The only remaining authority figure in their lives seemed somewhere beyond their reach.

They discussed a plan as Sara drifted off into her reverie.

"The kids are picking me up later for dress rehearsal at the theater," said Lisa to her sister. "You stay tonight, and I'll stay tomorrow while you go to band practice."

Lynette nodded. But something in Lisa's words caught Sara's vagrant attention.

"What did you say?" She had a sudden and distressed revelation. "Have you two been 'baby-sitting' me?"

"Well," said Lisa, slowly, "you haven't been yourself since Dad died, and we don't like to leave you alone."

Sara looked up. "Come to think of it, I don't remember being alone since…."

The girls glanced back and forth in embarrassment, each waiting for the other to speak. Sara tried to focus on what she really could remember of the three months since Gary's death. *Not much—the time was only a blur of aching loneliness.*

Lisa couldn't stand silence and always felt the need to fill it. "Mom, you've forgotten a lot of things lately. You're okay in the classroom because the kids need you and that keeps you busy, and you seem independent in outside activities because people expect it of you. You put up a good front of 'carrying on' when people need you. But when you come home, you fix dinner, then you retreat into the sewing room all night." She dropped her head. "We haven't wanted to upset you even more."

"We've never had so many clothes, Mom," interjected Lynette. "Please stop sewing."

"I guess I'm just trying to kill time. I can't sleep, and time goes so slowly at night. I hate not having him here...." *God, there's such an emptiness in my life.* "I keep expecting him to walk through the living room door and...."

"We aren't complaining, Mom," said Lynette. "We just worry about you, 'cause you're forgetting so much."

"Because," corrected the mother and teacher, automatically.

"That too," retorted Lynette with a sly grin. That had always been their private family joke. Whenever the "teacher feature" in her or in Gary "poked out," one of the kids would just say, "That too," or "Whatever," and they would all laugh. Remembering, Sara tried to smile. "Come on, now, girls, I can't be all that bad, can I?"

"Well," began Lynette slowly. "You're still quite competent in most things, Mom, but you scare us to death when you're alone--like when you walked out into Lake Tahoe on our picnic. You said you were 'trying to find Dad, and you'd heard him call you from out there someplace.'"

Lisa shook her long, fashionably straightened, blonde hair. "You can't even swim! You could have drowned, and we would have lost you too."

"I don't remember doing that. I must've just walked into the water--to cool off."

The two girls exchanged glances.

"No, Mom," said Lisa. "You scared us. And don't forget you lost the freezer, too. How does somebody 'lose' a 16 cubic

foot freezer? Did you give it away, lend it to someone, sell it--
what? Was it stolen?"
"I don't know, Lisa. I don't know!" Sara buried her head in
her hands and sobbed. "I'm sorry. I'm not being a very stable
mom. It's just that we were always a team, your dad and I. My half
can't seem to function alone. I should be able to take over all we
both did together, yet I can't seem to concentrate on anything
but...but missing him." She could feel herself suffocating. *Can
someone die just by wishing it?* "He was always there, my best
friend since I was ten. I can't do without him now." Her sobs came
out jerkily, leaving the young girls staring at each other helplessly.

Later, after many hugs, Lisa went to dress rehearsal while
Lynette settled down with her homework. Sara was again in the
sewing room. Halfway through a seam on a flowery t-shirt she was
making for Lynette, she rose and walked to her bedroom--to the
closet she had shared with Gary. His clothes had hung there,
freshly pressed, ready for his next day of teaching, since the day
he'd died. Though the kids had encouraged her to take the clothes
to Goodwill, she couldn't. She pressed his favorite tweed jacket to
her face to catch his indelible aroma of blackboard chalk and Old
Spice. She couldn't forget the joy they'd found in making love,
knowing she would never be able to touch him again.
Forcefully, she moved the clothing to one side, dragged out
a metal box, sat on the bed and opened it, rustling through the
papers until she found the multiple pages of application forms she
and Gary had dreamed of one day filling out together. She was
determined to fulfill their dream now--for him. *I must do
something...something....*
Just before three in the morning, long after Lisa had
returned home and the girls were asleep, Sara walked to the corner
to drop the bulging envelope of completed forms into the mailbox-
-before she could panic and change her mind.
The children's concerns of the evening had made a deep

impression. Though she had struggled to maintain the illusion she was carrying on normally, for them, she knew now the image was a false one. She was forced to admit she felt quite lost. She had made no plans at all beyond Lynette's eighteenth birthday. She had no vision of existence for herself beyond that milestone. She thought quietly. *What could that mean? There was no answer.*

Weeks went by, as Sara forced herself to pay attention to daily events, finished up the school year, and tried to remember things important to the girls. Then a large manila envelope arrived.

Her school Superintendent knew Sara was struggling whenever she was outside of school, and he approved her request for a year's leave of absence.

Sara's mother lived close by, and she explained her decision at their next dinner together. "I've got to get out of here for a while and find out how to be a whole person again, Mom. I feel so empty." She paused for breath. "I'm scaring the girls, and that scares me, too. I've been offered a teaching job in Germany." She looked down at her hands, roughened from trying to weed the recalcitrant garden. "I'm no good to anyone if I can't get myself together. Maybe if we go where nothing is familiar, it'll be easier."

Her mom nodded, with no trace of surprise.

Sara raced on. "Lisa and Lynette might even enjoy living in a foreign land for a year to travel and learn the language." Her voice broke, and she dabbed fruitlessly at a torrent of tears. "Honestly, Mom, I'm afraid of what I'll do, if I stay here."

"I haven't wanted to step in and say anything unless your depression got worse," said her mother. "Apparently the kids got to it first. A year away is a good idea—it might help you and the girls get back on track."

"Gary was my whole life. There's nothing left for me now." Sara gulped back sobs. "Was all that a mistake? Is there such a thing as loving someone *too* much?" Her throat ached from some vague constriction. She could barely breathe.

Her mother put her arms around Sara. "No, dear. It's never a bad thing to love, but it's just not in your personality to do anything half way, and that may always cause you pain. Gary adored you, but he feared that if anything ever happened to him, you'd be vulnerable because you worry too much about the needs of others and you never protect yourself. We talked about it sometimes. I've almost felt he *knew* he would die first. He protected you, and you brought out the best in him. It was a loving teamwork that most people never find. But he always knew that life without him would be difficult for you. This job might be an opportunity for you girls to go to Germany and learn how to live on without him."

The teens fussed at first. Their compromise was that Grandma would stay with them through the summer while Sara, the newly accredited Department of Defense overseas teacher, searched for an apartment and learned to manage alone in Germany. In early September, after their favorite summer activity-- band camp--Lisa and Lynette would join Sara to share a new European adventure. Psychologically, it would mean change and many adjustments, but Sara now realized that staying where she was could bring only disaster.

Her mom and the girls went to the airport and waved Sara off. As the sun floated down somewhere over the Atlantic, Sara's thoughts drifted out to her dead husband. *Gary, if you can hear me, you know how I've loved you, and now you're not here. I don't know where to channel my energy or who to trust. Help me know what to do, please. I don't want to disappoint your faith in me or let our children down.*

Soon she was lulled into a quiet peace by the beauty of ultra blue bands spreading across the sky and blurring into deep purple. There was a strange sense of warmth that seemed to fill the awful void in her heart for a precious moment. *Thank you, my love. I understand. You'll be with me.*

4

Seven years later – 1980 in Germany   The
meeting was far too long, and Neil Sedgwick joined the gaggle of
lieutenant colonels who made a break for the door as soon as their
colonel, the Brigade Commander, said, "Dismissed."

"There goes more of our scarce time," declared Bruce Etna,
who commanded an Artillery Battalion. "The Old Man says, 'If the
Soviets cross that Communist Border, they'll have an initial
tactical advantage because they'll know where and when the attack
will come, while our forces have to wait until we're attacked to
respond,' as if we didn't know that! Hell, that's been the political
fol-de-rol policy our forces have abided by since the Cold War
started. *Every* new Brigade Commander gets into a frenzy over it."

Neil phrased his tightly controlled response to sound more
positive than negative. "It's always a revelation for anyone new to
divided Europe. But during our last NATO military exercise, our
trigger-happy troops got excited and fired first. We can't afford
that in a real attack. These are good kids, but they need training to
respond *only* after being fired upon--a nightmare scenario for the
covering force, but it's American policy."

Skip Davis, commander of an Infantry Battalion chimed in.
"If the Soviets cross that border, our only defense in the initial
phase will be for you Combat Engineers to blow all the bridges
before they can cross them. We can't allow our enemy the
advantage of a Remagen Bridge." Skip was referring to a famous
episode of World War II, when the Americans were able to gain
the advantage of crossing the Rhine River because the retreating
Germans failed to blow up the Ludendorf Bridge at the village of
Remagen.

"But no one wants to be in the unenviable position of either
starting a war by blowing up the bridges too soon, or losing a war
by blowing them too late," said Neil. He smiled, seeing some irony
in the discussion.

Of course, no one not in the military would have understood the conversation of these battalion commanders who formed the combined unit, or Brigade, led by their new full colonel. It took battalions of Infantry, Artillery, Engineers, and Cavalry, with its helicopter Air Cavalry arm, to work together in any crisis at the Communist Border across Europe. These units were tasked to defend against frequent threats from the Soviet forces during the Cold War, and these commanders and their predecessors had done their job admirably throughout the era. Had the American Army not been stationed in Europe after the end of World War II, the map of Europe would have looked much different. Over the two or three years of their involvement as lieutenant colonels in command of their respective battalions, the officers depended on each other militarily and supported each other's units. Sometimes, they also become friends.

"It's already January. What do you have, Neil, one more week to finish your engineer battalion command?" asked Jeff Fenten of Cavalry, falling in stride with the others. "Did you get assigned the TDY (temporary duty) at Grafenwohr for the six months left before you report to Carlisle Barracks? My command finishes in June, so I'm right on schedule. I guess I'll meet you at the War College." He grinned at Neil.

"Yes, and the Grafenwohr job will hold me to about the right timing. I'll be at the War College with you this summer. They first want me to redesign the gunnery ranges out there in the boonies for the new generation of Abrams tanks and Bradley Infantry Fighting Vehicles that can fire while moving."

"Sounds like the kind of challenge you like, Neil," said Jeff. "But getting the funding for those changes will be a hell of a lot harder than designing the plan."

"Well," said Skip, "the general apparently figures you can do the job." The tall man smiled. "Will Faye and the girls stay here on Post in government housing while you're out at Graf all week?"

Neil nodded. It was hard to speak comfortably about his fractured home life. "I'll just get home on weekends, but I'm anxious to dive into the new job." *I'll have to think through how to go to the War College alone.* Neil was still optimistic where the Army was concerned, and he loved his job. However, his lack of optimism about his home life was his most carefully kept secret, even after sixteen years. Faye's angry tirades had only gotten worse over the years. He hated leading a double life, but it was not good form in the military to have a faltering marriage--not if you wanted to get promoted--and he'd always looked forward to the additional responsibility of the next promotion with strictly managed ambition. He struggled to change the subject from his personal life. "Our young troops seem to enjoy the activities set up for them lately, don't they?"

Les Jacobs, Commander of the remaining Infantry Battalion, agreed. "Getting them more involved does seem to help the barracks drinking problems. I'm letting a few go on leave next week for a Ski School in Austria."

"Some of mine are going too," said Neil. "I'd like to go myself, but I don't know what Faye has planned. This weekend, I'm getting away for four days to a warmer climate."

"Yeah, I heard from my wife that you're taking Faye for a romantic getaway," teased Les. "You lovebirds make the rest of us look bad?" He laughed raucously, slapping Neil on the shoulder. "My wife thinks I'm a bum for not taking her away, too."

Neil sighed and reluctantly took up the burden of Faye's fairy tales. "You can join us in Greece if you like." He desperately sought something to change the subject back to safer ground. "At least I'll forget about the Colonel's directives. Maybe by the time I get back Tuesday, he'll have a new policy to worry about."

"I wouldn't count on it," said Skip, not noticing the look of naked exposure on Neil's face. "He even thinks the introduction of female soldiers into the maintenance barracks will calm all these young soldiers' fistfights. Fat chance, with their hormones! I'm glad I'll be out of here soon, too." The men shared their laughter.

Reaching the parking lot, Neil plopped his briefcase on the car seat and turned to his own thoughts. *Lovebirds, indeed! What a chore it is to keep up with Faye's deceptions. They have, over many years, forced me to be someone I'm not. I wonder if my colleagues can see the hypocrisy I feel in struggling to maintain this rigid status quo and keep the peace at home?*

As soon as his engine flared to life, Neil scrunched his shoulders and headed home. *Home—what was that supposed to mean anyway?* How long had it been since he and Faye had spoken civilly to each other about anything besides the weather or the children? Not in years, in spite of futile attempts with marriage counselors. *Oh yes. I remember another topic. She whooped with joy when she found I'd received a traffic citation for speeding last month, saying it served me right. But other than that, nothing.*

He unconsciously shifted the Chevy down for the cobble-stoned streets of the 'hill' where upper ranking officers lived on the American Army Post. *What will be Faye's problem tonight? It's always something--always the minute I get in the door. I dread being alone with her for this Greek weekend. But we need to plan for our separation, and a quiet divorce.*

He waved automatically to a neighbor's children playing by the corner. *Yes, it had been our joint mistake to marry so young, right out of West Point.*

But their little girls weren't a mistake. Katy was doing wonderfully since she chose the challenge of attending German school when they'd arrived three years ago. She'd learned enough *Deutsche* to take all her subjects in the foreign language. Unfortunately, since German schools also had classes on Saturday mornings, it interfered a bit with their weekend time together. But he was proud that Katy was bright, full of life, and ready to take on such a challenge. And seven-year-old Micki was doing well at the American School on post. She was still too young and shy to manage such long hours and as much homework as the foreign school required, but she loved second grade.

No, it wasn't the girls who were the problem. Was it Faye, or himself, or some combination of both? Of course, he didn't know many lieutenant colonels whose marriage hadn't taken a hit during battalion command. It was a scarcely kept secret that the long hours and stress of dealing with equipment, training, and discipline for almost a thousand men took its toll on the leaders.

Some officers were able to pull their marriage back together when they relinquished command, *if* it had been strong beforehand. But those who had cracks in the foundation in the first place went straight to the divorce courts. "That's what it will be for me!" Unconsciously, Neil had spoken aloud. There had been major chasms in his marital foundation from the beginning.

Ironically, he realized that if he had a job at some factory, a divorce would be no one's business. But the divorce of a high-ranking officer was a blot on his efficiency rating--not openly--but known under the surface. He knew the drill. Divorces could be messy, and the Army didn't like a mess. His marital unhappiness had to stay underground at all costs. Separation was a first step, then a quiet and cooperative divorce so no one would know. The Army was, after all, his life.

Neil forced his mind to happier thoughts. The Ski Club was planning a week of ski lessons at the famed Sigi's Ski School in St. Veit, Austria. He'd love a nice break between finishing the most difficult command of his military career and starting his new engineering duties at Graf--a turning point of sorts. He had the consummate professional's need to keep improving in whatever he did. Lessons from a professional ski champion would be productive. The girls would be in school and Faye made it abundantly clear she would be glad to be rid of him anyway.

On a whim, he negotiated a quick u-turn and swung by the Officers' Club to sign up for the trip. He found he'd be joining another thirty-five officers, wives, enlisted men, and teachers who could wangle a week off by scrounging together leave, sick days, or other purpose days. He agreed to room with the school's counselor whose wife didn't want to learn to ski, either.

Neil drove home, feeling much better, enlivened by looking forward to the ski trip. *I hate it that I can't look forward to going home to Faye, but sadly, I can't. She makes it clear she hates me. How have we put up with each other this long?*

With practiced ease, Neil swung the car into his driveway, grabbed his briefcase, and held out his arms to Michelle, their dark-haired, elfin 'Micki,' as she ran into them.

"Now, *this* is a homecoming," he said with conviction. The shy little girl was always effusive with hugs offered to her father. Faye was, as usual, angry. He rarely knew the cause. Hers was the anger of a moment's emotion--not wanting to actually address a problem, but to stew about it until someone noticed. Over the years, Neil and the girls had instinctively learned not to notice more often than necessary, as her temper could easily get out of hand.

"What do you mean you're going on a week-long ski trip?" Faye still had the annoying habit of spitting out words when offended. "You're already going to Greece with me while my girlfriend watches Micki. Why do you need another vacation?"

"It's not a vacation, Faye." He struggled to keep the fatigue out of his voice. *We've been here so many times, and it's always the same.* "It's ski school--lessons with a pro. It'll do my skiing style some good, I hope. I'll sign you up too, if you'd like to go. They have beginner classes. You might like to try something new."

"I wouldn't waste my time!"

Her voice always set his teeth on edge.

"You know I have no interest in all that silly sports stuff of yours--a grown man going off with a bunch of ski bums and loafing for a week. All right, go! But be sure you trim the winter evergreens beforehand. I won't want to look at them once we get back. My lady friends and I are going on a shopping trip to the German porcelain factory."

"It's only January…" Neil stopped, recognizing the futility of logic. "Look, Faye, it doesn't matter if I go skiing or if you go away shopping. None of that matters anymore, because we'll be going our separate ways soon. I've already told you that this temporary assignment at Grafenwohr will be a separation for us. It'll give us each a chance to learn how to manage alone."

Faye paused on her way out the door. "You wouldn't divorce me here in Europe and embarrass me in front of my friends, would you?" Her voice still sounded calm.

He matched her tone. "No, Faye. I know how much appearances matter to you. We'll wait until we get to Carlisle

Barracks where few know us. We can decide how to divorce amicably and quietly so the girls won't feel the brunt of our unhappiness and the brass won't stunt my career."

"You'll change your mind by the time we get to Carlisle, Neil." A cloying sweetness crept into her voice, as though she were soothing a small child. "You just need a separation from your job, not from me. You'll see. Besides…" She jutted her chin out toward him with a barely whispered snarl, "I'll see you rot in Hell before I'll go quietly into oblivion and allow you to make me a divorced woman." Faye shook her finger under his nose. "I don't care if we're happy or unhappy--you're staying!"

"I agreed to go to Greece hoping it would give us a chance to discuss plans to separate calmly," said Neil, shaking his head in resignation. "I see now, the trip is a mistake, too."

"Mama was right. People think you're a good man because I've kept you so."

Neil started to turn away to avoid the taunt, but he made the mistake of adding, "Faye, I'm happy you've at last found you enjoy factory shopping for nice objects for the house, but please spend some money on yourself as well. I want you and the girls to have all you need. Safety pins in your skirt waistband and ragged sneakers are hardly appropriate.

"This skirt is fine," she screamed. I have to save for our old age."

"I'd just like you to have nice things. I'll see that you're comfortable in your old age, Faye. Go ahead and buy yourself some new clothes. He took a deep breath and broached the topic that was *really* bothering him.

"Faye, why did you tell the other wives about our trip to Greece?"

"They're *my* friends! Why shouldn't I tell them?" She arched her neck back to the point that she was sneering down at him.

"By the time they told their husbands, I got hit with all these hints about some big romantic getaway. It's foolish and embarrassing." He waited for her acknowledgement.

"Well, you needn't be so aloof and pompous. So what if I want a little of the respect you get? I've made every effort for the wives of your unit to like me, yet I'm never sure they do. You meet people on this big old, dignified, intellectual level. I can't keep up with their conversations. I don't understand half of what they say."

"If you'd read more, you would, Faye."

She smirked, ignoring the suggestion. "And so what if telling them my husband is taking me someplace romantic makes them tell their husbands? They're just jealous."

"There's *never* been romance in this marriage, Faye! You're living in a fairy tale, and I don't want to be part of it anymore." Frustrated, he turned to face her. "The image of a marriage is all that matters to you. You've never helped me make it a real marriage. It's unprofessional to have your fantasies creep into what my colleagues think of us."

"Well, you aren't doing all that much to be praised?" She wouldn't meet his eyes.

"Why haven't you ever wanted us to be friends and lovers?" He asked the question wistfully.

"Why can't you forget about this lovey-dovey stuff and act like a decent man of almost thirty-nine?" She flung the words back at him. "Damn you, why should I care what you want?"

"Let's not get ugly, Faye. The children…"

Faye again raised her voice. "Let the children hear me. Marriage isn't what it was advertised to be anyway, so get over it. And your assignment in Grafenwohr is *no* separation. Not from me!" From a high screech, she suddenly lowered her voice to a purr. "Besides, we wouldn't be going to Greece together if there were any *real* problem, now would we? I have my rights as a married lady." She stalked out.

Neil could hear her mounting the stairs to pack her suitcase. She'd be asleep by eight, as usual, and thus the argument would end. That was the *only* way they ever ended. But it would give him more time with Katy and Micki.

He found the girls cowering in the dining room, Katy's arm protectively around Micki's shoulders.

"Hey, girls," Neil said, more heartily than he intended. He realized they had overheard the argument, again. He had a sudden spasm of anxiety realizing what the girls' lives would be like if the courts gave them exclusively to Faye. *I must find a way to stay in their lives in any divorce—a shared custody at least.* "What'll we do tonight?"

"Mom said you had to go up and pack," said Katy, her voice trembling.

"Mom can do her packing now, and I'll do mine later, after you girls are in bed."

"Daddy," croaked Micki in her throaty little voice, "will you and Mommy have fun in Greece? You don't have any fun at home."

Neil rolled his eyes to the ceiling, trying to think of a way to answer the little girl. What could he say? "Micki, my dear, we always have fun when *you* are around, but since you won't be with us in Athens, we'll have to suffer and make do without you." He accompanied his recitation with melodramatic flairs of his arms and head, until the little girl was giggling and had forgotten her original question. She climbed into his lap and snuggled against his chest while he leaned over Katy's homework.

Katy looked straight at him with her fourteen-year-old eyes, and he knew she was aware he'd been play-acting. "Pretty good?" his arching eyebrows signaled her.

"Good enough," came her audible reply.

Neil evaluated his life. His career and his children were all he had. In seven months, he'd be at the War College. *Only good leadership positions will come after that, if I can just keep things going levelly, and no catastrophe befalls. It's been my dream. I might still be in position to do something worthwhile for my country, and for the Army.*

He pointed out a math question Katy had skipped. *Here in this room is the most precious legacy of my life. Katy is far too wise for her years. She knows I'm unhappy and worries about me, but she can't appear disloyal to her mother. Then here's Micki, already asleep in my arms--the child who was to cement Faye and me together forever. At what cost? Is it really better for the children to be with both of us, no matter how much we argue— when our arguments obviously scare them to tears?*

Neil automatically responded to a question from Katy, while juggling the sleeping Micki on one arm, scribbling a similar problem so Katy could see how the formula worked. Her smile lit up his day, but lately, that light had come less often.

Katy needs to be happier. We all do. What would make us happier? Having someone to love and encourage us, someone who could share activities with the girls and me just for the sheer fun of it. Military life can be a good life, if two can share the travel and opportunities. I'd like someone who would enjoy making love with me all night, if we wanted. Neil couldn't help smiling at the very idea of making love instead of the robotic sex he'd thus far experienced. He wasn't sure he even knew what lovemaking was.

I want a wife who can discuss a differing point of view without it escalating into an argument--a life's companion--that's· what I've missed. God help me, I want a loving person Faye will never be, and apparently I've disappointed her in not being the Prince Charming she envisioned. I don't know what it is that she wants. How long must we be yoked so unhappily together?

"Dad?"

Neil looked up to see Katy's concerned face staring at him. "What is it, Hon?"

She put her arms around him. "Daddy, you were smiling at Micki before, and now tears are in your eyes. What's wrong?"

Neil struggled to recover his thoughts. "I'm fine, Katy. Just thinking, I guess. I'm fine." He put his free arm around her. "We'd better get Micki to bed, and you need some sleep too. Your mother and I will be leaving early in the morning. Can you get Micki off to school and remind her she'll be staying with the neighbors at night? And are you sure you'll be okay here alone? You can call Mrs. Sutton day or night should you have any problems. She said it was all right. You still have her number, don't you?"

Katy nodded, with that same sadness still in her eyes.

Her sadness is for me. God, how do I get her to be happier if I don't even know how to be happier myself?

Neil lifted Micki into his arms and they climbed the stairs, as Katy turned off the lights. After tucking in the girls, he tip-toed into the room he reluctantly shared with Faye. Her bags were packed by the door, as were his. He threw up his hands in defeat. How long had he been asking her to let him pack his own things?

Once in the shower, Neil turned the water on full force and let it tumble down his angry muscles. *God, why can't Faye see that her endless discontent festers under my skin like a boil? And, damn it, I'm lonely. That's what scares me most…loneliness. We have different values and different lifestyles. We live a lie. I'm married to a stranger I know far too well. And damned if I know how to either get out of it, or to make it any better.*

But of course, there was the career need for staying wed. He certainly knew that by the time officers had reached lieutenant colonel, only the most competent were left. From this point on, the raters would look for something beyond their competence. Should someone drink too much, or his teenager get in trouble, or his marriage fail publicly, a military career could stagnate. Though the joke as a young man was, "If the Army wanted you to have a wife, it would have issued you one," by the time one reached battalion command, the saying was, "If you can't handle your wife, how can you handle commanding troops?" Officers still single or divorced did not often rise higher. *But is it worth moving ahead in my career to stay in an empty marriage? None of us are happy.*

Neil lathered himself with soap and rinsed, first with hot, then cold water. *God knows I need the cold shower,* he thought, *though I swear I'll never touch Faye again. I'm tired of being humiliated and rejected. To her, I'm nothing but a meal ticket.*

He spoke to the mirror. "We've never had anything in common. She never reads anything except those dumb old 'true' romances, or she watches TV, so there's nothing to talk about. She must see that we're no good together. We're suffocating each other. Why can't she just admit it, and let me go quietly?"

He laughed, ruefully. *Boy, you've had it! You're so desperate for someone to talk to that you'll talk to yourself? This*

has to end!
    Neil dried with the towel much more rigorously than he intended, almost rubbing his shoulders and backside raw. What should he do? He didn't want to sleep with Faye. He didn't want to touch her—even accidentally.
    Early in their marriage she'd said, "You're disgusting! The least you could do is cover your nakedness in bed." He had liked the caress of cool sheets against his skin, since there was never any other caress. He would have preferred warmth, but he was no longer willing to beg for hers--not any more. So, though he would have preferred to sleep naked, pajamas had become a necessity.
    Of course, she was asleep, or pretending to be. She didn't respond to his, "Good night, Faye." *The least she could do is find a new way to reject me. This one is stale.*
    He lay in the dark, way over on the opposite side of the bed, trying to force sleep to come. *We must help the girls understand that divorce is not the end of the world. We can help them see why they will alternate homes. God knows I'll need to share custody to counteract Faye's angry influence. We must make Katy and Micki know that we both still love them. My God, if we could manage to work together on just this one most important thing in our lives, maybe we both could really be free of this incompatible marriage of pretense, and both of us could make new lives before it's too late?*

5

1980 in Germany   It was a leisurely Saturday
evening. Sara had just finished a phone call to her teen-aged
daughters, now at college in the States, when there was a knock at
her door. There, carrying his guitar was Michael, one of several
friends who'd come to rely on Sara since her arrival in Germany.
He announced cheerfully, "I came to sing for my supper."

Never surprised by drop-in guests, Sara laughed at the
young man good-naturedly. "I thought you had a dinner date with
Charlotte, that cute little German girl."

"She fizzled out, and I thought of your Saturday night
soup." Michael lifted the pot lid and smelled the aroma. "Gee, my
favorite kind."

"They're all your favorite kind, flyboy. I'll bet you finished
your new guitar arrangement, didn't you?"

"How'd you guess?" He pulled the guitar from its case and
plopped on a kitchen chair, strumming a few chords as she set the
table. "Can we do some harmonizing after we eat?"

Sara nodded as they settled down to soup and homemade
bread.

"Are we having cookies for dessert?"

"And how did you know I baked cookies today?"

"You always bake cookies, Sara. Why do you think men
love you so?"

She laughed. "Gee, and I thought it was because I was wild
and glamorous."

Michael grinned. "Oh, yeah? That too. How are the girls?"

"Beautiful! Lisa's on the Dean's List, and Lynette says
she's struggling with literature, while adoring trigonometry, of all
things. I need to get checks in the mail for their books this week."

"They're smart girls. It's hard to imagine you have girls in
college."

"Gary and I got married young. I was still eighteen when

Lisa came along, so….” She shrugged her square shoulders.

“I heard you were picked for that international think tank in Munich. Congratulations. Are all the others really generals, admirals, and embassy people?”

“They just needed a woman’s touch among all those ‘big brass’ males.” She leaned forward conspiratorially. “They each see a problem from their own specialty. But being a literature major, I go for the theme of the problem--the big picture. Somehow, they say this qualifies me as a ‘catalyst’.” She sipped her cola and grinned. “At least, the group provides intellectual stimulation. I enjoy research on international issues.”

“A lot of outside reading?”

She nodded. “But I like the challenge.”

“Gee, Sara, you were a basket case when you came to Germany--now look at you! You know everyone on Post, and we all come to cry on your shoulder and get your advice when we fall on our faces, literally or figuratively.”

“With you, it’s usually literally.” They laughed together.

“It’s hard for me to remember when you were so timid.”

“I *was* pretty frightened then. I was looking for a way to become a whole person again—instead of the incompetent half I’d imagined myself after Gary died. But folks here kept me too busy to think much, so I stayed. This became a safe place to recuperate.”

“You always worry about our problems--about what everyone else needs,” Michael said with a sheepish grin,

“That’s funny. My mom tells me that’s my biggest fault--my fatal flaw.”

“I’m waiting for you to let some nice man into your life.”

Sara sobered and was quiet as she put the dishes in the sink and led the way to the living room where Michael could play and sing his favorite songs. She knew he was serious and caring, not merely facetious. Finally, she got up her nerve to answer.

“I’ve befriended a lot of men in Germany. But most are too young or already married. Guess I have a sympathetic face or something, because they keep coming to talk about their latest crisis. I don’t mind. We’re all human--trying to get along in the world. Just living day to day can be confusing sometimes."

"But Sara…."

"If you're asking if there's been any romantic interest—I date, but I seem to run away if it gets serious. I guess I'm afraid of losing again if I let myself love someone, Michael. Does that make sense to you?" She laughed at herself, "No, I guess it wouldn't." She sighed and realized she'd need to explain. "I appreciate your concern. I enjoy men as friends, just as I enjoy my women friends, but I'm not looking for one to whom I can give my life--not the way I did with Gary. It makes one too vulnerable. I'll never feel that for anyone else--a once in a lifetime thing, I think. Do you sort of understand?"

As Michael shook his head, she tried to divert his attention away from her private emotions, by adding, "Hey, aren't you going to play me your new arrangements of 'For the Good Times' and 'Help Me Make It Through the Night?' We can harmonize."

###

After music, counseling, laughter, and fortified with lots of cookies, Michael left to patch things up with Charlotte. About eleven, the phone rang. On the other end of the line, Katy whispered. She could hear noises outside, and she was alone. Sara promised to drive straight over to the on-post housing unit of Lt. Col. Neil Sedgwick.

"I'll knock four times, Katy, so you'll know it's me, okay?" At the girl's assent, Sara hung up, slapped on her sneakers and raced for the car with laces flapping. Her Mustang almost knew the way to Post alone, since she'd been teaching at the school for seven years. Her tires hummed over the German road--her thoughts racing ahead to Katy.

I wish they'd have left Katy with me in the first place--but I know she wanted to try staying alone. Sara saw the Sedgwick family casually at church, where many of her single friends attended the only Protestant service the Post had on Sundays. But she didn't feel she knew Faye. The woman rarely did more than nod curtly. It was easier to feel comfortable with the rest of the family. The girls and Neil were active in Ski Club, where Sara had been secretary, chief bottle washer, trip captain, and nursemaid to a succession of presidents since she'd learned to ski.

At the last meeting, it had been Neil who asked Sara if Katy could call her in case of emergency while he and Faye were in Greece. "You and Katy seem to get along well, and I don't feel quite comfortable leaving her alone. She thinks she is so grown up, but Old Dad here worries too much, I guess." He had seemed almost apologetic in his concern. Sara enjoyed Katy and instinctively understood the young girl's yearning for more independence, so she had quickly agreed.

Ski Club was a big part of life on Post. Sara's days were divided between club activities and the myriads of fifth graders who swept into her class every year, bringing with them a long list of overseas and stateside school records. She loved giving children the stability of a teacher who stayed in one place while Army families kept moving every three years.

Sara's friends and her children at school kept her too busy to miss her old life--except in the lonely hours of the night when she could almost feel Gary's remembered kisses. *Never a morning dawns that I don't miss his cuddling, and never do I climb into bed that I don't long for his warmth and passion.*

As always, tears still came, and she grabbed the box of tissues she carried in the car. *I mustn't think about that now. Katy needs me.* She jerked herself back to reality as she made a sharp turn off the highway toward the base housing.

She had to smile when she saw the Sedgwick house. Every light blazed. She remembered the nights as a child when she had listened to scary radio shows like *Inner Sanctum* from her hiding place behind the sofa. Kids were all alike. She ran to knock four times. Katy opened the door and almost pulled her inside.

"Thank you for coming to the rescue," said Katy breathlessly. "The noises probably weren't anything, but I would like some company." The girl visibly relaxed. "Do you want some hot chocolate and ice cream?"

"Goodness, I hope that's not all you're eating while your folks are gone." Seeing the crestfallen look on Katy's face, Sara added, "Of course. Hot chocolate and ice cream sounds wonderful. Lead me to the kitchen and I'll help you."

They chatted over their midnight snack until Katy asked, "You won't tell Mom and Dad that I got scared, will you?"

"Of course not. Would you rather stay at my place until they get home Tuesday?"

"Oh, Dad called. They'll be coming home tomorrow."

"Why, that's half their vacation time. Did something happen? Are they sick?"

"He said that the trip was a disaster, Mom didn't like it there, and they were coming home on the next plane."

"That's too bad. Your dad seemed excited about finally seeing the Acropolis when we all gave him ideas about it at Ski Club meeting last week."

"They're probably just fighting again. Nobody really knows them. My Mom and Dad are like green chips and blue chips. They don't belong in the same game."

What an astonishing statement from a fourteen-year-old. Sara felt it better not to comment, so she changed the subject. "Your dad signed up for the trip to Austria for ski lessons. Doesn't your mom want to come along and learn to ski? It'll be fun."

"No way! She hates his sports--hates his job--doesn't want to try. She'd rather he just leave her alone and go by himself, or with Micki and me. I love skiing and would like to go, but we'll be in school that week, and I have some heavy tests." She refilled the hot chocolate. "The trip will be a good break for Dad to get away, though. I think he needs it after his command. He seems so tired and so sad. I don't know if he'll be able to take me skiing as often, once he's at Grafenwohr. He'll only come home on weekends, and I'm not even sure where Grafenwohr is."

"It's a training base about an hour or so east from here." Sara recognized the loneliness in the young teen. "Maybe next time your Dad can't get away for a weekend ski trip, you can go along with me. If your folks say it's okay, of course."

"Will the Ski Club let us do that--your taking responsibility for a minor and all?"

"I think we can work it out." She took mental note to ask Neil if he'd sign a power of attorney, in case the girl ever had an accident or needed a doctor. "Do you want me to stay until your parents get home?"

"No, 'cause then they'll know I called you, and I didn't manage it all by myself."

"I'll never tell." Sara couldn't help smiling at Katy, remembering her own secrets.

The two went through the house, checking door locks and windows. Finally, Sara tucked in the young teen, regardless of her elevated status of fourteen years. "I'll let myself out, Katy. Don't forget, if there's a trip your dad can't take you on, call me. If it's okay with your mom, I'll take you on the bus with Ski Club."

Katy smiled, and nodded vigorously. "She won't care. She always likes to get rid of both Dad and me."

Again, Sara felt uncomfortable answering, so she simply waved good night.

On the drive home, Sara wondered at Katy's candid comments about the blue chips and green chips, and her mom wanting to get rid of her. The parents had always seemed in public like the perfect, respectable couple. Everybody said so. Was that only an act? What did Katy see in them that others didn't see? Of course, the child could be way off base, too. Neil had made offhand remarks at times, but Sara had always attributed them to the stress of his responsibility as battalion commander.

But, even if Katy was right, and there really was a rift between her parents, it certainly wouldn't be the first time in military history! As she drove along the dark highway toward her apartment in Wernsdorf, a tiny village a dozen miles off post, Sara tallied the battalion commanders she had seen fold up their marriage at the end of what was the toughest assignment of their career. There was even a joke that a battalion commander went home from Germany with a cuckoo clock, a new baby, or a divorce. And, of course, should it be divorce, she knew it would have an inordinate and unfair impact on the officer's career and his future in the Army.

Sara thought with sadness of yet another recent example of this phenomenon--the Infantry Battalion Commander, Skip Davis, who'd been trying to juggle his intense job and his problematic home life in such a way that his superiors wouldn't know. For Skip, hiding his family problems had resulted in a strange sort of double life that seemed to alienate him from his colleagues. *If they had only known what he was going through,* Sara thought, *perhaps they could have understood him better. But I couldn't have told them. He swore me to secrecy.*

She had become Skip's friend and confidante purely by accident, when she had encountered him with his little boy, Stefan, one slow night at the Officer's Club. No one else was there, and it seemed anti-social for each to dine alone. Skip said his German wife had been too busy to fix dinner when he got home late. Sara had sensed the comment hid a rift with his wife, but she said nothing. She had the three-year-old giggling right away and had made the comment, "Stefan can come visit me anytime."

A week later, there had been a knock on her door late at night. An insomniac ever since Gary's death, Sara was still awake. She opened the door to the lieutenant colonel, dressed in fatigues and carrying the sleeping Stefan in his arms.

"We've been called out to the Border on alert. The commies mustered their tanks again. Can you please take him for tonight and drop him at the sitter's in the morning?" He held out a crinkled piece of paper with the address of the sitter on it.

Sensing the urgency in Skip's voice, Sara nodded. "Of course." She led the way to her guest bedroom and turned down the blankets.

Skip placed the little boy there, covered him, kissed him on the forehead, and turned to Sara. "I'm sorry. I didn't want anyone to know, but I'm going to have to confide in someone before I go crazy." He blurted out in a rush, "My wife's an alcoholic. She was dead drunk when I got home, and I didn't dare leave Stefan alone with her. I had no idea at this hour of the night where to take him. You'd mentioned that you liked kids, and that you didn't sleep much, so I thought of you.

"It's okay, Colonel Davis. He'll be fine here."

"Please, call me Skip. I've just trusted you with my hellish secret, so I guess we'll need to be friends. I'm sorry. My sergeant is waiting in my jeep outside. I took a flying leap of faith. I don't know what I'd have done if you hadn't been home or had been unwilling...."

"Don't worry—Skip—Stefan is fine. I'll take him to the baby sitter as many days as necessary until the alert is over. If we should have to evacuate the kids, I'll take him along, so don't worry. Now you get going. The communists won't wait." She tried to smile encouragingly, though she realized she had just taken on a new responsibility.

It had been a week before Skip could return to get the boy, and Sara and Stefan had become great friends. Skip's wife hadn't even asked where the child had been. Skip hadn't told her. It became understood that Sara would take Stefan whenever Skip went to the Border, just so he wouldn't need to worry and could concentrate on his command.

Skip worked long into the night, and was wonderful with his troops, but in spite of three trips to Vietnam, three returns barely clinging to life from wounds received, and three sets of decorations for bravery, Skip's commander still seemed determined to break the man. "He already suspects something about my difficulties at home," Skip had said. "Military commanders aren't supposed to have marital problems!"

How idiotic, Sara had thought. *It's unrealistic to pass over a good leader because of a failed marriage. He should be judged on his command decisions, not his personal life. We're all merely human, and all humans have problems of one kind or another.*

When tensions with his superior officer became particularly tense, usually over something innovative Skip wanted to try, he might show up on Sara's doorstep as late as 2 a.m., wordlessly jerking his thumb in the direction of his long, yellow Pontiac, wanting her to walk with him along the old canal downtown. She would slip into her tennis shoes and go along, realizing his needs were critical. He walked fast, but in silence.

By the time they'd reached a playground on the canal banks, Skip had usually worked off his personal demons, and the two would sit in the children's swings, swaying back and forth, until he could talk about whatever problem was on his mind.

Rarely did Sara comment. It seemed enough for him to have her listen. After an hour or so, Skip would sigh, snuff out his last cigarette, offer her his hand to rise, and they'd walk back to the car and drive much more peacefully to her apartment. He would walk her to the door, thank her for her time, and kiss her on the cheek as he left.

Only once had he moved to kiss her on the lips. She had gently said, "Skip, I understand, and I'm not mad. But you're already having enough problems. You don't need me to complicate your life further." *I'll never fall in love again, anyway,* she thought. *I can never give myself away again, unless it's totally, and for keeps.*

"Sorry, Sara. I shouldn't have done that. I'll probably never be free. The German government would never let me take Stefan to America should Helga and I divorce here. To them, she's a German national with a German child, yet I know he's not safe with her." He put one hand to his brow as though he might think of other options.

"I have to get them both to the next Stateside assignment, and Stefan must be old enough to go to American school. Then the German courts won't have jurisdiction." The tall man slumped against the doorframe. "Helga's parents won't take her back, though I tried that solution. German law demands I keep an 'invalid,' as they call a drunk, if her parents won't." The man sighed. "She keeps promising she'll get better, but her promises last only a day or two. I guess my only option when I go back to the States is to hire a caretaker to watch her, or put her in a treatment center, probably for the rest of my lifetime and hers. We'll be leaving in another two weeks when my command ends. My colonel suspects about Helga, and with him doing my efficiency rating, I know I'll never be selected for the War College, or get another command."

His voice grew soft. "Thank you for listening when I needed to talk, and for the late night walks. I want you to know that I couldn't have made it through the pressure of battalion command without knowing I could talk honestly, at least to you."

The next evening when she'd returned from school, there was a huge bouquet of flowers on her doorstep with a card that only said, "Thank you," and her nosey German neighbor upstairs just grinned smugly.

Now, as she pulled the Mustang into her own garage and shut down the engine, Sara said a silent prayer hoping Skip could find a way to keep his little boy safe, and a way to get Helga sober.

Yes, she'd already seen lots of evidence that battalion command was the place where both marriages and careers either became stronger, or folded. The third option was to continue on-- pretending--hypocritically becoming a façade of what a real marriage should be, just to keep the career going to the next promotion. She supposed it depended on how much a couple wanted that promotion and how much they supported each other. Certainly she could think of at least five marriages that had not made the cut.

Though many military marriages were strong, she'd watched many fail as well. Sara's thoughts returned to Katy's strange remark. According to Katy, it didn't sound like Faye supported Neil or his career at all.

Oh, well, it's not my problem. I just care about Katy. I know she would be devastated if she didn't have her father around. She seems such a 'daddy's girl.'

6

1980   "But you *knew* I wanted our getaway to Greece, and then you bring me home early," complained Faye, flinging her suitcase into the closet unopened.

"You hated it! You know you hated it." Neil seemed tired and angry, planting his feet firmly in a stance Faye saw as defiant.

She didn't know quite what to do. He hadn't said a word since the plane left Athens. "That's just something you made up to justify our coming back. I thought it was nice, Neil. Really. Now don't be mad at me," she simpered. "Greece was just fine."

She knew she had gone too far by spoiling the only vacation they'd had in a year, and she started backpedaling to get to safer ground. "There were only a few teensy little problems, and you handled them quite well." *Damn, she could see in his eyes that he took that statement as patronizing.* "There was no need to leave." She looked across at her husband of many years and reached out to touch his arm in a rare gesture.

He jerked away and headed for the shower without speaking.

"Now, Dear, you don't need to be mad at me, do you?" She followed him to the door of the bathroom.

"Faye, you ruin everything you touch, even the wonderful Greek history I'd been looking forward to for months. I thought at least we could *try* to enjoy it together."

"What on earth did I do?"

"Where should I start?" Neil mimicked Faye's sing-song voice. "The streets were too dirty, the hotel bellman was too slow, the sun was too hot, the outdoor café probably had roaches, Greek wine wasn't as good as German. Damn it, Faye, you made a scene when the wind turned the umbrella inside out, and you even objected loudly and profanely about going to the Acropolis because it wasn't a flat path. It's on a hill, for Pete's sake! Don't you read anything besides trash?"

"They were just *little* things. We didn't need to leave."

"Faye, when will you get it? Little things pile up. Over sixteen years they've piled up to a mountain too steep for me to climb anymore." He stood still a moment.

Faye felt as though he were staring right through her. She held her breath.

"In fact, I'm tired of trying!" He closed the bathroom door, shutting her out.

She banged on the door with her fist, screaming, "You dumb son of a bitch. Get out here and listen to me"

There was no answer. She pounded one more time to emphasize her words, "I'll be glad when you're dead!" She walked slowly back to their master bedroom, wondering what her mother would tell her to do now that she'd angered her husband again.

Her unfailing instinct for self-preservation kicked in. Perhaps if she poured each of them a glass of wine before bed, he would calm down. *I only said what was true. Greece was too dirty. I had a right to say so. He's being stubborn and trying to blame everything on me. He just looks for an excuse to be mad.* She folded her arms and sulked.

She cited her husband's long list of faults until she ran out of them. But she didn't want to be alone, either. She didn't want to be divorced and deserted and without support. She liked being known as a married wife, an officer's lady, and she intended to stay that way. "Women, alone, are low class," her mama had always said. She assumed that was the reason single women working on Post weren't invited into the Officers' Wives' Club, even though they qualified as the equivalent to officers and could use Officers' Club facilities. *They don't belong with married ladies*, she thought.

Faye tried to think of something good to say about her husband--an exercise Chaplain Stewart had suggested. But it was harder for her than finding the things about Neil that she detested.

Oh, she heard those other women at Wives' Club meetings. They talked about their husbands' dedication to the Army and *their* dedication to their husbands. Since the birth of the Army, they said, the wives organization was meant to bond the ladies together so that in wartime, they could support each other when their husbands were deployed to combat. There were lots of jokes about the mandatory coffees, teas, and white gloves of the old days, but it was a long tradition, and it had given comfort in every major war, they said. They seemed proud of the tradition, loved the camaraderie and fun, and their OWC friends became friends for life. They talked of enjoying the lively social life in the military, the opportunities for travel, and the pageantry.

Well, I hate all that military stuff, Faye thought. Though she did her duty to host the coffees and bake the breads, she didn't relate to the other women in a comfortable way. Because she felt an outsider, she put her own spin on their camaraderie, attributing their activities to social climbing.

However, she couldn't avoid hearing much talk about rank as a status symbol. Well, she could play "Mrs. Lt. Colonel," smile, and shake hands in a reception line with the best of them. They never knew how much she hated it.

The wives also talked about the long working hours and limited family time of battalion commanders. No other job seemed to be so conducive to failure. They talked of the many things that could go wrong before the next promotion to the rank of colonel came along, *if* it came along at all. But according to Faye's calculations, Neil didn't need to put in such long hours, and he certainly didn't need to bring his work home with him. He was constantly being called out on alert, or to bail out some soldier caught in the German jail downtown. The latest ugly episode had been over his taking some soldier to the hospital in Erlangen in an ambulance. Why couldn't the company commander do it?

"Faye, that young man's foot was run over by a road grader," Neil had said. "He needed a cardiologist and an orthopedic surgeon. Why can't you understand? We work hard at safety, and still, sometimes one of my men gets hurt. If they hurt, I hurt. I'm responsible for the welfare of these young soldiers too, not only the company commander."

"No, you are responsible to me."

"Even if I'm home, Faye, we don't have anything to talk about," he'd said, "so what difference does it make?" He'd added, "If you can't support and encourage me in my job, then don't demand the things my long hours and good name provide for you. If you can't understand my dedication to my men, then at least don't get in the way of my efforts."

She had thrown her hairbrush at him, and said, "Damn you, I just wish you'd fail!" It had not been a pretty argument, but she had her rights too. *I guess I told him*, she thought.

Even at home, Neil played games with the girls or took them for walks in the old, historic city. They seemed almost relieved when Faye told them she didn't want to do whatever silly thing they were doing that day. She wanted no part of it.

It wasn't that she wanted him to do anything with her, though. She preferred to be alone to read her ladies' magazines or watch TV. After all, the stories were much more like real people, weren't they? Secretly, the stories aroused her, and she could imagine being touched in ways the heroines so vividly described— feeling that kind of passion. Yet she felt guilty about enjoying the stories, even as her free hand slid down her body in response to the torrid love scenes. She could imagine the handsome men and glamorous women—together. But somewhere inside she knew she didn't feel anything similar with Neil. In her make-believe world, sex seemed sensuous and beautiful. In a real marriage, she thought it disgusting.

Faye thought for a minute of Merle, Les' wife, who had commented about how much fun their family had when Les took them for a surprise picnic. Faye didn't enjoy surprises--or picnics. And Skip's wife never attended any of the Officers' Wives' meetings. Faye had heard rumors about his wife. She wondered how Skip would fare in the promotion game. Faye went dutifully to every meeting. *Neil should appreciate that,* she thought. In her absence she secretly feared she'd be gossiped about.

All those meetings were for anyway, she told herself, was to show off new clothes and brag about husbands. Well, she didn't like to buy new clothes, and she didn't see anything in Neil to brag about. Les's wife had mentioned that all the men thought Neil would make colonel first. Faye couldn't imagine why. She didn't see him simply bursting with attributes of high rank. She didn't really want him to go further in the Army. But, on the other hand, if Neil were destined for higher rank, it would mean a better salary, and a better retirement check—more security for her. If he kept insisting on a divorce, it would even ensure a better alimony--or a better widow's insurance. She smiled at that idea.

   Besides, there would be more prestige. She could picture herself walking out of the church, Neil with his new, colonel's insignia on his uniform, and with her two beautiful children. The "Model Couple" again. She'd just wait and see.

   Hearing Neil banging around in the bathroom, she remembered that he was still angry with her. *In order to wait and see, I'll have to get him over being mad now.*

   Faye's basic technique when she'd gone too far, even though she believed Neil was always in the wrong, was still to calm him down with a glass of wine. Sometimes he wanted sex, and she would just tell him to "get it over with, damn it!" but once that disgusting chore was done, or he couldn't do it, he'd leave her alone for weeks. *Thank goodness I don't have to resort to this silly masquerade often--only when he's really angry with me, like now.*

   She tiptoed downstairs to open a bottle of wine, grabbed a pair of crystal goblets and hurried back up to the bedroom. She was relieved he was still in the shower. She slipped out of her old cargo pants and grudgingly put on the filmy nightgown she'd worn only a few times in their married life. *Hopefully, this idiocy will be over quickly.*

   But as the banging stopped and she heard only silence, she thought of her disgust, hurriedly changed clothes, shoved the wine, goblets, and negligee under the bed, and turned out the light. *Why should I try to make up? He can get over his anger any old way he chooses.* She shut her eyes tightly and assumed her customary sleeping position at the farthest side of their bed.

   Of course, she would hear him come to bed. It was always the same. If she could lie quietly and make no movement when he whispered "Good night" to her, he would leave her alone. *Let him do whatever disgusting thing he must to mollify his oversexed body. I don't care, as long as he leaves me alone. He runs marathons, skis, and plays tennis, is Post racquetball and handball champion. That should work off all the physical needs he claims he has. He needn't bother me. I know he'll soon be lying there, waiting for me to stir. I won't! His so-called "lovemaking" makes me feel dirty. It's always made me feel dirty. I hate him.*

But until Neil came to slide into bed, Faye could relax. She lined up the day's events and calculated when she would have to face their outcome. *So he wants a divorce, does he? We'll see about that! Sixteen years,* she thought. *Sixteen years of my life doing my duty as a wife, even though his touch disgusts me.*

She knew she'd been drawing into herself—for years. She thought of the most recent time when she had given in to his attempt to have sex and she had hated him for it. Good grief, hadn't she *told* him not to touch her, and he still probed here and caressed there? Finally, she had just told him straight out, "You have five minutes to finish this ugly business, or you can damned well forget about the whole thing."

He hadn't even been able to continue. *Not much of a man,* she thought. *The hero of her romance magazine would have raped her right then and there.*

And what had been Neil's answer? "You're absolutely right, Faye. Let's forget about the whole thing." He had turned over and gone to sleep. Well, she guessed she had shown him! But secretly, she wondered what the marriage counselor would say.

"Faye, you're trying to shelter yourself from a disintegrating marriage," he'd said during their last counseling session--alone. Though he was intensely religious, Neil had given up on the counseling a few years back. Ironically, their chaplain of years ago, Leo Stewart, was now stationed in Germany too, and so it was to him, again, that she had gone for personal counseling.

When she had recited her current list of Neil's transgressions and had outlined her demands for a better marriage, Leo had actually insulted her.

"*'I...I...I*,' Faye," he had mimicked. "That's *all* I'm hearing from you…what *you* want. It's all about *you*. That's narcissistic. No wonder Neil is talking about divorce."

"He doesn't mean that. I know he doesn't."

"Perhaps you should try to think a little about what Neil needs after all these years, instead of always what *you* want. Marriage is supposed to be a partnership, you know."

Faye bristled in her bed, just thinking of the counselor's so-called advice. *That chaplain is nothing but a phony--a man. Why else would he take Neil's side?*

"I think you should try…" It was always Leo's same suggestion. Most of the time, however, she hadn't "tried," because the minister kept pushing her toward more communication, more intimacy, suggesting that since she obviously didn't want to be a loving wife to Neil and didn't want to enjoy his companionship, he would eventually find he needed someone else to love him.

Preposterous! There could be no other for Neil--never. She thought him as loyal and boring as an old shoe, and his loyalty, plus his religious upbringing and his Puritan family would always keep him at her side. His father could also be enlisted to negate any urge for him to run out on his duty to her. She felt confident, at least on that score. He'd stay, no matter what. Besides, she was sure no one would ever want him, anyway. *I won't think about today's counseling session. That minister is prejudiced and always takes Neil's side now. Seven years ago he was on my side.*

But she couldn't help considering that the minister had asked her what her biggest fear was, and what she thought Neil's biggest fear was. She was not sure of either.

Perhaps her fear was being left with no income or power to control life, and those two were one and the same in her eyes. Her mother had always equated them. Her thoughts drifted back to her childhood, and the uncertain life her mother had endured with a war-hero husband confined to a wheelchair for years before he died. Faye remembered nights of listening to their arguments when her papa had been drunk to ease his pain, and her mama had been tired from working two jobs. Had she perhaps been influenced to hold on to Neil just because he wasn't much of a drinker and was healthy enough to earn a good living? She knew she didn't love Neil? She had been disappointed that he hadn't fulfilled some yearning for excitement as much as her storybook heroes. *But I've given Neil a respectable life. Doesn't that count? He makes me so angry.* She pushed back the memory that Neil had often said he didn't want her kind of life. *What kind of life does he want?*

Faye intended to stay the respected married lady to which his rank entitled her. She covered her eyes for a moment thinking of the loss of her carefully cultivated "respectable married lady image," should Neil leave her. *How would I explain that to my friends?* Waves of nausea drifted over her, but she forced herself to control it. That will never happen, she told herself. *He owes me.*

But, against her will, she focused again on the minister's question. What was Neil afraid of? Nothing. If he was afraid of anything, he certainly never talked about it. Of course, he hadn't talked about much of anything for many years--just his dumb old engineering unit and skiing. She had no interest in those.

Actually, they didn't talk at all. He got up and left for work without turning on the light. She hated being awakened. She had dinner waiting at night, so they could eat quickly. She liked to watch television while they ate, so there was no time to talk. She retired early to read, while he read in the den. By the time he came to bed, he came quietly, without turning on the light. Weekends, he jogged while she went shopping with her girlfriends. She was glad they had little contact. They existed more comfortably the less they actually saw of each other. The whole thing with the minister was bogus anyway. There was nothing wrong with their life, not as long as she kept an eye on their finances.

As to that *other* side of marriage, she was getting pretty adept at avoiding it. She knew when she'd gone too far and needed to get all sweet and clinging to save the image, but she also knew that, most of the time, she could avoid him altogether. Avoidance was easy--just lie still and outlast him when he came to bed.

Faye forced her mind back to other subjects. She would have to arrange a conference with Micki's teacher soon. The teacher was mistaken. She'd said there was something wrong with her Micki. *She's young, that's all.* Faye knew that the child liked horses more than people, but that was nothing. Why, she, herself, had always hidden away to talk to her teddy bear as a child, and she'd turned out just fine, thank you.

The teacher had shown Faye several of Micki's drawings of the family. The two children were always in the middle holding hands with dad behind them and a distant mom way out on the margin. That stupid teacher had said Micki's drawings, plus her withdrawal from activities into her make-believe world meant there was a "…potential psychological problem within the family?" *I know better. The child is simply shy, and I'll go right down to that school and give that idiot teacher a piece of my mind.*

Of course, she hadn't told Neil about the conference. Children were the woman's job. Making money was the man's. Someone had to keep the roles straight. She would keep everything straight, and there was nothing wrong with any of them.

"There's nothing wrong with you," her mother had said once, echoing Faye's current determination. She could still hear her mother's beloved voice. "Nothing you won't fix one day with some man."

"What, Mama?" Faye had asked at the time. She must have been about six then.

"Faye, straighten up and look people in the eye."

She had been quiet and frightened.

"Faye, speak up and take charge." The child tried to do so.

"That's my good Faye. You take good care of Mama, and Mama will teach you how to have a secure home."

As that small child, she had felt stifled, suffocated by the pressure of all her mother assured her was necessary to be a "real" woman. She knew now, Mama was right.

"Men are only useful to give you children and a secure home, Faye. Now, you remember that when Mama says so."

Faye shook her head slightly to force away her unsettling memories. *Why should I find them unsettling? Surely I'm right about demanding my rights as a married lady. I should've married someone better than Neil, and I've told him so often enough!*

No, in spite of everything, she believed she had been a good wife and mother, and Neil would never leave her. She'd see to it! And narcissistic? Indeed! Why, she had looked up the word later, rather than let the counselor see she had no idea what it meant. It meant manipulative or self-centered. Well, the counselor was wrong! She was sure she'd never been either of those things.

Her forceful thoughts wavered from surety for a mere second. Yes, she had felt a disconnect creep between Neil and herself for a long while. He'd said he wanted a divorce for many years now, but she knew that wasn't anything really definite--just a pain, but not enough to worry about painkillers. She had hoped to change his mind in Greece, while he wanted to talk over plans for separation and divorce. Somehow the trip had only made things more uncertain, since they'd had no time to talk over either topic.

But Faye smiled, secretly glad the other ladies were jealous that Neil had taken her. Their husbands couldn't get away for such a trip. They were still convinced she and Neil had the perfect marriage. Faye felt sure of that, since she had nurtured the belief. She would never let anyone know how much she hated him, or that marriage itself, in her estimation, was never like those liaisons in the romance magazines--those in which she identified with the romantically-pursued lady, the desirable lady, the sensual lady....

She heard Neil emerge from the bathroom, grab a comforter from the hall closet, and head downstairs. She started to say something, but she didn't want to be the one to give in. *He'll get over it. He'll get cold on the sofa, and he won't want the girls to find him sleeping there in the morning. He's so conventional.*

Sighing, she finally drifted off to sleep, confident she would allow no problems with Neil. She dreamed peacefully of the romantic hero in her magazine who was touching...touching....

7

A week later - St. Veit, Austria   Sara started
the week-long ski trip as usual, with everyone chatting on the
German bus, sharing fried chicken, snacks and cookies made by
the wives and teachers from the school on Post. Paper cups were
constantly refilled from bottles of wine brought by the men.
Michael popped the top off a bottle of Schnapps and dramatically
threw it away. He took a swig and passed the bottle on. No cork
ever went back into a bottle. Skiers shared everything generously--
an impromptu rambling feast with folks literally walking up and
down the aisles appropriating whatever appealed to them until all
felt well fed. It was the camaraderie of friends bound for a
challenging week of their favorite sport.

Early on, people in the military community had found Sara
to possess both organizational and nurturing skills, so she was one
of the Ski Club officers in charge. She hadn't minded the extra
duties. One of them, self-prescribed, was introducing the "lone
wolves" and the most quiet young GI's to ensure all had a good
time. She took this responsibility seriously, bouncing up and down
the aisle, visiting here, asking questions there, and mixing new
people so they'd be acquainted by the time they reached Austria.

On one of her patrols down the aisle, Casey, a bachelor
pilot and a good friend, stopped Sara to refill her wineglass. She
wore an Austrian tourist ski scarf around her throat that proclaimed
"ski the big ones," and Casey was *nearly* toasted enough to
mention where the scarf's words lay. But he caught himself in
time, knowing Sara would have had no idea of the words'
significance. Instead, he only said, "Sara, would you look over my
new resume in case I decide to retire from the military this year?"

His seatmate, Neil, overhearing the question, said to Sara,
"Do you really help people write their resumes?"

"Sometimes," she replied, "if that's what they need."

"Do you ever look over speeches or articles for

publication? My battalion guys said my change of command speech was a bit wordy and…."

"Yes, I heard." She smiled, sympathetically.

"Then you already know I might need someone to critique my briefing for next week when I report in at Grafenwohr." His returned smile seemed tentative.

"Do you have it with you?"

"Yes. I figured I might have free time to work on it when we're not skiing. But I'd appreciate your telling me what you think of it--as an expert, of course." He laughed.

Neil's laugh was a surprise. He seemed so somber when Sara had seen him at church or around Post. She'd heard from a couple of the guys that he was a bit demanding of his unit, stiff, ambitious, and something of a loner. *That's probably an unfair assessment.* She chided herself to give the man a chance to be jovial. After all, she was aware that such comments were almost routinely made about those in positions of authority.

"I doubt you'll have much spare time," she said, "since the ski school leader waiting for us in Austria, Sigi, is famous world-wide for skiing and partying everyone to death on these ski weeks. But we might find a few moments to look it over. Let me know when." She started to move on down the aisle.

Neil turned to Casey. "She seems helpful, doesn't she? My daughter, Katy, certainly likes her."

"I heard that," said Sara, turning back to the two with a grin. "Katy's a great kid. You are a lucky man."

"I meant to thank you for being willing to help Katy if she needed it. She wanted so to try staying alone while we were gone."

"Yeah, Sara's like that," intervened Casey. She'll help anyone that needs it, though she kind of forgets to take care of herself. Can't do without her around here." He grinned with mischief at the object of the conversation.

"It sounds as though you like her especially well, Casey," teased Neil. Both he and Casey spoke as though Sara weren't standing right beside them. "Is she a girlfriend?"

Though Neil had directed his question to tease Casey, Sara

could feel his eyes on hers. Hers remained amused, waiting to hear what Casey would say.

"No, unfortunately," Casey answered. "Not because I haven't tried. She looks after all of us, but she runs like Hell every time anyone gets romantic." He turned to Sara, who was blushing and wishing she hadn't stayed to listen. "Don't you, Love?"

"Hm," she said quietly, with a soft smile that turned up the corners of her mouth ever so slightly. "You've all been special friends, Casey. You'll be the first to know if I'm ever in the market for a good man." She turned away to introduce a teacher to another friend sitting behind Casey on the bus. After chatting awhile with the two, she returned to the front of the bus and her seatmate, Joan.

Everyone on the bus seemed occupied so, with her rounds completed for the moment, Sara drifted into her own thoughts. *Tuesday will be the anniversary of his death—always hard to maintain control of my feelings. It's not that I don't miss him other times. But I can usually keep the old stiff upper lip except when I remember that terrible night—the phone call, that frantic trip to the hospital. We didn't even get to say goodbye. He was already gone--probably at the scene of the accident....*

"Penny for your thoughts," interrupted Joan.

"Nothing much. I guess sometimes a casual conversation reminds me that I don't really know where life is taking me."

"Hey, join the club. We all wonder about that."

"I guess I'd hoped the trip wouldn't have to be this week, of all times. It's sort of a bad week for me. But it was the only week we could reserve Sigi's popular Ski School, so I made reservations anyway. You know what a character Sigi is."

"It'll be a good trip. We all needed to get away." Perhaps sensing Sara's discomfort, Joan left her to her solitude.

All Sara wanted was to have Gary back, tender and sexy as ever. No one else could ever compare with him, so why bother? She wondered if the pain would ever go away in her lifetime. Her friends kept her busy but they could never know her thoughts. *If I let my thoughts show, no one would understand.* So she smiled at everyone equally and hugged her secret love to herself. Unaware that she did so, Sara had wrapped her arms around her knees tightly, holding herself in to keep the shattered pieces of her heart from spilling out where others could see.

Saturday's skiing took one's mind off everything else. Sigi's Austrian ski instructors knew only two words of English— "Follow me." With that, they hurtled down hills at breakneck speed. Skiers in their various ability levels hurtled after them, trying desperately to keep up. Anyone who thought he'd get to rest at lunch was sadly mistaken. The skiers collapsed on the outdoor benches of little mountain *Huttes,* but instructors drank a warm beer, rose with the familiar two words, and everyone was off again.

After the first day of such skiing on Saturday, the beginners and intermediates improved rapidly. By Monday, the advanced skiers had learned to leap over a blind precipice instead of stopping to peer over the crest of each hill and *decide* if they could handle the slope or not—no time for that. The ski instructor screamed over the top with advanced students following him blindly, each in his own heart fearing he was following to certain death, but each too intimidated to say so. Soon, they felt confident in their ability to recover in mid-air, and they took a bit of pride in themselves.

But each day also brought incredible fatigue. Leg muscles, plus other muscles no one even knew they had--all were sore. Large quantities of aspirin helped. So did the beer. Ski Club members usually danced and partied all night on ski trip evenings, but here, they collapsed at the dinner table and were in bed shortly thereafter. Sara did make an exception Sunday evening to look over Neil's proposed speech at the group's dinner. After reading a few paragraphs of dry facts, she asked him to just tell her about what he really wanted his listeners to know.

"You mean, just talk to you?" said Neil, incredulous. "Don't you want to go over the speech and suggest changes?"

"Maybe later. For now, just tell me what *you* believe this project is all about."

Neil began tentatively, but soon warmed to his topic--what he wanted the area to provide for soldiers' training--how to fire tank weapons in battle while moving. When he became particularly animated in explaining his vision, she stopped him.

"There--right there! *That* should be your opening. Introduce your vision, and then show why it needs to be done your way. You'll have a dynamite speech." She turned over the paper and jotted down an opening on the back incorporating Neil's vision, exactly as he had said it himself, and wrote 'evidence 1, evidence 2, evidence 3 underneath.' Then she wrote a breezy summation, again using his own words just as he had spouted them off while he was excited. "Here's your beginning and your ending. Fill in the 'evidence' from your old speech, but otherwise, scrap it."

The incredulous way Neil looked at her was disconcerting, as though he didn't know whether to laugh or cry.

"What's wrong?" she asked.

"You! You understood what I was trying to say."

"You have great ideas, Neil. You just need to give them to your audience more directly and not get bogged down in what you think a speech should sound like. You know your engineering--just tell them--so they'll be as inspired as you are."

"How do you know about engineers or tank trails?"

"A lot of my friends are in your engineer unit or in cavalry. They talk about their jobs all the time. Also, I read a lot--to keep up with what's going on--that's all." With that, Sara rose, yawned and said, "I'm heading to bed, whether my roommate Joan does, or not. Let me see your speech when it's finished, okay?" She waved goodnight to others as she headed out the door of the restaurant.

It was Austrian custom at the end of a day's skiing for each class to stand in a circle, raise one ski in the air, and join the instructor in a chorus of three cheers, *"Schi heil, Schi heil, Schi heil,"* which meant about the same as "three cheers for skiing."

By Tuesday evening, Sara's advanced group was the last

finished. All were so exhausted from strenuous mogul skiing without rest periods that they could barely slide in prone on their backs. But the instructor demanded his salute. Slowly, each managed to raise one ski from their position flat on the snowy ground, and croak, "*Schi heil, schi heil, schi heil.*" Not one student skier could get up! Every muscle, every tendon was weak as hot butter. As the six of them tried to roll over on the ground to get their skis off, the beginners and intermediates, who had not been pushed nearly so hard, took pity on their helpless comrades, carefully removed their skis, and helped them onto the bus.

"I've never heard so much moaning and groaning," said Joan, who was a beginner. She was answered by yet another chorus of groans from Sara and the other advanced skiers. The bus took them to a lovely indoor-outdoor swimming pool and somehow, in the warm water, all began to perk up a bit.

Sigi, the bronzed Austrian Olympic downhill racer who now prided himself on his 'run-'em down, then build-'em back up' method of teaching the sport, told them, "Today *ist der* turning point. Tomorrow, you *vill* be besser. First, we must have our party tonight, *und* tomorrow *vill* be *besser.*"

Sara was sure a party was out of the question, especially for her group, but no one could argue with Sigi. Soon the whole crew was bundled up and walking a mile up the hill in the snow to Sigi's party hall. They enjoyed a hearty dinner and Sigi's jovial speech followed by party games and dances to the music of an 'oom-pah-pah' band. Hoots of laughter filled the air as the men were arranged in a circle, each with a Tyrolean hat on his head. When the music stopped, each participant had to find a head to place the hat on, even as the hats kept disappearing. If there was no longer a bare head, the person stuck with a hat was out of the game. It was a subtle variation of the old children's favorite, musical chairs.

After several rounds, Sara noticed Neil hang onto his hat a little too long and she wondered if he was deliberately allowing himself to be sent from the game.

Neil smiled as he stumbled to her table and grabbed a beer.

"You did that on purpose, didn't you?" Sara asked.

Neil winked and said, "Of course not. I just couldn't move fast enough for all those young kids. He leaned across the table and whispered, "Besides, I'm tired."

Sara grinned. "Me too. I was trying not to let it show. Normally, I love to dance, but tonight I'm ready to walk back to my hotel and get my body together for this upswing to '*besser*' Sigi promises for tomorrow. My muscles tell me they haven't received his message yet."

"Hold on a minute, and I'll walk back with you. It's too cold for you to go out in the storm alone, and these kids look like they can keep up with Sigi all night." Neil chugged down half his beer and left the liter glass on the table.

They retrieved jackets and hats from the foyer. "I hope no one notices we're chickening out," said Neil with a shy smile.

Sara pulled her collar up as they stepped out into the night. It was a relief to get away from the almost deafening sound of the music. Large snowflakes fluttered down on the fields—the kind that come near the end of a storm. There was no wind. The only sound was that of their boots crunching the newly fallen snow on the stairs. The entire effect—snowfall along the street of a tiny Alpine village with mountains towering above—was awe-inspiring. "Isn't it beautiful?" she whispered. "So silent, so…"

"…calming?"

"Yes. It's wonderful, but cold." She shivered, zipping up her ski jacket.

At that moment, they stepped onto ice and slipped to the ground. As they each struggled to get up, their boots slipped again, until they were lying helplessly on the icy road, weakened by their own uproarious laughter.

"Are you hurt," Neil sputtered.

"I don't think so," said Sara, "but the others coming down this hill after the party are in for a surprise."

"They'll be too drunk to notice."

Finally, on hands and knees, Neil managed to grab a fencepost at the side of the rural road and pull himself to his feet. He offered his hand to Sara. She took it gratefully.

"We'd better hang together here," said Neil, "or we'll surely hang separately."

Sara laughed at his historical misquotation, and they joined arms, sliding down short stretches of hill before grabbing again onto fence posts to stop, erupting into giggles at their clumsy efforts to stay on their feet. Resting once at the side of the road, Sara asked, "Why have I never heard you laugh like this before?"

Neil sobered, answering slowly. "I guess I rarely have much to laugh about."

"Work? Home? Relationship? Community?" Sara inquired, using her breezy questioning ritual for all friends having problems.

"All of the above. Battalion command has been stressful, as has family tension. It feels good to leave all behind for a week."

"Your girls are special."

His shadowy smile was reflected in the brightness of the falling snow. "Yes, they are, aren't they?" He sighed. "I don't know what I'd do without them. Life, otherwise, would be tenuous and lonely. Sometimes I don't know where to go next."

"I know what you mean. Life doesn't always turn out the way we expected when we were young and starting out, does it?"

"But, I see you smile all the time. You seem to keep everyone else happy."

"Only so I don't have to face my own loneliness in a crowd, I guess. After all, the *alternative* to smiling," she pouted for effect, "doesn't help either, now does it?"

"You have quite a reputation for listening to others. Does anyone listen to you?"

She was silent--grateful Neil didn't intrude on her private thoughts by persisting.

Finally he said, "It seems funny. I've kept my counsel alone for so long. Don't know why I troubled you with this." He changed the subject. "Thanks for the help with my speech. It's amazing that the ideas were there all the time and I just couldn't see how to put them into words."

"Did it come together easier after we talked?"

He nodded. "Surprisingly so. I may need you around to

look at articles and speeches for me in the future."

"Any time. But for now, it's getting cold and I think we'd better get ourselves down this next slick stretch to the corner."

They joined arms again and whooped noisily as their boots acted almost like skis. "Wonder if we should *schuss* or *zig-zag*," wheezed Neil.

"I don't know." She giggled. "Let's try a *schuss* to the corner--race you."

The two slid down the icy road, totally out of control, stopping only when they encountered a lamppost on the corner, grabbing onto it for support. Filled with fatigue and laughter, they rested beneath the glow of its eighteenth century, candle-style gas lamps. When their breathing calmed, and only puffs of white condensation came with each breath, they faced the uphill climb on the village street to where the Ski Club had booked rooms in three different *Pensions* on the square. Looking at the climb to come, Neil again offered Sara his arm. "I fear going uphill will be about like going down."

She smiled. "Actually, this has been fun--more so than I expected for *tonight*." She wished she hadn't emphasized that--she hadn't meant to allude to tonight as anything unusual. *Did he hear? I hope not. I can't think about tonight, or I'll start crying.*

To her relief, Neil was silent as they trudged and slipped their way, arm in arm, up the hill toward the square, skirting the tiny chapel and graveyard in its middle. The chapel was the center of the darkened town and was illuminated by floodlights.

"Would you mind if we stepped into the churchyard for a moment?" Neil asked. He grasped Sara's arm firmly to help her up the icy steps, clinging to the ancient railing with the other. "These old Alpine churchyards fascinate me. Some of the early families must never have left the valley, to judge by names on the markers-- all the same. Many lives must have been a bit incestuous."

"Look, here's the tombstone of a married couple who died in 1765. I wonder what their married life was like so long ago."

"One would hope for their sakes," mumbled Neil, "that it was more loving than today's marriages."

Sara turned at the sound of his sarcastic voice. "Has marriage been a disappointment for you? I loved it, while I had it."

"What happened? I know you're in Europe alone now, but I've seen your girls."

"Gary died suddenly--a long time ago, but it still hurts to think of him being in a graveyard--like this." She swept her arm around the churchyard, taking in all the dead.

"I'm sorry."

Sara could tell Neil didn't know what to say. Neither did she. But she could feel the tears she'd fought all evening rise to the rims of her eyes, and she turned away so the man wouldn't see. *What a night to visit a graveyard in such a silvery glow!*

Neil finally spoke into her silence, "It must be painful to lose someone you loved so much. What are your plans now?"

"I don't know. Just continue along the way I have been; I guess, though sometimes it's hard to keep smiling all the time when I ache inside." *Why am I telling him? I've told no one else.*

"Believe it or not, I think I know what that ache inside feels like--the holding everything in. It's the helplessness I feel in wanting something *more* from life, to communicate with someone who gives a damn." Neil fell silent.

"I guess people can feel lonely with the living *or* with the dead." Somehow, in the dark silence of the departed souls around them, Sara felt their isolation. No one else would hear. "It's just that tonight, it's an anniversary of sorts, and it's painful to feel so alone." The tears started falling despite her efforts to remain stoic.

"Here," Neil said, pulling his handkerchief from a ski jacket pocket, clumsily dabbing at her eyes. "I'm sorry if I made you cry. I can't stand it when a woman cries."

Sara looked up at his face, a rugged, but kind face, now looking at her with sympathy--or was it empathy? He had said he knew what it was to feel alone too.

Neil wrapped a bulky arm around her and placed her head against his chest as he patted her on the back, trying to comfort her in the cold. "If you feel like crying, just go ahead. Sometimes I feel like crying too."

"Like right now?"

"Yes--like now, and for most of the years of my adult life."

They huddled together clumsily, bundled in their ski suits, both minds far away, each with their own inner sadness. Sara didn't quite know when he pushed back the fold of her cap until she could feel his warm breath on her ear. She turned to say something, but he bent to brush the tears from her cheek with his mitten. "It's okay Sara. You're the only person I've ever met who might understand this kind of emptiness."

She shivered. *Was it from the cold or something else?*

"I think I'd like to finally talk to someone about it," he said with almost an embarrassed tone. "I've held it in so long... But you're getting cold, and it's pretty foolish for us to stand out here in the snow. Let me walk you over to the restaurant in your hotel and we'll have a glass of wine and commiserate together."

His laugh sounded forced, and Sara sensed his pain was right up there with her own, dangerously near the breaking point.

He took her arm as they threaded their way down the steps of the chapel, across the road to her hotel, and into the lobby. When they entered the restaurant doors, however, they found the room darkened for the night.

"Oh well," said Neil. "I guess we didn't need a wine anyway. Do you think they'd mind if we just sat here at a table and talked awhile?"

"I doubt it," said Sara, as Neil helped her out of her ski jacket and hung it, dripping, along with his own on a wall peg near the door. They sat quietly on the *Eckbank,* the padded corner benches usually found in Bavarian and Austrian restaurants to go with their ornate tables. These tables were already set for breakfast.

They removed hats and gloves, and Neil took her frozen hands in his, rubbing circulation back into them. They laughed, as he apologized for "bending her ear" outside in the cold, when they could have been more comfortable in this dark, antique restaurant.

"It's okay," she said. "I'm glad we walked back together. You're right that it would have been a dangerous journey alone. Thank you for looking after me."

His chuckle was warm. "We looked after each other. It was fun, wasn't it?"

She nodded. "I've enjoyed being able to laugh with you, especially tonight."

"But, you have many friends."

"Yes, but usually they need me to talk about their problems. I almost feel as though you and I could talk together about both of us--about what makes us both lonely…." Her voice trailed off as though she'd said too much. She shrugged.

"I know." He laughed softly. "It's funny to be able to tell another human being that I know what they're thinking. It's never happened to me before, but I *do* know. I'll bet we could almost finish each other's sentences."

In silence, they examined the details of each other's faces in the shadows. Sara broke the stillness. "Do you want to tell me what makes you feel lonely?"

Neil pulled her against his shoulder. "Lay your head here. It's hard to talk about something so personal when I'm looking directly in your eyes. I wouldn't want you to laugh. I've never told anyone—in fact, I guess I've become quite a hypocrite in trying to pretend for so many years that everything is okay. It's not okay, and I really don't know how to make life better."

Sara only nodded in companionable silence, not at all uncomfortable listening.

Neil continued, "I think my loneliness stems from never feeling I could hold someone and not have her pull away from me as somehow--well--unworthy. Does that make sense?"

"But you're married. I've seen your wife at church. Surely, she…."

"That's about to change. I haven't told anyone else yet. You can't imagine how tired I am of waiting and waiting for her to--to love me. I know now it's never going to happen. God, I hate to admit that. It makes me sound really pitiful, doesn't it? When I go to Grafenwohr, and then to the War College in the states, I'm going alone."

"Have you told her?"

"Yes, but as always, she never hears what I'm saying. She only hears what she wants to hear--only pictures us as some phony 'happy happy couple.' She won't face the problems. Actually, I've been telling Faye I wanted to leave since shortly after Katy was born when she began snubbing me so completely…I feel like some type of factory reject--unfit to love anyone--like my dad used to say, 'fat, dumb, and ugly.'"

His voice broke in mid sentence, and Sara could feel his chest throbbing against her shoulder. She reached up to touch his cheek. "Don't--you are *none* of those things, and don't blame yourself alone. It takes two people to want to save something. Perhaps you can make her understand, or perhaps you can agree to try to put it all back together."

"It's too late for that. We've tried counseling before. It made things worse. She apparently sees me as a meal ticket, and she doesn't know, or even want to know, about my dreams--nor will she share her own. We have nothing to talk about. I guess that's why I was so surprised that you immediately saw what I was trying to say with the engineering speech--that you had confidence in me. No one ever has…." He stumbled on the words. "I've been intellectually lonely as well as all the other ways. I didn't have anyone to compare, so I guess I've assumed over the years that *all* women rejected their husbands. Now, I realize I was deluding myself, because you apparently never rejected yours. Maybe lots of couples can share their lives, and love each other the way I used to dream was possible. I don't have those dreams anymore." He turned to stare at the blackness outside the window.

"I believe in loving someone totally, and easing each other's burden as a team, so perhaps I'm the wrong person to understand what Faye may think. Have you ever tried to talk to her like you're talking to me now—openly and honestly?"

Neil put his other arm on Sara's shoulder and looked into her eyes. "I *have* tried. There's never been any response from her except anger and profanity, and it hurts that the girls hear her. I've tried, but I can't seem to understand or predict her mood changes." He shook his head suddenly, as though to clear away cobwebs and asked, "What about you? How are you managing to make a life for yourself alone? What do you miss most--honestly?"

"I guess just being held, being needed, being loved by someone who wants only me, and who wants me to be a partner and share his life." She looked down at her hands. "When Gary died, something in me died too. I'll never have that feeling of trust and warmth with anyone else, so it hurts to remember when life was good." Her tears flowed again, but she was no longer ashamed of them. Neil seemed to understand.

He cupped her face in both hands and brushed away her tears with his thumbs. "I can't even *imagine* that 'warmth' part of loving you describe. I've never had it."

"Sometime you will," Sara tried to reassure him, but when she looked up, his eyes pierced hers with a dark, brooding intensity. She was surprised when he kissed her, clumsily, reaching his arms around and holding her to him.

Neil muttered, "I'm sorry. You're so understanding and soft. Your warmth is all I ever dreamed about. I've waited so long to be able to communicate with someone. You can't imagine…."

Sara started to pull away, but the glow in his eyes stopped her. He kissed her more slowly, more fervently, and she found herself relaxing in his arms. She could feel his loneliness, his need, reaching out to her—and her own need was responding. Suddenly she felt the warmth, too--the warmth she thought she'd never feel again. She felt it in every place Neil touched her, stinging as though welding their bodies together, touch by touch. It crept around her shoulders and through her lips, deep into her body. She could no longer pull away from this man. His kiss made her feel reassured—needed, almost whole and alive again. It was enough that they could hold each other in the beauty of the moment, drawing strength and sustenance from each other. In a moment of mutual trust, they melded together. She felt his breath quicken, and their sadness slipped away.

8

Neil was on cloud nine. He had crept into his room at the *Gasthaus* across the street to keep from waking his roommate. But as he lay in his own bed, he could feel only the remembered warmth and soft lips of Sara. Happy and contented with the lady he had found and the intimacies they had shared, he was amazed by the intensity of feelings he normally suppressed. He felt wonderful.

Yet, his thoughts were morally conflicted. *My God, what have I done? I took advantage of her vulnerability--of her loneliness. But, if I admit it, I was lonely and vulnerable too.*

Perhaps he'd only been hungry for a quick mind and a sympathetic heart to relieve the stress of Army responsibilities and his empty marriage. Was that a justification for infidelity? Was that justification for drawing in another wounded soul to assuage his own loneliness? What had brought them together? It was an accidental mystery he couldn't begin to explain.

But above his guilt, he also felt exhilarated and refreshed, as though he could whip tigers. He laughed at his own metaphor. But that's how he felt--as though there was nothing he couldn't face--nothing he couldn't accomplish. He could hardly wait to see her again. How could a woman so sense the need of his mind and body, and give it, willingly, lovingly, no matter what her own personal fears might have been?

That thought sobered him again. *What if she had felt forced to do it for me, when she really thought it ugly? No, That's Faye who always talks of her disgusting duty to put up with me. Sara felt my need and came to me willingly. Maybe it was her need too. Perhaps we were simply good for each other at that moment. I didn't realize I was as vulnerable as she.*

They hadn't planned it. It had just happened, as though the Fates had thrown them together for a blind moment--perhaps emanating from the shared laughter and the shared loneliness. He'd never had anyone with whom he could share.

It wasn't as though he had meant to be adulterous. The

word scared him and stirred up a painful memory. It had been many years ago, as a young lieutenant, that he'd been given an R and R in Australia with some of his men after a particularly tough firefight in Vietnam. The soldiers saw his celibacy as both comic and abnormal, and had secretly hired a prostitute to lie with him after he fell asleep in his hotel room. They thought it a big joke, since he had emphatically expressed his moral distaste at their choice of infidelity. Apparently the woman had been touching him as he slept because when he awoke, she was immediately on top of him. He had climaxed almost instantaneously. He wasn't sure, even now, whether he felt more guilt for having sex in such sordid circumstances, or for having betrayed his wife. His friends tried to get him to discuss his ugly encounter at the Pink Poodle Hotel. He had ignored them and forced it out of his mind, until now.

Of course, now that he thought of it, what had there been to betray? Faye and he had not made love before he deployed to the war zone. They had, instead, bargained. "You may touch this and perhaps that, but nothing else."

But being with Sara had not been even close to that early experience that had made him ashamed. He felt no shame now. Sara had actually made him feel warm and loved and all right with the world. No prostitute could ever do that, and he marveled that some men wasted their time and money on such women.

Then there had been that humiliating experience in Virginia, when he and the family were visiting Faye's best girlfriend, Marsha. As usual, Faye had retired with a book at eight o'clock. "I want to read the best part alone," she had said. Marsha suggested a brisk walk along the beach.

"Great idea," said Faye. "You two go ahead without me."

But Marsha apparently had ideas of her own. Once they were far down the beach, she turned suddenly and literally attacked him, unzipping his pants as though she were quite practiced at the operation. He'd never known a woman to behave like that and was taken aback, thinking her actions some kind of joke. Even as he clutched at his clothing and told her "No," that they had to get back to the house," he had been a bit aroused by the encounter, especially since it had again been a long time since Faye….

Nothing really happened, because he tore away and jogged all the way back to the house alone. But guilt had consumed him, and he never wanted to look at Marsha *or* Faye again. Marsha's attempt had been so animal and blatant, so business-like and unfeeling. And worst of all, he felt somehow that Faye had manipulated him--as though the two women had conspired on this plan. *Could such a thing be? Was it a test?* Marsha hadn't even kissed him--only jerked up her clothing and grabbed at him. Neither had said a word.

"You're back already," Faye had complained with a semblance of disgust. "I wasn't to the good part of my story yet."

Neil had gone straight to the shower and scrubbed himself almost raw, feeling unable to cleanse away the stench. He felt sick from this dirty little secret he couldn't explain. Nothing was said. Neil had made an excuse to take his daughters downstate to a National Park in the morning. Marsha had hugged Faye goodbye and hadn't even looked at him. What had it been to her? Nothing. What had it been to him? Equally, nothing.

There it was. So far in his limited experience, sex had been linked with either shame, or the humiliation of Faye's cold refusals, excuses, and mandates.

This felt different! He lay alone in the dark and could somehow imagine that he still felt Sara's body against his. Loneliness had been the crux of it. They had both been hungry for the warmth, reaching for the warmth. *Dear God, I've never felt like this. Is this what making love is supposed to feel like?*

But what if Sara should regret it today--not even speak to him? Of course, he had been rather insistent in the restaurant, but it felt so natural after their shared confidences. She had seemed to understand his need, and she seemed to feel it, too.

He had known she was vulnerable. *Oh God, I'm at fault. Maybe I forced her. I don't know!* But they'd both been tortured by the same repression and loneliness—and had found comfort together. He had been vulnerable too, and it had all happened so fast. *Damn, Faye shouldn't have left me so alone all my life!*

His conflicted thoughts raced, wondering what he could say to Sara today that wouldn't cause her to run away from him. *Please God, don't let me do or say the wrong thing.* Contented and satisfied as never before, he fell soundly asleep.

###

During the morning, Neil looked for an opportunity to talk to Sara, but she seemed busy with everyone else at breakfast. Watching her, he smiled. She was not especially beautiful—though not plain either. The fluid grace of her movements turned heads, yet he could not quite say what it was about her. She had a quality of gentleness or depth that somehow attracted even strangers to her side. He tried to smile at her, but she was gone with her advanced group before he could catch her eye.

Almost at noon, he caught sight of her at the ski lift and managed to jockey through the line to join her on the long T-bar ride up the mountain. "Have you been avoiding me?" He averted his eyes. "You don't seem quite your exuberant, outgoing self."

"Not really, but I didn't know what to say. I feel so bad for both of us."

Their words blurted out simultaneously, "I'm sorry." "I hope I didn't mess up a friendship because of last night." "I didn't mean for that to happen." "It was sort of an accident." Finally, frustrating each other's apologies at every turn, they both broke into laughter.

"I couldn't sleep, at first," confessed Neil. "Ira snored through all my nighttime ruminations, but I was thinking of you. Then I felt so satisfied, I slept like a baby."

"I couldn't sleep…."

Neil sensed some concern in her voice.

"That wasn't my normal behavior, Neil." She shook her head as though confused. "People regard me as ultra conservative. I don't know what got into me."

Neil was momentarily distracted by the way wisps of hair escaping from under her ski cap blew in the wind. "It's not my

norm either. In fact, most people think I'm an up-tight so and so."
He laughed, nervously. "Here we are, both considered such pillars
of the community, such conventional souls, yet so helpless...."

"I'm not sure what caused it. I really didn't see it coming."

"Maybe we were just sharing the warmth we both needed
for a moment--both of us in some type of crisis. I should have
caught myself drifting toward you sooner. I never meant to
compromise you."

"It wasn't entirely your fault, Neil. I hadn't believed I could
feel that way again, so I suppose I had no guard up. I should've
been able to push you away like I have everyone else. I responded
to your kiss with definitely mixed signals. I even confused myself.
I suppose we should be ashamed of ourselves, but...."

"You enjoyed being together too, didn't you? Please say
you did."

"I did." She smiled with downcast eyes. "But we both
know this can't happen again! We slipped up this once. We'll have
to stay apart from now on."

"But I don't want to stay apart!" *This was going all wrong.*
"I loved talking and laughing with you. I've never had so much fun
before. Can't we just stay friends and...and...be more careful?" He
scrambled to move his left ski back into line where it had swung
dangerously out of the track. "We were both so very vulnerable."

She thought over the idea of friendship, and suddenly
snickered. "You'll have to admit, it was rather improbable that we
managed all that on a narrow *Eckbank* bench, emerging from
bundles upon bundles of ski clothes. What would my mother say?"

Neil joined her in laughter. *Is she feeling better?* "I never
could have imagined it that way. If anyone had ventured in, they
wouldn't have believed their eyes."

"I'm glad no one did. This secret is safe with us, isn't it?"

His arm tightened around her waist in answer as he pushed
her toward the dismount. "Always friends, right?"

"Absolutely. Just more careful friends, okay?"

They went over the crest together and let go of the T-bar,
sliding off to the right.

"Well, look at that!" said Neil. "It looks as though both your class and mine are actually being allowed to eat lunch today."

"Okay, my forever friend. Race you to the *Bratwurst*." With that, Sara took off down the ski slope at a speed Neil could barely follow, but she waited with the others for him at the *Hutte's* sun-drenched tables on the snowy mountainside terrace. The whole gang of "Wild Bunch" skiers shared in mugging for the cameras, laughter, and hi-jinks until the now familiar, "Follow me" separated them into different groups again.

The two *Pensions* across the square had sleeping rooms only, with patrons of all three houses joining together for breakfast and dinner at the restaurant in Sara's *Gasthaus.* The group was so companionable Neil didn't think anyone noticed that he and Sara chatted through dinner. They both, rather self-consciously, made it a point to circulate around to visit with others, as well. Later, the larger share of people decided on a disco down the street to continue dancing. Neil said he would go out with this group. Sara declined, which was unusual for her. Neil knew she loved to dance.

He was sitting in the sauna later, also in the restaurant building, and was surprised when Sara opened the door. He pulled his towel over his lap.

"I'm sorry," she said. "I thought no one was here. I thought you were going with the group to the disco, so I stayed here."

"Too many sore muscles. Ira suggested I'd better heat some of the pain out before tomorrow, instead."

"I'm here for sore muscles too, but I'll come back later." She turned to go.

"Stay, Sara, please. I'll be good, I promise. It's okay."

She hesitated, and Neil patted the bench above his encouragingly. He knew his grin must be pitifully repentant. He relaxed when she finally smiled and climbed to the upper shelf.

"I guess no one will think this unusual," she said. "The Austrians run around nude, and we at least have these bulky bathrobes and big towels."

"Are you concerned about how it looks?"

"Not exactly--not for me, but in your position…."

He noticed that she seemed a bit tense. "This is my first time in a sauna. Ira insisted this would cure my sore back."

Sara motioned to Neil, and he dutifully looked away while she placed her robe on the hot bench and laid down on it, covering herself modestly with her huge bath towel.

"May I look now?" asked Neil, with a grin.

"Sorry to disappoint you--nothing to see." She returned the smile. "You're supposed to stretch out and relax."

"How was the rest of your ski class this afternoon?"

"Exhausting, as usual, but not as bad as the first days. Maybe Sigi is right that the rest of the week '*vill be besser.*'" She paused. "Do you have races Saturday, too?"

"Yes. I'm scared I'll make an absolute fool of myself. Will you come cheer me on, even if I do worse than everyone else?"

"Sure." There was a long pause.

"Sara? Don't you think it's funny that we both happened to be together last night, and we both turned up here tonight? Doesn't that seem like a mystic plan or something?"

"Maybe we both were just given sore muscles at the same time, for *penance*."

He chuckled at her wit. "I feel as though something is drawing us together." Shyly he ran his foot back and forth along the smooth sauna bench below.

"We don't want to have this conversation, do we?"

"I don't know. Do we?"

"We've already agreed we'll forget all that happened and just be friends."

"I've thought about you all day, and right now--the way your hair curls up in little tendrils around your face from the heat, the smoothness of your shoulders with the sauna glow on them…."

"It's difficult for both of us to forget such closeness and urgency, Neil, but we must. You're not free. We're both far too vulnerable, and neither of us needs any more pain in our lives. Last night was an accident. We shouldn't repeat it."

"But I really loved it!" He turned and touched the hair on the nape of her neck, gradually sliding his fingers around to the front of her throat.

She took a deep breath. "Even though I can't think of a good reason right this minute when you're touching me, I know there *is* one--at *least* one reason not to continue that I'll be able to think of later, when I'm alone."

"Do you know what I want most this very minute?"

"I'm not sure I should know."

He reached out his fingers, picked up the edge of her towel, and pulled it slowly toward him. "I want to see all of you." He smiled as she looked at him with pleading eyes, the beginnings of tears barely visible at the corners. *Oh God, did I say that out loud? What is she thinking?* He fumbled to explain. "Let's face it, last night it was too dark to look at each other. Oh God, Sara, I said that all wrong, too. I'm so bad at this."

"I'll admit I'm not exactly an expert either, but we must stop here because right now, my good intentions are slipping away, feeling you so near. Unless you are really, truly *free* to care for someone, Neil, you need to stop now. I'm afraid...."

"I do care," he said softly. "I didn't know this kind of feeling existed before. I've told you the steps I've already taken toward getting my freedom." His fingers pulled the towel further from her shoulders as she lay quietly. He could almost see her breasts quivering slightly under the towel's edge.

Neil sucked in his breath. "I love the glow of you in this light. I never imagined..." He reached out one finger to touch, but she suddenly swung her legs around in one fluid motion and sat up, startling him.

"European sauna etiquette demands that no one can touch. And, if one person is naked, all are expected to be." She playfully snatched his towel, laughing as she threw it across the small room.

By the time he retrieved it and both had rescued the tense moment with laughter, they were sitting up, and again covered decently with their towels. But he could feel something drawing them together. He reached for her hand. She did not pull it away.

"You're supposed to pour that dipper of water over the coals, now, Neil. When the next session of steam and heat cools down, we should be about cooked to perfection. Then we must go find some snow to roll in, some ice-cold air to rest in, or each go back to our respective rooms for an icy cold shower. Heat, then cold is the rule."

They sat quietly, breathing in the pungent eucalyptus until the steam died down.

"We need to go back to our rooms now, Neil, really, and separately."

"Can't we go roll in the snow somewhere, together? I don't want to leave you."

She smiled at him. "We need to part now, while we're still able to. If we wait longer, it'll be harder." They helped each other on with their bulky robes and walked out of the sauna, closing the door behind them.

Sara reached on tiptoe to kiss him on the cheek. "Good night, my dear forever friend. I need that cold shower, and I can see that you do too."

"Wait--please. I have an idea." Neil walked toward the end of a hall and climbed what looked like a blind staircase up to a trap door in the ceiling. "Aren't we on the top floor? Don't you think there might be some snow on the roof, or at least some cold air?"

"You're crazy, Neil," she said, watching him push open the trap door and raise his upper body into an attic.

"I was right. Come up here and see. There's an attic window open to the sky, and we can watch the stars while we rest in the cold air. That *is* what you said was proper form after a sauna, didn't you? Heat, then cold?"

Slowly, Sara climbed the stairs enough to peek over the edge. "We can't go up there. It's not open to the public. They're using it as a kind of drying room." She turned to go back down, but Neil knelt on the attic floor and extended his hand to her.

"Please, Sara. I want us to cool down, together--just for a little while--please."

He wondered what she was thinking as he waited for her. *Did I go too far? She was fearful before? She's still hesitating? Maybe she doesn't want to be with me as much as I want to be with her? Am I rushing her? She's known such pain? But so have I!*

His hand still reached down for hers, and finally, with a quiet sigh, she gave her hand into his care, slowly and with such seriousness he felt he was truly taking her into his protection. *It feels good to have her trust me so. I know it can't be easy for her.*

He helped Sara up into the dark attic, let down the trap door behind them, and led her to the wide window opening. It was slanted, as in all European attics, so that they could see the sky, but they were above other rooftops. It was no longer snowing, and stars shone down, flickering in the cold night. A shooting star whipped across the sky, and it pleased Neil. "There, did you see that? That was a sign just for us. You must admit this is peaceful."

"And it's certainly cold enough for the 'cool down phase.'"

He helped her off with her robe. She stood still, looking to Neil like a naked Greek statue in the starlight. He caught his breath. *She seems almost unbelieving, unresponsive. What can she be thinking?* He took off his own robe, and threw both over a railing. Taking her hand, he drew her to the windowsill. "Now," he said, with a note of pride in his voice. "We can cool down in the great outdoors, watch the stars, and just talk to each other." *She's still silent, still searching my face for something...what?*

Finally, she stepped in front of him, laid her head back against his chest and said, "Let's look at the stars together, then. That can't hurt."

He put one arm lightly around the front of her shoulders, pointing out what he thought was the Big Dipper, and perhaps he was right about Venus. They surveyed the rich night sky for several minutes, comparing their knowledge of the stars.

Very much aware of her body so near, he felt her shiver. "Do you see what they've been airing out here in this attic?" He reached for one of many eiderdown comforters lying over the railing, gently wrapped it around her shoulders, and stood with their bodies touching and his arms around her. "You're getting *too* cool now, and I can even fix that. He pulled several comforters to the floor, creating a nest. "See, we were meant to be here together. They left these just for us. Come," he said, gathering her again into his arms and pulling her gently to the floor. "I'll keep you warm…as long as you'll let me."

He turned her face to his with both hands, and kissed her soft lips, feeling her response. He couldn't seem to stop kissing, as though they were reaching deeply into each other's souls for solace. No one had ever kissed him so--*my God, I can't even find a word for this feeling!* When they at last paused, breathless, he reached out his hand to caress her cheek. She met him warmly, softly smiling--he had never felt such a glow inside himself.

He finally found his voice. "I feel weak, just from kissing you, as though I have no more of myself, and I've blended completely with you."

"I know," she whispered. "I feel it too, like one person. I didn't know I could ever feel this way again." She closed her eyes. "But what can come of our feeling like this?"

He sensed sadness in her voice, but also a certain resignation, as he pulled her closely to him in the nest he had created. For a moment they lay side by side and watched the silent stars, as he struggled for an answer. "I don't know yet. This is all very new to me. I've never felt like this before, but I'll not be able to let you go."

When she turned on her side and lay her head trustingly where it seemed to fit so naturally into the indentation of his shoulder, he felt as though they were alone in their own cocoon where no pain could touch them further. She trembled as he ran his hand down her side. He had never before kissed a woman's breast, but he was drawn to kiss hers upturned to him. They moved to some mysterious sensual beauty as their bodies responded, together—together….

"What a beautiful word," Neil murmured into her ear as he pulled her body closer to him. "So new to me—but I have this overwhelming feeling that we're meant to be together, always."

9

Faye was surprised when Neil came bounding in from his ski trip Sunday night, whistling something inane and tuneless. He tossed Micki into the air as she giggled. The girls had stayed up late to welcome him home.

"You must have learned a lot about skiing, Dad," said Katy with delight. "You're so happy."

He laughed boisterously as he regaled Katy and Micki with his exploits on the slope and his awe of Austrian ski instructors. "You should have seen your old dad on race day--probably the slowest parallel turns in history, but at least they were parallel!".

"When can you teach us?" asked Micki, excited from his exuberant performance with wild gestures showing his terrific new jumps and turns on difficult slopes.

"Soon, girls." He promised Katy with his eyes. As always, she got his message.

Faye had not found his tales humorous. "You sound conceited about all that nonsense. A little too much confidence, don't you think?" Oh, yes, she knew he had lots of confidence, too much of it in fact, at his job. Why, she'd even go so far as to say she considered him cocky. She couldn't help noticing that this triumphant return differed dramatically from their return from Greece. She muttered to the walls, "He ruins Greece for me, but his ski trip was all smiles."

"What was that, Faye?"

"Nothing. The girls have waited up long enough. They must go to bed now."

"Aw, Mama," whined Micki.

Neil kissed the little girl on the head and winked.

"I'll tell you tales about the Master Marauder of the Austrian ski slopes next weekend. Good night, Pumpkin. I'll come tuck you girls in, since I'll have to leave for my first week at Grafenwohr early, before you get up in the morning."

When Neil climbed the stairs later to get his gear ready for the morning drive to Grafenwohr, Faye followed him, but he was no longer laughing. He went in immediately to take a shower.

Faye yanked open his duffle bag and threw his dress uniforms and fatigues into it automatically as she considered their frugal exchange of words. Yes, he had confidence and seemed all-powerful about his work, but normally, at home, the confidence faded. She could usually persuade him to do anything she wanted him to do. This time, however, he'd returned exuberant, almost defiant. And, he had put away his ski gear at the ready, as though he intended to go skiing again soon.

Well, she'd see about that! No more skiing, since he'd be out at that miserable Grafenwohr all week. She hated it whenever his unit had gone to Graf for training, not because she missed him, but because the soldiers would have to wash off all this sticky, ugly, gray mud when they returned with their equipment. Anyone could tell where they'd been.

Snatching a shirt from the closet, she deftly folded it into his bag. She began to wonder if Neil had, indeed, gone over the edge. He was acting strangely. They'd been on a teeter-totter of ups and downs for years, mostly downs, and she felt a bit miffed that he seemed to have enjoyed his ski trip more than his trip with her. But if she'd said that out loud, it would have only made the breach more obvious. She stood still, holding a pair of Neil's socks in her hand. *But why, when he came home, did he say that his dreams lay elsewhere…what dreams? He's never told me of any dreams. Dreams are for children.*

"Why are you doing that?" asked Neil, as he entered the bedroom drying his neck with a towel. "I'm capable of packing my own duffle after all these years in the Army. Please stop mothering me, Faye." He took down extra clothes hangers from the closet and pushed them forcibly into the bag he had wrested from her fingers.

"You have somewhere to stay in Grafenwohr, don't you?"

"They've given me a cottage out in the woods near the gunnery range. The phone number is on your nightstand, in case of emergency. It's a military Class C line, though, which means I can't call out, but you or the girls can call me."

"Don't expect me to. There's little enough news during the week. Anything important can wait until you come home on weekends." Faye tried to smile at him, but it felt phony, even to her. She turned away, picking up her latest magazine.

She watched as Neil paused, holding his 45-caliber pistol in his hand. It was Army issue, 1912, practically worthless unless at close range, he'd said. He had preferred his rifle for actual combat. He shrugged and shoved it down the side of the bag. "I guess I'll need it in case we get called on alert." Then he stood tall and faced her squarely, almost commanding her attention.

"Don't forget, we're using this separation to learn to get by on our own. We can talk about divorce when we're Stateside."

Faye shuddered, feeling uncomfortable with the turn this discussion was taking. *He's different, somehow—more determined or something.* "I heard you, Neil, but I don't for a moment believe you mean that." *After all, how would I ever manage my finances, if I were alone? He's just trying to frighten me.*

Neil's eyes grew steely gray, and she knew for self-preservation she would have to deflect his angry words of leaving, yet again. She smiled in her most ingratiating way, attempting to pat him on the shoulder--an uncharacteristic gesture. "You can't get by without me, old husband, and I'm used to you. We've had sixteen years together, and we've been happy, haven't we?"

"Have we? When?" He moved away from her touch.

"Haven't we always prayed together with the children at church on Sundays? Your religious views alone would keep you with me. Your duty is to me. Haven't I always done what was expected of a wife and mother? You could never leave me." Her voice hardened suddenly. "You wouldn't dare...."

Faye turned away to search for something--anything--that he might have forgotten. She hoped to recover composure so he wouldn't see her anger. It might give him an edge. *He's complained for years, and always he settles back down. I'm not going to worry myself about this because he's going to get over it.* Yet, her sweaty palms reminded her of the old insecurity resurfacing. She could think of nothing to say.

"I just want to be sure you understand, Faye. I'll see that you have more than enough money to live on, and we'll both take care of the girls." He sighed, adding, "You'll get along just fine. You always do better when I'm not around."

"You'll be here on weekends, though, and we'll have a good time then."

"You're not listening to me, Faye."

"But, damn you. I don't *want* anything to change." She struggled to keep her voice from whining. She knew he hated that.

"I do!"

She caught her breath at the forcefulness of his answer. *He's looking straight at me as though seeing me for the first time.* "You'll get over it, Neil. You've thought you wanted to leave before, but you always got over it." If she saw him turn away and curse under his breath, she ignored it, and smiled sweetly. "You really have no reason to leave me. You'll feel differently by the time we work this out."

He turned away, picking up the duffel bag to load the car. "Not this time." He glanced around the room and sighed. "Not this time, Faye. I'm tired of being lonely and hopeless. You know, you have never in our lives together even once said that you loved me."

"Well I suppose I do love you, but…"

"That's the problem, Faye. There should never be a 'but' attached to those words. There's got to be more to life than this. I…want…out!"

Faye's voice was steel edged. "You leave me and I'll take you for all you've got!"

"Unfortunately, Faye, that attitude doesn't address the problems in our marriage," Neil said in a quiet, tired voice. "And you've never shown any willingness to actually discuss them. You simply curse or threaten."

She ignored him, and turned away to busy herself with some needlepoint, making a large show of looking domestic. "I'll have time now during the week to play bridge and read. This will be a pleasant vacation for both of us, and we'll be together, afterward…."

Neil shook his head and turned for the door.

"I'll see you when you get back," she called after his retreating form. "Don't wake me when you leave in the morning."

The door closed.

He'll be running for home before the first week is out. He wouldn't dare leave me. I'd ruin him first, and he knows it! She heard the chatter from the girls' room as Neil kissed the children good night. Then she heard him thunder down the stairs to load the military sedan he'd be using for trips back and forth in order to leave the family Chevy for her.

However, soon her stitches slowed, and her anger spilled out. How many times had Neil expressed dissatisfaction with their marriage? *Too damn many to count*, she thought. But she also knew Neil was a conventional creature of habit. *He always comes back to the children, and I can always convince him he needs to stay here with them--and with me.* The last was an afterthought, and it was unsettling.

Should she get Neil to go to counseling again? Apparently Chaplain Leo had changed his mind about who was right and who was wrong. He and Neil had acted like it was old home week clapping each other on the back and promising to get together for a beer or a hike. *That won't help the chaplain's listening to my side of the arguments. I don't have confidence in Leo anymore.*

Faye was angry that Neil might really mean to leave her this time, but a fleeting thought popped, unbidden, into her head. *Neil's my security—I can't let him leave, but I really don't care about him.* The intensity of the idea startled her. *I'm sure he knows--it's been no secret. Actually, I've told him so often enough.*

That's what marriage is, though, isn't it? Having security with a man forever--being sure he won't leave you destitute.

She felt justified. She always knew she could have married better. Why, Neil had come from nothing--a side-hill farm in Maine in a family of eleven. Had he not been awarded an appointment to West Point at 17, he would have been there still, trying to run the farm for his father. Surely, she was the only woman who ever would have married him. He'd been so shy.

Why without me, he's nothing! Yet he always seemed to expect something *else*—some kind of closeness she didn't want to be a part of. She didn't even like him, yet this uneasy truce had lasted many years--for the children. They had played the game well, and they seemed on the surface to be quite conventional. She liked it that people in the community accepted them as well matched and on the way up in rank. After all, she was careful never to curse at him when his superior officers or their wives were around. *He should appreciate that, at least,* she thought. However, she would look forward to his being gone all week. She smiled, thinking that was less time he might expect her to be "wifely." And she'd have time to do things she liked to do.

But what could she do to make him realize he must continue on in his duty to her, beyond fixing his favorite pot roast? She certainly couldn't say how much she loved him or how much she missed him—because she didn't! But, she didn't want to be considered a divorced woman either. *He'll come around. He always has. He damn well better!*

Then she sighed, remembering the biggest advantage of all—and she held it in her hands. Neil's ambition, his dedication to the Army—why, she'd often thought his blood oozed Army green. His desire to succeed would always be in *her* control. How did she know? Because Neil, himself, had mentioned with sadness that many a good officer had been denied their next promotion because of a weak marriage, or worse, a messy public divorce or a discovered romance. They'd seen it happen again and again in the military, most often at battalion command level. A man would have to choose between his goals in the military and his desire to end a marriage. Why, one colonel they knew had run away from his wife and five kids with the wife of his adjutant. Adultery brought a court martial. So that colonel's career ended. He was demoted and censured! Good riddance! A marital breakup was apt to be messy, and Neil kept saying the Army didn't like messes.

She knew a very few officers had managed a quiet divorce on grounds of mutual incompatibility, and they had still gone on to one more promotion. They simply showed up at their next duty station unaccompanied by their spouse. But there were very few, indeed. It was quietly done—unless their wife contested the divorce! Perhaps that was what Neil planned to do. She smiled. *Neil should know I'd never agree to an uncontested divorce. I'm not going anywhere quietly!*

Neil will never be able to call me weak. And we look good in public together. Therefore, he'll never divorce me. He knows the public fury of divorce would ruin his career without my having to tell him--and I'd make damned sure it was public! I can always remind him of that fact, should he keep pushing.

"Use whatever advantage you need to hold on to your security and your good name, Faye." That's what her mama had always said, and she knew her mama was right.

Faye glanced again at the framed, yellowed portrait of their family hanging over the bed and smiled her secret smile. The picture always gave her confidence--after all, the Model Military Family could not be divorced, certainly not by the whim of some low-life--a mere man. She slid into bed and turned out the light, feigning sleep. She hadn't heard Neil's footsteps, but she didn't care where he slept, and he'd be gone in the morning.

As she listened to the girls giggling in their bedroom, still too excited to sleep, she remembered that she also had the upper hand in another way. Neil would never in a million years leave their girls. *I can make sure the girls owe their allegiance to me, and Neil will have to stay or risk losing them. He'd never, ever, take that risk!*

10

Sara's fifth graders were excited all day Monday--because their teacher was back from Ski School and because they gave their reports on the Civil War. One by one, they demonstrated their understanding of that complex catastrophe from a ten-year-old point of view. Sara was pleased with their progress in research skills. Teaching was her joy, and her children knew she loved them like her own flesh and blood.

The children proudly hung their projects on display and hugged her goodbye. She hummed as she put away books and did the lesson planning that concluded her teaching day. Teaching was the only career she had ever considered. She assumed the Army was the only career Neil had considered, as well.

Her mind wandered to her companion of the Austrian nights. She felt content. Was it because of the unexpected turn her ski trip had taken? Why, after so many years of running from every interested man who came along, was she suddenly feeling such strong emotions for *this* one? She wondered what he was feeling.

For the remainder of the week they had been powerfully drawn to each other. Though they constantly vowed each time would be the last, like magnets, each sought the other's eyes in the crowd—knowing it would never be the last.

They had enjoyed simple things—a shared wine, exploring an old ruin, a walk in the snow, and starlight. They had talked endlessly--about everything—as though both had bottled up communication for too long. They debated--argued--challenging each other's views of education, religion, politics, the military, music, books, living in Germany vs. the United States--breaking into delighted laughter at probing each other's minds. Sara had shared her understanding of great literature with a man who only read books on military engineering tactics, opening a new field of study to his insatiable desire to learn. He confided that he loved to read dramatic poetry aloud, but no one ever wanted to listen, and they laughingly tried to recreate *The Midnight Ride of Paul Revere* and *The Highwayman* from memory. In the latter poem, both were moved by Tess's sacrifice to protect the man she loved. They had arrived in St. Veit as indifferent acquaintances, and had gone home as respected and intimate companions--a magical transformation.

In the quiet nights, Neil had confided his loneliness and the emptiness of his life-- being trapped in a relationship long dead. Sara shared her own fear of caring again, and found herself empathetic to his needs--wanting to restore the faith in himself that Faye had destroyed with her belittling remarks, unpredictable anger, and the demeaning act of pushing him away.

He saw himself as unfailingly strong, in control, the ancient standard bearer in his career, yet he lost confidence completely in his home life. He was brilliantly stubborn on some subjects and unforgiving of mistakes in others. Could he forgive his own youthful mistake of marrying as he'd said, "too young and for the wrong reasons?" Yet, it was obvious that Neil had been neglected for years. His exuberant surprise and joy in every warm, intimate response spoke volumes to Sara's perceptive understanding.

Sara's own feelings were in conflict. A relationship with a married man, even one who was separated, was against everything she had ever believed about the sanctity of marriage. She and Gary had enjoyed a loving, giving relationship. Perhaps they'd been unusually lucky. Had her marriage been as loveless and empty as Neil's, would she have felt such sanctity? Neil had been so lonely. Should she feel guilty for accepting his love when Faye so obviously didn't want it? Sara wondered if her previous beliefs had been too rigid, failing to take such painful circumstances into consideration, or was she rationalizing now? She tried to think within the realm of logic, but what was this haunting remembrance of Neil's lips on hers? She hadn't felt so complete since Gary died. Was she allowed to feel giddy as a teenager—just thinking of Neil's kisses?

Sara erased her thoughts. She was expected at the Officers' Club for dinner with friends. She would keep her secret, and Neil's.

###

"He's married!" Casey forced her to listen to his fierce whisper after dinner. "Don't be a blamed fool. Haven't you been hurt enough, losing your husband?"

"But Casey," she had cried as they moved out to the hall for privacy from the partying group inside. "They're separated. They don't even love each other. They never did. You know I couldn't give myself to someone I didn't feel could love me too."

"Sara. Be realistic. He can't!" Casey wiped his brow with a handkerchief, obviously feeling some of the pain he was now causing her. "He can't afford to love you. His whole career will go up in smoke if anyone ever suspects."

"I don't understand why. Officers are only men underneath the brass. It's not always their fault if they can't keep a flimsy marriage together. No one can, alone."

"He isn't even your type, Sara. He's pompous and holier-than-thou...."

She smiled. "I thought that too—before. The only thing that saves him is that he genuinely *believes* his rigid values. He's precariously balancing this 'shiny knight' image with a deep fear that he's missing out on life. It's a delicate conflict." She led her friend over to the sofa and they sat down together. "There's something more inside this man than just the image, Casey--something that touches me, that makes him as vulnerable as I am. I know it could be dangerous for both of us, yet I find myself filled with tenderness every time he reaches out to me. He has such responsibility at Graf. He needs someone to care--and so do I."

Sara gasped, suddenly realizing Casey knew their secret. "How did you know?"

"God, the way you two looked at each other--he simmered. Anyone who happened to look his way would have seen it in his face. Besides, you two were missing much of the time." Casey looked down at the tops of his flight boots.

Sara was alarmed. "Do you think anyone else noticed?"

"Probably not--except maybe our core ski group who worry about you and want you to be happy. They'll fear you'll be hurt, but they won't say anything. When you disappear, I notice." He looked troubled. "You aren't already in love with him, are you?"

Shyly, Sara took her friend's hand and squeezed it. "I know you worry about me, Casey, and I appreciate your care. But Neil and Faye already have planned this TDY duty in Grafenwohr as a separation. Neil told me so. They plan to make it final when they return to the States in six months for the War College. Have faith."

"She'll never let it happen, Sara. Women like that are in it for the image, for the security, for the prestige." Casey paused, apparently considering whether to go on. "And Neil may not realize it, but that military image is ingrained in him, too. If a crisis comes, he'll be forced to seek the safest ground, the status quo. You're the one at risk here."

"But she doesn't love him, Casey. She ridicules him and his work. She prostitutes their marriage vows. So much of his lifetime has already been lost, and so much of his emotion has already been blunted. He doesn't even know what loving is! He thought his pretense of a marriage was 'normal' because he's never *had* anything else. I'm the lucky one to have had it, at least until Gary died." She searched Casey's eyes to see if he understood. "Casey, he melts my soul." Her hands joined over her heart. "I haven't felt so alive in years, and I believe him when he says he feels the same way. I'm terrified to care again, but he needs me. I could see it in his eyes--*feel* it in every move of his body."

"He's a man, Sara! This is nothing but a fling to him. He'll forget it as soon as he's back to the real world. He breathes 'duty, honor, country.' Don't let yourself feel so much for him. You need security--take what you need this time instead of what he needs. Assume you've had your first little fling, too, and forget him."

Casey bit his lip while watching the tears run down her face. Her hands shook. If he had meant to shock her, he had done so. He blurted out, "My God, Sara. It's too late. I see that 'startled rabbit' look in your eyes. You care for him already, don't you?"

She was silent. But Casey's question hung between them until she couldn't ignore it. "I tried not to care, Casey, but I think it's impossible. He needs...."

"Sara, you don't understand. Even if he cares for you, when

the Army swings its promotion guns, love will play second fiddle.
You'd have been a lot safer falling for someone who didn't have
prospects for high rank—the War College--all that stuff. His life
will never be private since he'll have general's stars hanging all
over him. They watch those people, and they're considered an
asset belonging to the Army. He can't afford to think about you."

Sara smiled at her dear friend through her tears. "Neither of
us chose this, Casey. It just sort of happened to both of us. There
were too many obstacles for it not to have been meant to be.
There's a softer side of Neil struggling to get out. He's learning
that there's something more to life than feeling belittled and
unhappy. It's going to be okay, Casey. I must trust the man I'm
seeing emerge from what he calls his 'little box.'"

Casey shook his head sadly. "Just let me know when you
need help. I'll always be there." He started to turn away, then
added, "And Sara, if you two intend to continue on this dangerous
path, you'd better see Doc about birth control. I don't want you left
with a souvenir." Casey ran down the stairs and drove away.

Sara stared after him a moment, then drove home to
Wernsdorf, silent and shaking. She didn't want to remember
Casey's warnings. She only wanted to remember the magical
nights spent with Neil in an Alpine attic with stars watching over
them. After their first discovery of the attic, both had thought
they'd be able to avoid each other on Thursday night. But Sara had
found herself tiptoeing up the stairs, just so she'd know the last
two nights were not her imagination. Neil had been standing by
their window to the sky. She climbed up, let the door back down to
its flat ceiling, and joined him there.

"You came." he said. "First I just hoped you would, but
then I knew you would. Isn't this the craziest thing between us?"

"I knew you'd be waiting. I don't know why I came. I
shouldn't have, yet...."

He had laid his finger over her lips, then opened his arms.
They stood linked together in front of the skylight. "You have
nothing to fear, Sara. I promise."

"I know, but it's terrifying for me to think about caring

again. I loved Gary, and he died. I'm trying *not* to care." She could not lie to him. "But I'm afraid I already do."

He chuckled. "So I'm irresistible already? That's wonderful! I've never been considered irresistible before. You know feeling like this about you is something I've always dreamed about. It's just never happened to me. Don't you feel that too?"

She replied by laying her head against his chest.

He bent to kiss the top of her head and nuzzle her neck until she laughed softly and lifted her arms around his neck. In silent communication, by unspoken mutual consent, they gently undressed each other in the moonlight, removing each piece of clothing with kisses, intense passion, and promises. He pulled her full length against him, unhurried, with great tenderness. They sank to their pallet of comforters, where he cradled her against his huge frame. With bodies touching, they felt contentment even in simply lying quietly together

They had discovered the sense of touch anew, as though they had never learned as children the feel of flower petals, snow, or their own skin. Sara found when she gently touched the little hollow in his shoulder that his body quivered. "Are you cold?"

"I never knew the skin of my shoulder was so sensitive." He laughed sheepishly.

"No one has ever touched you before, have they?"

"I'm almost forty years old, and I'm admitting to never having been touched by a woman. When you simply run your fingers along my throat, there is something--I feel electric-- energized somehow. I never knew there was such a thing...."

She laughed softly. There, in what they now thought of as their private nest of comforters in their own attic, she taught him the joy of sharing soft touches and kisses. His body responded as she moved from her finger tracing along the inside of his forearm to little nibbles and a soft movement down his back. Each time, she quieted him and focused only on the gentle touches. Eventually, when he could hold back no longer, they found intense pleasure in coupling slowly, quietly, with long undulating movements, kissing deeply all the while. She could *feel* his enjoyment of her tenderness, and she could tell it was for the very first time in his life. Quivers of pleasure spread throughout his body--and she knew in her heart he would never be the same.

I'll never be the same, either! My happiness already comes in pleasing him.

In spite of her occasional moments of fear in letting herself grow to love someone again, they had met the next night, and the next. She could feel Neil's pleasure in discovering the latent masculinity Faye had denied him over many years of the "get it over with now or forget it" brand of sex that he said had frequently left him without desire or almost unable to do anything at all.

Sara rejoiced in his soft chuckle and "purr" of contentment as he discovered his own power for the first time. He was like a child with a new toy. The complete freedom of touching fascinated him, as did his new feeling of being cherished and valued.

"I know now there's more to living and loving than what I've endured," he said. I've yearned for this--this something *more*-- all my life, and yet I've never known for sure this kind of intimacy even existed. Please love me, because no one else ever has."

The quiet remark seared Sara's heart. *Dear God, what has Faye done to him? What power has she exerted over him for so long that he has accepted her view of himself--that he must beg for love? No one has the right to make another feel worthless.*

By their last night together, Sara had felt the changes—both his and her own--the escape they had provided each other. Yet she wanted to be sure they were both clear about the surprising week. *Had it happened only because of the shared isolation?*

"Neil." They lay quietly in each other's arms in their attic, watching the stars.

"Hm?" He stretched lazily and turned to look at her face.

"I want you…"

He grinned. "Again? Wonderful. It's always been once, or more often not at all, until I found you. I'd love to try a third."

Her low chuckle came to his ears.

"No, my dear, I mean there's something I want you to do when you go home."

He nuzzled his face into her neck. "Anything you want, my love…anything."

"This whole week has had such a dreamlike quality. I'm afraid we'll wake up to a painful reality when we go home. This attic is our 'never, never land.' Perhaps we're two different people here. Your feelings from this week may melt away the minute you're back in the real world. I want you free to make that choice."

He seemed puzzled. "Haven't you enjoyed this powerful intimacy between us?"

"Yes." She laid her head back on his chest. " But if you get home and feel differently, you must tell me. If you think you can make your marriage work, we'll just call this week a small interlude in an otherwise blameless life, and always be friends. This whole week—sharing time with you—it's been wonderful for me, too, wonderful in a way I never thought I could feel again."

"You know it's been that way for me, too."

"I know." She took a deep breath. "If you want me to love you, there will never be any half-way about it, because I can't hold back just part of me. I'll either love you forever, or leave you when we go home. I want you to decide for both of us."

His voice was husky as he stroked her face with the tip of his finger. "I understand what you're saying. But going home won't change anything. I'd already given up on my marriage before I came here, before I even knew you." He smiled, and added with dry sarcasm, "in this Biblical sense. My marriage to Faye was a mistake from the first. It'll take some time to get a divorce. She won't give it willingly. Until then…."

"Let's leave it at this. When we get home, you think about what you truly want. Let me know if this was all some cosmic mistake, or if you still want to see me. Either way, I'll understand."

Neil hugged her tightly and whispered in her ear, "It'll just be a matter of our being discreet until I can find the right time to make the break--just until I can get back on Stateside soil and get a nice, quiet, non-messy divorce. I'll reassure Faye that nothing financial will change. That's all she'll worry about--that, and how things will look to others. I've needed to get out of this marriage for a very long time. Trust me." He looked into her eyes.

She had nodded, knowing it would have to be his decision, not her own. "We need to get back before our roommates miss us. We're lucky they both sleep like rocks."

He kissed her, and she melted against him. "I've never known a kiss could reach so deeply into my soul. It's like a promise," he said in breathless wonder. He hugged her full length against him, letting his fingertips run down her spine.

She touched his cheek and gently pulled away to return to her room. The next day would bring a reluctant bus ride back to their normal routine. They sat together on the bus, chatting about books. Neil folded a phone number into her hand. As others fell asleep, he gently laid his hand over hers under the jacket he'd thrown over them both for warmth. She smiled, knowing that was all the big man dared for the moment--but his touch was enough.

###

And now Casey had hit her blatantly with the fear she was denying to herself.

Is Casey right? If the chips are down, will Neil feel compelled to choose his next promotion over my feelings for him? Am I endangering his career? Has this week together meant as much to Neil as it has to me? Would Faye fight to remain in a marriage Neil described as "cardboard?" Perhaps Neil is dreaming. Sara faced the thought--perhaps she was dreaming too.

He's a good man struggling with a bad situation. I won't allow him to be forced to choose. I'll give my love only to help him be happier, never to hurt him.

However, she did make an appointment to get a diaphragm at the German hospital. She couldn't face going to the military dispensary where she knew the doctors. Suddenly she craved anonymity, but Casey was right. She didn't want anything to force decisions no one was ready to make.

Casey had implied Neil would forget their love affair as soon as he was back in the military milieu, but Sara's heart knew better. She was already dedicated to restoring the missing emotional side of Neil's nature that he had subverted to intellect, to duty, to his need to constantly prove something. She sensed that he needed her softness for balance. *Faye has put him down far too long, making him feel like a failure,* she thought.

But what should she do with the phone number Neil had put in her hand? Did he want her to call him in Graf? She could tell from the number combination that it was a Class C phone, so he couldn't call out on it. *Does he want to end this? Did he realize he wanted to save his marriage after all? What is he feeling?*

Finally, exhausted from tossing her options back and forth, Sara knew if she picked up the phone, the ball would be back in *his* court. If it had only been a fling to Neil, she would know—she would hear it in his voice.

Twice, fingers shaking, she misdialed the Class C number. Finally, she did it correctly. His voice interrupted the first ring.

"That was quick," she said. "Were you right by the phone?"

"Shamelessly waiting for your call."

"How did you know it would be me?"

"I only gave my number to you and my family, in case of emergency. Faye would never call in a million years. It *had* to be you. That sixth sense between us again, I think. I'm glad you called. It's pretty lonely here. I can only hear night sounds of crickets, owls, and the firing of artillery on the training range."

"What will you be doing out there during the week?"

"Walking the ranges and measuring--engineering stuff, challenging during the day. It's harder at night. I remember our attic and our stars, and I feel lonely."

"Surely, you have the usual writing and paperwork to do."

"I have an article for the branch magazine I'm working on. I brought it out here, but I find that it misses my point a bit."

"Do the same thing we did with your speech. Talk it out and use only the points you believe in. You can do it. You have such original ideas."

"You're the writer, and you believe in me. I'd rather talk my ideas out with you."

"We can look at the speech when you get back to base--if you want to." She left him an easy out, just in case.

"Deadline is Friday, so I'll have to try it alone, I guess."

She held her breath as he framed his next statement.

"It'll give me a project to do while I wait to see you again."

"I didn't want to bother you, Neil. I just wanted…."

"You aren't going to hang up, are you?"

"You have the article to do."

"I'm not doing more on it tonight. I'll be going to bed soon. I have an early start tomorrow. Please talk to me awhile. Hearing your voice will soothe me to a sound sleep, don't you think?"

She couldn't help laughing. "Does talking really make you sleep better?"

"I'd love it if you'd call me every night. I would feel less lonely out here. Of course, I'd much rather have you right here with me. I almost feel like our week in St. Veit was something I'd waited for all my life, but never hoped to have. I thought I dreamed it all. I need to hold you again to be sure it was real."

"It did have that quality, didn't it? Almost as though we could shut the rest of the world away and escape for a little while." She sighed. "But you may not want to continue now that you're back to your old life."

"I do want it, Sara. I do want—I need to be with you." There was a sharp intake of breath on the other end of the line. "Hey, I've got an idea. Do you have any qualms about driving an hour alone to come have dinner with me here, tomorrow evening?"

Sara paused, running two separate kinds of ideas through her head. One was purely practical. Could she drive to Graf after school, have dinner with Neil, and drive home to get enough sleep for her class the next day? *Probably*. And did she have any other obligations tomorrow night? *None that couldn't be postponed.*

But the other kind of idea was emotional. If she saw Neil again and the fire between them had been imaginary--would it be a tremendous disappointment for both of them? And if they both felt the same attraction, back in their real life setting, a military setting, would she be endangering him? She shuddered.

"Sara, are you still there? You don't have to—but I'd love to have dinner with you--if you aren't already busy—just to talk."

"Where should I meet you, Neil?" She heard the sigh of relief in his voice.

"Ask at the gate for the Officers' Club. I get off work about five. I'll meet you there, and we'll have a steak. It'll be nice to share a meal that doesn't involve *Bratwurst* or *Sauerkraut*."

She chuckled, remembering how many such meals they'd had in Austria. "I'll be there. I had an idea for an article for a teaching magazine, on American children who opt for German schooling--like Katy. I'll interview her, then I can pick your brain this time."

"Great! I'll be looking forward to seeing you. It'll make my work day go fast."

"You'd better get to sleep now, though, if you'll be getting up early. Consider yourself officially tucked-in, read a bedtime story, prayed over, and kissed goodnight?"

"I can feel that kiss. Thank you. Good night—my love— and Sara?"

"Yes."

"I know you're scared, but I *do* care."

"I know. So do I. Good night."

She hung up the phone and lay back on the sofa for a moment, breathing deeply. Their coming together had been so strange, as though planned by some higher power--relative strangers that somehow fell into each other's rhythm. There had to be some purpose in their finding each other. That first night was not even making love—it was more of a basic need to relate to another human being--to have someone understand the pain and to *care* about it.

In a moment of blind faith, we tore away the facades and exposed our raw nerves to each other--the pain we'd each hidden from others. What have we begun, and where is this going to take us?

11

Neil greeted her in the foyer of the Graf Officers' Club. He removed her coat and took her arm to escort her into the dining room. He hadn't greeted her with a kiss, and suddenly he realized she would have noticed the omission.

He looked down at Sara's face, and her eyes said it all. "*This might forever be forbidden in public. Is this the kind of relationship I want--one in the shadows?* He knew what she was thinking and squeezed her arm to show he knew. They both laughed, a bit self-consciously. But, by the time they were seated, the tense moment had passed, and Neil could see her conflicted emotions relax. The light definitely shone in her eyes, and he hoped she could see its answer in his, as well.

"The drive out was beautiful--full of caves and canyons. I hadn't seen it before."

"It only leads here to the NATO training centers, and to the East/West communist Border, so I guess the road isn't high on any priority list. But design for these training bases will be changing."

"And that's your job here? Redesigning? Pretty heavy responsibility, isn't it?"

He nodded. "Responsibility is what makes the Army." She could hear the pride in his voice for the Army, *his* Army.

As they waited for wine, ordered, and then sat quietly, Neil said, "I'm so happy you cared enough to come."

"It makes me sad when you say that. If I say 'I'll be there,' I'll *be* there! I always do what I say I'll do. And I *do* care enough."

"I know. I don't know why I said that--the habit of many years, I guess." After a pause, he added, "Damn it! It's *not* just a habit! No one ever *has* cared."

She reached out to caress his hand before withdrawing hers to her own lap. "Is it a problem for us to be seen together here, in a public place?"

"I'm not sure. I don't think I know anyone here at Graf except the general I'm working for." He grinned. "You and I are both so darned conventional."

The waiter brought steaks, and they continued talking as they ate--enjoying the intellectual sparring and the companionship. *Like old and trusted friends*, Neil thought.

"What about the War College and your next promotion."

"I hope those won't be in jeopardy. I've wanted this divorce for so long, that I feel Faye wants it too. She certainly gives enough evidence she doesn't want me around. But it needs to be peaceful. We have our girls to consider. Of course, if she finds out about *us* before the divorce, it won't be peaceful at all!"

"I want you to be sure about that before you disrupt anyone else's life."

"Meaning yours?"

"Meaning yours, Faye's, the girls--everyone." She sighed. "I can walk away now, and you can continue on as you were, with no one ever the wiser. Do you need more time to sort this out?"

"Time together, or time apart? What are you thinking?"

Tears came to her eyes, but he could see her fighting to control them. "I wish I knew. I guess it's all up to you--whatever you're feeling now." Before he could answer, Sara whipped out her notes and began firing questions about the reasons behind his allowing Katy to go to German school, in her best journalistic interviewing style.

Fifteen minutes whizzed by before Sara sat back, under control again and satisfied with the answers she'd received for the article. There was another moment of awkwardness as they toyed with dessert. Neil's eyes followed her every gesture.

"What are you planning to do now?" he finally asked.

"Type my article and submit it to *The Education Journal*."

"No, I mean *now*. Will you stop by my place long enough to look over my article, too? I did what you told me to do, but I want more time with my favorite critique partner."

"Okay, but only for a few minutes. It's a little over an hour's drive back."

He paid the check and rode with Sara in her Mustang, giving her directions until they turned left at a chapel and drove into a field where a tiny cottage sat alone, well back from the dirt road and surrounded by trees.

"How darling it is! I never knew anything like this existed as Bachelor Officer Quarters on a military base anywhere. It's like a doll house in a fairy tale."

"I never saw anything like it either until they gave me the keys." He opened the door and they stepped in. "As you can see, it's pretty spartan--only the bare necessities."

He pointed around the living room that held a couch, a desk, a rickety coffee table--all out-dated government furniture issued from the warehouse. The kitchen was only big enough to bump into each other. There was a small bedroom with one twin bed, a nightstand supporting a phone, and a bureau, plus a small bathroom. Both a pot-bellied stove and a fireplace shared the living room--which meant the cabin was very old--before modern heat.

"I had a momentary vision of Washington's cabin at Valley Forge," Sara said.

"I told you it was fairly spartan."

"It could be quite livable though, if you brought in something for color. It's kind of cute." She traced her fingers over the wobbly table. "You might need a nail or two here."

"I won't bother decorating for only six months, though I would like a few books."

"It's so quiet out here in the woods, isn't it? I don't hear a thing but crickets."

"Later the tanks and artillery will be firing on the gunnery ranges. The howitzers sound like they're coming right through the house, but that's music to a military man's soul. I sleep well." He grinned. "I like its being out here away from everyone else. The privacy is nice in case you should decide to stay." He watched her eyes for a reaction.

"I have to get up early," he continued, "so you'd have time to drive back to school. You should have a change of clothes with you, as per evacuation rules. You knew I'd want you to stay. We can read each other's minds, remember?" He smiled and waited.

She took a deep breath. "Did you plan this when you asked

me to come?"

He laughed. "Let's just say I hoped you'd come and not want to leave me here all alone." He pulled her into his arms to kiss her.

She arched back to look at him with mischief in her eyes. "You know it's impossible for me to think clearly when you kiss me. I really shouldn't be in your house. Someone might see the Mustang, and that would be irresponsible of us both."

He kissed her again, and he could feel her weakening. "Don't think--just stay, please. We can build a fire in the fireplace, and I bought a bottle of wine. We'll have to use the two water glasses that came with the cottage, but…"

Still she hesitated, and he pressed his advantage by helping her off with her coat, seating her on the sofa, and busily building a fire with wood stacked beside the fireplace.

While the fire caught and grew, he came to sit beside her on the sofa and take her in his arms. Their tender kisses were interrupted when smoke suddenly filled the small room. Coughing and with eyes watering, Neil banged open sticky, paint clogged windows with his fist and fanned fumes with his jacket. Sara ran out to the porch, coughing.

"That wasn't exactly the big, romantic finish I'd been anticipating," he croaked, wiping tears of laughter and smoke from his eyes as he joined her there.

"I thought you were the big Maine woodsman." She was lost in giggles. "What happened? All that fire and no place to go with it?"

He roared with laughter. "I forgot to open the flue--poor planning on my part. The outside world interferes with my passion—it's intolerable!"

Neil finally got the fire to an almost smoke-free condition, reseated Sara on the couch, and poured two tumblers of wine. Just as each thought they had their laughter under control, the other would sputter and start all over again.

"You looked so funny," she said, trying to keep a straight face. "The confident old military commander and outdoorsman choking on his own fire."

"Cheers," he said, sheepishly suppressing his grin, as they clinked glasses. "To us, and all our tomorrows."

"Will we truly have any tomorrows?" She was serious now.

"Now that I know what loving is, I'm determined to have it the rest of my life."

"Last week in Austria was beautiful. I haven't felt so alive for a long time." She started again. "But we might need to chalk it up to an accidental experience, like both of us learning to live again. Should we take this step tonight, we'll be...."

"...Deliberately learning to love," he finished her sentence. "I can't let you go away tonight, because I'm afraid you'll get scared and not come back."

"I'm scared already, Neil."

He set their wine tumblers on the coffee table, and folded her into his arms. "Don't be, my love. Please don't be afraid."

"This combination of urgency and contentment is scary, Neil. I'm afraid to let my feelings go, afraid of loving you too much. I'm terribly afraid of losing someone I've come to love, all over again. I couldn't stand it again...."

"You'll never be able to get rid of me, Sara." He held her tight as she nestled her head on his shoulder, her body still shaking.

Artillery fired all night, rocking the tiny cottage with each impact as though they were on ground zero. "I'm here with you, Love," he whispered. "Nothing can harm us."

###

Late Friday afternoon, Neil strode across Graf's south gunnery area with a team of subordinate officers, checking distances between static live firing ranges. Even with gray mud spread liberally over his boots, Neil was clearly in command.

Neil poured over two sets of data—measurements for all existing gunnery ranges, and space requirements for the new weapons systems. On paper, they wouldn't mesh.

"Is this project even possible, Sir?" asked Captain Baker.

"Oh, we'll get it done, Captain, one way or another. Right now, the ranges can't accommodate the new equipment. If soldiers are to fully utilize the capabilities of the new weapons systems coming to us--and the leap in technology is considerable--they must have ranges where they can practice shooting while maneuvering." He looked out to the horizon. "We need to somehow adapt these static ranges to accommodate the new Abrams tanks and Bradley fighting vehicles that can both shoot on the move. They'll require more room and a different design."

"Wouldn't it be easier if we just built a new range, Sir?"

"We can't, Captain. There isn't any more real estate in Germany available to us, so we must make do with what we have in Grafenwohr, Hohenfels, and Wildflecken. We've done measurements at all three ranges, and only Graf can be modified for the new Abrams. Hohenfels might be okay for the Bradley, but more tests will be necessary. Wildflecken can only handle static firing--nothing on the move."

The men looked skeptical.

"Take heart, men! We're engineers. We'll persuade them! The General will back us and clear any logjams that we can't. Some will throw obstacles in our way--there is resistance to change out there. Coordination is the key, getting people to work together. There are those saying, 'It can't be done!' But I'm here to tell you, this change will happen!"

"But Sir," said the young man. "Won't the Range Safety people and the operators of the equipment be in conflict?"

Neil grinned, as he waggled his hand in a movement like rocking a boat. "I'll try to get the safety people to admit they have a little built-in wiggle room so they can lower their standards a bit. Then I'll try to convince the operators to build in a few restrictions on live fire training maneuvers--then go back to the safety people-- who will try to say there isn't enough room for live fire, and so on. I'm sure I'll be going back and forth *ad infinitum* but, in the end, we *will* get the Army ready for its new hardware. Once that's done, we'll need funding appropriated and workers. This first planning phase will be tricky with so many 'nay sayers,' but the funding phase may be even harder. We'll cross that bridge once we build it. Understood?"

"Yes, Sir," came the unison response.

"Then stand down and have a good weekend," ordered Neil, and the men began gathering up their equipment to head back to the main Post.

Flushed with adrenalin at this latest challenge, Neil hurried back to his quarters to jot down notes for his next design operation. He thumbed through a book lying on his desk--School for Soldiers, a documentary about West Point sent him by a fellow grad.

West Point had been his ticket out of the impoverished farmland of Maine. He knew in his heart that he owed a debt to the military for saving him from the mundane farm work he would otherwise have had no choice but to embrace. Yes, his colleagues thought him a 'self-made man,' and he had done what he needed to do in Vietnam and here on the Cold War Border, along with thousands of others, but it was the Army that had given him a chance in life. Today had been a good day. The general had chosen him for this job, and he felt confident he could do it.

Neil started the drive home to see his girls. Only after his military day ended, could he think of where his newly complicated life could lead. But he certainly liked the "complication."

He smiled as he thought of his Tuesday rendezvous with Sara. Though the single twin bed was small for his big frame and occasionally provoked laughter from an elbow in the neck or some such accident, the two of them were so entwined, they scarcely noticed. They found they could sleep comfortably in each other's arms, or with her body on top of his, or spooned around each other. His preference to sleep naked hadn't offended Sara. Far from finding him "disgusting," as Faye had always said, Sara had dropped her nightgown and snuggled against him, saying, "I can feel the warmth of you all over, and we fit so nicely. I love it." He felt positively transported when she wriggled with pleasure. It was a brand new delight for him to feel he could give pleasure to a woman and not be pushed away and rejected.

On Wednesday evening, Neil had waited for Sara's "tuck in

call." They talked for two hours about their days' work and her evening's volleyball competition. He felt he could reach out and touch her, even when they couldn't be together. The sensuous chord she touched within him hummed at the sound of her voice.

Neil had asked her to come out for an additional visit to Graf on Thursday after school and they had dinner at a local German restaurant. The owner came out to greet them and share a glass of wine. They knew the ancient *Gasthaus* would be a favorite for future times, They made plans to spend at least every Tuesday and Thursday night at Neil's cottage in Grafenwohr.

Sara had brought books from the Post library which they would discuss after they had both read them. They discovered Sara held more of a humanitarian view of the world, while Neil's view was more pragmatic and militaristic. He looked forward daily to a good discussion or debate with a "worthy opponent," as he considered Sara.

During Thursday night, he suddenly roused to Sara's hugging him tightly, murmuring, "It's all right, darling, I'm here. It's only a bad dream."

As he struggled awake, he felt the usual cold beads of sweat on his forehead and realized his body was shaking. *No, not the dream again, not now.* "I'm sorry," he managed to mumble, feeling embarrassed that she had seen him so out of control.

"It's okay, Neil. Everyone has nightmares. You were yelling, and you flailed out to hit the top of the bed. Was it bad?"

He could hear the concern in her voice, and realized she wasn't screaming at him for disturbing her sleep as Faye always did. He could never tell Faye. *I don't know if I can explain so Sara will understand?*

"Was it something from Vietnam? I've read of screams and hitting, before men realized they were no longer in combat. I figured it was sort of an 'occupational hazard' for the wives of combat veterans." When he couldn't answer, she held him quietly. "Do you want to tell me? You don't have to, if…if it's too bad."

He felt her closeness and realized he *did* want to tell her. He began relating the harrowing incident he had never been able to talk about before--to anyone. Slowly, in a shaky voice, he began the story of the helicopter that had been shot down in Vietnam with eight aboard. The aircraft burst into flames as the right side fuel cell exploded upon impact. Survival depended upon where one was seated. "The pilot, the left door gunner, my battalion commander and I all got out. The co-pilot, right door gunner and battalion Sergeant Major seated on the right disappeared in a ball of flame."

Neil shook his head as though to clear cobwebs. Sara softly caressed his chest with her fingertips, comforting him, much as his mother had when he was a child. In Sara's warm patience, he was finally able to quiet his labored breathing to go on. "My radio operator was sitting to my right with his radio and secure unit on the helicopter floor. We'd been talking just before the B-40 hit. We were at a low level and the explosion sent us spiraling down—fast. Everyone was shouting and trying to hang on. The pilot yelled instructions, still trying to auto-rotate down to soften the crash. We could tell it wouldn't work." He knew Sara could feel his shaking and the sweat pouring from his body, dampening the sheets, but she didn't move away.

"When I went out, I grabbed my radio operator by his web gear and dragged him with me. And amazingly, he dragged his radio gear along too! I only had minor burns and scratches, but his clothing was on fire. We got him away from the burning wreck, rolled him on the ground to snuff out the flames, and removed his clothing. His skin was a shiny red and black. He hadn't regained consciousness before we were evacuated by another helicopter."

Neil wiped sweat from his brow with his forearm before continuing. His heart was beating fast as it often did when he dreamed. "I was surprised to learn that he died later, and I've always wondered if it was from the flames or the explosion. But the survivors and the fatalities were split down the middle of the aircraft with the line drawn between my radioman and me. I've never been able to get over the randomness of the selection—who lives and who dies. I've always felt guilty for having lived."

"There was nothing you could have done, Neil. It was decided by the time the aircraft hit the ground. That's God's choice--not yours. I understand survivor's guilt, but holding it in for so long probably makes it surface in these violent flashbacks. Vietnam vets seem unable to talk about their fear and the pain of losing friends."

She made sense to him, and for that night, the shaking finally subsided. He fell asleep peacefully in her arms.

Now it was Friday, and as he drove along the mountain road, Neil was forced to think of what awaited him at home. He knew Sara would be going to the O'Club for dinner and dancing, mostly so she could allay questions from her friends about where she had been the *rest* of the week. But he was going home to visit his girls. He wondered what Faye would be like this weekend. *One of the most difficult things about trying to live with the woman is the fact that I never know from moment to moment what will set her off, or what might come out of her mouth.*

"Get those dirty boots out of my house." Faye screamed her first words as Neil walked in the door. He stopped obediently and slid them off his feet, hopping to the back porch to deposit them for later cleaning. As he looked them over, he couldn't quite see that they were as dirty as all that, but it was fruitless to argue. He was determined to walk on eggs to keep from arguing in front of the girls for the short time he'd be home on weekends.

During dinner, he joked with the girls while Faye was absorbed in her TV show. Suddenly, she said, "Well, you're pretty chipper for one who's supposed to have been working all week."

"Now Faye, you knew I'd been assigned TDY to work in Graf during the week and I'd be here only on weekends. Why are you angry about it now?"

"Don't mind me," she whined, "I'm stuck with all the problems. You have to drive home during next week to take the car to the garage." She turned to glare at Micki for dropping her fork.

"It's only an electrical problem. You don't need me. Just drop it off at the garage and take a taxi home."

"You know driving annoys me. I don't like it. No! You have to do your share."

"I was under the impression my 'share' was to work and provide you with a decent living." He could feel his anger rising. "If I take a day off in the middle of the week just to take a car to the shop, that's neglecting my share for the Army, now isn't it?"

"Always the Army!" She grumbled to herself and then added loudly, "I should have married someone besides you. I could have done *much* better than you!"

"Yes, Faye," Neil said quietly. He gritted his teeth and decided not to mention that she had never even had anyone else ask her for a date. He didn't want to say something hurtful. Some words could never be taken back.

"Well, I hate the Army, and I hate you," she shouted.

Yes, Neil thought, *those are some of the words I meant.* Still, he decided not to argue. He vowed to spend his weekend time with the girls and not bother Faye. If he avoided her tirades, perhaps they could generate a type of "truce." If he pressed the matter prematurely, Faye could endanger his career and make life unbearable. *I can think of at least a half- dozen military colleagues whose career went down the tubes with their marriages, and I'm determined not to let Faye do that to me. So I will wait carefully-- very carefully.*

He had relaxed his fear of Faye finding out about Sara, though. It was apparent that Faye, as usual, didn't really care enough about him to notice the changes taking place inside him-- his happier outlook, his more buoyant step, his increased confidence--as long as they didn't affect *her* security or status. For years, it had hurt him to know she didn't care about him. But now, Faye's lack of interest suited him just fine.

They both kept their silence the rest of the evening. Katy and Micki wanted to go downtown to climb the police station tower from which one could see the ancient city spread out before them. Neil had promised to take them several times before and had made friends with the police chief who held the keys to the tower. But always some task of Faye's "honey-do" list took precedence. He'd promised again for Saturday afternoon. Faye said nothing-- just tensed the muscles around her mouth and left the table.

But the morning brought more argument. Neil was preparing for Saturday's early morning run—the habit of a lifetime for most military men, when Faye screeched that he couldn't take the girls downtown because he had to mend the screens.

"Faye, it's January. We won't use the screens for months. I do everything you ask of me, but this time, I promised the girls...."

"You promised *me* that you would see to all the household chores, and you are gone all week, so it's time for you to do some of the things *I* want you to do."

"Why don't you come downtown with us? You haven't been to the tower either."

"I won't tag along while you play with children. You must do what *I* need done."

"Faye, I promised the girls at dinner last night, and you said nothing then, so don't say anything about it now, please. I won't disappoint them again."

The woman leveled her gaze to his as he bent to tie his running shoes and, out of the blue, hissed, "If you ever touch one of our girls, I'll see you in Hell! You'll be sorry if you've ever molest one of them."

Neil was frozen in place. He gasped, unable to think of anything to say to such an appalling accusation. Angry words finally made their way to his tongue. "Are you crazy? Wherever in Hell did you get such an idea? It doesn't even make sense. I would *never* hurt those girls. What gives you the right to say...? How can you say such a thing to me?"

"Just remember what I said." With that, she turned and stomped back into the kitchen obviously aware she had stunned him and triumphantly nailed him to a wall.

Neil slammed the door on his way out the back of the house.

12

Neil headed blindly into the woods behind the Post. He didn't hear the birds or feel the dirt under his pounding feet on what was usually his favorite path. He ran faster than normal, trying to force Faye's ugly words out of his mind. His anger seethed—then suddenly exploded into abject fear. *What if Faye accuses me of such horrendous acts in court when I try to get the divorce? Any court would award her full custody if they believed her lies. I'd lose my girls forever.* He also knew Faye could affect that "martyred" look whenever she chose. Some judge might believe her. That kind of accusation would also end his military career. *There's no way to predict what she might do or say if she's angry enough. Her volatile moods scare the hell out of me.*

Gradually, under the strenuous exercise, he settled into the natural rhythm that had served him well all his life. He fought to let his mind cool, to gain control. He tried to remember another time--jogging across hardscrabble farmland as a young child, managing the family farm, himself, when his father needed to take an additional job in town. Then, running had often worked out the frustration he felt in not having money to go to college to feed his hungry mind. He hoped running would help again now, but this fight with Faye was beyond anything that had come before.

I can't handle being with Faye when she becomes abusive. Maintaining her status quo shouldn't result in arguments about our children or off-the-wall accusations. How could she say such a thing to me? Where does she even get such ideas? Television? Who knows? Damn! Her venom sticks in my mind. It always will!

For many years, Neil had tried to find excuses for Faye's mercurial behavior—her explosive mood swings. But he had never found the key to helping her stay calm. He knew Faye had also had a difficult childhood. Her mother raised Faye and her three brothers alone, in the projects of New York City's suburbs. He felt Faye should have wanted more peace for their children. They had both been insecure young people, making the mistake of marrying before either had dated others. His drive for a military career must have seemed like a stable future to Faye and her desperate mother. He had provided Faye and her mother whatever they had wanted, but it was never enough to raise a smile, much less a thank you.

Perhaps she *did* hate him. Otherwise, how could she hurl such horrible verbal tirades at him? And there had been angry threats of physical assaults--times when she brandished a butcher knife at his neck and said, "I'd like to run this right through you!" He'd never even known why she was angry. He had tried to believe her threats were mere isolated incidents of her mercurial personality.

But *these* ugly words hissed at him were indelibly imprinted in his mind. He had no doubt she would do him harm if she thought she could get away with it. She had never been a wife, a lover, or even a friend. He just didn't care any more. Her unfair words hurt too deeply.

If Faye had ever controlled her mouth—the profanity, the "pieces of her mind" she felt compelled to spew out to every tradesperson--or to me, or to our girls--perhaps we might have found some common ground years ago. But now it's impossible.

He recognized that Faye was the consummate game player, though. Her anger was never used near the military establishment. She showed quiet deference, publicly, especially to anyone of higher rank. *No, her venom is reserved for the girls and me.*

He forced his mind back to reality in time to notice that he had not turned where he usually headed back to his house. Instead, he had kept running down the path toward Wernsdorf. In his reverie, where were his feet taking him? He suddenly knew. He had run almost all the way in the early morning fog.

The surprise and pleasure in Sara's eyes as she opened the door made the fatiguing distance worthwhile.

"You're tired and cold," she said, pulling him into the warm vestibule and hugging him. He collapsed, exhausted, onto the floor of Sara's foyer. Fearing his heart or lungs had failed, she grabbed the phone in panic. As she started to dial the hospital, he couldn't keep a straight face and dissolved into laughter, taking her hand and pulling her to the floor with him.

"Dear, I'm just going to lay back and soak up all this pampering and loving." His big 'pussy cat' grin vanished when he saw the terrified look on her face. "My joke wasn't funny, Love, I'm sorry. I should have known you'd have been scared."

"Death can be very sudden and quite permanent, Darling. I never want to see it happen to someone I love again. Please promise me you won't ever die." He had promised. He would have promised her anything. Soon, however, he quelled her fears and they were laughing uproariously

"Why on earth did you exhaust yourself to run so far?"

"I was going home, and I've discovered that home is wherever you are."

The tears in her eyes he knew were tears of joy. She drew hot water, peeled off his running suit, pushed his exhausted body into the bathtub. She sat on its rim, bathing him lovingly, touching him tenderly. He loved her touch. He pulled her into the big German tub with him, clothes and all. It didn't take him long to remedy the clothing matter. It was a memory in the making--one neither would ever forget.

After splashing and playing for an hour, they laughed as he redressed in the sweaty running suit and Sara drove him to the outskirts of the base where he got out and ran the rest of the way home. It was a lovely way to start a Saturday morning. His mind had eased, and his soul was refreshed. He could worry about Faye's lies later. After this first time, the long Saturday morning run, which he thought of as 'self-discipline,' often became a part of his weekly ritual.

He had asked Sara to meet him at 1400 hours, so they could take the girls up the police tower together. Their afternoon with Katy and Micki was fun--one of many more to come. Neil had come to relish just enjoying life, another new experience for him. They'd climbed the police tower together to enjoy the view. Micki hopped around on first one foot and then the other, clambering for her father to hoist her up to the railing, where he held her tightly so she could see the city's rooftops. Afterward, they stopped for ice cream. Katy wanted Sara to accompany them on another Saturday outing, and Sara invited the girls to her apartment sometime to bake cookies.

"Mama never laughs like you do," exclaimed Micki.

Neil and Sara exchanged glances. Neil grinned happily, but he could tell Sara worried Micki might say something to her mother that would compromise him.

Sunday morning they saw each other quite chastely at church, but Micki and Katy ran to Sara, giggling and excited-- already planning another outing. There was little she could do except greet the family. Surprisingly, Faye hadn't seemed bothered that her children had enjoyed an afternoon with Sara and Neil. Instead, she said, "Take them whenever you like. It gets them out of my hair so I can read and relax. It's only fair that Neil do his share of baby sitting when I'm stuck with them all week."

Sara looked stunned, but Neil simply nodded and grinned. He elaborately mentioned to Faye and everyone else present, that he would begin leaving home on Sunday evenings so he could get a good night's sleep before starting each new work week. "I can also avoid those icy roads so early on Monday mornings," he added. When he glanced her way, he knew Sara had understood, and she would be expecting him at her apartment.

Their first Sunday night, Neil arrived at Sara's ground floor apartment and parked his military sedan in her garage where it wouldn't be seen. Her Mustang remained on the street. He vaulted over her balcony railing like Romeo rushing to the arms of Juliet. They laughed hysterically when Sara's nosey German landlady on the second floor almost fell over her balcony leaning out to watch Neil make the leap. Grinning, he gave the woman a snappy salute.

They talked for hours, sharing ideas, debating to their usual "draw," lying on Sara's soft white rug. By the candlelight of the harem lantern she said she'd once bought on a whim in Casablanca, they listened to love songs of Barbra Streisand, eventually finding their way to Sara's big German bed. They both enjoyed the cuddling, the sense of touch. Touching had become a language between them, a peaceful discovery. They softly made love and drifted to sleep contentedly in each other's arms.

A mini alarm clock Neil bought her as a gift woke them for breakfast. Then he was off for his early morning drive to Graf. He felt energized--ready for his strenuous workweek. He'd not known such camaraderie before, but now he smiled, thinking that sharing and supporting each other felt so very right. An Army officer needed a partner in the quest. Sara had somehow become that partner when Faye, over many years, had abdicated the role.

Tuesday and Thursday evenings at the cottage in Grafenwohr, they discussed passages from library books Sara brought, mostly on their common interest of international relations, debating amiably, and laughing over differences of opinion.

Sometimes, to catch him in a weak debate argument, Sara would insist they switch sides on the issue to see if each could prove his point against his own argument. It sharpened tactics Neil would need to counteract objections in his staff briefings. Sara brought intellectual complexity into his life--something he'd always desired in a partner. Faye's ignorance of world issues and her disinterest in learning anything new had grated on his nerves all through their years of marriage.

Neil was surprised to find Sara thought him unforgiving of mistakes in others. She teased him unmercifully, exposing his image as the 'ancient standard bearer' who was always stubbornly and militarily 'correct.' She asked what would happen if Neil ever found himself making a mistake. He merely laughed and ran his fingers through her hair, tousling it gently. "My love," he said, "I might be wrong, but I will never be in doubt."

In rare moments alone, Neil wondered at this intricate pattern of three lives. It was a hectic schedule, but he relished the time he could spend with Sara, loved his job, and dreaded Faye's tirades for the brief time he was at home. Seeing his girls was all that made those treks back to Post on Fridays bearable. *How long can we keep this pace without slipping up and causing a disaster? Yet what would I change, if I could? Only to get the divorce faster.*

Neil noted that each time Sara drove out to join him at Graf, she brought little things to make his bare cottage more home-like--a couple of sofa pillows she had embroidered in his favorite colors, a throw rug beside the fireplace where they frequently lay to talk or heartily make love, and a wooden mug she'd hand-painted in German *Balenmalerei*. She brought a pair of *real* wine glasses and a tiny wooden candlestick with an elfin face painted on, the only candlestick available at the sparsely stocked Graf PX. "We need candlelight," she said. "This little guy smiles with us."

When Sara used her key to the cottage to fix Neil's dinner, simple though it had to be in a mini kitchen with few utensils and a single hotplate, he was touched. With anyone else, he would have stiffly controlled his emotion, but with Sara, he had simply held her closely. "You cared enough to surprise me."

"You're learning to trust," she countered with the low chuckle he had come to love. "I'll always come to you, whenever, wherever you need me."

"Forever? No matter what? As life companions?"

"Forever. No matter what! I promise."

His spirits soared. Sara's presence made the heavy responsibilities of his job and the trials of his difficult home life much easier. Her natural, relaxed way of kissing him on the nose or the kneecap with equal glee, rubbing the soles of his feet when he was tired, or the lobes of his ears while he read made him laugh and feel cradled in her warmth. Sara hung a couple of her school outfits on the door handle of his closet, and put her cosmetics— 'Charlie' body lotion and lipstick plus a toothbrush and hairbrush, in his bedroom. Her needs were simple, and this saved a stop at her apartment on the way to school. Neil felt proud that she had made a home for him in this primitive little cabin.

Sometimes Sara would wake, lying pensively beside him. Even with his eyes closed, he could sense her watching his chest rise and fall--listening to his breathing. He knew she was checking to be sure he was alive, and he lay quiet to let her work it out herself. She had lost so much before. What did she fear? That he would die? That he would leave? He vowed to reassure her during their days together. They both had been creatures in crisis. Now he felt sure the crisis had been resolved, together.

Sundays involved keeping up Faye's image of the perfect family. She demanded they go to church together, eat a hearty dinner, and insisted on calling the afternoon "family time," though Neil couldn't interest her in actually participating with the family. Like everything else in their life together, it was a sham. Neil found himself wishing they had developed something to talk about for when they were stuck with one another. But, then, he'd spent years unsuccessfully trying to push back her angry words, so silence was infinitely better.

He played games with Katy and Micki, but Faye would not take part, simply retiring to a corner to read her latest romance magazines or watch television.

"Are you taking me to my doctor's appointment?" she whined.

"Is there anything serious you're worried about, Faye?"

"No, just a routine check up—next Wednesday."

"Then I can't make an extra trip or take an extra day off-- unless it's an emergency, of course. I take a military sedan each week so you'll have our car for such occasions. I'm making presentations to the evaluating board all this week"

Faye pouted awhile and then spat out her words with a jerk of her head, "Actually, I'm glad you're gone during the week. It makes it easier not to have to put up with a man around."

Neil thought it better not to answer the taunt. He was content to wait for confrontation, since he knew what kind of power Faye wielded over his life, his career, his girls, and perhaps even Sara. He fervently hoped Faye didn't realize what she could do to them all. She had not mentioned her ridiculous accusation of child molestation again, but Neil knew she would drag it out and make the charge, should she ever decide it was to her advantage. Involuntarily, he shuddered.

"I just don't want any of your changes upsetting the system I've established," she continued. "I have my friends here, and I don't need you coming around."

Neil weighed the fact that Faye didn't know how his own inner changes had already affected her "system." He even tried throwing out an invitation to Faye to join him in Graf for a formal Hail and Farewell party coming up for an outgoing commander.

"Now, why would I want to drive all the way out to that God-forsaken place? Just because *you* are there?" She snorted, "I'm not interested in what you do out there."

Neil smiled. He had known she would refuse. He had gone to almost every occasion during his career, alone, for lack of her interest. But, by her own words, she had given him *carte blanche* in Graf as long as it didn't upset her precious status quo.

Occasionally, Neil was present when his daughter phoned Sara. He watched silently as they laughed and chattered. He could tell from Sara's face that she loved his daughter. It pleased him.

Sunday afternoons with Faye seemed to last forever, but by around 1900 hours, Neil had packed his duffle, kissed the girls good-night, and driven out to Sara's, vaulting her balcony railing to begin another week. His weeks flew by in warm succession.

One such Sunday evening, perhaps two months into the rhythm of their routine, Neil said, "Faye and I don't say much to each other except what pertains to the girls. She's never interested in talking to me anyway. Since she doesn't know who I am, inside, I feel impervious to discovery." He reached out to take Sara's hand. "She doesn't know my thoughts like you do. My total silence gets us through the weekend with fewer fights."

"Doesn't she wonder why you no longer ask her for sex?"

"The last time she consented, months before I knew you, she stared, eyes wide, at the ceiling while gripping the bedpost and yelling, 'You have five minutes--do it now, or forget it.' That totally turned me off, so I forgot it. For years I've had trouble— almost like impotence--in doing anything--feeling rebuffed. She never liked it, and she made me feel like I was forcing her. I think she's relieved that I don't ask. Sometimes I feel she knows about us, and is just biding her time until she can hurt us in some way. It scares me what she might do or say to tie me to her forever."

As they sat on the floor in the living room, quietly listening to music, he could feel something was on Sara's mind. He waited.

"Neil. I've been thinking about the girls. Katy knows there's a rift between you and her mother. She worries about you, and I know she can't talk to her mother."

"Has she said that?" Neil was curious. "Faye seems to consider motherhood her calling, and the Army, mine."

"I'm sure she's fine in meeting daily needs, but she's rather withdrawn and moody, and that influences the girls. They're shy, and they think inwardly more than outwardly. I've raised teens, and it's not uncommon at Katy's age, struggling for an identity, to need more openness than Faye is willing or able to give. I can see that the girls need *you* for balance in their lives. I'm afraid of what would happen to them, if you left them with her full time."

Sara had the look of a sacrificial lamb, and the fear in her eyes startled Neil. "The girls will be with us, you and I, at least half the time," said Neil. "Katy would choose to be with me, and Micki would follow. They already love you."

"Yes, and I love them. I'm hoping very hard that they can be with us. They need the sense of fun, laughter, and self-confidence we can give them. But, should Faye be unwilling to share custody, or should she discover our life together, we must be prepared. The girls might need you. Maybe you shouldn't hurry to make the changes we've talked about."

Neil was aware of Sara's head thrown back with eyes

closed, as though searching for strength. Her movement and her words made him dizzy when she continued. "You've told me much of your problem with Faye was the difference between your views of sex, with the lack of spontaneity and her denying you warmth and companionship."

Neil watched in some crazy slow motion as Sara timidly drew out two library books from under the couch. "I've been thinking that if you read her some books about sex and showed the tenderness you've learned from our being together, there still might be a chance to solve your differences and make a safe home for Katy and Micki." He saw that Sara's hands were shaking.

Neil exploded, blindly hurling the books at the wall, tipping over his wineglass onto the coffee table. "How can you suggest such a thing? You don't know all she has done to me, the angry words—the lies. You know I can't stand to touch her!"

To his chagrin, he felt tears flooding his eyes, and he laid back, prone on the floor, his arms over his face to hide his shock and despair. "Don't you understand? Faye has brought me nothing but anger, accusations, humiliation, or threats. She has never *once* in her whole life come to me or touched me of her own free will. She has never loved me. How many times can a man be rejected and not give up?" Almost too incoherent to finish, a sob tore from his throat, "God help me, I wish she'd just die!"

Immediately, he felt Sara by his side on the floor, rocking him in her arms as he tore from his insides the frustrations of sixteen years of emotional loneliness.

As though from far away, Sara's voice murmured into his ear, "Shh, darling. I'm so sorry. I just wanted you to be prepared in case your loving me could jeopardize custody. I had no idea this sadness was festering so deep and painfully inside you. I'm sorry."

Neil felt her tears mingle with his own as she smothered his face in kisses.

"My Darling, forgive me. I was afraid she might use our love to hurt the girls. I thought if you gave your marriage one more try, we could protect Katy and Micki, even if it destroyed us."

"And what about you?" He'd said it slowly and painfully,

between gasps for air.

"Darling, I'm not strong enough to watch her hurt you or hurt the girls." Their faces were both wet, and somehow the shared moment strengthened Neil.

"Do you love me? That's *all* I need to know." He was holding his breath, waiting.

She threw herself on top of Neil and hugged him all over. He could barely breathe. She was practically strangling him, but he felt amazing relief from her reaction.

"I do--so much I can't even think straight. But I wanted to give you one final chance to leave me, if you needed to do so to save Katy and Micki. I thought I could help you and Faye work out her frigidity, like a counselor or something. I didn't want you to ever hate me for not helping you fix your marriage."

"Sara, Sara, Sara." He folded her in his arms and kissed her tearful face. "I could never hate you. You've brought only good into my life--brought out the best person within me--a loving person I didn't even know I had inside." He sat up slowly, leaning against the front of the sofa, and pulled Sara into his lap. "My marriage was a disaster almost from the beginning—dead long years ago. You had *nothing* to do with that."

It was now his turn to rock her in his arms and reassure her. She had given him a gift--the chance to sacrifice his promises to her if he had thought it would save his children. He recognized the pain and fear it must have cost her to offer him that choice.

After a while, their shared trust folded over them like a blanket. Her body relaxed against his shoulder.

"I don't know what I would have done if you'd taken me up on the offer, Neil. I was scared for you, for Katy and Micki; and even for Faye, in case she did love you and just couldn't show it."

"You are a unique individual, my love." He was finally able to see humor in the situation and chuckled. "No one but *you* would feel sorry for the shrewish soon-to-be-ex-wife of your lover." He tried to suppress his grin. "I want you to know that I sincerely appreciate your generous offer to help us out with our sex life, but I only want a love life, for the rest of my life, with you!"

He sobered and cupped her face in his hands to look into her eyes. "I'm ashamed, Love, that I didn't realize how deeply I felt anger, until you suggested I should go back to her. I guess I hadn't acknowledged it, even to myself." He kissed Sara softly. "I'm sorry that my outburst scared you. It certainly surprised me."

"I understand, Darling." She nodded. "You've just held it in too long. I think I'm still afraid to trust that life will be kind to us. I want nothing except the chance to make you happy forever."

He held her tightly that night, aware he had the power here in his arms to be the loving person he'd always wanted to be. Now that he knew what love could be, he was determined that he *would* have it. Sara had stayed by him through a disclosure that had terrified even himself--the dark secret anger he hadn't realized he'd developed over the years in response to Faye's verbal abuse and rejection—her lack of love for him. In that moment, he accepted that Faye's hatred of him was real, as well.

Sara had understood his anguish and inner turmoil. As he watched her sleep, he thought, *I'm grateful you were beside me when I finally faced my true feelings. One shouldn't have to confront such painful truth alone. I realize now the only way to fix my marriage is to get out of it. I can't live a lie anymore. I can hardly wait to get to the United States and get this mess over!*

He noticed Sara's sleep was uneasy and restless, and her hands were cold to the touch. He snuggled against her body to warm her. Just before he fell asleep, his eyes were drawn to moonlight reflecting off the brass of his uniform hanging on the window frame in the bedroom's semi-darkness. Though he had worked diligently for the chance at West Point, without the Army, he would have spent his life following some old plow horse in Maine. He smiled, imagining the eagles that would soon replace the silver leaves of his rank insignia. He would someday make the Army proud. He knew Sara backed him all the way and was already proud of him. Faye would never be, no matter what he did.

13

Faye watched as Katy hummed tunelessly and bounced around the kitchen in imitation of the latest dance fad while she set the table for dinner the next Friday night.

"Stop that silliness, and behave," said Faye, more sharply than she intended.

Katy stopped, but she saw the trace of resentment in the girl's eyes. Katy expected her dad home from Graf momentarily, and Faye recognized the eagerness her daughter exhibited knowing she'd be with her father soon. Faye refused to allow their closeness to make her feel insignificant. After all, children needed both parents. She cut carrots into her pot roast, smelling the richness of the beef and vegetables blending flavors. She was a good cook, so Neil would be docile when he came home for dinner, and perhaps not mention the divorce. She would simply go on protecting the image—Neil was too conventional to fight the image.

Faye knew the girls loved her too—in a different way. *I can't be silly the way Neil is—he's over the top in entertaining the girls I wouldn't stoop to playing and giggling with a child.*

But Micki had wailed one day, "You never play with us, Mom. You're no fun. You just yell at us for stupid stuff."

This uncharacteristic exchange from a shy Micki had left Faye breathless. "*You,* young lady, are rude and insubordinate. Your father makes a fool of himself enough for both of us." That had silenced the child. All she needed to do to get the girls quiet was criticize their father. *He makes that really easy*, she thought with a smile.

She continued to muse to herself as she stirred. *Lately, Neil seems too happy to be normal. The girls whoop their pleasure with him, and greet me with mundane acceptance. After all, I'm the one who took on the disciplinary duties while Neil ran around playing soldier, went off to war, and came home to act like he'd never dumped all the responsibility in my corner. He owes me.*

Faye shook her head and changed the subject with Katy.

"Annie Painter called to invite your father and I to a Beer Fest in Erlangen next Saturday night. I told her I wasn't interested. It's not my kind of thing." Faye scowled at the idea. "Annie was very insistent, though. You know her, Katy. She goes to our church. Her husband, Ira, was your dad's roommate on that stupid ski week. He seems to think a lot of your father."

"Everyone *else* does, Mom," said Katy with a sharp look at her mother.

Faye ignored the subtle emphasis. "Ira only wants a beer buddy. I don't like German Fests--all that drinking and noise."

"Fests are an old tradition, Mom. You and Dad should go. You never do anything together. Dad would enjoy it. Maybe you would too. I'll stay here with Micki."

Faye mulled over the idea. She had a week to decide.

"I'm not really interested," Faye told Neil when he arrived for dinner.

"Call Annie back, Faye. Tell her we'll go." "Ira mentioned he really wanted to go to this Fest, and it won't hurt us to accommodate his friendly offer. Ira's a nice guy--a little crazy sometimes, but okay. Annie adores him. They're a happy couple."

The implication was not lost on Faye, that the 'happy couple' designation did not fall on her shoulders, but she ignored the comment. She wanted to keep control of the situation.

She walked into the den to use the more private phone, but it was not Annie she called. On impulse, Faye dialed Merle's number, the wife of another battalion commander she knew casually from Officers' Wives' Club.

"What are you two doing a week from tomorrow?"

"Les has been doing some hobby building with our boys on Saturdays. He said we could go to the movies when they finished. How about you?"

"Neil insists we go to the Erlangen Beer Fest."

"Oh, that's a good fest! We'd love to go too, but Les

promised the boys."

"I was hoping you would go along."

"You'll have a good time, Faye. By the way, Les said you had car trouble and Neil might have to drive in from Graf to take the car to the shop again. Is it *that* serious? Can't you take it in?"

"It conked out on me again, and I told Neil he'd damned well better get in here and get that car fixed! We women have to keep these men in line, don't we?" Faye laughed. "I save up these little extra chores to keep Neil busy."

"Doesn't he object to those extra things cutting into his limited free time? Les would."

"Why, Merle," Faye cooed, "You know how 'helpless' I am. Especially if I need him to do what I want him to do." She laughed. "I finally talked him into having my own bank account, too. I simply demanded my financial independence."

"But you have no job, Faye--no income. Won't that just cause extra paperwork?"

"We've argued about it so long, Neil gave in and agreed to fund it. He can afford it! And he *owes* me. Why, he sent all of his eight brothers and sisters through college with *our* money."

"Why, that was really a nice thing for him to do. You sound like you object to his helping them."

"Well, I just don't see why he should spend our money on them. They aren't his responsibility. He kept saying that being selected for West Point gave him his ticket out of poverty since his family couldn't afford to send him to college, and they needed a chance to be successful as well. Because he was the oldest, he thought it was up to him to provide for their success. What a bunch of boloney! But now the last one has graduated, so I know he has more money now."

"But he's always given you anything you've wanted, Faye. You make it sound like you've done without in some way."

"As a woman, I just need more independence. I don't want him knowing any of my financial plans. After all, The Women's Liberation movement says we need equality in everything. We have to be assertive to get it. We can't just let men walk all over us. There's a lot about it on television."

"Oh, Faye, you believe everything you see on television." Merle laughed at her. "Why, you even try every health remedy television advertises, and you always believe it'll work. Get real! Women's equality is only needed for wage parity. Those women are crazy, marching around and carrying signs. Who looks good without a bra, anyway?"

"Well, they're right on this, Merle. You need your own bank account, too. Of course, I don't think women should stop with equality. I think we should shoot for superiority." She laughed wickedly. "Don't you think so? Neil is such a dumb shit, he doesn't even know we women are already superior."

Merle gasped and announced suddenly, "I have to go, Faye. I heard one of the boys call."

"Bye." Faye hung up slowly. *Merle was in a hurry-- something strange in her voice. Oh, well. She just doesn't know how to control her man.* Faye laughed about Neil's inability to guess her motives. He kept saying that she was "…all over the map," and he "could never predict what she would do next, nor what her mood would be, so he and the girls had to walk on eggs." She smiled. *According to my mama, I need to be unpredictable, to keep a man, any man, guessing. It's all part of the game.*

She sighed, and reluctantly made the call to the Painters to accept their invitation.

When Faye returned to the den, she found Neil reading and announced as usual that she would go up to read her magazines in bed and watch television. He mumbled, "Good night, Faye, sweet dreams," and returned to his book without looking up. Both girls were settled for the evening, Micki in bed and Katy doing her homework.

But Faye changed her mind, descended the stairs again, and went next-door to borrow a recipe from her neighbor, Ruth. She and Ruth settled in for a lengthy visit. Around 10:30 or so, Faye returned home to find the front door locked. Furious, she yelled loudly and leaned on the doorbell until Neil rushed to the door.

"Who the Hell do you think you are, locking me out of my

own house? How could you be so dumb?"

Neil looked bewildered. "What are you doing out there? You said you were going up to bed, so when I got up for a drink of water, I locked the doors for the night. I'm sorry."

"I decided to go next door. I come home and I'm locked out!" She stomped around the entry hall. "You did it on purpose to embarrass me. You're a pig for doing such a thing." She liked Neil's confusion whenever she accused him of something.

Neil ignored the epithets. "You never said you were going outside. It was an accident. You might have told me you were going out, instead of to bed. I've already said I was sorry. Can't you accept my apology and let the matter drop?"

"Some accident!" Faye defiantly placed one hand on her hip. "I don't have to tell you anything. I'm an independent woman."

That seemed to be the point at which Neil lost his temper. "You and your Women's Lib ideas! When has anyone ever stepped on your independence?"

"Why should you care that I'm my own boss and I'm in control? I can do as I please, and you damn sure can't stop me."

"I've never *tried* to stop you. What's your being your own boss got to do with my locking the door for the evening believing you were already in bed? Faye, you *must* learn to control your temper! This is such a silly argument. You get mad at the drop of a hat, and then you stay mad for a week. You just cannot do it. It's a strain on me, on the girls, and on any pretense of family life."

"Well, I'm my own person. I'm not going to let you dominate me. And since we're complaining, Mister, is there anything *else* you want to complain about?"

"No one wants to dominate you, Faye. And since you're asking for my complaints, there are far too many things that have come between us over years of tension to name just one. We've been totally dysfunctional as a family for years." Neil paused a moment, and then sighed. "Okay, if you really want to know, one of my biggest disappointments was that you knew I wanted more children—I would have loved to raise a son. But you went out and had your tubes tied and got breast implants while I was away on temporary duty. You knew I'd never have agreed with that decision. You didn't even tell me about it until I got home."

"It's my body, I'm no slave, and I don't ask your opinion. I didn't want to lose my figure for another baby. You can like it or not, I don't care. That was a long time ago."

"Yes, it was a long time ago, but when you do something with such impact upon a relationship, it should be a joint decision. I've never quite gotten over that we didn't at least talk it over first. And if you were intent on doing the breast implant thing, why didn't you get silicone implants that didn't feel like rocks. No one would want to snuggle up to those, long time ago, or ever since."

"Did I ever ask you to snuggle up to my body at all? I don't want you. I never should have married you! I could have done *so* much better than you. You're over-sexed anyway."

"You know, Faye. I think I just may be normal, but how would you know? There's never been any intimacy between us. You're asleep when I come to bed. I dress in the dark and fix my own breakfast before work because you don't want to be awakened. Implants and tube tying seemed like only a couple of the things we should have talked over before you made a decision. But none of it matters any more. Your constant anger, criticism, ridicule, and the fact you've never wanted me to even touch you for any semblance of a marital relationship ruined our marriage years ago. There's no longer any reason to keep it together. Clearly it doesn't even exist except on paper. I've told you we'll end this chaos when we get to Carlisle. We'll both be happier for it."

Faye screamed her usual profanity at Neil. She could tell he was trying to keep his voice down, but she didn't care. "Let the children hear! You make me mad all the time. How dare you question my right to go out at night without telling you? How dare you lock me out of my own house? You did it on purpose. And how dare you keep hurling that idea of divorce at me!"

"Faye, you get mad over such little things, even accidents, then you run around saying they were on purpose. Your constant anger doesn't help either of us any. You won't even talk to me in a normal tone of voice."

Faye watched, smiling faintly, as he ran his fingers through his hair in frustration.

"No one is questioning your independence," he said. "In fact, you can have all of it you want! Neither the girls nor I ever know what you'll do or say next, or why you get mad so suddenly. Some things we should've been able to talk over--that's all I'm trying to say!" He sighed. "A marriage should be a team endeavor. You've seemed to turn every minor action into an act of personal defiance, just to prove how 'liberated' you are. After this assignment, when we get to Carlisle, you'll be liberated completely. You should welcome that as much as I will."

He added one last comment, "Sadly, Faye, giving everyone 'a piece of your mind' simply means you don't ever listen to the concerns of others. There could have been a middle road years ago. I'm tired of accepting your anger just to keep the peace. There has never been any peace in this marriage."

He fell silent, unable to say anything further. Faye could tell he wished he'd never argued at all, as he put his head in his hands. She knew he was defeated. She could out-shout and out-wait Neil anytime, and whenever he grew silent, she knew he had given up the fight. It was always the same. Neither he nor his silly words mattered, anyway. She always won in the end—just by waiting.

Ignoring his voice, his ideas, his talk of ending their marriage, Faye stomped deliberately up the stairs, knowing the noise exacerbated Neil's sense of helplessness. He wouldn't *ever* be able to get a divorce. The arguments were all just a part of the game to her. She smiled and picked up her brush for the nightly 100 stokes of her lovely blonde hair.

14

Sara woke with "frabjous joy," feeling she now understood the phrase from <u>Alice in Wonderland</u>. She, like Alice, was in a wondrous new land. She hugged her knees as she watched Neil move around the bedroom very early Monday morning, donning his fatigues. Neil's often-expressed happiness was gradually relaxing her apprehension that her world could vanish in a heartbeat, the way it had with Gary's death. Neil's love was peeling away her safety net, one layer at a time.

Even when Neil had to leave first for the drive to Graf, she didn't feel lonely. She could still snuggle down in the blankets and feel his warmth and smell his clean masculine aroma. She loved remembering the happy cascade of laughter that flowed through them in the gentle afterglow and Neil's little purr of contentment.

God, thank you for knowing how good we are together. He makes me feel I've given him some marvelous gift just by loving him for himself alone, with no status, no price. After not believing that I could love again, I do! And it's glorious!

Sara could sleep well again, for the first time in years.

On Tuesday evening, they debated Neil's latest engineering magazine article over dinner in a Yugoslavian restaurant in Weiden, and went to the opera. On Thursday evening, after dinner in Eschenbach, they sat in their favorite spot by the fire, watching dancing sparks and flames flicker ambient light around the cabin.

Neil was contemplative. "I've changed during these months we've been together, haven't I?"

"Tremendously." She teased, "You're more mellow, less driven. You ooze confidence, laugh out loud, lift me off my feet for spontaneous hugs, and you now find comfort in sharing a random caress on the shoulder or pat on the rump." She touched his face. "I see something peaceful and warm emerging in you."

"I can feel it happening. It seems like whatever problems come, even at work, they all fade away in just relaxing together."

Sara playfully sang the words of a new Carpenters' hit, "I can take all the madness the world has to give, but I won't last a day without you."

"That's it, exactly. We recharge each other for the next day's 'madness.' My dear love, we are committed."

"We've both changed. You've made me feel secure. It feels good to love you so."

Mornings, Neil went into "North woods Maine" mode and thumped outside into the snowy dark to bring in wood and oil for the stove. He hummed, seeming to enjoy the mundane chores of their preparing breakfast and packing lunches together.

When Sara emerged from the shower and dressed, he watched as she applied Charlie perfumed lotion to her arms and legs and brushed her hair. Sometimes, the tenderness he was now able to show would result in their making love just one more time, though that required a mad scramble to grab breakfast on the run and not forget books, lunch sacks and paperwork for the day. Laughing and content, they'd tumble out of the cabin into the snow, each heading away to jobs they loved, refreshed and ready for a new day. Their time together was joyful, and life was good.

After school one afternoon, Sara received a call from Katy. She could tell something was on the young girl's mind, so she invited her for shopping. They laughed together over silly toys on sale in the open market downtown, enjoyed *Gulaschsuppe* at the *Gasthaus* by St. Michelsburg Abbey, and walked several legendary ice-encrusted cobble-stoned streets before Katy got around to talking about what was bothering her.

"You always find something good to say about people," Katy observed. "How do you keep from putting people down?"

"I don't know--habit of a lifetime, I suppose. My step-mom always told me, 'If you can't say something nice, don't say…'"

"…Anything at all," Katy finished, and they both laughed. "I've heard that too--but it's hard. Why aren't you ever mad?"

"Everyone gets angry once in awhile, Katy. I get angry when someone hurts others. I try to find something good about a difficult person to focus on, or try changing the subject." Sara could see where Katy's questions were going, but she wasn't sure how to head them off.

"What if you can't always find something good? What if you can never tell what's going to make them mad at you, even when you love them?" Tears loomed close.

Sara put an arm around Katy's shoulder. "Sometimes it's difficult finding the good in people. If you genuinely can't, then you find something good inside yourself, like forgiveness. Try to give them the benefit of the doubt. Maybe they don't realize they're being mean, or don't know how to control themselves."

"It's hard to believe the words aren't on purpose. They come out so suddenly and loud. Sometimes I don't want to talk after that, but if I leave the room, she gets even madder at me."

"Maybe, instead of fighting back with equally angry words or leaving the room, try saying something like, 'I don't think you meant to hurt my feelings, but I don't quite know what to say to you now. Can we talk later?' Do you think that might work?"

Katy was quiet a long time as the two strolled across the square and paused at Neptune's fountain, now silent for the winter months in its icy rigidity.

"I *am* trying, you know," said Katy softly.

"I know you are. Communication isn't easy. One day you'll find you can rise above that kind of hurt, and you'll feel confident in your ability to do so. Remember, she is special to you too."

Katy brightened a bit. "You know my dad likes it that you and I talk together."

"Does he now?"

"We have good talks on the weekends, but he doesn't always understand my feelings, either. And he's busy trying to pretend Mom isn't screaming at him."

Sara laughed. "Men think they aren't *into* feelings. It's part of their 'mystique.'" They walked to Sara's parked Mustang, and drove toward Post, as it was getting dark.

"Could you possibly make him see that I'm growing up?"

"You mean, you want me to intercede on your behalf, young lady?"

"I know he likes to talk to you as much as I do, and I know he listens to you. Could you make him understand that I'm no longer a little kid, and I'd like to be allowed to do more grown up things--to have a little more freedom and privacy?"

"It's hard for him to see you grow up. I've told him that."

"You mean, you already knew?"

"I've raised teens too, remember?" She smiled knowingly.

"I love him so much, but I might hurt his feelings."

"No guarantees, Katy. He won't want to believe, but perhaps I can make him aware enough so he'll at least notice when he accidentally puts you in Micki's age group. Okay?"

"Thank you." With a quick hug, Katy ran into her house.

Driving home, Sara thought more of the conversation. She hated it when Faye said mean things to Neil and the girls. Faye's anger was frighteningly sporadic. She'd seem relatively calm for a few days, and then would suddenly, for no apparent reason, spew out ugly words over some imagined slight. Sara couldn't figure out what was wrong, but it was easy to see why Katy had difficulty keeping on Faye's good side.

Of course, interceding with Neil on their next night at the cabin probably wasn't quite what Katy had expected. Neil simply couldn't see the young girl's need for privacy or more freedom.

"She's a mere child and I have to look out for her…"

"She's fourteen. She needs space to have friends over and chatter. She can't talk to Faye, and she knows you still see her only as a child. She's growing up, my dear."

"Sara, she's my little girl, and…"

"No, Love, she will always be that in your heart, but she's growing into a beautiful young woman, and you must let her spread her wings."

Sara never won this debate, but Neil at least promised to be more attuned to Katy's needs, and Katy appreciated Sara's efforts. Neil liked knowing his daughter could talk comfortably with Sara, and he was happy that she loved his girls, whether he was with them or not.

"They'd be safer with you," he commented one night. "I really *try* to avoid an argument and use a reasonable voice to counteract Faye's anger, but at some point I lose patience. She becomes so argumentative and profane. And guess what I get back with every argument? Women's Lib stuff. I don't care if she becomes independent. In fact, I wish she would! She's so damned helpless—not strong like you."

The comment hurt Sara's feelings, but she didn't allow tears to show. She realized Neil didn't understand that she was much more vulnerable than Faye. *Why can't he see more clearly through Faye's pretense of helplessness? And why doesn't he understand that my only strength comes from his love?*

Sara's friend Casey stood by on Friday night at the O'Club, as always, gauging her level of anxiety. "I guess I have to eat enough crow to say you seem happier than I've ever seen you, Sara," he offered one such night. "I guess I was wrong about Neil."

"He's working long hours. He says he needs me there to relax. He's so dedicated, but he has tension both at work and at his house. And Faye will never go out there to share an evening."

"I don't suppose so. She doesn't even go with him to events here on Post."

"I know. He always says he goes to everything stag because she isn't interested in joining him at anything. I've tried, but I can't understand Faye. "Why does she waste the time she could share with her husband by playing 'helpless' and making him do what she could easily do herself? It would be more fun to enjoy his time at home together? She has deliberately destroyed what could have been such a good military life for them all."

"Sara, all women aren't the same—you know that. Most

are happy and supportive in the military lifestyle. But Faye likes Neil to do things for her because she feeds on control."

"The other night when Neil said 'she's helpless and I'm independent,' I thought it so ironic--and a bit painful. Gary always tried to protect me but, with him gone, I had to *learn* to be independent. Gary certainly never intended for me to have to hold my own with garage mechanics, or 'jury-rig' the washing machine, or travel alone. But now Neil doesn't see my *emotional* vulnerability--only the strength I've had to learn in everyday things. He thinks Faye, the manipulator, is 'helpless.' Funny, no?"

"Yeah, Faye's as helpless as a Mack truck. You try to take stress off his shoulders, but then I see her putting it right back on."

"Maybe that's why he feels a balance with me. But it's wonderful that once again my life revolves around someone I love—someone who needs me. It feels good, Casey, really good."

"Well you two are practically living together, and he seems happier too." Casey nodded down at her. "You're a good influence on him. I still have this gut feeling that things are going just too well to stay that way but, for now, I see you both blossoming."

"Is it so obvious?" Sara smiled at her friend, shy that he could see through her so. "Neil and I enjoy our life together. We make a good team. I just melt when he says, 'my love.'"

"Well," said Casey slowly, as though he hated the words. "I hope I'm wrong, but Neil hasn't confronted Faye yet about filing for divorce, has he?"

"He's told her of his intentions, but he feels it'll be safer to actually file when they're settled in the States."

"I don't think it'll make any difference. She can go to a lawyer and accuse him of any wild charge, or sue him, or ruin his career as easily there as she can here—maybe easier at the War College because there, he'll be under the military microscope."

"You think his choice will be about what she can do to his career, don't you?"

"I don't want to think that. I like him. But I haven't seen him lose any of his ambition yet, and this *is* the Army, after all."

"Actually, both of us are more worried about protecting

Katy and Micki. We think we can give them more love and less unpredictability with us. And Faye makes it clear she doesn't want Neil around, or she would show more affection. She doesn't."

Casey remained quiet, biting his lip.

"Casey, Neil says he'll protect us, so don't worry so much. Admit it! I'm happy, he's happy, and we both love his girls. My girls are going to love Neil too. Everything *must* turn out okay with all that good feeling sashaying around."

"I won't deny this is the best thing that's ever happened to either of you. But I've never known the Army to be lenient on an officer with either a girlfriend or a divorce. If Faye finds out about you, Neil could be court-marshaled. I'd still suggest you wait to see if he can make his dreams work, and what it will cost you."

"Of course, there'll be a price. We plan to take care of Faye quite well financially. Neil says her security, and her image, are all she'll worry about. Together, he says we can face anything."

Casey was silent for a moment, apparently exasperated by Sara's inability to see the danger he saw. Sara turned sharply to see what caused his silence.

"I'm not sure that's the 'price' I meant, Sara. I think you're in fantasyland, and you are the only one that will be hurt. I'm trying to warn you as strongly as I can. When he sues for divorce in the States, you two won't *be* together. He'll be alone to face her. Is he strong enough?"

The question hung between them.

"He will be, Casey." Sara wanted to believe that since she and Neil loved each other, nothing could go wrong. She quickly put the conversation behind her. Casey shrugged and sighed, giving up to the inevitable. Sara's trust in Neil was unshakable.

At Sara's apartment after his morning run, Neil had talked of their Sunday evening plans, but somehow Saturday evening hadn't come up. So when Faye and Neil met the Painters to drive to the Erlangen Beer Fest, they found another attendee as well.

"We invited Sara to go with us over a week ago, and she promised," said Annie. "This will be such fun!"

Sara choked back her surprise at seeing Neil and Faye, and mouthed the words at Neil, "I didn't know." She felt trapped in an impossible situation, and a bit nauseous.

"Neither did I," he mouthed back, trying to subdue his grin. He merely laughed at Sara's concern when she desperately suggested that perhaps the van would be overcrowded with five, and she would be happy to remain behind at the Officers' Club.

"No you don't young lady," Neil said, heartily rejecting her plea. "You're not opting out. You're here, we're here—we'll *all* go teach those Germans some new tricks."

It was too late to refuse to go without drawing even more attention to her discomfort. Neil simply grinned, nodded at her, and helped all three women into the van. Sara recognized the mischievous twinkle in his eye, and knew he intended to have fun with this occasion. She worried, thinking of possible disastrous scenarios that might give away their relationship. *How is Neil going to handle this situation? He seems to be thinking it's just a lark.* His only reaction had been to mouth the words, "Don't worry," and throw a huge 'stage wink' her way.

The main feature of the *Festsaal,* or beer tent, in addition to food shops ranging around its perimeter, was a huge dance floor and a raised dais holding an enthusiastically-loud band--sometimes more enthusiastic and loud than talented. Drinking songs interrupted frequently by toasts of *Ein Prosit* and cheers of "*tiki-taki, tiki taki, hoy, hoy, hoy,*" filled the tent with revelry. A dedicated people watcher, Sara enjoyed the light and color of the German Beer Fest tradition. All sorts of people hung out together, simply shouting, singing, dancing--forgetting all other cares.

Actually, with the joking and clowning Ira and Neil were doing, and the hubbub of the setting, Sara found herself relaxing, and it seemed that the others were having a good time, as well--at least she and Annie were able to enjoy the occasion. But for Faye, it seemed difficult. Sara resolved that Faye should enjoy herself, and tried to engage her away from her tendency to sit silently with a disapproving stare when everyone else joked and laughed. After all, Sara rationalized, Faye was facing packers coming to take furniture to Carlisle soon, and she probably needed a break, too.

"Those two are drinking far too much," Faye finally commented aloud.

"Yes, but look at them," answered Annie. "They're enjoying themselves, and Fests are just boisterous fun. I'll drive us home if my old Ira gets too drunk. Relax, Faye. We don't get out to see this very often with the guys working so hard."

The men wanted food to dilute their liquid refreshment, so they ordered roasted chicken, *Bratwurst* with *Sauerkraut*, and curly white radishes quite different from the red American type. "Don't forget to order my *Apfel Strudel*," called Ira to the waitress.

Since Sara wasn't a beer drinker, the only alternative was either a too-large tumbler of wine, or lukewarm lemonade.

"Guess we'll get three lemonades," said Annie.

Sara pointed out the amazing ability of the buxom German waitresses to carry eight or more two-liter beer mugs at one time.

"They're way too big-busted," complained Faye. "They wear those disgusting low-cut dirndl dresses to seduce their drunken customers. They're probably hoping for big tips."

Sara wasn't sure how to answer, since most of the skillful ladies with the beer mugs were in their fifties or sixties, a bit old to be seductive. She kept silent.

Ira danced polkas first with Annie, then Sara. Then the band started playing the "*Enten Tanz*," which meant "duck dance" but by some mystery of translation was called "chicken dance," and all nationalities joined together to shake and wiggle their way through this silly, favorite novelty tune.

Neil grabbed Sara's hand and pulled her onto the floor. Though Sara panicked to see if Faye was concerned about this turn of events, she saw that the woman had just waved Neil away from her as she would a bad odor. Thus the two enjoyed several dances in a row, polkas and Sara's favorite, the German fox trot.

"See," said Neil. "She really isn't interested."

"I'd hoped she would join the fun and have a good time."

"Probably won't happen, but try if you're game for it. She might respond to you--everyone else does." He grinned wickedly. Sara could see the beer was taking hold and had to laugh with him.

The band played *Kufstein Lied*, which encourages friends and strangers sitting at the huge trestle tables and benches to link elbows and sway back and forth together, or *shunkel*. Sara finally got a chance to pull Faye out of her silence and into the group activity. After all, it was hard *not* to *shunkel* when everyone else was doing so, since at a crowded table you'd get bumped repeatedly if you tried to sit still. In the *Kufstein Lied,* the whole group *shunkels,* and then, on the chorus of "*Oleo-li-o-li-o-olido-o-li-di-a,*" swings up to their feet and back down in a wave.

Everyone except Faye laughed uproariously when an old German man swooped up on the bench, grabbed Sara's hand and pulled her to her feet on the "O-li-di-a" part. Neil and Ira moved up to the bench. Then it became obvious the old man intended to go to the table. Wobbly as he was, he again pulled Sara with him, using her for support, and she was swept into the swirl of *shunkeling* on top of the table. Neil joined her to help hold the old man steady, while Ira reached down to bring Annie into the mix. Sara nodded at Neil, indicating he should grab Faye's hand and bring her up.

Faye shook her head and drew away from Neil's hand, but Sara said above the wild noise level, "Come on Faye, this is fun. Look, this old guy has started something."

Sure enough, a glance around the room showed probably a thousand people all swaying together on top of tables and singing heartily as the band swung into yet another chorus. Sara had a flash of concern, wondering if all these flimsy fold-up tables could hold the weight, but apparently they'd been doing so for centuries.

It was an event not to be missed. The next time Sara reached down, tapped Faye's shoulder and nodded, Faye reluctantly, as though her hands might get dirty, accepted the hand of the German man to her right, and made her way onto the table.

Neil looked at Sara and grinned. "This *is* an occasion, and I intend to have another couple of those two-liter beers, one for each hand." Faye's eyes rose to the heavens, but there was no longer an opportunity for her to sit down.

People rotated in and out of the tents in a constant flow, for fresh air to chill drunken heads, or to explore the rides and fun houses down the Midway. A myriad of little booths sold everything from wooden toys to gingerbread *Lebkuchen,* and hot, spiced wine, or *Glühwein*. The whole event was colorful, noisy, and full of good-natured people, both German and American.

When Ira complained of his head spinning from the beer, the group roamed outside to this Midway. Neil grabbed Sara's hand. She tossed her head toward Faye to remind him to grab Faye's as well. That maneuver kept everyone in tow while they threaded their way through the milling crowd. Neil had wanted Sara to see Faye's uncooperative behavior, and his demeanor said as loudly as if he had shouted, "See, I told you so. Now you know because you've seen that trying doesn't help much, does it?"

Sara didn't feel as uncomfortable any more, though she still felt a bit alarmed that Neil almost seemed to enjoy the awkward situation that should have been every man's worst nightmare—the presence of both his wife and his love at the same event.

After a visit to a haunted house and several rides on the octopus, which made Ira sick, Neil proposed they ride the giant Ferris wheel, with each seat swinging under a huge, dangling umbrella, both rocking and rotating in a slow spin while it circled in the traditional manner as well. Ira and Faye both declined, so Neil grabbed Annie and Sara's hands and ran for the seats like a schoolboy. Laughing, the three were closed in by the attendant and rose immediately from the ground—up and over. The wheel was high. One could see all over Erlangen with its hypnotic city lights.

Neil began rocking the gondola vigorously, especially each time they rose over the top of the wheel's arc, until he had both Annie and Sara screaming and begging him to stop. They both feared he would tumble over the side. Roaring with laughter, he held both their hands to "keep them from being scared," but he continued to rock and lean out, in spite of their protests.

Sara had a strange flash--*of what*? Not fear of the Ferris wheel, even though the operator had deliberately left the trio on the wheel and replaced everyone else because of Neil's signal that he didn't want to stop. It was more an insight that Neil was somehow declaring his independence at the top of this high place. Was it independence from Faye, from day to day responsibility of Earth, from control, as he rocked and spun the gondola, or from a rare moment where his career could not possibly be touched, as he swung far above it? It was an eerie moment. When he turned to look at her, Sara raised her eyebrows in question, and he suddenly smiled. She knew his exhilaration was once again calm and in control. Then, she laughed, realizing he had probably never been *out* of control—was he was merely entertaining Annie?

"You girls have had enough by now," he said as he signaled the wheel operator on the next trip down, and the trio was set free from their captivity above the crowd.

They passed a shop where the smell of honey roasted almonds emanated from huge copper kettles stirred by a fat, jovial German. Seeing her favorite Bavarian treat brought a squeal of delight from Sara. "We must have some," she cried, as she moved up to the man with her *Deutsche Marks.*

Sara held out the paper cone of nuts that were so hot she kept changing hands to avoid burning them. Faye at first declined, saying she hadn't seen them before and had no idea what might be *in* them. But after the others ate heartily, licking the hot burnt sugar coating from their fingertips, Sara finally persuaded Faye to at least try them. When Faye actually smiled and accepted her second clump of nuts, Sara felt good about it, and it lightened Faye's glowering mood a bit, at least for a few minutes.

After one more trip into the beer tent, with a few more beers for Neil and Ira, the women decided Annie would have to drive home, and they went about steering the two exuberant and expansive 'pillars of the military community' back to the van. It was hilarious to watch them dancing down the Midway. A rare night, indeed, where everyone seemed to let the day-to-day cares float away in the anonymity of this foreign setting.

Neil and Ira began a boisterous bragging contest, about their skiing ability on the recent trip, about their magnificent manly accouterments, their glorious career paths, their cooking talents, their accomplishments in drinking, dancing, and fighting, until Annie and Sara looked at each other with flaming grins and launched into a mocking rendition of "Oh, Lord, it's hard to be humble, when you're perfect in every way," a recent hit novelty song. Faye looked as though she would die of disgust.

When they reached the second line, "I can't wait to look in the mirror, I get better looking each day," the men were collapsing in laughter, leaning on the women's shoulders and, when Sara elbowed her and grinned, even Faye joined in the singing.

But the moment quickly passed, and Faye complained about her husband all the way home. Both Annie and Sara found Faye's comments excruciatingly out of place. The men didn't notice, as they both fell asleep immediately. Sara felt a moment of insight, realizing Faye mistook the 'scrambled eggs' of throwing a marriage in a pan, stirring vigorously, and dumping them on the plate with disdain, for marriage that should be the 'omelet,' lovingly tended and nourished, liberally spiced with warmth and good fun, and turned carefully with consideration. *My God, what Faye and Neil might have had, and Faye ruined it all with anger!*

Every time Faye made some comment that she was "doing Neil a favor by having to put up with him," Sara cringed. She could see Annie didn't know how to respond, either. If Neil had wanted her to see Faye in action, Sara felt he had definitely been successful. Her empathy for Neil rose 900 percent, as she fought to keep from screaming at Faye, "Why didn't you ever love this good man? He begged for your love for sixteen years!"

It was obvious the woman would not have listened to reason. Faye had deliberately thrown Neil away, never even knowing his real value…and never caring.

15

Once home, Faye found herself embarrassed by the whole boisterous evening. "You were far too drunk. I was humiliated," she accused Neil.

Sober, after his nap on the way home, Neil answered, "Oh Faye, lighten up once in awhile. I thought you enjoyed yourself a little bit there, for a moment--a rare occasion, yes? All the rest of us had a great time. There are so many wonderful and fun things to do during an assignment in Europe. Why can't you just let go and enjoy them like everyone else? This military lifestyle with its travel and pageantry and camaraderie is an *opportunity*, Faye—an opportunity most people can never experience."

When met by her tight-lipped silence, he continued. "Old Ira will have a hangover in the morning, but he'll still be bragging that he drank me under the table. I'll just get up in the morning, go out for a four mile run and get all that beer out of my system before church." Neil laughed, apparently remembering only the good fellowship.

His laughter angered Faye. "I'm going to bed." She flounced out of the room and stomped up the stairs.

"Fine, that's a good idea," he said forcefully to her retreating figure.

She could still hear him, downstairs, humming a few bars of the song Annie and Sara had called 'his theme song.' "Oh, Lord, it's hard to be humble…."

She slammed the bedroom door.

"How was your evening, Mom?" Katy was up early Sunday morning for church as the family gathered for breakfast.

"Just as noisy and chaotic as I had imagined. Of course, your dad and Ira Painter were drunk--even singing. You'd think grown men could act properly."

Katy laughed. "Oh, Mom, that's what Fests are for—doing crazy things, laughing, singing, welcoming the hops harvest and all. You need to relax and learn the traditions."

"I'm getting sick and tired of being told what I need to do. You sound just like your raving father."

Katy's laughter stopped abruptly as she recoiled. "My *father* is not the raving one," Katy muttered. Her eyes burned as she turned away and left the room. Neil quietly shook his head, apparently not wishing to make the scene worse.

Faye pretended not to have heard. *I'm tired of the girls thinking their father is so perfect,* she thought.

Neil's wristwatch had stopped. Faye watched him remove the back with a small screwdriver and take out the dead battery, placing it on the kitchen table between them. He asked if she could please pick up a replacement on her next shopping tour, since the Post Exchange at Graf was limited and didn't carry such things.

Faye reached out her right hand and flicked the tiny battery, sending it flying into Neil's chest. "Get it yourself!' she fumed. "I'm not your damned slave." She stomped away to the kitchen sink. *I guess I told him,* she thought to herself.

Since Episcopalian was the only Protestant service available on Post, Protestants of every variety attended Leo's service on Sunday morning. Faye took it upon herself to unofficially greet people at the door, but behind the smile she was collecting juicy tidbits to share later with her cronies about parishioners' clothes, their demeanor, or their private lives.

When Annie and Sara entered, Faye nodded regally. Neil pulled the two women to the bench next to him. Annie was apologetic that Ira's hangover was beyond his rising this morning and she had let him sleep in. Faye didn't see Neil quietly folding his hand around Sara's as she reached for the hymnbook between them, but she could hear their conversation as she approached.

"Sorry if you ladies had to put up with me last night," Neil said loudly. "I heard that I was really an obnoxious drunk."

Sara quickly moved her hand away. "Not at all," she said. "You and Ira were just having a fine time. We all had fun."

Annie nodded vigorously beside her.

Neil grinned impishly, and Faye wondered what had prompted the smile.

After the service, people stood talking outside as the minister approached. After shaking hands with Neil, Leo asked when they could go hiking together again. Neil replied that he had been quite busy out at Grafenwohr.

Faye noticed that the chaplain raised his eyebrows, smiled, and said, "Yes, I *know* you've been busy out there. I'm *glad* you are enjoying the *challenge* so much."

She wondered why the chaplain emphasized the words.

Annie again apologized for Ira's indisposition. "But I love that man, and I love seeing him have a good time." She grinned at Faye, "You know how it is. You love your husband, too."

"I'm married to him, aren't I?" Faye said, turning away.

Chaplain Leo blanched, but kept his tongue.

Neil didn't comment.

Fortunately, to break the strained silence, Katy came running down the aisle with Micki. She approached Sara with a hug. "Will you come skiing with me next weekend?"

"When did this all come up?" snapped Faye.

"A couple of West Point buddies asked Katy and me to go skiing next weekend, Faye," Neil said. "I hadn't a chance to tell you yet, but you can go along if you like."

"I wouldn't bother. I don't approve of ski bum trips."

"Please, Sara," Katy persisted. "Dad said I could invite any friend I like since he'll be skiing with his friends, and their sons won't want to ski with a girl. Please come ski with me."

Faye chimed in, aiming her words obliquely at Sara. "Yes, go along with Katy. She doesn't have any friends of her own, and her father will be drinking with his buddies and ignoring her." She looked sideways to see if Neil had noticed.

Katy's face fell, and Sara cringed. No teen wants it

announced to the world that she has no friends. Neil was stricken, and his glare at Faye showed it. Faye, for her part, realized she had put each witness in his or her place. She smirked broadly.

The minister flinched, but Faye didn't care.

Faye *did* notice the response from Sara.

"Katy," Sara intervened quickly. "Are you sure you want me instead of one of your school friends? I'd like to ski with you, but I don't want to take one of their places."

Why, she seems to think Katy was embarrassed by what I said. How dare that woman interfere with what I say about my own daughter! I don't think I like that.

The grateful sigh in Katy's voice was audible. "No, I'd rather have you, Sara. I'll take one of them another time."

Neil let out the angry breath he'd obviously been holding.

"Okay, that's settled," he said. "Katy and I will both have a friend to pal around with. Shall we drive down to Austria together?"

"Oh, I can't," said Sara. I have a teachers' meeting after school. I'll come alone when it's over. Where can I meet you?"

Before Neil could answer, Katy interrupted, "May I ride with Sara, Dad? Then you won't have to drive from Graf to pick me up. You can meet us at the lodge." Neil glanced at Sara.

"Katy, I'd like your company, if it's okay with your mom."

All eyes turned to Faye. Her anger at their making plans boiled to the surface, even though she'd already refused to go. *Neil could at least have cancelled the weekend with his friends.* "Good riddance" she said with a burst of air from her pursed lips. "This way, I'll not be bothered with either you *or* your father."

It escaped her notice that Leo, the chaplain who had once proposed another child to stitch their sagging marriage together, now shook his head sadly at the whole exchange.

As Faye turned to stalk out of the church, she heard Katy say, "I'm so excited, Sara. Dad can write out the directions to the ski lodge, and we can meet him there by dinnertime on Friday."

The others were too busy making plans together to notice Faye's exit. Seeing that she had not made the impression she planned, she scowled angrily.

Sixteen

The drive to Austria on Friday was filled with laughter and 'girly' conversation as Sara took extra care to put Katy at ease. She had been appalled by Faye's act of embarrassing Katy at church the previous Sunday. The young girl had a million things on her mind--friends, hairstyles, boys, school--and she was determined to share every one of them within the four-hour span of the trip.

Katy finally blurted out the topic Sara was dreading, but knew would be coming.

"I still don't know how to get along with my mother. She seems to hate my dad, and I love him, and that makes her mad at *me* all the time." Katy's stare was straight ahead at the hood of the Mustang as though there were answers outside in the snow.

My God, what do I say now? Sara stalled for the time it took her brain to kick in. "Well, Katy, a lot of adults just don't know how to talk to teenagers, and we've already talked about the idea that she may hurt your feelings inadvertently."

"My dad doesn't do that. My teachers don't. You don't. It's just her. I tried looking for the good like you said, but it's too hard for me. And I hate it that my dad has never been happy at home."

"He loves you and Micki, Katy, and your parents have been married a long time."

"I think Mom makes his life miserable, and I've overheard her say she wished he was dead. That scares me to death. If my Dad were dead, I'd have nobody." The tears welling in the corners of her eyes began to roll down her cheeks.

Sara had a moment's insight. *Neil and I must make sure the girls aren't separated from him,* she thought. She reached out her right hand and patted the girl's arm. "Your dad isn't going to die, Katy. And your mom's probably saying things she doesn't really mean--in a moment of anger."

"She doesn't care if she hurts him with the terrible things she says—she just blurts them out like an explosion."

"Well, Katy…"

Katy was agitated enough to interrupt. "Sara, I overheard her when they thought I was upstairs in bed. She said she would poison his food because she deserved someone better than him. There's *nobody* better than my Dad! Mom said she didn't even care if she got tried for murder. I think she means it, all right."

Sara's stomach wrenched, and she struggled to keep her voice calm.

"It must just have been a way of joking, Katy. Your father wouldn't stand for threats, or something so scary being said in the house with you girls there to hear it."

"Well, he *did* stand for it! He didn't say anything. He never fights back—always tries to 'keep the peace,' as he calls it. He just walked out and closed the door."

"I'm so sorry, Katy." Sara didn't know how to relieve the girl's obvious anxiety. "Perhaps he didn't take it seriously." Sara wanted to believe that no one would say such a thing. But as a teacher, she knew the psychological statistics of family abuse. Thirty-five per cent of spouses who got to the stage of threatening their husband or wife with just *how* they would like to get rid of them, actually wound up committing murder.

Is Neil in denial about his perilous home life? Is he ashamed to admit a military officer could be an abused or a threatened spouse? Or is he simply accepting the path of least resistance, assuming he can handle any such violence, if it ever materializes. After all, I've heard him discuss hand-to-hand combat in Vietnam, fears of fragging by drugged soldiers, and good Army training. Maybe he's over-confident. Finally, Sara spoke aloud. "You may have misunderstood…."

"They don't even *act* friendly, Sara. Remember, I told you about the blue chips and green chips? I think my dad has wanted to leave ever since I can remember." She took a tissue to dab at her eyes. "If they got a divorce, where would Micki and I go?"

"I wouldn't worry about that now Katy. You'd be old enough to choose, and wherever you chose, Micki would come too, as soon as she was old enough."

"You mean Micki and I might be separated?"

"Probably not. The courts are careful to consider the children. If they both agree to divorce amicably, your parents would share custody and the two of you would stay half of the time with each of them. And of course, this is all purely hypothetical."

Katy nodded. "That sounds better. We'd all be happier if they weren't together. I love my mom, but it keeps getting harder to…. Sara, I think she hates me--not all the time, but sometimes."

"There's no way she could hate you, Katy and, of course, you love her. It's awkward for mothers and daughters to talk sometimes, that's all. You both have to keep trying. It'll be easier once you're through the teen years, and you'll forget all about the difficulties you're experiencing now. Trust me on this one. Okay?"

"I'll try, but it scares me that maybe Micki and I are the reason they should be apart. Are they unhappy because of us?"

"No way, Katy!" Sara was emphatic. "If your parents aren't able to love each other, that certainly doesn't keep *both* of them from loving you girls. Love of your children and love of a spouse are two completely different things. You girls have nothing to do with their unhappiness. Don't ever think that! No one has any way of knowing what their real problems are with each other—they may each have simply brought a difficult childhood into their marriage, or chose the wrong person, or had differing expectations. They'll have to work their problems out together, *or* separately. But either way, I guarantee you that neither of them would want you girls to feel it was your fault."

"My dad has been so lonely—me too. It's much better for us both now that you're our friend." Katy looked at Sara with such clear-eyed warmth, that Sara caught her breath. What could she say? Fortunately, Katy took the choice of words from her.

"I don't think I ever want to get married, Sara. I don't want to risk being unhappy like my parents. Dad seems happier to be out at Graf all week than he was when he was at home all the time."

"Maybe it's easier for him out there than facing the arguments at home, Katy. He loves coming home to you girls."

Katy was quiet for a time, staring at the road ahead through the moving windshield wipers. "Did you love your first husband?"

Sara was determined to reassure the young girl, but it was painful talking about Gary. "We were lucky to have had a good marriage, though we married quite young. We loved each other, and we'd always been best friends. His death devastated me. I wanted to die, too. But I had children to raise, so there was no choice except to go on doing the best I could for their sake."

"So, good marriages *can* happen? They aren't all like my mom and dad's?"

"Oh, no, Katy! If two people trust and love each other, marriage can be wonderful! Just be absolutely sure before you jump into marriage that you know each other really well, that you have lots in common, that you can talk out problems without becoming angry, that your feeling of love is real. There's much more to choosing wisely than just being anxious for a wedding."

"It's a lot to think about, Sara, and it seems like just the opposite of my parents. They have nothing in common that I can see. No wonder they seem to hate each other." She paused. "Do you think you'll ever love someone and get married again?"

"That's a hard question, Katy. I thought for a long time that I could never love anyone again. I was afraid for fear I could again lose someone I loved. But now, I'm beginning to hope I'll marry again. If I do, I promise I'll let you dance at my wedding, okay?"

Katy finally laughed and said, "That would be super!" Her smile continued as she innocently said, "I wish you were my mom. We have fun together, and I can talk so easily to you."

Sara quickly looked out her left window to hide her sharp intake of breath. She tried to keep her response light. "Hey, wouldn't that be great? I'd love having another daughter or two." "In the meantime, we can be good friends, and I'll be only a phone call away whenever you need me."

Katy smiled, sighed, and looked out the window at the Austrian countryside. "I think we're almost at the lodge. We should be turning pretty soon."

Grateful for a change of subject, Sara answered, "Good. You have the map and you can tell me where to turn. I'm getting hungry, aren't you?"

17

Neil's West Point friends and their sons were good company on the weekend ski trip. But they found that the lodge was full. It had only three rooms for three persons each, and no single or double rooms, though that had been the request when reservations were made. The hotel manager was apologetic.

Katy solved the problem without a moment's hesitation. "Well, that works out fine," she said jubilantly to the West Point couples. "You all have your family in three-person rooms, and Dad and Sara and I will just be a family too. This will be fun."

The other adults didn't bat an eye. Neil quietly smiled and said to Sara, "Do you think you can put up with my resourceful daughter and me for the weekend?"

"I guess so." Sara's voice was barely audible. Neil knew that she worried more about his squeaky-clean reputation than he did. Discovery for him would be most traumatic, yet he found that he didn't worry about it anymore. *Have I fallen so deeply in love that I'm throwing caution to the winds?* He chuckled at his own affirmative answer.

Katy ran off with Sara's bag to their designated room. When she saw the king sized Austrian bed, with a single bed about three feet away, she said, "Oh, look, this is great! I want the single bed because it has a light so I can finish my homework and read at night. Sara, you can be right across from me so we can talk all night if we want to, and we'll just stick Dad on the back side of that big bed where he can't bother us too much."

Sara gasped and stammered, "It might be better if...."

But Neil quickly interrupted her and agreed, smiling broadly. "That sounds like a good idea, Katy. Let's do it." He tossed his bag on the far side of the big bed and said, "What about my taking you ladies to dinner? We can unpack later."

Katy jumped up quickly and took her father's hand on one side and Sara's hand on the other, leading them out of the room. "I'm starved," she said happily.

Sara raised her eyebrows at Neil and mouthed the words, "Be good."

He nodded, but he also grinned mischievously across the top of Katy's head.

"This is going to be the greatest weekend," squealed Katy. "We're a family!"

After dinner, the trio went for a late night walk along the dark, narrow Alpine valley road leading to the next village. The air was fresh and crisp with not a cloud in the sky. The stars were brilliant. Spring was coming to the Austrian Alps. Tiny rivulets from the melting snow could be heard gurgling beneath snow pack. Katy was ecstatic to find tiny Edelweiss flowers poking their blooms out of the ground in available bare spots. Neil tossed snowballs skyward ahead to listen as they splattered on the roadway. Katy was happy to be in the company of loving adults. Neil was happy to be with the woman he loved. Sara was happy to have found that she could love and be loved again.

But Neil could *not* be good. Back in their hotel, even while Katy and Sara talked across the space between their beds, and Neil pretended to be already asleep behind Sara, his hands were reaching out to softly caress her hip, her thigh, her back, when he knew she couldn't jerk away or say anything without his moves being obvious to Katy.

Even after Katy was asleep, Neil reached for Sara. When she protested, he put his finger to his lips saying, "Shh, you'll wake Katy." Their compromise was that Neil would curl up behind Sara and put his arm over her after Katy was asleep, but Sara insisted there would be nothing more. Neil kept gently touching her, trying to woo her away from her resolve, teasing and pulling her to him, but to no avail.

The worst scene came Saturday night when Neil and Sara had already bathed separately and had gone to bed while Katy was taking her shower. Neil could not control his passion and desire. He was quite insistent, and Sara almost had to fight him off.

"She's in the shower, and she'll be in there a long time."

"Neil, we're *not* going to risk her finding out about us in that way."

"But she loves you, and I love you. She'll know about us sooner or later."

"Well, walking in on our having sex is not the way for her to find out about our love--trust me. That would add trauma on trauma for a young girl like Katy. We can't."

"But she's still in there." He reached again to pull Sara's body to his own.

"Look, my love. You have two ways of handling this. You can tell her right now when she comes out of the shower. We can all sit here and talk over our future together. Or we can control ourselves until our usual nights together and tell her after the divorce is in the courts. The one thing we are *not* going to do is to make love right now, and have her walk in on us. I won't allow that to be the way your little girl finds out about love, sex, and marriage. She's already confused enough."

"But she'll be in there a long time yet..."

Sara jerked out of his grasping arms and stood up at the side of the bed. Just as her feet hit the floor, the bathroom door opened, and Katy emerged, bundled in her terry cloth robe with her hair piled up in a towel.

"What's wrong?" she asked, seeing the breathless look on Sara's face.

"Oh nothing," said Sara. I was just waiting for you to get out because I forgot to brush my teeth." She immediately walked into the bathroom, closed the door, and stayed a long time.

By the time she returned, Katy was asleep, and Neil welcomed Sara back, thoroughly shaken. "You were right, my love. I was wrong. I'm so sorry. I don't know what got into me." He buried his head on her shoulder and kissed her neck. "I promise I'll be good. I didn't think beyond wanting to hold you in my arms this whole weekend. I love you so deeply, I'm afraid I've lost sight of anything else that could go wrong." He sighed and confessed, "I'm ashamed that I never even thought what such a shock would do to Katy. I should have known better. I also realize now how you would have felt had she walked in at that moment and found us."

He nuzzled her ears and apologized again and again.

"That was *too* close," he added. "I'm thankful you sensed it somehow and knocked some sense into me." He held her quite chastely for the rest of the weekend.

Neil had not opted to sit Katy down and tell her of their love right then, either. He didn't want his daughter involved until he had his life straightened out permanently.

Yet, many times over the weekend, both Neil and Sara had the distinct feeling that Katy *knew*—perhaps even was promoting the relationship. On their strolls in the snow, Katy would walk between them, holding both their hands. But then she would skip off to inspect a cow peeking out of a barn or climb on a pile of rocks, and she would carefully put their hands together while she went exploring, expecting that their hands would still be joined when she returned to get between them again. It was like her own personal 'family game'--perhaps what she dreamed a family should be, instead of what was real. Both smiled at this routine in wonder, holding their breath, not sure where Katy was heading with this. She seemed so innocent in bringing them together.

Vigorous days of skiing filled with laughter were followed by evenings when the congenial group told stories and enjoyed Austrian dinners together. Neil's buddies reminisced, laughing at old outrageous tales of study *and* mischief at the Military Academy. Sara smiled at their camaraderie, and Neil felt she understood that these men were his friends for life.

On the final afternoon of skiing, anxious for that last carefree run, Sara fell, jamming her wrist deeply into the ice as she tried to catch herself when pitching face first into the snow. "I must have crossed my tips and not realized it in time," she cried.

Neil helped her up while the other men looked for something to wrap her wrist. Neil insisted they use ice. All three officers had differing proposals over how best to rig a sling for her arm to keep her from moving it until she could get home to the clinic for x-rays. Sara was in obvious pain, but the three men could not agree and kept turning her first one way and then the other. The women dissolved into laughter, watching them.

"I can see now why the Army only allows *one* commander at a time for each unit during a war," said Sara, laughing at the three. "You guys would lose the whole war while you argued how best to dynamite the bridge." The men looked at each other and, after a puzzled moment, joined in the women's laughter. Katy wrapped Sara's arm with snow packed inside her scarf, and the party skied down slowly, with Neil carrying Sara's poles.

"At least it happened at the end of the trip," said Katy, almost in tears with worry, even though Sara assured her it was an awkward, but not a serious injury. Since Sara's right wrist was now painfully incapacitated, and she could do little with only her left hand, Katy and Neil were faced with the awkward problem of getting her out of her boots and ski suit and into her street clothing for the drive home. Together they tugged Sara's slacks over her long underwear and tucked in her blouse. Neil stepped back to let Katy do the zipper. But when Katy got the zipper stuck up the front of Sara's slacks, she simply handed Sara over to her father, assuming he could fix anything. Embarrassed in front of Katy, Neil performed surgery on the recalcitrant zipper. He and Sara both blushed beet red, and he was in awe that Katy obviously didn't see any problem at all.

Neil and his friends each drove one of the cars down the steep mountain of hairpin curves before Sara could take the wheel herself to drive Katy home on the flatter, straighter roads with her uninjured arm. Switching cars again, Neil hugged both Katy and Sara, trying to comfort his daughter who cried at leaving their beloved Alps and their "family" vacation. Finally, he could tear himself away to drive alone to Grafenwohr.

During her 'tuck-in' call to Neil Monday night, cradling her new plaster cast on a pillow, Sara described an invitation to dinner from Katy for Tuesday evening. "You must help me think of a way out of this. I'd be uncomfortable at her house, and I'd miss seeing you at Graf."

"Just go," he said. "Katy will love having you there."

"Faye is only inviting me because of Katy's insistence."

"When I called Katy from Graf's O'Club to be sure you'd made it home safely, she was still excited about how much fun she had on her 'dream weekend.'"

"I'm glad she enjoyed it--so did I. But do you think she mentioned our sleeping arrangements to Faye? Faye would certainly not be sympathetic to our dilemma."

Neil chuckled, tickled by his daughter's enjoyment. "Katy was so jazzed about the whole weekend, she told her mom how the three of us shared beds and a room and had been 'family' for the whole weekend. The three of us 'family'--isn't that great?"

He was surprised at Sara's tears. "Oh, *no,* Neil, I can't go now! What can I say to Faye? She'll assume the worst, and we tried to be so careful with Katy there."

"Katy was so innocent and excited about the whole thing, Faye shouldn't think anything at all. And besides, it's not Faye you're going to see, my love. It's our little girl, Katy, and she'll be hurt if you refuse her invitation. Go. It'll be okay, I promise."

Sara cried out, "Neil, sometimes you are *so* naïve!"

He laughed, thinking Sara worried too much about things he could easily handle.

18

When Sara arrived at the Sedgwick government quarters, Katy flew to the door to admit her, while Micki stood back, silently letting her dark eyes do the talking. The shy little girl was a special favorite of Sara's, and she immediately greeted her with a hug. The child beamed. Faye entered the living room with a wan smile, but Sara felt a definite chill.

"Katy was simply insistent that you wouldn't be able to feed yourself with a cast on your arm," said Faye, "so we have some lovely salad and crepes for dinner."

"Thank you so much for your kindness. It was a stupid fall and it's almost impossible to handle pots and pans left-handed. I've been eating sandwiches. This is so nice of you."

"Well, Katy and Neil seem to think so highly of you." She turned partially away and added, almost as an afterthought, "Of course, we *married* ladies know you single women have no way to fix things for yourself."

Sara tried to assess the tone. Was there some seething resentment? She couldn't be sure, though she recognized Faye's stance on single women being somehow inferior to married ladies. Nothing was said about the sharing of rooms or the ski trip, however, and Faye seemed almost civil. Sara feared it might be an act, hiding her true feelings. She concentrated instead on Katy and Micki who both bubbled with excitement.

Micki always had horses on her mind. She rode them, petted them, or just watched them whenever she could. One too-friendly horse at a nearby petting zoo had even bitten her, but it had not changed her passion for equines. She grabbed Sara's hand excitedly, and said, "Sara, come upstairs with me. I want you to see my pretty horses. I told you about them--remember?"

Sara started toward the stairs hand in hand with the little girl, but Faye stepped in her way and glared down at Micki. "No one wants to see your dumb old horse collection, Micki. Stop bothering our guest like that."

The child's face froze in horror. Sara tried to salvage the moment, saying, "Micki, I'd love to see your horses. Perhaps we can go upstairs to see them after dinner."

But the damage was done. Micki ran to the kitchen to hide in a corner. Sara cringed as she saw Faye accost the child again on her way to the oven. "I told you to be seen and not heard." Faye pinched Micki's arm as she went by. "Now, behave!"

Before Sara could think how to comfort Micki with Faye present, the front door opened, and Neil walked in! Katy rushed into his arms, obviously delighted.

Faye returned to the living room. "What are *you* doing here? We only have ladies' food. We don't want you here!"

Sara caught herself in an audible gasp, but Neil's glance told the story. He had come because he worried about her discomfort in being alone with Faye. He had known his greeting from Faye would be less than welcoming. Faye hated surprises.

"I don't need anything to eat. I just had the evening off and decided to come to surprise the girls and enjoy your guest." He smiled at Sara and shook her uninjured hand, squeezing her fingers to let her know everything was all right. "I hope your wrist is better," he said, but his eyes added another message, "I'm here now." Sara understood the unspoken words and smiled. Then he turned to Faye and continued, "You ladies go ahead with your dinner. I'll just fix myself a sandwich and grab a beer."

Sara did feel better with him there, but she marveled at the racing speed with which he must have driven the mountainous road after work. He relaxed in an armchair.

Faye screamed, "Don't you dare sit on my furniture in your Army uniform! I just cleaned today. You'll get it all dirty. And you get those boots off my rug, too!"

Neil sighed, reached down, removed the boots, and slid dutifully to his sock feet to get away from the 'clean' chair. His tired sigh hurt Sara. She felt the sting of Faye's manipulating Neil, and it was all she could do to stumble through the evening. She was desperately looking for something good in Faye, as she'd told Katy to do. It was hard.

The meal proceeded with Katy and Micki's bubbly interchanges with their father and Sara, while Faye sat in stony silence. But when Micki bounced in her seat, accidentally toppling her milk glass, the child thrust her hands stiffly into her lap and shut her eyes tight as tears began to well. She knew what was coming.

After a pause while she knit her brow in a gathering storm, Faye screamed at the little girl, "You dummy! You're so clumsy. You just keep making more work for me."

Micki burst into loud sobs, Katy cowered in her chair, and Sara was near tears as well. She reached under the table to take Micki's hand in her own and squeeze it tightly.

Neil calmly told his wife: "Lighten up, Faye. Little girls sometimes spill their milk." He quietly rose and mopped up the mess with a towel, patting Micki on the shoulder as he did so. In her rage, Faye was almost incoherent, mumbling curses under her breath, but she finally seemed aware Sara was in the room and made an heroic effort to bring herself back under control, complete with a huge sigh.

Sara couldn't speak from shock. The girls were silent.

Though Sara's sprained wrist throbbed wildly, since she had chosen a clear head over the prescribed pain pills, she hoped she could make it through the evening. She was grateful Neil had come to keep her from facing it alone, but her relief was short-lived.

Katy made comments about her 'home family' and her 'ski family,' asking when her 'ski family' could go again to Austria.

Faye's eyes narrowed. "There will be no more goofing off like skiing, Katy." Though she addressed Katy, she was looking straight at Sara. "Any weekend time your father has off from now on, will be spent at home helping me get packed for our move to our new duty station in the States."

Sara immediately caught the barb Faye put in the words 'at home.' Neil didn't seem to notice. He was smiling broadly that Katy and Sara got along so well, though he did remind Faye that he and Katy had already paid for the Ski Club's Hintertux trip.

Faye scowled and banged the dishes as she collected them.

Finally, Sara could make her escape, thanking Faye profusely. Neil and Katy walked her to her car.

"I wanted you to see my reception for yourself," Neil whispered. "Do you understand better now?"

Sara nodded at Neil, but addressed her comments to Katy. "Thank you for inviting me, Katy. It was kind of your mother to help me by fixing dinner."

"Can we have dinner together again, Sara?"

Sara nodded. "At my place next time—when my arm is healed."

Neil shook her good hand, winked, and strode back to the house arm in arm with Katy. Sara could hear him say, "Well, Katy, are you getting through the week okay?"

When Sara met him in Graf on Thursday, Neil repeated the conversation that had followed her departure. Mimicking Faye's nagging voice, Neil acted out the harsh scene that had transpired with his estranged wife.

"'Katy told me all about it, Neil! How could you have that woman in your bed?' She spat out the words like acid, as usual. 'I don't want my house defiled by her presence. I hate you for bringing her here.'

"I just told her, 'I didn't bring her here. You invited her.'

"She said, 'I had to. Katy wouldn't shut up about her. I had to see for myself.'

"So I told her, 'Ask Katy. She'll tell you the beds were her choice, *not* Sara's or mine. The rooms we reserved weren't available. Katy will tell you that she was with us at *all* times. If Katy told you about our sharing a room, she would certainly have told you if she thought anything was going on, so forget it. It was an accidental shortage of rooms, and nothing happened there.'

"Then she got even more vicious." Neil's voice mimicking the woman rose. "'You'll never change. And you'll never make your next promotion!'

"'No, Faye,' I told her. 'I *have* changed. And whether I do or don't make any more rank, it's a long way off, and it has nothing to do with our arguments here. Graf is our six months of separation, and we're still getting a divorce when we get back to the States. Get used to the idea.' I felt confident I had the last word."

"And did you?" asked Sara, her heart racing with anxiety.

Neil grinned. "No, not really. She said, 'Think what you want--your duty is to me,' and she threw a vase at me that normally sits on the hall table. I didn't even look at the fragments. I just told her, 'I'm driving back to Graf for an early briefing. I assume you've destroyed this vase in the same way you destroy everything else.' I grabbed my boots from the back porch and carried them out, barefoot. I'm afraid I slammed the door on the way to my sedan. I got back to the cabin about midnight."

"Oh, Neil, how awful," said Sara, as she put her arms around the man.

"She'll shed a few angry tears sweeping up the pieces of her favorite vase--a wedding present from her mother. She'll wish she'd picked something else to throw, or that I hadn't ducked. But it's rather fitting that she shattered a wedding vase as she shattered our marriage. The incident was just an example of 'Life with Faye,'" He shook his head. "We'd make such a good soap opera."

But a shadow moved across Sara's face. She couldn't sleep, realizing she saw more to worry about than Neil did. Faye's motives and her hatred were becoming more transparent every day. Neil represented her "married woman" status, and Faye would never let him go quietly and be left "single" and, therefore, in her own eyes, "inferior."

During their next quiet Sunday evening, Neil took Sara's hands. "After all that drama, let's get away for a week."

Sara was surprised by the idea, but nodded. "When?"

"I knew you'd be off from school next week for Easter vacation, so I already put in for leave. We need to put our exclusive and permanent relationship to the real test," he joked with a flash of his mischievous grin.

She raised her eyebrows. "So what would be the real test?"

I think the real test is if we can face the challenge of traveling together for more than a weekend without fighting." He smiled and squeezed her hand. "What do you think?"

Sara was amused, remembering his descriptions of taking Faye to Greece. "Are you worried--checking me out?"

"They say if people can travel comfortably together, they can live together comfortably, forever."

"Oh, really? Who said that?"

"Me." He laughed out loud. "But you always say I'm an expert in my field, so...."

She took his hand as they walked into her kitchen for a cup of hot chocolate before bedtime. "Where do you want to go?"

"I wanted to surprise you. We both love history, and I've always wanted to visit a rustic German hunting lodge." He laid a yellowed book about antique buildings on the table as they sat down. He pointed. "I made reservations at this one."

"It's beautiful, Neil. How old is it?"

"The book says about four centuries. What do you think?" He reached across the table to take her hand. "Thursday after school, you can drive out to Graf. We'll get an early start on Friday morning. Here, you can see, it gives directions in the book. It seems to be way out on a back road." He laughed. "Probably on some goat path, but I'm sure you're a good navigator. It says they specialize in wild game."

"You made the reservations for Good Friday night, then?"

"Yes. We'll have all day to drive leisurely out to the lodge. I told them we'd stay four or five days--a low-key time to relax, read, sketch, whatever you like, and then we can stop on the way back anywhere you want. We'll be back in time for next Friday's trip to Hintertux with Katy and our 'Wild Bunch' ski buddies. It will give me extra time to drive your marvelous Mustang."

Sara knew Neil loved her car as much as she did. "It sounds wonderful. How are you able to be gone for that long?"

"There's a commander's conference in Frankfurt. I just mentioned it in passing and she made the assumption I'd be going there. I didn't say anything to dissuade her thinking that. I didn't even bother to remind her that I no longer command a battalion. She never wants to know about my work, anyway, so… I simply took a week of my leave that was on the books." He paused for a moment. "Of course, as always, she had a price."

"What was it this time?"

"You and I won't be able to be together at Graf on Tuesday night this week because I have to take a day off from my real work and drive in to Post to complete the list of chores she has 'saved' for me. It's always something, and she is so damned helpless that she can't do anything for herself. I wish she were independent like you, so I wouldn't constantly have to stop my work assignment for the Army just to drop the car off for repair, or change a light bulb, or a vacuum cleaner bag. The list is silly and endless."

Sara cringed, remembering the times she'd heard Faye brag to the ladies with a laugh, "I have to keep Neil busy so he's too tired to get frisky." *Faye could save you trouble by simply doing what she could easily do for herself,* Sara thought. *It makes me sad that she has taken advantage of your naiveté and your desire to please all these years and then bragged about her deception.*

But out loud, Sara could only say, "Never mind, darling. Do whatever you feel you should. We'll have the rest of the week together."

Neil smiled at her and said, "Thank you for understanding, my love. I do still have responsibilities to her for taking good care of the girls--a sense of duty to set her up comfortably, and take care of her security."

While Sara agreed that Faye should be well taken care of financially and that she should not suffer unduly from a divorce, she pushed back into her subconscious the disappointment she felt that Neil still didn't seem to realize that the girls weren't happy at home with Faye, any more than he was—that all of them were actually victims of verbal abuse. *He must begin, soon, to see for himself.*

Ever since Neil's unexpected outburst of frustration toward Faye, he and Sara had grown closer. It was as though by his sharing the deep anger and resentment he didn't even know he had, they had shared everything, and they had come through it stronger—trusting each other completely. But Sara had also noticed that Neil now only referred to Faye as "she." It made the woman seem further out of their lives than she really was, but he simply wouldn't mention Faye's name.

He also was becoming quite confident of getting out of Faye's life safely. "She doesn't want me," he kept repeating whenever Sara asked how Faye felt about the divorce.

"Are you sure we can get away without getting you into trouble somehow?"

"Yes, my love, don't worry so much." He came around the table to lift her to her feet, and walked her from the kitchen to the bedroom, flicking off the lights with his elbow as they passed. They laughed and snuggled together as they lay on the bed while he nuzzled her neck with kisses. As always, their relaxed, spontaneous play led to sensual love-making and, as always, Sara could feel Neil's happiness swell to match her own.

19

The week spun by quickly, as Neil waited to greet Sara when she arrived at Graf on Thursday evening as planned. "I was singing along with my car radio all the way," she said, happily, "even though it looks like we'll have a severe Spring snowstorm."

"And seeing your loving smile makes my heart sing," he added with a grin. "I'm really corny tonight, aren't I?" After dinner at their favorite restaurant in Vilseck, they contentedly lay on the floor in their little cabin, watching the changing patterns of firelight on the ceiling and making up stories of dramatic "scenes" they could imagine in the flickering shadows. These were spiced liberally with debate over their latest readings on international policy makers--an odd combination of fantasy and hypocrisy, they decided with shared amusement.

With the morning, even more snow had fallen, but they managed to get away early on slippery roads, and head southeast from Grafenwohr. Passing a monument on a hill, they decided to explore it—a fortuitous surprise--*Valhalla*. Neil was both an opera fan and a military man, so he was fascinated by the topic of *Valhalla*, the heaven-appointed place for brave soldiers. "Here's where I'll be one day," he boasted with a grin.

"Don't make it anytime soon," she countered. They spent a pleasant hour hiking around the aristocratic monument.

Their next stop was at the ruins of an old Cistercian Abby. They delighted in finding they shared both curiosity and the willingness to scrap any time schedule for a good bout of exploring. "I was afraid you might be too 'disciplined' a traveler for me," Sara explained through her laughter.

"And I worried about you for the same reason," he said. "It's super to find we feel alike on this topic of such great import to lifelong traveling companions. I love seeing the world through your eyes. You always give me a new perspective." He whistled as he drove the Mustang through the white countryside.

In Regensburg, lunch at the ancient little bratwurst stand by the riverside restored their energy to enjoy a walk across the lovely old stone bridge in the falling snow.

"I'd like to swim the Danube someday," Neil said.

"I'm glad it's too cold for that today, my dear." She bundled up her coat.

In the late afternoon, with the Spring snow falling more heavily, they followed directions in the book to find their hunting lodge. *Haus Auersberg* seemed much further than they had estimated, the hour grew late, and the storm increased its fury.

"The directions in the book seem to keep leading us east," Sara remarked, fumbling with a road map that held no clues. "At least, I *think* this is east. I can't see a thing, but we're going toward the Communist Border of Czechoslovakia, aren't we?"

"I'm sure we'll come to the lodge's turnoff any minute now," assured Neil. But the snow had become a blizzard, blotting out all landmarks and heaping high banks on both sides of the narrow unpaved road they had entered a long way back. Lack of visibility and swirling snow had slowed them to a crawl, but there was no sign of civilization where they could stop, either to rest, or for further clarification of the directions.

"My 'brave heart warrior' looks a little nervous." Sara tried to joke, as they plowed forward. "We passed that little farming village of Phillipsreuth some time ago, and I seem to remember it was close to the East/West Border with Czechoslovakia."

"We should find the driveway any minute," repeated Neil, stoically.

This would not have been a problem had they both been civilians. But anyone stationed on a military installation was restricted to stay outside five kilometers from the communist Border, except when escorted or on orders. The one-kilometer zone was restricted to military units on guard duty. Neil and Sara were both aware that the hour was getting late, and they had no idea how much further ahead their lodge might be.

At last, inching along in the darkness with blowing snow obscuring the road completely, a sign ahead became barely visible. Neil stepped out into deep powder. Obviously no other cars had come this way. Framed in the dim headlights, he reached up to brush snow from the sign with his gloves. They had to find out where they were, and quickly. They were exhausted from fighting the snow on unfamiliar, slippery roads, and there was no way to turn around without getting hopelessly stuck in the high snow banks on both sides of the narrow "goat path" Neil had predicted.

Neil climbed back into the driver's seat and slammed the car door behind him. His shoulders slumped. When the snow had fallen away from the sign, it had said, "*Achtung! Grenze* ahead! You are within the one Kilometer zone of the Border."

"You saw it too, I imagine. We're inside the one K."

"Yes," she said quietly, knowing the consequences of their being caught there. At the very least it would mean a reprimand in their official files. At most, it could spark an international incident--with capture, ransom, interrogation, spy charges, or worse.

"I can't imagine how we passed the five Kilometer warning sign," said Neil.

"It must have been covered in snow and we couldn't see it among the drifts."

"Well, my dear. What do you suggest? I don't relish the idea of keeping you in the car all night, when the likelihood of our being found frozen stiff is about all I can promise you. There's no way to turn around or back up until we can see better in the morning, yet we *cannot* go on ahead."

Sara peered through the murky window. "Neil, Look across the road on the left. Could those trees be outlining the snow banks of a driveway over there?

He wiped off the condensation frozen on the inside of the windshield with the back of his glove. "You could be right. I'll go check." He again climbed out of the car and hurled himself against the wind in the direction she had pointed.

The car was almost immediately swept from view in the diminished visibility, and he wondered if he could find his way back. But finally, his large form bumped up against the window, and he opened the door, covered in snow. Sara quickly brushed the snow off his head and face. "Before you get frostbite," she said.

"It's a driveway," he puffed. "It might be the one. There's a dim light way down. At least, I hope it's a light. Everything's so dark and snowy out there, I can't be sure. Shall we try it? I don't think we have any choice but to find shelter somewhere—soon!"

As Sara nodded, he added, "You need to know that if I'm wrong, we could be taking a hell of a chance going down this road. It's very narrow. It could be a dead end, and we can't turn around. We'll be stuck. Or, since it's lightly marked at this point, the road might cross the communist Border and we'd be up the proverbial crick without a paddle. I'm sorry I got you into this mess."

He tried to make light of a disastrous situation. They'd both been stationed on the Iron Curtain Border for enough years to know it would be no laughing matter should they be caught. But Sara reached out and touched his cold face. "Let's go, my love. I trust your judgment. And don't feel you got me into this. I wanted to come, remember? We're in it together, whatever happens."

He leaned over to kiss her on the nose. "You're something else, you know that? We make a great team." He started the car again and, even in that short time, wheels were frozen to the snow, straining. The chains finally caught and the car spun sideways as Neil struggled for control. Slowly, they pulled ahead and, though sliding heavily into the snow bank where Neil tried to make the turn, they began to make some headway. The snow on both sides of the narrow drive was much higher than the car itself.

Sara laid her hand lightly on Neil's thigh, and he could feel her message in the touch. *She's with me, no matter what.* He grinned slightly, feeling he was lucky to have her, but he was also aware he had brought her into a potentially dangerous situation.

Neil kept wiping the windshield with his glove and peering out through the small cleared hole. Sara grabbed a polishing rag from the glove compartment and took over the job so Neil could concentrate on his driving. Minutes clicked by.

"I think it *is* a light down there," he said, with a note of hope in his voice. Finally, they could make out the shape of a huge old house with snowdrifts almost up to the rafters. The light turned out to be a lantern stuck on a pole at the back door. As they stopped the car and Neil got out to try to raise someone in the house, the back door opened and a man emerged, bundled up and obviously expecting them. He identified himself as the innkeeper, shook hands heartily, and welcomed them inside.

"I was afraid you were lost in the storm," he said as he helped Neil and Sara out of their coats and told them not to worry about the snow falling from their clothes and boots. A young girl immediately swept up the snow and threw it back out the door, while an older lady, the innkeeper's wife, bustled them into the warm kitchen where the smell of food brought them up short.

"Wow," said Neil, rather unprofessionally, "Whatever you're making sure smells wonderful." The woman, introduced as *Frau* Benz, beamed at them both.

"When you've warmed yourself a bit, you'll have your dinner in the study while I get your bags," said the man. "Then we'll show you around the great hall and the lodge."

Neil and Sara both relaxed, realizing only then, that their bodies had been tense.

"Well, my love, we lucked out." Neil said, wrapping an arm around Sara's shoulders.

"I wasn't worried."

He smiled, knowing she wouldn't admit it, if she had been.

The innkeeper, *Herr* Benz, said, "I'm sorry to have to bring you in through the kitchen. The door to the great hall is blocked by snow, and my son and I won't be able to get it uncovered until the storm slows down a bit."

"Do you expect it will stop tomorrow?" asked Neil.

"Later tonight," he answered. "Come now and have dinner. You must be starving."

The two were shown to a large library. Their table was set elegantly near a fire roaring in a fireplace probably eight feet tall. It towered over Neil's six foot three frame. He examined the antique marble mantle with interest. "Would you look at this," he said, running his fingers over the smooth woodwork. Old world carvings of animals in wooden railings surrounded a spiral staircase that wound up to more library shelves on a second floor.

They explored the room--Sara finding the gilded covers of original works, Dante, Chaucer, and Shakespeare. "All my favorites," she said breathlessly. "Oh, Neil, this is perfect! I'm glad you found out about this place." She squeezed his arm with glee.

"We were lucky," he said again, as he escorted her to her seat at the gracefully hand-carved antique table. Crystal goblets gleamed in candlelight near elegant gold-bordered plates. Sara's excitement was evident when Neil seated himself opposite and took her hand across the distance. "You know darling, it feels as though we've always been lovers and friends, and one is as important to me as the other. I love being here with you. But, when the storm is over, we'll have to leave."

Her eyes grew large. "But we found the right place. We're here safely, now. And we're warm again while that blizzard rages outside. Why will we have to leave?" Seeing his strained face, she added, "What is it, Neil? What are you worried about?"

"Are you forgetting the sign?"

"No, but I assumed once we were here, it wouldn't matter. There's no place else we can go in this storm. No one knows we're here. The Borderline could even have turned the other way at this point. Surely, they would have noted it in the book if this house was actually *within* the one K zone, wouldn't they?"

"I'd like to think so, but we'll have to find out. Let's not worry about it until after we get some food in us. I'll ask the innkeeper later."

"I didn't see any guard towers or razor wire fences."

"They aren't as prevalent on the Czech Border as they are on the German. Besides it was too dark and snowy to really see anything. Thank goodness. If any communist guards were out there, they probably couldn't see us either."

Frau Benz and the young girl entered with steaming bowls of soup and hot homemade bread. It was the beginning of a marvelously romantic evening.

After a sumptuous meal of venison and a delectable chocolate fondue dessert, their host suggested that he take his guests on a tour of the old lodge.

The great hall was festooned with trophy heads of almost every animal hunted in Europe. Interspersed between the towering, and now snow-blocked, windows of the hall were hand-painted targets, the border of each telling the story of that particular competitive hunt, and who won the target. "I've seen such treasures before at various hunting clubs in Germany," said Sara. "But these are particularly exquisite." Together they tried to decipher the difficult Old German phrasing.

Their innkeeper was delighted by their interest and regaled them with stories of the glory days before World War II, when great hunters from as far away as Bulgaria and Canada had come to his lodge. "Not many people can make the journey anymore. We are honored that you two have visited our home."

"Are we the only ones here?" asked Sara.

"Yes. And though we'd like to entertain such lovely guests for a fortnight, I know you will not be able to stay with us long."

"I'm glad you understand," said Neil. "How did you know?"

"The Border has been a terrible problem for us, but we are glad that we are at least on the proper side of it--barely. We are particularly grateful that the American Army is here to keep the communists from taking *all* of Germany. Though your license was almost obliterated by snow, I saw the green military plate when I got your luggage. I knew you wouldn't be able to stay, but you at least needed shelter for this night."

"Thank you, Sir," said Neil, "for being so understanding of our predicament. We had no idea exactly where your lodge was situated. We were trying to follow the directions in the book, but it made no mention of being so near the Border."

"What book is that?"

Neil gave the name, and the innkeeper smiled. "That edition is very old, from before the war, and before the division of Germany into free and communist blocks."

"It's from the Post library at Graf. I should have looked at the publication date," said Neil. "My mistake, and I'm so sorry. I'll pay you for the days we reserved...."

"No, please. Don't give it a thought," interrupted their host. "As I said, we are grateful to you Americans for being here. There will be no extra charge." The man pulled aside a drapery of the great hall and smiled. "Look. The snow has finally almost stopped, and my son is already clearing a path from the front door."

Sara peered from the window and exclaimed, "Oh, Neil, some of the stars are coming through the clouds. Look how brightly they shine there in the darkness. Can we go out for a walk, now, please?"

He noted her hands clasped together like a child, and chuckled. "Three hours ago, we were anxious to get *inside*, and now you want to go back out? The boy has dug the path through walls of snow at least four feet deep!"

"But, how beautiful it is! Can we, please--for just a few minutes?"

Neil turned to *Herr* Benz. "Just how far away *is* the Border from your house?"

The innkeeper smiled slyly, and said in a conspiratorial stage whisper, "It's best if you go out the *front* door, and go *only* in the direction of the path my son cleared."

"And the back door we came in…?"

"The lantern is on the Czechoslovakian Border line. It has no wall at this place because of my driveway. There are guard towers further down the drive."

Neil sighed and looked at Sara, shaking his head. She thought of something else. "*Herr* Benz, will the *Grenz Politzei,* (the formidable German border patrol charged with arresting folks found too near the Border) come tonight looking for us?"

"I'm sure they will."

"The car…"

"Buried, Madame!" The man made a low bow. There was a pause as Neil and Sara absorbed that information. Then all three broke into relieved laughter.

"I know we'll sleep safely tonight with you protecting us, *Herr* Benz," said Neil. "Thank you. You'll never know how much we wanted to come."

"My pleasure. Now, your wraps have dried in the kitchen so I'll get them for you and you can have your romantic walk under the stars--out the front door, of course."

The snow had become the quiet, crispy cold type that no longer stuck to their bulky coats. It only gently kissed their eyelashes and drifted away. After walking a little and watching some of Neil's favorite stars from the front of the old hunting lodge, the two agreed they would be content this night in such a warm and friendly place, regardless of any danger.

The room to which they were shown had a regal, high ceiling, an enormous four-poster bed for which they had to climb hand-carved wooden steps, the most elegant of antique furnishings, and a curved bathtub on clawed feet. They were treated as royalty. The innkeeper discreetly withdrew to leave them complete privacy.

In such a beautiful setting, their lovemaking was elegant as well, until they broke into laughter at becoming entangled in the deep, old-fashioned goose-down comforters. Remembering their first clumsy efforts at lovemaking in ski suits, Neil murmured contentedly, "How far we've come together, my dear--as lovers, as friends, as life companions."

After a huge breakfast, which the two consumed with the family in their cozy kitchen, Neil and Sara said their goodbyes. The son of *Herr* Benz had left the table a few minutes earlier to dig out their car, and they were given advice on how to make their getaway, hopefully without encountering any patrols of the U.S. military or the *Grenz Politzei*.

"We hope you two will return to us someday when the Border no longer divides our country. We would be extremely happy to see you again."

The two men shook hands heartily. "Until then, *Herr* Benz," said Neil. "And thank you for everything."

The couple was grateful that the day had dawned gray and drizzly, hoping the weather would cover their getaway from too close a proximity to the Border. After what seemed like a tense eternity, they finally were far enough away to breathe easier, and had come to a highway that was actually *on* the map.

Neil brightened considerably. "Well, my love, where would you like to go now? We still have the rest of our week together."

"Can we go to Passau? I've read about three rivers, the Inn, Ils, and Danube Rivers, that supposedly come together in three different colors." Sara glanced at the map. "It's only a little out of our way to the south."

"Done!" Neil tried to grin brightly.

"You were really worried back there, weren't you?"

"If we'd been found in that lodge by the *Grenz Politzei, or* the communist Border Patrol, it would have been a 'career ender,' for sure. Never in a million years could we have explained our presence within mere inches of the communist Border. With my security clearance level and not even armed or accompanied…." He sighed, and looked over at Sara. "And our presence there *together* would have been impossible to explain, too. Do you realize how lucky we were?" He feared a catastrophe had been averted by sheer luck. "It was reckless of me not to check out the location better." He grinned. "I guess all I could think of was a romantic getaway alone with you. I wasn't watching what I was doing. For an officer, that could be fatal."

"I guess I'm just beginning to realize how important your career is, and how easily it could all be swept away by one little mistake." Sara was silent for a long time.

He reached out to squeeze her hand. She closed her eyes, laid her head back on the seat, and squeezed back. For a moment, he had no idea what she was thinking.

20

Sara was happy as they spent four days splashing their way through continuous German rain that had replaced the snow in the ancient and picturesque town of Passau with its 15th century fortress. Neil declared his enjoyment of the successive defense systems of the old Episcopal stronghold from an engineer's standpoint as well as from religious antiquity. But they chose to spend their last day of adventure in the cabin they had made their own. Neil lit the wood in the fireplace, while Sara prepared sandwiches and soup.

"Do you mind if we just stay in by the fire?" she asked.

"Great. Come here and sit by me, Love." He held out his hand to Sara from his cross-legged position on the rug in front of the fireplace. "It was a super trip. I feel at peace with the world."

She nestled into his lap and sighed contentedly. "Did we pass the test?" she asked, mischief in her eyes.

"With flying colors. You never once complained about either me *or* the weather." He kissed her on the cheek and laughed. "I figured you would have pushed me into the Danube River by the third day we walked in the rain."

"It could have been a temptation," she said, grinning as she brushed her palm over his short military haircut. "But it gave us a chance to feed our breakfast bread to the swans and find quaint little museums."

"The changing colors of the three rivers probably won't show up in all my rainy day photos, though." Neil leaned back against the sofa, smiling with satisfaction.

"I liked strolling along the rivers and falling asleep in each other's arms with the sound of the Danube slapping against the sea wall below our hotel room."

"An interlude I'll never forget." His smile was contagious.

As Sara's warm chuckle filled the room, he added, "I feel lucky to have you. I think we've crossed some invisible line, sharing so much together—having pure fun with someone I love, someone who has also become my best friend. We make a great team, you and I."

She only nodded and hugged him tighter.

"After all," he said, "how many people do we know who've had their car buried within the One K zone? You didn't even flinch when we had to make our shaky getaway. We'll have lots of traveling to do once we're together--for always."

She snuggled against him, in response to the 'always.' "Where shall we go first?"

They liked the planning. "Do you have a preference?"

"We've both been overseas so long. There are things I've never seen in the States." She paused to think a moment. "Oh, I know where we can go first. Remember that book we read together, Killer Angels, by Michael Shaara?"

"About one of my favorite heroes, Colonel Joshua Chamberlain, commander of the 20th regiment of Volunteers—he was from Maine, you know."

"How could I *not* know? You've told me a hundred times that all men from Maine are great, so I guess it must be true." She caressed his cheek with her fingers. "Let's go to Gettysburg and find the place on the hillside where Chamberlain and his men turned back the Confederate attack--you know the one--when his maneuver saved the Battle of Gettysburg for the Union, and no one had even tried it before."

"Great! I love the history angle. We'll do it this summer when you visit me at the War College. Gettysburg is very near."

"Will I be able to come see you by then? Will it be okay?"

"Of course. Six months of separation from Faye will be over. I·should have papers filed. Even if all isn't quite settled yet, we can still meet and go to Gettysburg. I know a quaint old inn at the edge of the meadow where Pickett led his battle charge. How will that be?"

"I'll meet you there in August, before I come back overseas for the fall semester."

"Will you have to come back here? Can't you wait in the States with me?"

"I'll have to come back, unless you're free by then. I still need a job *somewhere*--two daughters in college, remember?" She traced his brow with her finger. "Of course, if you have everything worked out by August, just *try* to push me back on that plane! I'll already have my letter of resignation written, so I can send it then and stay with you."

He considered a moment. "Will you listen to us? We've moved on to the next step, haven't we, my love--we're making plans for our future."

"I can see that." She smiled, mischievously.

"You know, I want to be with you always, even when we're so old we can barely toddle along on the seacoast of Maine, hand in hand."

"Me, too, Love. But, are we ready to move through the upcoming minefield?"

"Oh, I'm sure the confrontation will come--soon as I get back to the States. But I've been dodging broadsides for years. Our marriage went downhill like a snowball headed for hell. But you're probably right that it could take more time to get custody settled and paperwork done for the divorce than the time between June when you leave, and August, when you and I meet."

Sara silently watched the man she loved work out his timeline.

"How about this?" He hugged her. "We meet at Gettysburg in August, and I'll make love to you once for every Civil War Monument there, and then you can teach overseas until Christmas break. That can be our compromise. Nothing bad can happen in that short time apart. I'll be getting the divorce while you're making reservations for Katy and me on the Ski Club's winter trip, and we'll fly over to Germany and join you."

"Katy will love that. I know she'll be anxious to ski with us again. She's already looking forward to the Hintertux Ski Club trip to Austria coming up this weekend."

"By winter, I'll have told Katy about us. She'll be old enough to choose where she wants to live and it's my guess she'll want to be with us. I'm sure Micki will follow. Then you'll hand in your resignation after the holidays and fly home to the states with us." He kissed her on the cheek.

"It sounds wonderful. I'll tell Lisa and Lynette as soon as you get the divorce. I know they'll love you too. But you probably need to prepare yourself for the confrontation, darling. Will you be strong enough? You're so good at thinking through the potential problems for the military. Have you thought through all the contingencies of *this* battle?"

"I wish I could avoid the drama, but in the end it will turn out all right."

"Do you have doubts?"

"Not about *us*. But I'm sure Faye will make it difficult. Yet, there's been a breach between us for so many years, a divorce should be a relief to her too. I'm optimistic."

"Are you sure? Has she *said* divorce would be a relief?"

"No, not exactly." He paused. "But she has said that she'd like to see me dead!" He laughed. "Does that count?"

Sara didn't laugh.

"Oh, don't worry, darling. She says that all the time. She'd '...like me dead even if she had to poison my food and knew she would get caught,'--that sort of thing."

Lines of concern appeared on Sara's brow, remembering that Katy had overheard something similar. She felt the need to warn him. "You know, don't you, that people who threaten such things have already worked it out psychologically to the stage where they're capable of acting? With poisoning, you would never even know it. Counselors know all about the danger of that type of thing. Threats are a form of spouse abuse."

He laughed at Sara's concern. "I don't worry about it. Remember, I've been trained to handle combat. I can certainly handle a woman's angry comments, abusive or not. Besides, she knows there's no hope for our marriage. We gave up trying to fix it years ago. We simply avoid each other as much as possible. The only feelings I had for her disappeared with her constant rejection. There's only disgust and indifference left between us." He sighed. "It's no way to live a life. Why would she want to stay when she knows she hates me?"

"I pray you're right. But status seems to mean a lot to her, too—that of being a married lady, an officer's lady. You'll have to reckon with that."

"I do feel a responsibility to set her up securely in the States—give her the house we own in DC, make sure she can live independently with school, or a hobby, or a job. I'll fix up the family car so it's dependable for her, set up alimony, living expenses and medical care. I'll convince her to share the children so they won't feel torn between us. That should keep it all quiet."

"Neil, we both know she doesn't share anything with you now, so why do you think she will share the children to save them harm? And you know she won't do this quietly. Perhaps we should tell her now about us, so she has time to make her own plans."

"Trust me on this one! The only safe way is to wait until you're out of country. It's hypocritical to pretend to the community that ours is a good marriage, when it's been a disaster, but that's the choice left to a military officer if he wants his next promotion." Neil's frustration escaped in a sigh. "But I know her--she'd make a bigger scandal in front of her friends here, and ruin my career if the divorce was on grounds of adultery, so she mustn't find out about my love for you." He took Sara's hands in his. "We must, at all costs, keep her from knowing about us until we leave here. She could hurt you. I want her a continent away from you before I file papers. Stick with me, please."

"We'll do it your way, then, but I'm afraid this secrecy will all blow up somehow. You know, don't you, Neil, that it's too late now for me to ever stop loving you, ever?" She put her arms around his neck and buried her face in his shoulder. "That makes me the particularly vulnerable one of this threesome, doesn't it?"

"You're fearless, my love—this will all be behind us soon."

They set to work sharing notes and suggestions on his magazine article for half an hour, with bodies almost joined at the hip and shoulder, Neil turned to brush her forehead with a kiss. "I love having you close enough to reach out and touch, even when we're working."

"It makes the work go quickly, doesn't it?" She mused aloud, "Sometimes I think everything since West Point has gone so smoothly for you that you just *feel* invincible?"

He smiled with eyes crinkled in fun. "I *am* invincible, my love--just ask me!" He grew serious. "We rely on each other, don't we? I'll never be the same person I used to be."

"I should hope not!" Sara chuckled, chiding him gently. "You were a pompous, holier-than-thou, love-starved oaf when we met. And now…" She paused for a moment.

"And now?"

"Now, you're wonderful," she said, kissing him playfully on the shoulder with a loud smack.

He roared out his appreciation. "Do you know how happy I am right this minute?"

"I know." She said it quietly. She was happier than she had ever thought she could be again—with quivers of delight never far from the surface.

"I promise I'll be free to make a home for us by Christmas."

"By Christmas? Really, Darling?"

"Don't worry. I love you, and I can do this."

"I'll wait for you, Neil. You know I will. God help me if I'm wrong, because if you changed your mind now, I couldn't survive it." She looked trustingly into his eyes.

"My love," he said slowly, meeting her gaze, "now that I know what life with love can be, I'm no longer willing to live without it. You've made that happen for me." He patted her playfully on the backside. "Now stop worrying. Just leave it all to me. Let's hit the shower." He wiggled his eyebrows, suggestively, and she couldn't help but laugh.

"It's a plan, then." She reached over to the coffee table to rescue their glasses of wine, smiling as she clinked his wine glass. "Here's to making love once for every monument in Gettysburg, and the three of us skiing together again in December."

###

Neil was late for the ski bus on the Hintertux trip next afternoon, having had to make a quick flight to Heidelberg during the day. He called her at the Officers' Club to tell her of the helicopter's emergency landing as soon as he could hike to a phone. "I knew you'd be worried. I'm thankful you're with the rest of the group. Hopefully, the bus can wait an extra twenty minutes for me. And can you pick up Katy? She should be all ready."

Sara didn't worry Katy about the emergency landing, but assured the ski group's Wild Bunch Neil would come soon. They weren't worried. Sara, however, had to pretend she was not particularly concerned about his flight. She didn't like pretending.

But once in Hintertux, alternating with Neil at skiing with the Wild Bunch and helping Katy, she quickly forgot her concern. They spent their evenings watching stars and searching for Enzian flowers on their after-dinner walks, with Katy holding their hands together as usual. This trip, Neil and Katy shared a room and, as soon as Katy fell asleep, Neil came to Sara's room for privacy. It was safer and more comfortable for both.

"We share so much. I'm happier than I've ever been in my life." He cupped her face softly with one hand and smiled at her. "I want to shout it from rooftops that this sweet, long-legged, intellectual creature loves me." He winked, full of mischief.

"Neil, I know keeping our happiness secret bothers you as much as it does me."

"It does. I want to tell Katy the truth, though I feel like she already knows--the way she keeps saying how, '…just the three of us have more fun together.'"

"Especially when she keeps making references to how unhappy you were before, and how happy we all are in Austria together with this 'family thing' she loves." Sara grew serious. "I think Katy misses laughter too, Neil. She worries about you so. When she cried because we must go home tomorrow, it hurt terribly not to tell her that we'll all be together soon."

Neil agreed, and held Sara closer. "We'll do it soon, my love—soon."

21

Faye mentioned buying a new car when they reached the States during Neil's next weekend at home. "Not right away," he said. "I'll fix up the Chevy so you'll have a dependable car just for yourself. I'll be getting an apartment near the War College while we work out a divorce settlement, so I won't need one for awhile."

Ignoring his reference to their pending separation, she said, "We will *too* want one! We'll be near enough to visit our parents. Plus I've heard the War College has quite a social life. We'll have fun being back in the States together."

"We might have had fun together in the early days of our marriage, Faye, but you never wanted me, and you never wanted the Army. Now it's too late. We're divorcing. You've not ever listened."

Faye screamed, "We will *too* need a car, and you'll live in *our* quarters, damn you." Neil bowed his head and went outside to rake the winter's undergrowth from the yard. Faye screamed after his departing figure, "I wish you were dead."

Faye deftly folded a few things into an overnight bag Sunday night while Micki watched. Neil's six months of temporary duty at Grafenwohr training area was almost over. In sixteen years of marriage, there had been many separations and reunions. For Faye, separations were much more comfortable than reunions.

She looked down, hoping Micki would smile. She didn't. Instead, the child ran to hug her big sister as she entered the room, and announced excitedly, "Katy, guess what? Mama and I are going to the little house in Grafenwohr with Daddy and stay all night. Daddy said I get to sleep on a real folding Army cot."

"That's nice, Mick." Katy returned the hug, looking quizzically at her mother. "Why are you going tonight all of a sudden? Dad's been stationed there for months, and you've never gone before.”

Faye picked up a hairbrush and nudged her blonde hair into its perfectly permed style. “Myrna Lester is meeting me tomorrow at the crystal factory, and Graf is much closer to Neustadt. I can save myself an hour and a half's drive in the early morning by staying at your Dad’s quarters tonight.”

Katy stared at her feet and muttered something unintelligible. A danger signal went off in Faye’s head and froze her hand on the hairbrush. “What did you say, Katy?”

“Nothing, Mother.” The girl paused a moment, with honesty apparently getting the best of her fear of rebuke. “Only I’d hoped you just wanted to be with Dad for an evening. But, then you do enjoy shopping at the German factories, don’t you?”

Faye eyed the girl narrowly. *Was she being sarcastic?* “Don’t be such a romantic.” She forced a laugh. “We’re old hands at the Army game. Dad can take care of himself. He doesn’t need me there.”

Katy hesitated, as though choosing her words carefully. She ran her fingers absently over her father’s bureau. “I feel sorry for him out there in that cabin all week. You’ve never once gone to see him. Have you ever even called him? When he comes home, you two never speak.” The girl rushed to get it all out in one breath.

That’s more talking than Katy has done in a long time, thought Faye—*to me, anyway. She and her dad talk for hours on Saturday nights, and both girls go off with him on explorations, if I can’t think of some chore for them to do here at home instead.*

“I know your father better than you do, Katy,” she finally answered. “A Lieutenant Colonel’s wife must keep up her social obligations. I’m too busy to be calling or running all the way out there. Your father isn’t lonely. He loves his job, and the Army, and you girls…” She had started to add, “…and me,” but the words died in her throat.

Before she could recover and finish the statement, Katy had turned and walked down the hall without a reply. Faye slowly went back to the job at hand. *What am I to do with that girl? She seems at a difficult age right now, and I don’t like her tone one bit.*

As usual, Faye's eyes swept across the bedroom wall to the yellowed news photo of the "Model American Military Family" stepping from the chapel on Easter Sunday, years ago, even before Micki was born. The three of them seemed to represent an important milestone, and she was proud of the framed clipping. The faces smiled out at her. "We've made it this far in happily ever after," they seemed to say. Unconsciously, she brushed her hair into the same style as the picture.

She frowned as she thought of comments she'd heard since then about her husband. "Brilliant," they called him, "dedicated." Battalion command had brought him high evaluations. Even the Corps Commander had said, "He'll make a great general." *Why have they said nothing about me? He'd be nothing without me.*

Her mother had always taught her to aim high and stay in control, and it had paid off. When she met Neil, they'd both been shy. Now, though, he'd become outgoing, militarily prominent, and he seemed almost embarrassed by her avoidance of all but the most socially important functions. *Well that's tough. I didn't ask him to change. And I've shaken all the right hands.* Neil would be getting his eagles soon--probably during War College. They'd be going to Carlisle in a month. *I'll soon have it all!*

What did it matter that Neil seemed merely polite and businesslike when he came home on weekends and kept insisting they were "separated?" He was too smart to risk his future by discarding his wife of sixteen years. She knew ways to stop him. He was just trying to startle her into…what? She could think of no actual reason, so she dismissed the thought.

The phone rang, breaking into her reverie. "Oh, Hello, Dorothy." "Yes, I'm going tonight with Neil and stay at Graf so I can get an early start shopping. Shall I bring you anything?" "No?" "Well, he went out there on Sunday nights during the winter to avoid battling the morning's icy roads. Now that it's spring, he still likes to get more sleep Monday mornings, he says." "Yes, they tell me he's doing very well there." She emitted a prideful laugh. "Gee, Dorothy, you make it sound like he'll be promoted again soon." "Yes, more money sounds good."   Faye had realized since their arrival in Germany that she enjoyed the fruits of Neil's increased rank and salary. Shopping had become a hobby. *He can afford it,* she thought. *I'm only spending what's rightfully mine.*

"Yes, Dorothy, you and I may hate the Army, but it does provide security in retirement benefits as long as our husbands don't get themselves killed." *Or don't want a divorce.* She thought. *But I'll never let him divorce me!*

Her confidence faded for a second as her eye caught Neil's packed duffel bag on the floor. When she told him she and Micki were going to follow him out to the cabin and stay overnight this Sunday evening, he'd rushed out suddenly--to make a phone call, he said. *Now, why couldn't he have made a call from home instead of from battalion headquarters?* He'd been acting strange lately.

"I like his being gone the extra night--that's less time I have to put up with him, right?" Faye laughed as though with a fellow conspirator, though Dorothy was only a casual acquaintance. "Yes, as a matter of fact, he did act surprised when I said I was going to Graf with him. You'd have thought I'd interrupted some plan by going along." "Dorothy! How you talk! He's getting older, thank God…he never expects all *that* on his nights home and not if I go out there, either. He's too tired, and gracious, I sure don't miss it!" *He hasn't touched me for over a year,* she thought silently, *thank Goodness.*

Faye rang off with an expansive farewell, and picked up the photo of her mother near the phone. Dorothy's prediction that Neil would be promoted soon put Faye into a good mood, and she playfully said to the photo, "No, Mama, Neil's idea of a divorce is just a whim. We're going all the way together--or else!"

The front door slammed. A few muffled words were exchanged between Katy and her father at the door before Faye called down the stairs, "Come up and get the bags, Neil."

"I picked up my military sedan from the motor pool," he said, balancing a clinging Micki on one arm. "You two can follow me to Graf in the family car. You'll be able to leave early in the morning for your shopping date with Myrna." His voice betrayed no emotion, yet Faye felt some resignation in his tone, as though he wasn't pleased with her sudden decision to tag along.

The highway twisted through the dusky hills, a scenic route. But the strange animal-like rock formations and caves held no interest for Faye, as she followed Neil's staff car through the evening light. Micki was quiet, hugging one of her stuffed horses.

I get so tired of reminding a seven-year-old that nobody is interested in her dumb horses, and Neil is no help. He encourages her! Surely when we get back Stateside, our family will be perfect—like the picture. In her thoughts, though, something seemed wrong with the picture? The separate faces somehow remained separated--blurred, not refocusing into a unified whole. *Neil wouldn't leave me. After all, I'm making the effort tonight to go with him to Grafenwohr. Sure, it's only to meet with Myrna, but I don't even like Neil's company. He should appreciate the fact that I'm making an effort to come out here at all!*

She laughed aloud at her silly apprehension, shaking it from her mind as they pulled into the training area. Her laugh caught Micki's attention, which she then turned to the taillights of the staff car they were following.

"Why does Daddy keep going faster and faster? Are we almost there?"

"It's your imagination, Micki," Faye snapped. Yet she felt the need for acceleration in her own tingling foot on the gas pedal. *Why this sense of urgency?*

As she drove into the woods leading toward the firing ranges, she mused over Neil's activities—working, skiing, opera performances. *In our early days, he used to beg me to go along, and I told him I wasn't interested. He doesn't ask me anymore, thank goodness. I don't want to be included in his stupid plans.*

Micki interrupted her thoughts. "What's that noise, Mommy?"

The ka-rumping of the artillery ranges seemed all around them. The sound made Faye nervous, though Neil had said the artillery was never aimed toward the roads.

"Why does Daddy have to work clear out here, anyway?" asked Micki with the usual inquisitiveness of seven-year olds.

Faye hadn't ever asked because she hadn't wanted to hear Neil explain. "Just some dumb thing that keeps him flying around in helicopters and computing all night," she answered.

All this Army nonsense is so—so--damn, we're in a bumpy part, she thought angrily. *Ruts, tank trails—why can't they put a lieutenant colonel in decent officers' quarters instead of out here in the woods? He's content to put up with any kind of quarters and any kind of inconvenient schedule. He should be demanding more.*

The color of dirt at Graf was depressing. Faye glanced at the banks on both sides of the road in the waning light. "Gray, gray, gray. Even the mud tattles on every vehicle that comes into this training area. Damn him and the Army to Hell."

"What, Mommy?"

"Nothing," she said with a disgusted flick of her head.

Jolting into a long dirt driveway, she watched, amazed, as her normally calm, dignified husband bounded from his staff car into the tiny cabin, not even stopping to get the bags or carry Micki, who was now squealing for her attention.

"Hurry up, Mama. Daddy's trying to get into the cabin before we do. It's a race!" The child giggled excitedly as though her father's speed was some kind of game.

Faye didn't answer. *Something is strange. Damn it. What's his all-fired hurry?*

Faye followed through the open cabin door hesitantly, although she could not have said why. It was a tiny two room and bath frame structure, with an old-fashioned stove smelling faintly of wood and kerosene. The living room seemed cozier and cleaner than she had imagined for his bachelor-like, temporary existence. There were a few healthy plants around the room. *Ivy? At home, he forgets to water the lawn unless I scream at him to do it.* Some pictures hanging on the cracked walls gave a more lived-in feeling to the room. Lots of cool greens and blues--none of them were familiar to her, though. *Would Neil bother buying them at the Post*

Exchange for a temporary assignment?

A small red candle sat on the tottering coffee table, its holder winking one eye from a round wooden face. *A candle...with a face, yet. Not like conventional old Neil.* The unmistakable residue of a recent fire lay in the fireplace. A blue and green sofa pillow nearby captured her attention. She picked it up idly. *Looks handmade.*

The desk seemed cluttered, as though it had been quickly disturbed--recently, too. Picking up a book that had fallen to the floor, she read School for Soldiers. *Just more damned Army stuff.*

She threw the book on top of the stack. Next to the books was an ugly stuffed duck--the kind you win at a carnival for knocking down milk bottles. The room felt strange to her--as though it belonged to someone she didn't know.

"Look, Mama," squealed Micki. "Ghosts!" The little girl had already invaded the adjoining bedroom. Faye entered and noticed where Micki pointed at the closet door. It seemed some article of clothing had been pulled from a hangar—apparently so suddenly that the wire coat hangar on the doorknob was still swinging, swinging, rocking back and forth. Faye and Micki stood watching, hypnotized, until it stopped.

With an increased but ill-defined confusion, Faye walked further into the bedroom and glanced around. *Nothing too unusual,* she thought. The single small bed was neatly made, though not exactly in West Point style. She was glad Neil had a couch in the living room since she sure wouldn't sleep with him, especially in such a small bed where his body would actually touch hers. She slid open the bedside table drawer and noted his gun inside. Across the room, a hand-painted wooden mug of old Bavarian style sat on the dresser with more ivy entwining its leaves around a bottle.

The bathroom door opened and Neil emerged. Scanning the room quickly, he almost smiled--looking more relaxed than he had seemed earlier.

But his tentative smile froze as he followed the direction of Faye's gaze and arrived on the half-full bottle of 'Charlie' perfumed body lotion sitting on his dresser.

There was a pause that extended into what seemed like hours. Faye heard a voice that was not hers, from a long way off, from a picture somewhere on a wall scream, "What is that?" A hand that was not hers grabbed the bottle and hurled it at the man in the picture. She heard the crash against the wall. He had ducked the exploding glass.

From somewhere she heard Neil calming Micki and offering her a new horse book to read on the folding Army cot he'd erected in the living room. From somewhere came the sound of broom and dustpan, as he quietly swept up the shattered remnants of the bottle and its contents and threw them away. Somehow he moved in an effortless slow motion, though her own limbs seemed rooted in Grafenwohr's gray mud. Her thoughts were on the gun. *Could she reach it?*

But Neil came back then, took her hands in his, and guided her to the government-issue chair by the government-issue bed. In her mind, she tore up that smiling photo. *That* was what was wrong with it. That phony fairy tale of a Model-American Military Family did not exist! Perhaps it never had. She had known! She had not accepted.

At last, Neil broke the aching silence. "Don't you think it's time we talk?"

With force, she pulled herself to her feet and put her head in the air. "There's nothing I care to talk to you about. I'm tired." She turned, stalked into the living room, shut the door behind her, and lay down purposefully on the couch. *I'll show him!*

"But Faye," Neil called through the door.

"Leave me alone."

She could hear the creak of springs as he tossed and turned for hours.

Faye's momentary lapse of control submerged into ice while she plotted her revenge. As Micki lay sleeping peacefully on her Army folding cot in the corner, Faye lay open-eyed through the night.

22

When the phone rang Monday night, Neil relaxed and smiled at the photo by his bedside of the woman to whom he now spoke. "Do you have any idea how good it is to hear your voice?"

"Of course I do, darling. You love me--remember? Now tell me what happened. Are you okay? I know we left some things out in plain sight Friday morning."

"Well, Love, I barely beat her into the driveway and bolted inside ahead of her. I raced for the bathroom like a weak-bladdered three-year-old, gathering photos, bathrobe, and your clothes from the hanger as I ran. I stuffed them under towels in the bathroom linen closet, along with your toothbrush and hairbrush." He could hear the ripple of Sara's laughter.

"It sounds like some grade B movie. Did you get it all?"

"Not quite. She found your 'Charlie' bottle and threw it at me. I'll have to get you another."

"Oh, my God. What'd she say? What'd she do?"

"Nothing. That's the weird part." He took a deep breath, not quite sure himself what had happened. "After my initial shock, I thought for a moment we had a chance to really communicate--to confront the fact we both needed a divorce. But she just said she was too tired to discuss anything. She slammed the door and slept on the living room couch while Micki slept on the cot. When I woke in the morning, she was gone."

"Gone?" Sara was incredulous. "Just gone? Didn't she say anything at all?"

"Just gone." He was as bewildered as Sara. "I never heard them go."

"Then we don't know what she's going to do, do we?"

"If I were her, I'd be calling a lawyer, but I suppose she's shopping with her girlfriend, buying all the crystal in Neustadt."

"Something tells me this is not good. If she wouldn't let you talk about it at all, do you think she's trying to figure it out, or trying to pretend it didn't happen?"

"I don't know, and you know something, I don't really care. Perhaps now, she'll realize I mean it about the divorce."

"But she must be speculating on whose bottle of lotion that was--she knows no man would have been keeping it on hand."

"I doubt she'll want to know." He sighed. "I saw it as an opportunity to tell it to her straight and get all her anger out in the open. I hate living in secrecy. But since she refused to listen, I had no opportunity to talk rationally with her."

"If she doesn't admit it happened and doesn't have to talk about it, it didn't happen."

"What do you mean? That's crazy!"

"No, Neil, I'm serious. I think that's her strategy. She'll pretend nothing happened until it suits her purpose, and that will leave you having to bring it up all over again the next time."

"I'll bring it up as often as I have to. I've only been telling her for years! I still feel it would be safer to talk it out later, so she can do less damage to you, but I can't stand living with her hatefulness and hostility. If she wants to start the battle now, that's okay by me. She'll have to listen to me sooner or later."

"All this anxiety must have made your conference today especially nerve-wracking, Darling. I was worried about your helicopter getting back safely when I saw the fog. How did it go with the generals in Heidelberg?"

"I thought you'd never ask. I'm so glad you understand my duty concerns. Let me tell you what the general wanted to do about my cost estimates...." An animated hour later, he extracted her promise for coming to Graf Tuesday and Thursday, as usual.

"You don't think Faye will be watching you more closely?"

"Frankly, my love, I don't care. Just come on out. We'll go to Weiden for dinner and have a quiet evening together." They shared their usual tuck in and good night ritual, then he hung up the phone, kicked off his boots, and lay back on his bed.

He smiled. *Amazing how alive Sara makes me feel— especially since I've been dead inside for so long. It's a revelation to actually be loved. Where did my marriage to Faye go wrong anyway? A stupid question--at the very beginning, that's where!*

"Fat, dumb, and ugly"--that was what his dad had always called him--so often he'd believed it. Oh, he could prove his dad wrong by running eight to twelve miles a day not to have an ounce of fat. And he could graduate as valedictorian, max out his Officer Efficiency Reports and go up through the officer ranks, not to have an ounce of dumb--but the ugly? How does one overcome ugly? Maybe that was why he'd been sure as a young cadet that no one would ever love him--as surely as Faye feared becoming an old maid. *Of course,* they fell right into a disastrous marriage.

Having had no previous dates, they had nothing with which to compare, so each thought their strained relationship was normal for all marriages. When Faye's view that "nice ladies didn't want sex" surfaced, not long after Katy's birth, it had seemed to confirm his dad's old edict of "...living according to God's law and having sex only to propagate children--Don't *expect* love."

So instead, Neil had thrown himself completely into his work. There, at least, he had excelled, though neither Faye nor his dad had ever acknowledged that fact.

The furrows compressed on his forehead relaxed as he remembered that Sara hadn't seen him as either ugly or unlovable. She had bounded into his little cabin, breathing fresh air into all its corners with the verve of a hyperactive child, making him laugh, making him feel, and making him enjoy life again. *Lord, where does she get all her energy and her smiles? She loves me,* he thought, smiling at her picture. It had only taken Sara's love to erase the ugliness from his mind. She had chuckled at such a notion, telling him he was "beautiful" and loving him warmly until all his inhibitions, built painfully from sixteen years of Faye's "no's," fell away. Sara propped him up when he was down and healed his wounds from the arguments at home.

Thinking of her, he drifted off to a contented sleep without even removing his clothes. It had been a long and uncertain day.

Nothing kept the pair from their Tuesday and Thursday

night rendezvous. They held each other especially close Thursday, each nervous about what would happen next.

"Nothing will happen," said Neil, as they lay on the rug by the fire. "She'll ignore it like she does everything else. If she didn't say anything Sunday night, she missed her chance. I was prepared to tell her I loved someone else and send her back to the States early, so she could begin divorce proceedings. She refused discussion and disappeared. I don't owe any more explanations."

Sara seemed quiet. "I'm worried about what will happen when you go home tomorrow night. You need to be prepared for whatever kind of strategy she decides to use."

"She probably won't mention it at all. The only thing I really need to be prepared for right now is my briefing for the Commander in Chief's Conference in Heidelberg a week from Monday. Everything in Army Engineering is riding on that briefing. General Grayson says he's relying on me to convince them we need the time and funding, since I was the one to design the new range requirements."

"My dear, that simply means General Grayson believes you can do it. He believes in you as I do. Your briefing will be great."

"Let's plan on looking it over next week when you're here. Then a week from Sunday at your house, we can go over it one last time before I fly to Heidelberg Monday morning.' I don't mind telling you I'm a bit nervous. This is probably the most important thing I've done. A lot is riding on my persuading them this project is necessary for the future of the Army."

"We'll make sure you feel confident with the speech before then. It'll be fine, you'll be fine, and you'll get the funding." She grinned impishly. "After all, who could resist a 'proposition' of yours?" She reached her arms up around his neck and kissed him.

He slid his hands down her long body, allowing himself to rejoice as always in her warmth, allowing his longing for her to take over his mind and his body. The rest of the world seemed far away as they held each other tenderly to make love. Later, as shafts of moonlight painted stripes across the bedroom, Neil recognized that, subconsciously, each was trying to reassure the other that nothing could destroy them

"What happened? Anything?" Sara asked Sunday night after Neil greeted her at her apartment. "I'll go heat some cocoa."

"Wait a minute, Sara." Neil took her hand and walked her over to the couch in her living room. He was tired and unnaturally tense. "I don't know how to tell you." He could hear the quaver in his own voice.

Sara put her arms around him and pulled him down on the couch. "Just tell me, Darling. Get it out where we can deal with it. What did she do? Did she go to a lawyer?"

"I feel so awful, and I don't even know how it happened."

"What happened, Dear?"

"When I got home, she'd sent the girls to a friend's house for the night. I should have known something was going on. She said nothing, so I read awhile and went to bed. As I sat on the side of the bed, she walked in wearing this dinky little baby doll nightie with no panties on. You could see everything. I was shocked and told her to go get her bathrobe, but she plopped on my lap naked like that, and started apologizing all coyly and telling me how much she loved me. I know that's a lie, and she's never been able to even flirt. It was obscene!"

Sara gasped. "What did she say?"

"I don't know. I was so confused, and it was so gross. She said something about having 'neglected me far too long,' and how 'she hadn't realized I was so lonely.' All the time she was talking and apologizing, she was kissing my cheeks and rubbing herself all over me. I tried to push her away, but I couldn't just throw her on the floor, though I felt like it. I told her we were separated--that I didn't want her to even touch me. She ignored my rebuffs, and hung on like a leech. I couldn't pull her loose."

Neil could see thoughtful lines gather on Sara's brow as she listened intently.

"Then she said that if I didn't have sex with her right that minute, she would know for sure that I had another woman, and that she would certainly be sure General Grayson knew about it before next week's briefing.' She also said that if there ever had been another woman, she'd be sure to destroy her as well, and 'she knew how to do it.'"

Neil put his head in his hands. Sara said nothing.

Into her silence, he started again, but his voice sounded like someone else's coming from far away. "She said that if she had been wrong and there was no other woman, then I should *want* to have sex with her after being gone so much—that she would forget everything that had happened, if I did it." His voice was shaky. "Her threats at you and at General Grayson scared me to death!"

Sara reached out to squeeze his hand.

"She cried and said she was so sorry for leaving me alone, and she was all kittenish and cuddly, and at the same time threatening and...." He pulled Sara's hand to his cheek. "And you know I have trouble when a woman cries..."

"What did you tell her?" Sara's voice was tremulous, and Neil knew she didn't really want to hear the next words he would have to say.

"I panicked, thinking of all the harm she could do to us. I did what she demanded."

"What?" Sara pulled her hand back, her face contorted in shock. Neil hurried to try to explain.

"She was so contrite and sorry, and I felt bad for her crying like that, and I did try to comfort her. That was a mistake. I was so embarrassed with her grinding all over me, and I didn't want her to know about us, or for her to hurt you. I tried to do what she wanted. Then afterward, I was sick and threw up."

Sara didn't speak. She rose and walked away, tears flowing down her cheeks. Neil noticed one arm hugging her stomach as though she would be sick as well. Finally, she turned to face him, and the pain in her eyes was like a punch to his mid-section.

"Were you that helpless in the face of blackmail, or just that helpless in the face of a woman's tears, any woman--or was it because your wife made you feel guilty?" Her quiet voice broke.

"You didn't even fight for yourself, or for us? You just did what she wanted? How could you? You've assured me night after night that you felt nothing for her--that you were prepared for anything she might try. Obviously you weren't!"

Neil rose and walked slowly to Sara. She stood, breathless, shaking her head as though to rid it of images that were too painful to contemplate. He could see the suffering in her face, and the truth crashed in on him. What he thought he *had* to do to protect Sara had hurt her immeasurably instead. Why didn't she hit him, or curse him, or scream? He deserved it. She deserved to be angry.

His actions had produced pain in the woman he loved, and her blame would have made him feel better. But then, it was Faye's way to scream and blame, not Sara's. Instead, he could see her withdrawing into herself and into an anguished silence. Her breast heaved with unheard sobs, as he watched her struggle to hold her feelings back. He ached to find the right words, knowing there were no right words.

He put his head against the top of hers and tried to put his arms around her. He felt numb, paralyzed. He was trembling, and he could feel she was as well, but she did not respond.

"God, Sara, I am so sorry. I didn't know what to do. I was so sure she would know all about us and destroy both of our careers, hurt you, and take the girls. I just couldn't think what *else* to do at that moment, short of hitting her, and you know I couldn't hit a woman. I thought I could just try to get it over with quick so she would leave us alone."

He noticed that Sara had not put her arms around him. Instead she pushed his arms softly away and turned to the wall.

"Are you jealous, Darling? I guarantee you don't need to be. It was just like going to the bathroom to relieve pressure on the bladder. There was no feeling to it at all. Her grinding around produced a minor, involuntary reaction in spite of my negative feelings, but my body wouldn't even perform properly. Being so threatened and grossed out was hardly conducive to stirring up the libido, even if I had wanted her, and I *didn't* at all. I felt sick to my stomach."

Sara could not seem to answer. Her face had drained of color. Neil's heart was bursting. *Why doesn't she say something?*

"Darling, you must believe me. With all those years of her hostility, I've been almost impotent with her. Not that she would've known the difference anyway, since our marital relations were never even close to satisfying. You know I don't love her…you know I was only trying to keep her from having proof--I *had* to somehow keep her from knowing about us."

When Sara still could not respond, he tried again to explain. "Sara, you could have been right there in the same room with us and there would have been nothing for you to be jealous about … We hate each other…There's just no feeling.…I couldn't even…."

"You don't get it, do you, Neil?" Sara walked back to the couch and sat down abruptly.

He could see her struggling mightily to keep her voice even. That quiet control made him feel her pain as though it were stabbing in his own chest. He followed her to the couch and sat nearby, hesitating to touch her--feeling he had lost the right to touch her by his own stupidity.

"This isn't *about* jealousy, Neil. This is about control! By your having sex with her, you just negated five months of separation--five months of our love--five months you had weathered toward an amicable divorce in the States. Before you went to Graf, you said you told her it was over-- that there would be nothing between you pending a divorce as soon as you got to the War College, didn't you?"

Neil stared blankly at her, not fully understanding.

"Now, *she* has control. It doesn't matter if the sex was consensual, or even if you couldn't perform it completely. In her mind, she got you to have some kind of sex with her. She can honestly go before a judge and say that you had sex during that six-month separation, and that nullifies it all. She used blackmail, Neil. Don't you understand? She would only leave you and your career alone if you 'proved' there was no one else by having sex with her, right there and then. She knows your weaknesses!"

Sara's voice remained forcefully controlled, hiding the

depth of her outrage. "She knows you can't stand tears. She knows threatening me would get your attention, and she knows threatening your career-enhancing presentation to the big wigs in Heidelberg would *certainly* get your attention. She knew before you got there that you would fall for this kind of trap. She planned. You didn't! So now, you're right back where you started--right back into a marriage you said you didn't want." She turned away.

Neil moved up behind her. "But Sara, I still want the divorce. I'll just tell her again…and again. She knows I want the divorce. It wasn't even real sex. I couldn't..."

"Try telling that to her lawyer, Neil. You gave her the ammunition with which to shoot you down." She turned to face him. "The court will say you reconciled with her. She 'll say you reconciled. It's true. You had sex. You couldn't resist her threats. You believed her tears. You reconciled. We have nothing left!"

To Neil's horror, Sara reached to the coffee table and handed him his car keys. He dropped them as though burned.

"No! Sara, I don't want her at all." He reached for her arm, but dropped it when he saw the expression of finality in her eyes. "Sara, you have to understand." He could hear his own voice rising. "It was nothing to me. Nothing! She knows it was nothing. She didn't even speak to me or come near me the whole rest of the weekend, all day Saturday, Sunday…nothing… When I left to come here tonight, there was nothing." Neil shook his head in disbelief. *Was Sara right? Had he ruined everything?*

Sara cried, "It was something to her, Neil! It was the sign that she's now in control of all our lives. Any time you say something about a quiet divorce, she'll demand that you 'prove there is no one else.' Just wait and see if she doesn't. Let me put it in terms you'll understand. If you had been on a battlefield, you wouldn't have let the enemy into the camp. Yet you succumbed to Faye's infiltration battle plan at home."

"But if I do it just to keep her from knowing about us and hurting you, and it's only until I get the family safely home, and you know I love you and she means nothing to me—that I can't even complete the act with her, why should you feel bad?"

"Neil, face reality!" Sara put her fingertips to her temples and took a deep breath, obviously in pain. "She already knows there is someone else. She probably even knows who it is. Don't you see? If she can trap you into this type of 'play-acting' with her, she can control everything you do, every emotion you feel. Of course, I know it means nothing to you. Of course, I know you love me, and I even know that nothing you've done with her would come close to the feeling we have for each other. But do you realize what a hypocrite that turns you into? Do you realize what your double life will eventually do to us? Do you realize that every time you touch me, I'll wonder if she trapped you into touching her first--if this is a week you'll have to 'prove' something to her…." Sara stopped talking abruptly and put her face in her hands.

He quickly put his arms around her, caressing her hair. "Sara, I'm so sorry. I thought I could do it as a kind of duty to protect us, so she wouldn't come after you, or my girls, or my career. I love you. I don't want her to touch us."

"She already has, Neil. You just don't see it. I thought *I* was the naïve one. She only has to yank your string, the one connected to your fear of discovery, and she wins. If you continue to respond to her threats like you did this time, you'll never be free. Do you have any idea how this hurts, and what it costs me to give you up now? Surely you know it's too late for me to take back my love and move on alone, as though I had never loved you so much, so completely." She broke into sobs as Neil pulled her tightly to his chest.

"I didn't know what to do. Please forgive me—I was so scared that I did what I thought was best to protect *you--us*." Oh, Darling, why didn't I know what to do? I felt so trapped. Don't you see what she could do to both of us if she knew?"

"It's too late, my dear. She has already done it to us."

There were no answers. Sara finally fell into exhausted, sleep on the sofa. Neil sat on the floor beside her, holding her hand in his, hugging her when she stirred and cried, sadly having resolved nothing except the new need to somehow win back Sara's confidence in him.

23

Faye stood in her bedroom and laughed at the mirror. She knew she had once again trapped her husband. She had the upper hand, and her mother had been right. "Do what you must, Faye, to maintain your status quo. No man can be trusted, and it's up to you to protect your own position in life."

"Yes, Mama," Faye heard herself say aloud. Then she laughed again. "The status quo is not *even* in jeopardy."

Ironically, Faye didn't really care that Neil had been unfaithful. She didn't want him, so perhaps another woman would simply keep him out of her hair. She only cared that he might possibly love this woman, and if so, he might fight for a divorce.

She would have to be careful not to cause a confrontation until she had proof that would stand up in court so she could threaten him with a divorce on grounds of adultery, not incompatibility as he had planned. Adultery would lose him his precious Army career, get him court-marshaled, and she would have no trouble maintaining custody of the girls. He would never be able to stand up to that. She smiled and wondered where he was at that moment. *It doesn't matter. I have control of the situation.* She picked up her magazine and climbed into bed, satisfied that she had her husband where she wanted him—on the edge. She snuggled down warmly to read a new love story.

Faye was surprised when Neil made an extra trip home during the week to talk to her. She ignored him as he followed her around the house trying to get her to listen.

She could see he was in distress. *Well, let him suffer, damn him. What a washout--he couldn't even get it up, and I had to pretend to enjoy his emasculated performance to achieve my goal. Where was my love story hero when I needed him?*

Outwardly, she smiled and allowed him to stew in his

discomfort all evening until the girls went to bed. She knew he would not risk arguing again in front of the children.

When they were finally alone, he said, "Faye, you know what happened between us Friday was a mistake—an error in judgment. It meant nothing to either of us. I still want a divorce."

"What divorce, Darling?" Faye cooed. "Why, we've reconciled, and I've already told my lawyer too." Inwardly, she crowed, *I've got him begging now!*

Faye smiled sweetly and began an innocuous and detailed description of her shopping trip with Myrna, insisting on a private showing of each of the elegant household items she had purchased. Each time Neil moved away, she would call him back to see yet another decorative, crystal treasure. "Don't you think this will look stunning in our entry hall in Carlisle, Neil? My great aunt used to have a similar ornament on top of her credenza in the living room. You probably don't remember my great aunt, but she…"

Faye became more animated at each anecdote she knew Neil would find boring. She relished her control in forcing him to listen to drivel about people he had never heard of or could not remember before he could get a word in edgewise to bring up his own topic of concern. She smiled, watching the man squirm like a bug skewered on a pin against the collector's velvet backdrop.

Eventually, Neil found a break in her monologue and tried again to tell her he meant to have the divorce. "Faye, you know you've never loved me. After sixteen years of trying to get you to care, I finally just gave up, accepted your hatred, and moved on."

Faye used her "patient mother" voice as she reminded him of his duty to her, and that their "sexual episode" was all she could have expected of him. "I told my lawyer what a tender reconciliation we had, Sweetheart. Now that you've *proven* to me that there is no other woman, I feel confident of our future. I'm sure everyone now understands that we are together, forever." She deliberately emphasized the last word.

"Then we'll start another six months' separation now, Faye. Sooner or later you'll have to listen to me. You may have trapped me this once because I wasn't prepared for your methods, but I made a horrible mistake. You know we need an amicable divorce."

Faye smiled, knowing he could do nothing as long as she kept calm and controlled in public. She could play the ever-loving wife as long as she needed to, until everyone believed she was sincere—until she would see him into his grave, if she had to.

"Why, you have no grounds for divorce, Neil. You can ask anyone! We've played the role publicly so long, no one would ever believe we weren't the happy couple we've presented to the world, now would they?" She smiled at him again, thoroughly enjoying the disgust in his expression.

"And we've been hypocritical by pretending to be that 'happy' couple most of our married life, Faye. We both know our marriage is in shambles--that we are a disaster together. We need to stop pretending and have no more tricks."

"Oh, ho, now it's a trick, is it? There was no trick, Neil. I'm your wife, and I can ask you for sex whenever I wish, as often as I wish. My lawyer said so. I asked him! You just might make general someday, since everyone else tells me you will, but you need to remember who is in charge here on the home front." She smiled again, in a cloying, suggestive manner, knowing it infuriated him. "I may hate you, but I won't *ever* set you free. Your duty is here, to me! We won't part until *your* death." She arched her eyebrows as she watched his voiceless rage.

With that, she turned away, and tossed one last phrase over her shoulder as she climbed the stairs to the second floor, "You'll pay for the rest of your life, you dumb shit. And I guarantee I'll outlive you, just to see that you do!"

Faye flounced through the hall into her bedroom, thinking, *Well, I gave him a piece of my mind! I hold all the cards, and I'll soon have him back in the States where he won't be able to see this woman again. He'll never be able to stand up to the scandal I know how to create.* She glanced into the mirror, smiled in a seductive way, and then laughed hysterically. She didn't even care if Neil could hear her.

The door slammed as he left.

24

Sara's friend Casey dropped by the next Wednesday evening to bring bottles of wine for her end-of-school-year party the following Saturday. He immediately noticed her quiet mood. "I can see you're hurting. What's happened between you and Neil?"

"I love him, Casey, but what am I to do? He's never had a military problem he couldn't solve, so he thinks he can handle anything. But he's helpless in the face of Faye's blackmail. I know now she'll tear him apart before she lets him go. I'm disappointed in him, yet all I seem to be able to do is try to comfort him in his sadness." She pushed back her bangs from her eyes in one sweeping, frustrated motion. "Faye's savvy, and she knows how to press her advantage to control Neil."

"I warned you, Sara. If she can't have Neil on her terms, she won't care what she does to him. She plays the game in public, but she talks openly about having grabbed on to a man that's on the way up, and that it's her duty to control him and keep his status for herself. What did you think she'd do if she found out? Set him free, so he could be happy?" Casey's voice dripped sarcasm.

"I don't know, Casey." Sara shook her head. "I expected her to be angry, but I'd hoped she would see the advantage in divorcing so the girls wouldn't have to hear them argue constantly. Actually, the arguments are pretty one-sided since when Faye gets abusive, Neil just walks away to keep the peace. I don't think there has ever been any peace between them. It seems so unfair that I'd make any sacrifice to make him happy, while she says she doesn't even love him. Why won't she just let him go quietly, so they can both make new lives without a ruining his life?"

"Why should she? She has her image on base as the Lieutenant Colonel's wife--the church-going, married lady--and she has her meal ticket. She doesn't feel it's necessary to love him, too! She'll put on that sad face and make everyone sympathetic to her side of this triangle, not Neil's, and certainly not yours." Casey shook his head emphatically. "Did you really think she'd allow herself to risk losing public sympathy, no matter what Neil might want--perhaps especially not to give him what he wants?"

"It's so hypocritical for them to pretend to the world that they're one big happy family. How can they do that?"

"But Sara, that's the way the military works. Only the 'happy families' get promoted. It's always been this way. The promotion boards look beyond the commander's skill to see how his personal life impacts on him. If he were sued for divorce on charges of adultery, it would be all over. You've certainly seen it happen before. What does Neil want?"

"He thinks he's neutralized Faye for now. I'm not sure I know what he wants any more. He still says he wants me."

"Sara, you know in your heart he does. Neil's just in shock. He thinks he's protecting you by going along with her demands. God, I don't know. Maybe he's right. Maybe she *would* hurt you, and he needs to protect you, *any* way he can."

"I'm not afraid of physical hurt, Casey. This pain is emotional and spiritual, I guess. I don't want him protecting me by giving in to her demands. He says he won't. Still, it would destroy me to leave him, too. I fear he'll never be free. What can I do?"

"You know all us men have feet of clay. We make stupid mistakes where women are concerned. Neil has never known love before. He's existed by keeping emotional life squashed, public life on track, and throwing all his energy into his duty to the Army. He doesn't know how to deal with Faye's threats."

"Are you saying I should just go along with this charade until they leave Germany? Is that the way you men think?"

"I'm saying that he'll be trying hard to reestablish your faith in him. I hope he'll stand up for himself, and you, now that he realizes how precarious his situation really is--and perhaps how little he knows about his wife." Casey thought a moment and then shook his head. "Maybe you should just run like hell."

"He's still expecting me at Graf tomorrow night. I suppose I should leave him before this kills me, but he needs more preparation for his briefing before the funding board. He's really nervous. The timing of this blow-up with Faye couldn't be worse.

He already has so much to think about with his project on the line." Sara bowed her head. "I guess I feel a duty too, to give him the support he needs right now. I can't desert him in mid stream."

"But your sadness is pervasive, Sara. You've got to protect yourself."

"How, Casey? I love him. I've believed in him, and I feel betrayed. It's too late now for him to decide to stay with Faye without hurting me too much to survive it. I'm so afraid." The tears and fears she'd been holding back finally erupted into sobs.

Casey put his arm around her shoulder and let her cry it out. "I find it impossible to imagine he can find an answer that won't hurt you in the long run. Please be careful."

"It's too late for me to be careful, Casey. I think it was already too late after one snowy night in St. Veit."

Tuesday, Sara thought over her options as she drove the now-familiar road. There didn't seem to be many. If Faye went to the authorities and ruined Neil's chances for promotion, it wouldn't particularly matter if she were married or divorced. A pay grade less for Neil would mean less income for them both, less retirement to split, and less alimony for her. *If Faye wanted to hurt Neil and me she certainly could do so, but she'd be hurting herself as well. If security is her main focus, why would she do that?*

But Sara knew Neil was too paralyzed by Faye's threats to believe they were a bluff to keep him in line. Over the years he'd accepted her derisive put-downs as fact. His self-confidence, so optimal in military matters, took a tremendous hit whenever he was with Faye. Their marriage was destructive to them both.

Will I be giving him back his key tonight? Is his inability to stand up for us the end, or does he really think he can rebuild six months and regain control of his own life? I want to believe him.

In spite of her pain, Sara almost had to laugh when she thought of her present scrambled situation. Hadn't the tables been turned full circle when she was expected to somehow forgive Neil for an infidelity with his wife? She was sure no one had come up with that angle before. As far as she knew, her situation was unprecedented. Loving a married man was never her intention.

And what of Faye? Ordinarily, Sara would have felt sorry for any betrayed wife, but since Faye had turned Neil out into the cold long ago, she now felt only sorrow that the woman had been so determined to ruin her own chances for happiness, *and* Neil's. What a marvelous military life they could have enjoyed, had Faye not had her own agenda, and had she lovingly taken part. How sad.

As Sara put aside her bag of school papers and picked up the rough draft Neil had left on the table for her, she heard his footsteps. They sounded sluggish--not his usual vibrant, clipped beat. She glanced through the window and was appalled at the sight of him. She could *feel* the pain in his body as he slouched in an uneven gait, the cares of the world weighing down his shoulders. *A difficult day at work on top of his personal crisis, no doubt,* she thought. *He'll need to relax and unwind to think clearly.*

She simply could not add to his already overwhelming burden. She couldn't. She knew that sharing the pressure was all she could do now for the man she loved, whatever the future held.

When he walked in, looking around for her, she impulsively jumped out from behind the door and nipped him on the backside. Catching him by surprise, she could grab him from behind and tussle his over six foot frame to the rug. As she tickled him, he burst into laughter until he couldn't speak for holding his sides. She knew he couldn't be serious after that.

When he got his breath, his first words were, "You aren't mad at me anymore?"

"Of course, I am, Darling! You're stupid about women, and you make lousy choices. But, I can't hurt you when you're carrying so many problems already. God help me, I love you too much for that." She flopped on top of him with her arms stretched up around his head, nose to nose, toes to toes. "Let's just go on from here. Our love is too important to be thrown away over one night of insane mistakes, don't you think?"

Neil, put his arms around Sara, there on the floor, and

sighed his relief. "I did the one thing I didn't want to do--I hurt you, Love. I was a fool. Faye is laughing at my unhappiness right now. I'm so sorry. I promise I won't fall into her trap again."

"Don't give me promises in words, my dear. I'll be looking for actions." Sara swatted him on the side and said, "Now, let's get busy on this presentation. I see something in the second paragraph that needs a bit more pizzazz." Sara could feel Neil's relief that she was still beside him, and they settled down to work.

"You can't imagine how Grayson was piling on the pressure--a really rough day. I've been wrestling with the 'powers that be' over funding. Their figures and mine still aren't close enough together, and now this nitwit general wants to skim eight million dollars off the top for some other project. That would shortchange my project and make it impossible."

Neil's frustrations tumbled out the minute he was in Sara's arms. She forcibly pushed aside her own pain and listened quietly.

"Grayson won't be doing the presentation, though he'll be there when I go before the Board and the Finance decision makers. The 'make or break' issue with the whole project will be on my shoulders, and it's hard to even think with so much else going on in my life—and the tension that Faye brings. I need you, Love."

"You can, and you will succeed. Forget everything else. We'll take the draft along to dinner at our special place."

Neil pulled Sara to him and kissed her softly, "You've been the one stable force in my life, and I almost lost you through my own stupidity."

She smiled sadly. "Yes, you did, almost. But I can see you need me, and I'll not desert you now. We'll collaborate through the good times *and* the bad. You know that, don't you?"

"I know." He folded the speech into his pocket, and squeezed her hand. "I want you to know that as soon as I can get that woman out of my life, you'll be the one in it. All I need is enough time to make it legal."

Sara nodded, squeezing his hand back, unable to say what was in her heart--that if he couldn't learn to deal with his wife's blackmail, Faye would never be out of his life.

On Thursday, after much talk, many promises, and another night of hashing out any last minute problems with the presentation, and with each other's feelings, they were sad to be spending their last night together in the cabin at Grafenwohr.

"It's been our home together," she whispered to Neil as they lay in his room. "I'm feeling bad about leaving you to go to California for the summer with my girls, but they need me too."

"I know they do, Love, and it will only be a short time until I get to meet them too. This cabin will always hold our loving memories," he said, "but we'll soon build our own home together."

With pain and doubt erased by forgiveness, their tender lovemaking in the little cabin was particularly poignant, and when Neil had fallen asleep at her side, Sara laid awake, thinking. She knew she could not desert this man, no matter what lay in the future. Was this the way it was meant to be? *God, am I doing the right thing in letting my doubts slip away and loving him so? Can he really understand that I'm committed to him for a lifetime? Does he know my whole life is in his hands?*

She had no more than let the prayer flutter across her mind when the answer came. Neil stirred in his sleep, reached out with his hand and mumbled something unintelligible. She lay still, watching, as he slid his hand up and down the sheet, anxiously searching until he found her body. He ran his hand softly up to her breast and cupped it gently in his hand. He slid closer, laid his head against her breast, and the words became clear. He was murmuring her name. *It's my name he calls in his sleep!* He snuggled against her, and the peaceful look came back to his sleeping face.

Sara smiled. It was such a confident, little boy gesture--not at all sexual--simply trusting, as though he were answering her prayer. *He knows.* She thought. *Deep down, he knows.* She settled her body into the position he had thus proscribed for her, wrapped her arms around him, and drifted off to sleep, knowing she would love this man, unconditionally, as long as she lived.

###

They both went to work Friday morning with sadness, knowing no place they ever shared could be quite the same as their little house in the woods.

The rest of their plan left little time for error. Sunday afternoon after church, they would be lunching with Lex, a friend and former commander visiting from his dead end job at the Pentagon now that his messy divorce was final--just one more victim of the hypocrisy required by a military system that seemed unaware some marriages had unsolvable problems. Sunday night, Neil would practice his delivery of the presentation during one final time together at Sara's apartment. On Monday, he would fly with Grayson and do his presentation in Heidelberg.

Neil's career could rise or fall on that one presentation, so Sara knew he was feeling particularly vulnerable Sunday night. They practiced his speech until, by the end of the evening, he was about as ready as he could be.

Sara saw him off at her door Monday morning, with hugs and promises to think good thoughts for him all day.

Neil seemed jubilant. "I'm confident, prepared, content, and well-loved," he happily crowed to the world in general. As he lifted Sara in the air to kiss her, he added, "Come kiss the world's greatest lover."

There in his arms, she rejoiced in the fact that he really did feel 'well-loved,' now. "It seems a million years from when we first found each other, Darling, when you believed yourself unlovable and you said, 'Please love me because no one else ever has.' Now, suddenly, you're the 'world's greatest lover?'"

"You've got that right. *You* love me, so that proves it." He hugged her again, emphasizing his boast and echoing her chuckle.

Neil had mellowed from a lonely man to a thoughtful and loving one. Most noticeable was his inner warmth, his belief in himself as being loved and lovable--a real glow of contentment that showed in his face as he smiled down at her.

Sara closed her eyes a moment. *That has been my gift to him for a lifetime. Dear God, whatever happens, seeing that confidence in him is worth it all.*

After Neil's presentation in Heidelberg and his helicopter flight home the same day to pick up his car, he would drive straight to the Frankfurt military hotel. Sara would finish her last day at school, and drive to meet him there. Once his car was shipped, they planned a few days of vacation together before her flight home to her family. He would stay on another three weeks to finish up preparations for the Grafenwohr range project, borrowing her Ford Mustang, getting household goods packed and shipped, and finding flights for the family to the States.

According to plan, Neil would start the U.S. Army's War College at Carlisle Barracks, Pennsylvania, get the girls settled into school, and wait for Sara to meet him in August for their reunion at Gettysburg. By Christmas, another six-month separation from Faye would be completed, and Neil would try again for an amicable and quiet divorce that he hoped would not ruin his career or take away his children.

Neil was confident he had every detail worked out for them to be together soon—that nothing more could possibly go wrong. Sara wanted to believe. She once again put aside her apprehension. The first stumbling block would be that the Heidelberg presentation must go well. One crisis would have to be all they handled at a time.

25

That evening, Neil lounged in the Officer's Club at Frankfurt's military transient hotel. The sign over the bar said, "Gateway to Europe," and it had been so for countless Americans defending against the communists of the Cold War. As he waited for Sara to arrive, he had a momentary chill thinking that perhaps she had thought it over and wouldn't come. Was he kidding himself that he could be loved—that he deserved a love like hers?

His anxiety calmed when he saw her enter the bar. He smiled, watching other eyes turn to follow her smooth, statuesque stride all the way across the room. He took pride in knowing she didn't even notice other men. Her eyes sought only his, and her smile brightened as she came toward him. After six months of intimacy, the warmth in her eyes still took his breath away. He wanted to sweep her into her arms. *Dignity, Neil, dignity*, he thought to himself. *You don't know who might see, and we don't need any more confrontations.* Instead, he took her arm to steer her into the dining room where they could hear each other speak over the hubbub of the bar crowd.

Sara excitedly asked, "How did it go?"

Neil couldn't resist a small diversion, for effect, while he ordered a Mosel wine for her and a Heineken beer for himself.

"How did it go? I can't stand this suspense."

Neil grinned ear to ear. "We did it, my love! The Commanding General approved the whole project just as I planned it. They didn't want to give us funding, but I finally persuaded them." Neil excitedly told Sara of the day's activities.

"Our helicopter arrived late, and General Grayson reminded me that the policy guidance of the Commander in Chief's (CINC) General Officer's Conference stated that all speakers would be general officers. There I was, the only exception, a lowly lieutenant colonel. I was first to give my briefing--totally nervous--felt like a sacrificial lamb, wondering if Grayson wanted me to do the presentation so, in case it failed, he would share no blame. I should have known better. He's backed me all the way, but you'd be amazed what goes through one's mind at a time like that. I could see my whole career going up in smoke, knowing it would be a tough sell."

The waiter brought their salads, but Neil was too much into his story for either of them to feel hungry.

"Remember, I told you the German civil engineers wouldn't contract for the work unless we could guarantee all unexploded ordinance had been removed? Of course, we couldn't guarantee that on a gunnery range! So we'd have to use Army Combat Engineers to do the work. But none of the engineering units wanted to give up their soldiers or heavy equipment for the time it would take to rebuild the ranges. I finally persuaded the Deputy Chief of Staff for Engineers that our plan was the *only* way to get the ranges modernized, and it would be good additional ordinance training for his men to disarm any shells they dug up. Miraculously, the CINC approved of using military troops for the operation. But there was opposition."

Neil took a breath long enough to grab Sara's hand across the table in both his big ones. Her delighted smile showed him she felt the excitement in his voice and touch.

"Once you'd lined up troops to do the work," she asked, "what was the hang-up that made it such a tough sell to the General Officers? You'd have thought they'd see the CINC's hand in the project."

"The war fighters assembled were not happy that I would close their precious gunnery ranges four months for each of the next three years. General Grayson backed me up. The CINC even nodded. Someone in front said I could have the ranges only from December through March because the commanders needed them for training during the summer months. I said I needed the prime construction season--July through October."

Sara mirrored his excitement. "What happened then?"

"The CINC, General Kimball, held up his hand. Everyone stopped. He said 'Approved. Go execute.' That was all! I floated out of that room. The whole plan is going to happen."

"That's wonderful! See, you had nothing to worry about. I knew if you believed, you could make the others believe too."

"If it's executed the way we've put it together, there'll be engineering journals filled with articles authored by officers who will build my range design. Careers will be made or ended on this program, mine included. But, in the end, the results will be obvious when our Army combat units have trained on those ranges. They'll be the best--unmatched anywhere in the world. Our Army will be ready for any future conflict."

"I know how much that matters to you." Touching his hand she said, " I'm so proud of your idealism, your work…and you."

"You've been my cheering section all along, my love—no matter how rough it got. Admittedly, it got pretty rough, for both of us. I hope you'll forgive me for that. I'm so sorry I disappointed you and let you down. But, for now, let me say how much I appreciated your coaching me on my presentation. You got me through it." The soft smile in her eyes rewarded his exuberant day.

"So what happens next?"

"After we get my car to Bremerhaven, as per orders, I'll have five precious days' leave before I put you on the plane, my love. Can you spare them with me?"

"I'm yours, Sir," she saluted, playfully.

"I want you to be—for always." He smiled warmly, feeling the pressure of the last few weeks float from his shoulders. "Did anyone ever tell you what a good sport you are?"

"Lots of people—just good old Sara, one of the gang. I'm tough, remember?"

She smiled, but he saw the glimmer of an old fear in her eyes. He knew she'd had to be tough before. He quickly kissed her on the cheek. "I'm hoping you'll never again have to be tougher than a marshmallow, Sweetheart."

"Are you too tired to go north tonight? I'll help you drive."

Neil was amazed. "In all my years of marriage, Faye never once offered to help me drive, even when I was practically falling asleep at the wheel on a cross country move." Neil's grin went all the way to his eyebrows. "Let's do it. We'll stop up the highway, and be much closer to getting rid of my car and having our wonderful days together."

They left Sara's car at the hotel and started north, stopping half way to Bremerhaven. In their exuberant mood, they could even wake with laughter and snuggle back to sleep when it turned out the town's church steeple was right next door to their hotel. Its bell rang loudly every hour, all night long.

They dropped the car for shipment the next day at noon, finding the sheer volume of government paperwork, causing a four-hour delay, would force them to return on the night train. While waiting, they engaged in a traveling dinner, having dessert first--strawberries atop Columbus Center overlooking the harbor. They walked hand in hand along the quay, and ate *Bratwurst* from a sidewalk stand. During a two-hour layover in Hannover, they found one store open at midnight, and shared an ice cream sundae.

Also, Neil felt, they shared a renewal of faith as they talked their way back to trust in their future. Again confident their feelings for each other couldn't change, they picked up Sara's Mustang and decided to explore castles along the Rhine River.

It was an idyllic time, whether walking leisurely along the parapets of centuries old castles or playing 'lord and lady of the manor' in stately drawing rooms. They hiked to the top of cliffs overlooking the famous *Loreley*, where German legend claims that mythical maids lured sailors to crash their ships onto the rocks. They picnicked, watching the barges on the river below from their car blanket. Resting, watching clouds drift across blue skies, and making love in the sunny solitude of the hilltop enhanced their joy in being free together to love, to plan, to envision their future together. At last, they returned to explore more castles below.

In the torture chamber of Marksburg Castle, the guide tasked Neil to demonstrate antique wooden handcuffs binding the neck to the wrists with a wooden harp. He accepted the good-natured teasing of a tour group of elderly people from a Rotterdam cruise ship. He even gave an impromptu talk to the whole entourage of exuberant seniors on the excellence of the castle's fortifications from a combat engineer's point of view. "This castle has never been taken by its enemies," he said, as final proof.

The peaceful days sped by far too fast, and they both knew parting would be difficult. At a terrace restaurant overlooking the river, they again broached the subject of their uncertain future.

"We're both so dreadfully conventional, aren't we?" Neil said. "This need for secrecy bothers us, yet I dread my classmates and colleagues finding out my marriage has been a lie all this time, and that I'm so in love with someone else. They'll be shocked that stuffy old Neil has had a secret life. Yet my feelings are so deep, I can't let you go. I know this whole plan puts us in danger, but I'd sacrifice it all to at last have your love in my life permanently."

"I feel the same way. It's painful to hold it all in when I want to shout from housetops how much I love you. I'll admit I feared you might decide that you couldn't leave her, and I feared being hurt. I know you wouldn't do that again on purpose, but…"

"But what, my love?"

"What if you aren't able to stand up to her, should she throw more blackmail in your path? You haven't always done it very successfully. What do you really, truly want, Neil?"

"You."

"But you know that could cost you everything you've worked for, if she chooses to make it hard. I won't be responsible for your losing your Army career, Neil--your vision of duty."

"I'm hoping that won't be a problem if I can convince her that a quiet divorce is in everyone's best interests."

They lazily watched boats go up and down the river past a tiny island where tolls used to be demanded of all who passed. It didn't escape Neil's notice that a toll is still exacted for everything one wants in life. Would he and Sara be able to pay this one?

Sara continued as though she had read his mind and known his concern, "And you, poor dear, are so worried about what a divorce might do to your girls, especially should Faye get sole custody. We mustn't take any chance you would lose the girls."

"In my family," said Neil quietly, "parents have stayed together 'for the sake of the children,' no matter how unhappy those couples were. I'm sure I'll take flak from my father about divorcing. That will hurt, because I've always tried diligently to please my father—usually with little success. But Faye despises me. Often, she'd say to me, 'I hate you!' Once those words are out there, a person can never take them back. It takes a lot of 'I love you' to make up for just one 'I hate you!' and I never heard any of those—never any kind words. I can't go on with this farce of a marriage. I can't climb back into the little box she's put me in. But I need a clean break with at least half time custody of the children. I can't leave them totally with her—totally under her influence."

"I know, Neil. We want to be sure the girls aren't hurt. I'm sure Faye loves them in her own way. Perhaps an amicable time-sharing plan might be worked out. Though it's not part of your experience, I know first hand what it's like for a child to listen to her parents feud for a lifetime. A clean break must be easier than that! Children blame themselves. I feared I was the cause of my parents' arguments until the day my father died. Katy mentioned fearing she might be causing your unhappiness and her mom's angry moods as well. That's too big a burden to place on a kid."

Neil nodded, listening quietly, knowing the whole thing could be difficult to keep calm and quiet and sane.

"The tension between parents who hate each other is so harmful to children. Read Spoon River Anthology, the story of 'Mrs. Bliss.' I helped Lisa learn the lines once for a school play. It's an agonizing epitaph of a woman whom 'preachers and judges' forced to stay in a marriage that poisoned her children's lives, her husband's, and her own. Always it was 'For the sake of the children,' a rather sanctimonious lie, since the children were suffering within the family discord. The lines are so painfully appropriate to your family situation."

Neil nodded his understanding.

Sara breathed deeply and plunged ahead. "Faye owns at least one-third of this triangle for her years of rejecting you. I wouldn't want her hurt, but she still doesn't see her part in it. The girls will choose to come with you, should you two split."

"That's assuming they're given a choice by the courts. Faye and I have nothing in common except the children, and I know she'll fight for them."

"But so will you." They rose to walk to the car. Neil felt his spirits rise with the clasp of Sara's hand, and some anxiety slipped away, though he knew it would be Faye's *method* of fighting for the children that could cost him his career.

They crossed the Rhine by ferry to the tiny town of Boppard, continuing to search their souls for any hazards in their plan. "I'm glad we can discuss things freely and openly--my fears and yours, too, Sara. Tell me what you're thinking."

Silently she stared into his eyes. He felt her gaze go to his very soul. *I wonder what she sees there. God, I wish I knew. Duty, honor, country, all in a tight box, she always tells me. Can she see my fears and conflicts there, too?*

"It frightens me that you haven't been able to tell her about us yet. I know you think it better to wait until you're Stateside, but it might be easier now. If you truly, as you say, can't stand to be with her, *she* needs to make plans. If there's a chance you would stay with her, whether to protect your career, or your children, or your reputation, or because you can't stand up to her, then *I* need to know. You can't have it both ways and be fair to either of us. You'll have to fish or cut bait soon, Darling."

He took her hand in both of his. "My love, I've already made that choice. You're the one I'll spend the rest of my life with. Never doubt it. There'll be nothing quiet about divorce if she finds out about you now. I must get you on a plane and safely out of the country, before she hurts you--then, I can proceed with caution."

"I know you think that plan best, and I bow to your judgment, but I guess I'm pretty sure she already knows, and she's already plotting. I think that's why she hasn't said anything further. I fear she's waiting to get you alone in the States, where she'll either threaten or persuade you that your only option is to stay married for the sake of your career or for the sake of the children— that she'll ruin *both* if you try to leave. What will you do then?"

They were hard words, and he could see her pain in saying them. Perhaps they needed to be said, because both of them were becoming anxiously aware of time running out. Sara's plane would leave in mere hours, and both were near to saying all the wrong things in their sadness, anxiety, and the uncertainty of parting.

"Be realistic, darling. For the girls to get old enough to understand and for your career not to be lost when we know Faye will make a divorce difficult, you'll have to wait ten years to make the break. She'll always find some way to keep you in her control. I can't live without you that long. What if we've already had all the time together we're to be allowed?" Her voice quavered.

"*Ten years*!" Neil angrily shouted the words at the very idea of it taking him so long. "I was thinking more like two *months*!" He grinned as he saw relief flood her face.

She wiped her eyes and smiled. "Suddenly two months sounds easy, doesn't it?"

Neil pulled over to the side of the road so they could hold each other. "Yes, darling, two months will be easy." He kissed her passionately, closing his eyes at the feel of her body and her soul in his arms. The moment moved him, and a wave of unreasonable tenderness swept over him. "Sara, I think I was searching for a warm, loving, communicating companion all my life, and I found you. Ours nears the perfect relationship. You don't think I could give that up now that I've found you, do you, Love?"

"It would be far too late for me, if you could," she said.

He hoped his reassurances were drawing away her fear. She'd been devastated badly in losing Gary, and now he had hurt her again through his own weakness--he didn't want her to be bear any more pain. *God, what am I to do? I have a duty to Sara, too.* "It's funny, isn't it? You fear I can't stand up to Faye's power if I move too slowly, and I fear losing our whole dream if I move too fast. I'm trying manfully to overcome past mistakes, Love."

He grinned at her pitifully until she had to laugh, and he added, "I will assure you yet again that it will only be a short time until Christmas, when we're together for always. Now, let's talk about where and when we'll meet for our sojourn in Gettysburg."

They stopped early at a hotel on the outskirts of Frankfurt, showered, and rested a while, nestling together and savoring each last precious moment—each touch. After a leisurely dinner, a long walk along the river, and a glass of wine at a terrace café, they returned to the quiet hotel for gentle lovemaking and a sleepless night simply holding each other close, each fearing what the rest of the world could do to them. Neither wanted to think about parting.

With the dawn came hurried kisses and goodbyes, and Sara flew away to see her children in California, while Neil drove her Ford Mustang disconsolately back to Grafenwohr, acutely conscious of being very much alone.

When the phone rang the next evening in Neil's cabin, he felt a shiver of pleasure hearing Sara's warm voice, even from long distance, "tucking him in" as usual.

They felt relief from the sound of each other's voices, relaxing the tension of their parting. Neither of them seemed good at goodbyes. Neil told her that both he and their little house were lonesome without her.

Neil knew his phone would ring nightly as long as he was at Grafenwohr tying up loose ends and arranging for work on the ranges to continue after he transferred to Carlisle. They could talk freely on his private phone until July first.

After that, he called and wrote Sara at her mother's home in California, even though she had no safe place to write him back. He wrote encouraging and loving letters telling her that their months together had been the happiest he had ever known

Two months dragged by, but on August 5th, Neil excitedly paced the floor of the airport near Carlisle, waiting for his "life's companion," as he called Sara in his frequent letters. She'd be in his arms again within minutes. He was nervous, fearing somehow, her anxiety might have kept her from coming. *What if she isn't on the plane? What if she fears the coming storm? Dear God, what if she doesn't feel she can take the chance on me any longer?*

26

As her plane descended into Harrisburg, Pennsylvania, the nearest airport to the War College at Carlisle Barracks, Sara could hardly contain herself knowing she would soon be in Neil's arms. Yet, even after all his marvelous, loving summer letters and phone calls at her mom's home, a shiver of apprehension engulfed her. *Will this be the time Faye shuts the little box and closes Neil in? What if he couldn't stand up to her? What if he's not there?*

She knew better than let fear intrude. He'd *always* been there. And as she walked off the plane, there he was, all smiles, rushing to lift her into his arms.

"I was so afraid you wouldn't be on the plane--that you might have changed your mind about me," Neil said breathlessly, covering her face and hair with kisses.

"And I was so afraid you wouldn't be here to meet me."

Neil gallantly bowed and said, "As sure as I'm standing here, you'll never again need to be alone. I'll always be here."

"And I'll always come to you no matter where or when you need me," she answered with a curtsy. They both laughed and shared an exuberant hug, glad just to be together again.

"Are we taking any risks by meeting here so close to the War College?" she whispered. "Mightn't other officers be here?"

"Darling, my love for you is so deep, and I've missed you so. I suppose we might be acting contrary to all reason, being carried away in what could be dangerous, but I don't care about risks. We've probably been acting contrary to all reason for almost a year. Right now, I can only feel my love for you overwhelming me, and I see its answer in your eyes." He smiled at her with such fervor that they both fell into infectious laughter.

Her heart swelled from her warm emotions.

"Come, my love, I have all sorts of surprises for you." Neil put her luggage in the car's trunk, seated her gently, kissed her again, and they headed for Gettysburg.

. "It's wonderful to see you so happy, Darling," she said.

"You make me a happy man, Sara. God, how I've missed you--your smile, your mind--I'm floating right now. I'm here with you, where I feel I can accomplish anything--anything at all--nothing else matters. Did I tell you how much I love you?"

"Yes, but I love hearing it again." She snuggled by his side as he drove out of town. The distance passed quickly as they interrupted each other with excited news, though it had been only a day since he'd last phoned her in California.

Their inn sat at the edge of a meadow across which Civil War General Pickett had charged toward the trees. "This action became known as 'the high tide of the Confederacy,'" said Neil. "I'm practicing a Staff Ride Tour on you tomorrow. I've been 'volunteered' to give it for other officers at the War College, so you'll have to see if first. Can you stand it?"

"We've shared so much about the history of this battle," Sara said. "I'm excited to be here in the midst of it all."

Drinks and dinner at the historic Old Dobbin House found each assuring the other that the two months apart had made them even more confident of their feelings for each other and of their need to have a future together.

As though by a common thought, they joined hands and walked onto the battlefield in the balmy night. The park had closed for the evening, yet the monuments and silent guns, ominous by day, were lovely in their own magical way. They strolled together until the night's quiet moonlight coaxed them into the shadows where Neil pulled her to him and cradled her head against his chest.

"Do you have any idea how good it feels for me to hold you like this again?"

She lifted her face to kiss him full on the lips as he brushed back her hair.

"You know, running my fingers through your hair never fails to bring a warm feeling of tenderness for you that overwhelms me. You're so touchable." He gently pulled her dark hair and smiled. "I love the feel of those silky curls. With you, my life becomes so warm and natural—so real."

Somehow, not quite sure when or how, Sara realized Neil had unbuttoned her blouse and loosened her bra while he kissed her fervently. Playful at first, soon both became consumed with passion. Clothes seemed in the way all of a sudden, disappearing in every direction. By the time they realized where his emotion had taken them, nothing else mattered, and they were making love in the huge rotunda of the Pennsylvania monument, their soft moans and cries of pleasure echoing from the ancient marble.

Afterward, on a lark, they romped naked in the fields like children, hiding each other's clothing, laughing all the while. During a pause, when they heard the sound of the night guards' horses, Neil snatched up their clothing and they hurried from the park, donning their clothes and laughing as they ran. But Sara could not find her panties, and Neil was hopping wildly on one foot as he tried to get his loafers on. Finally, he waved her panties with a mischievous grin and put them back in his pocket.

She could feel the breeze ripple over her body under her full skirt, and said she hoped they could enter the hotel with some semblance of dignity. "Surely, we must be too grown up for this sort of thing, Darling."

"Hey, why not? Neither of us ever got to play as kids. We both took on heavy responsibility much too soon. Now, we're free to simply laugh and love together. This was such fun, though I suppose it was foolish of us--taking the risk." He chuckled. "I can see the headlines now—'Pillars of the military and teaching communities found naked in the middle of Gettysburg's battlefield.'" Noting that Sara was nervously holding her skirt about her, he quipped, "Just walk in as though you *always* run around without your panties, Love." They paused outside the old Inn's door. "Don't give it a thought. It's our secret."

"Don't you dare ask loudly for us to go to the bar for a cola or anything. We'll just go straight up to our room, okay?"

"Now, you know I wouldn't do such a thing, would I?" But Neil couldn't resist patting her on the backside just as she walked in the door, which caused a surprised skip in her step. "Careful, Darling, you wouldn't want us to be considered daring at our age, now would you?" He wiggled his eyebrows wickedly, and she was laughing with him upon entering their room.

Neil pulled her to him. "Love, I always know what you're thinking by your lovely brown eyes."

"Really?" She looked up into his at close range. "And what do they tell you?"

"Right this minute, they're dancing with mischief. But sometimes you look at me with such devotion that I feel I could fall right into their depth and warmth. Other times they flash with excitement at a discovery we've made together. But I see them changing as we speak. I can see your desire in them too—now."

They again moved together, as though linked by magnets, gently peeling away the so recently-donned clothing, this time with soft touches as he kissed her lips, her breasts, her body. She felt the warmth rising from his groin and quivered with anticipation.

Though they had always seemed attuned to each other in marvelously synchronized passion, somehow making love again after the two-month separation brought more intensity. They moved deeper, stronger together than either had ever known, even more satisfying, if such a thing could be possible. Tenderness and passion took equal turns in glorious and multiple orgasms. But one final climax made Sara feel different, somehow. Arched as she was against his deep thrusts, she felt as though something inside her was breaking. She could not find her diaphragm afterward.

Neil joked about the "lost object" and asked her later if she had ever found it. She had, but it was in two pieces. She tried not to think of the possible consequences of such an accident, but she relaxed and forgot the moment of uneasiness when Neil said that he thought with their getting close to forty, probably nothing would happen, though he would love to have more children.

Later, Sara nestled her head in the hollow of Neil's shoulder, her long legs wound around his, as he folded his arms around her to hold her closely. She gently traced his chest with her fingers, knowing how he enjoyed the touching--their private language. Both savored the joy of simply being together, quietly, filled to the brim with tenderness and warm satisfaction.

Neil captured her hand and raised it to his lips, kissing the palm before closing it in his own. "Are you feeling what I'm feeling? Sort of overwhelmed with peacefulness?"

"I think so," she responded. "We're so very lucky, aren't we, to have shared this year together?"

"This is true contentment, Love--this marvelous feeling inside us. Nothing can ever go wrong again. We'll have lots more years together, because you're here by my side like this."

They talked for hours, making plans, enjoying each other's nearness, with gentle hands cupping shoulders or faces, punctuated by relaxed kisses that had become almost soft nibbles. Neither could let the other go.

Neil was proud to tell Sara that he had already overhauled the family car for Faye, but Sara found he had not yet served the divorce papers. "I fear what she'll do about the girls," he said, his anxiety plain in his voice. "If she tries accusations again...."

"I fear what she'll do to you, too, darling. But nothing is really good for the children, if it isn't good for you. You must be healthy and happy if you are to give them the love and time and support they deserve and need. Do you plan to try again?"

"Soon, but I wanted us to have this peaceful, quiet time together before I stirred up the hornet's nest." Neil laughed ruefully. "She won't make it easy, but I'll have it settled by the time Katy and I come skiing at Christmas time. You can count on us. Go ahead and make our reservations. We'll be with you, my love," Neil whispered into her ear, "for always. I promise."

The pair rose with the sun and visited the battlefield legally, hand in hand, as real tourists. Neil did, indeed, "practice" his Staff Ride performance on Sara. Neither could keep a straight face when he tried to pontificate on the "major significance" of the Pennsylvania Monument. He lifted her hand and kissed it. "You know, this monument will forever have more importance to me now. Whenever I bring officers here and tell them the Civil War story, I'll be thinking of our story, instead. They'll wonder why I'm grinning the whole time."

In the museum, Sara was impressed with a diorama showing southern General Armistead facing certain death rather than compromise his West Point friendship with the northerner, General Hancock, and General Garnett riding high in the saddle to his death believing it was necessary to regain his honor. The whole battle was rife with sacrifice for a cause each believed in, with the "duty, honor, country" she had always told Neil was ingrained so deeply into his blood, too. Of course, the highlight, for both Neil and Sara, was finding the actual rock on which Chamberlain and his 20th Maine had turned the battle with an end-sweep bayonet charge. Both reveled in the history, and in each other.

They drove through the Pocono Mountains to a cottage on the Delaware River. Again, they talked late into the night.

"My biggest worry is the girls," Neil said again. "She is so volatile at times. I can't leave them solely with her."

"We'll do nothing that would compromise their lives, but I truly believe they'd have more fun with us."

Sara grew thoughtful for a moment. "It's hard for me to understand why Faye has never enjoyed the military opportunities for friendship and parties and travel and education—even just the chance to do everything with you and the children. You're a wonderful companion. Why does she stay indoors and miss the whole world? She missed so much by not embracing your love and sharing your career. It's sad, because most couples have such a good time together, and it's such fun to be with you and the girls."

"I don't think 'fun' is part of her vocabulary. Believe me, in the early days, I tried to engage her in all the camaraderie, because I love it all—even the Hail and Farewells and the pageantry. I tried to make her love me too, at first, but I got the same negative rejections then. I guess our expectations were different. I think secretly, she wanted someone else. I've never known where her anger and hostility came from, but there's no way to make someone love you if they seem to hate you instead.

"Now, I know I just need to get away from the pain and

find peace with the one who loves me--you, my love. I'll have this fall and winter to straighten it all out--get the divorce, set Faye up comfortably, protect the girls, and still be able to do my duty to the Army. Then we'll have the rest of our lives to make each other, and the girls, happy. And you'll get a chance to enjoy all the Army fun—just you, Katy, and Micki, and I, together."

The gentleness between them made Sara's heart sing.

"It's only a matter of a little more time, darling," he murmured again and again, with jubilant hugs. "Only a little time."

Sara and Neil loved rambling through the beautiful countryside of upstate New York, savoring the breezes that presaged the coming of fall. But finally it was their last day together in New York City before Neil would put her on the plane back to Germany. They spent the morning studying dinosaur and gemstone exhibits at the Museum of Natural History--lovingly called "America's Attic," lunched at a sidewalk café, and did some people-watching in Central Park. To end their day, they journeyed to the observation platform atop the World Trade Center to watch the sun gradually descend over Manhattan, bathing the Hudson and East Rivers in golden hues. A passerby took their picture. Together, they felt as golden and beautiful as the rivers.

Yet the trip to the airport was difficult. They both felt the strain of parting. Spasms of silence were punctuated by each rushing to say everything through tears--until Christmas. Sara's absolute terror of separation made her almost sick.

At her flight's gate at JFK airport, Neil reminded her again how he had been at the Harrisburg airport even though she had been afraid. "So, my love, I'll always be there for you. Even if everything we've planned goes up in smoke, we'll be with each other again. No matter what happens, always remember that I love you so very much." He whispered this with his hands cupped around Sara's face, looking deeply into her tearful eyes. "I promise you, my only love."

She could not speak through the tears, but Neil was loving and full of promises. Sara knew his words would carry her through for the lonely months until they could be together at Christmas.

Once again, on a plane going back to Germany, Sara's thoughts were, by turn, jubilant and vaguely fearful. She needed Neil's communication and his touch, yet she felt apprehensive that he has not already taken more action. She understood his fear of open confrontation, but he had to be first to act if he was to have any chance at getting part-time custody and saving his career. *And God, I know how much his duty to the Army means to him. I share his concern, but I love him so much, and Faye loves only his prestige. Surely he deserves to be loved for himself alone. Please God, give him the strength he needs to make the hard choices.*

Sara arrived home to Germany to find comforting touches of Neil all over her apartment. Little signs of his caring—tiny love notes tacked on every surface and in every drawer she opened. An envelope full of four and five leaf clovers brought her laughter because Neil could stand still and pick up a handful of lucky shamrocks, while she could search diligently and never find even one. He said it only needed "concentration." Lovingly, she framed them to hang in her kitchen, where she could see and remember.

He had brought things from the small house at Graf and placed them back in her apartment. There were extra gas coupons in her car, which was also newly washed and waxed. And pressed flowers graced her pillow. *Blessed Neil. How I needed the reassurance you obviously planned for me weeks ago. I can't live without you now. I've come full circle to where I love completely and I'm vulnerable. I couldn't survive another loss—not your loss!*

Within a few weeks, Sara realized she would have a surprise for Neil when he arrived at Christmas. She hugged herself with joy, thinking how he'd laugh when he realized they were not too old after all. Neil loved her and would be delighted at this culmination of their love. She was happy with her surprise. She only needed to be patient for everything to be perfect.

Weeks went by with daily letters from Neil. Touched by his loving words, Sara bloomed with happiness. Their Christmas ski plans were complete--reservations were made, though she realized that perhaps by Christmas, she might be an observer on the trip.

On the evening of November 28th, Casey encountered Sara in the hall of the Officers' Club with a stack of letters in her hand.

"Are those all from Neil?" Casey could never resist teasing Sara about her "monopoly" on the Army postal system.

Her excited smile confirmed his assessment.

"All but this one with no return address. I'll check it first. Just let me take a glance at these, and then we can meet our friends in the dining room, okay?"

"Sure. No problem. I have to go pay my club bill at the office. I'll be right back. Wait for me."

Casey got only half way down the hall before he heard an agonizing groan from Sara. He turned to see her collapse, lunging against the edge of a heavy glass-sided table that held a lamp. The letters fluttered to the floor. One was open.

Thus unbalanced, the table turned over, its wrought iron legs stabbing the air as the whole weight crashed across Sara's body. The lamp smashed to pieces. Casey rushed to her, as others came running out of the dining room and bar upon hearing the noise.

Sara's face was ashen, and cold beads of perspiration glistened on her forehead. Casey hurried to lift the heavy table from her, helped by three of the other officers. Unconscious, Sara did not respond to his frantic calls.

Casey gathered up her letters and stuffed them into his pocket, quickly assuring the other Club patrons that he would get Sara to the hospital. Picking her up in his arms before anyone could stop him or ask additional questions, Casey hurried to put her in his car, ran to the driver's side, and drove recklessly out of the parking lot. He remembered her comment that she knew everyone in the Army Medical Clinic and didn't like to go there. He also knew that the on-post clinic had little in the way of emergency care in the evenings, so he drove the additional five minutes to the downtown German hospital's emergency room.

27

Faye and Neil – Carlisle Barracks, PA   "Philanderer, philanderer, philanderer, philanderer," Faye screamed, as she held out two letters so Neil could see the return address. The letters had been torn open. She kept yelling the hated word even after Neil acknowledged her accusation.

"Hush, Faye. Katy and Micki will be frightened. Faye, stop the screeching! Yes, I love her, but Sara had nothing to do with my decision. I wanted out of this marriage years ago. All you and I do is fight. I've been telling you for a very long time that we were unhappy and needed a divorce. You wouldn't listen."

A pasty white face appeared in the doorway. Faye faced Katy squarely and screamed, "Your father is a philanderer. He insulted me. That woman only acted like she liked you girls to seduce your father. He's a philanderer, a cheat, a bastard!"

Neil went to the door and hugged Katy, urging her quietly to go back to her room and take care of Micki, as usual, until the storm passed. Reluctantly, the young teen walked down the hall, looking back at her father for guidance as to what it all meant.

Neil again faced Faye. "Must you always involve the children in our arguments?"

"Why should I care? They need to know all men are cheats. I have two letters now, and that guarantees I'll win any divorce case, you dumb shit! These go to your Commandant at the War College. You'll be drummed out of the Army for adultery. And being on the Colonel's list--you can forget about those eagles too."

"Faye, you don't have to do it this way. And you don't need to scare the girls to death either. Let's sit down quietly and talk about getting a divorce for incompatibility. It's long overdue."

"You aren't getting a divorce. I am!" She spat out the words. "And it sure won't be for incompatibility! It'll be scandalous--all over the newspapers. I have proof you have a mistress. I'll bet you've even given me some damned venereal disease. I demand we both be tested. God damn you, I wish you were dead! I won't have it! I won't be left a penniless, divorced woman. I'll see that everybody knows what you've done." She was breathless from the tirade. "You'll pay for the rest of your life!"

"Faye, we both gave up on our marriage long ago. I've never had any sexually transmitted disease, either, so forget about that. And I'll always take care of you financially, so you won't be penniless. Sara is no mistress—she's the woman I love and want to marry. Let's get to the *real* root of the problem. You've never loved me. You've never wanted to take part in the advantages and fun of military life with me--the travel, the camaraderie, the friendships, or the chance to grow together and as individuals. You've hated every minute of it. You don't care if we break up our marriage. You only care what others might think about it."

"Yes, I care about what others think. Somebody has to preserve our family image. You certainly haven't helped it."

"No, I haven't, Faye. But had you ever wanted to be a real wife, even a friend, life might have been different for us. I've tried for years to avoid reciprocating your anger and profanity, hoping it would get better. It didn't. You refused psychiatric help and only would go to chaplains who perhaps didn't have the skills…."

"There's nothing wrong with me! It's you who've made me hate you. You're a bastard! Look what you've done."

"Faye, the mess our marriage is in didn't happen overnight. Love never happened between us. Neither Sara nor I meant to hurt anyone, and our relationship is very recent. We can make a loving home for the girls and share custody with you. The children's welfare must be the most important decision we *all* make."

"Don't you think you can have the girls, even part time, and don't think you're making any decisions either--I am." Again, she waved the letters. "See these? See?" She narrowed her eyes and jabbed her finger at his chest. "My lawyer is making copies for the commandant, the promotion board, and that woman's school superintendent. And I'm leaving. I'm taking the girls. You'll never get them back. Now get out of my way and get out of my sight."

"You can't do that, Faye. The girls belong to both of us. They're all that we did right with our marriage. No court will take them completely away from me."

"Do you want to bet on that, Mister?" Faye sneered. "These letters prove you committed adultery. No court will give children to a philanderer. And my attorney still wonders about what you might have done to them." She raised insinuating eyebrows.

Neil's face blanched pale in astonishment. "Faye, you wouldn't! No matter what anger has passed between us, you *know* me better than to tell such a lie...."

Suddenly, Faye began yelling the word again--hysterical bursts of laughter coming between the repeated epithets.

"Faye, stop it...."

"Come here, girls," Faye screamed down the hall. "We're leaving your philandering father now."

Katy came slowly out of her bedroom pulling Micki. The little girl cowered behind her sister, barely peeking out.

Faye could see Neil's horrified reaction. She knew she had him, as the old soldiers said, "by the balls." *Now* was the time to make her move! Neil would never again be so vulnerable as he was with his name on the proposed colonel's list and being in War College. He would never again be as vulnerable as he was at this moment when she marched the girls from the bedroom. She grabbed Micki's and Katy's arms and held them tightly to her. "Say goodbye to your philandering father."

"Mom, please...."

Faye didn't even hear Katy's cry. She stood defiant.

Katy jerked away and ran to her father. "Daddy, please don't let her take us. Don't leave us alone. Keep us with you." Her mother grabbed her arm. Clinging to Neil, Katy sobbed as her mother tugged at her from behind, screaming all the while.

"My God, Faye, let go of her! Get hold of yourself! You needn't be as vicious to the girls as you've been to me. Let me talk to her." He pushed away her hands. Faye's chest heaved in anger.

His arms around Katy, he finally quieted her enough to tell her, "Katy, you go with Mom for now, and we'll set up some type of visitation. I'll fight this in court. You'll be able to see both Mom and me, I promise."

"Your promises don't mean much do they?" Faye snarled, jerking Katy by the arm. Looking back with teary brown eyes, Katy was dragged toward the stairs.

Faye said, "I'll be in New York with my family, should you choose to meet my terms. Don't bother calling any of us until you decide to do so."

Neil's shoulders slumped as he watched them walk down the stairs, retrieve bags from the closet, close the door, and walk down the sidewalk. He ran to the hall window and peered out. Everything was spiraling out of control and had taken him so completely by surprise. He needed to think. *What were "her terms," anyway? What did Faye want?*

The girls stared back, as though waiting for him to save them. He was helpless. With Katy streaming tears and Micki carrying her little back pack over one shoulder, sobbing, he knew the image of that moment would never leave him.

###

Faye smiled, sure that she had made the right move. *I can sit tight and do nothing. I have time and conformity on my side. That woman is an ocean away, and Neil won't be able to face scandal.* "Hush your crying," she flung at the girls, bouncing off the curb with a jarring thump as she drove away.

The following week brought papers and injunctions. Micki became ill with the mysterious kidney problem that had plagued her since birth. Neil had often wondered if Micki's illnesses might be due to his exposure to Agent Orange in Vietnam before her conception. Frightening medical evidence was piling up.

He was not allowed to see the child. There was an injunction against that too, "until the mother's terms were acceded to." Micki called him, her hoarse little voice sobbing in whispers until she was almost incoherent. He knew Faye had not authorized the calls, and the little girl was running the risk of angering her mother further. Katy called to complain that she hated New York schools and wanted to come home. Neil was often near tears himself after trying to reassure the girls everything would be all right soon. *Would it ever be all right again?* He didn't know what to do next. The house was deathly quiet without his children.

###

Faye waited as Neil continued his military seminars at the War College. She knew each day would be torture, because he'd never know which day he would be called into the Commandant's office and his career ended on charges of adultery. They'd seen it happen before, even to a four star general. *He'll wonder why it hasn't happened to him already. I'll keep him on edge, and spring the trap whenever I choose.* She had also moved quickly to clean out their joint savings and checking accounts as well as a small fund set aside for Katy's college education.

Life was tough. Neil found it difficult to concentrate on his demanding studies while his whole world was crashing down around him. He blamed himself for waiting too long to file for divorce and totally losing control of the situation.

The final straw came when Faye called. "Katy ran away! You called her and told her to do this, didn't you?" She screamed into the phone until Neil had to hold the receiver at arm's length.

"Faye, calm down and tell me what happened. I didn't ask her to do any such thing. I'm as panicked as you are to think that she would leave alone."

"Something has to be done, you bastard. She's lost."

"I know, Faye. I'll start looking for her right away."

"You just stay right there! The police are looking. And you have to bring her back here immediately when she shows up. You have no visitation rights until such time as my demands are met. Damn it! You cannot keep her there. Do you understand me?"

"Yes, Faye. I understand you!" He threw the phone to the floor. Only after a few minutes did he carefully pick it up and put it back on its table. *Katy might be trying to call me, and the only thing that matters now is to find her safe.*

Frantically, Neil waited for Katy, or for the police to come say she'd been hurt. He felt panic rise like gorge in his throat.

When she finally arrived, tired and tearful, Katy was filled with protests. "Daddy, don't make me go back," she begged. "Let's just go away someplace together, please."

His heart hurt. "Katy, we have no place to go while I'm in the middle of War College, and I'm forced by the injunction to take you back to your mother. I promise I'll get visitation rights somehow after we get through this crisis. Now you must call your mother to let her know you're safe. I'm sure she's worried too."

The phone call was tense. "Mom, I'm okay. I'm with Dad, and I'm staying here." Tears filled Katy's eyes as she listened to the tirade from the other end of the line.

"But Mom, I really don't want to come. I don't know how to talk to you when you're so angry." Katy's voice became subdued. "You know I want to see Micki. Please don't put it like that. It's not fair to make me choose." The young girl nodded at the phone, mumbling, "Mom, I'm staying here." She hung up, hugged Neil, and said, "I guess I really made her mad this time, Daddy."

My God, what can I do? Neil thought, deeply troubled. *Katy doesn't understand being in the middle of all this.*

Faye wasted no time driving with Micki to Carlisle to take Katy back, against her wishes. Neil tried to reason with his wife. "Faye, the child hitchhiked to get here. Anything could have happened to her. She just doesn't want to stay with you. She wants to be here with me. What do you hope to accomplish by keeping the children away from me?" He shook his head, with a hand to his brow, trying to stay calm. "And you mustn't keep Micki away from Katy either. We need to settle this *now*, Faye. I refuse to have my children endangered and unhappy like this."

"You son-of-a bitch! All you need to do to settle everything is to accede to my terms. Then you can have the children with you whenever you want." Faye suddenly stopped yelling and smiled coyly, her tongue pinched between her teeth.

"All right, Faye. Just what *are* these demands that must be met in order for you to take away the sword hanging over my head with my children and my career and my life? I'm prepared to set you up comfortably. You'll have your security. How much do you want? Name a figure--anything. It's yours."

Faye smiled, knowing she had won. "My demands aren't about money, Neil. I already took all you had. You can't even write a check without me—didn't you notice?"

Neil looked up, surprised. "Then, what is it you want?"

"I demand we stay married, raise our children together, and you'll never see or communicate with that woman again. You'll toe the straight and narrow. One slip, and you'll lose the girls forever. The letters haven't gone to the Commandant yet. The loss of income would affect me--but I'll do it now, and sue for divorce on charges of adultery and child abuse, which you know will get you a court marshal, *unless* you come to your senses and agree."

Neil looked sadly at his tearful fourteen-year-old.

Faye saw her advantage. "You've made it abundantly clear that you don't want me to raise the girls alone. You keep saying they need you for some kind of balance."

Words choked in Neil's throat. Faye had the advantage of knowing he'd be heartbroken to give up his precious daughters.

Good! Faye thought. *I have him cornered.* "Just say the word and you can still have your children and your career--still go on to colonel and maybe even wear general's stars. You keep saying it's so bloody necessary that you make a difference for the Army. This is your last chance to decide, Neil. Make up your mind. Accept my terms, or I'll have your girls, your career, your reputation, and you'll live with the consequences of your choice."

She could see Neil silently searching Katy's eyes. *Father and daughter were thinking something...what? They seemed to communicate, sometimes without words.* "Well, what will it be, Neil. I can't stand here all day. I have appointments with my lawyer and the Commandant of the War College."

There was a long, silent minute. No one spoke. *God, what is my duty now?* Neil was aware that the tick of the German clock on the wall was inordinately loud, drowning out his thoughts, creating an unwavering noise in his head. His mind kept time with the strict conformity of its rhythm.

Finally, he knew what he had to do. Barely perceived, he nodded. His nod broke the eerie spell, and Katy rushed to his arms.

Faye could see his defeated eyes. She smiled. With his one curt nod, he had climbed back into the box where he belonged. She would exact her price, her toll—the sacrifice of this woman, and she didn't care if the two loved each other. She had the advantage of a long distance between them. She would still pin on the stars.

Faye picked up the phone and called her lawyer. "Drop the charges and the divorce proceedings," she said into the telephone. "Neil has agreed to my terms and a lovely reconciliation." She made sure Neil could hear the triumph in her voice.

Neil sank down on the stairs with his head in his hands. He was whipped. He had spent his life trying to be in control, and now, his life, his dreams, his plans were totally gone. He knew he would forever regret the decision he had just been forced to make, but he could see no other way.

Katy leaned her head against his shoulder, crying with him.

Faye smiled. She had beaten the whole game.

Neil sat alone in his den later, trying to sort out the pieces of his life shredded before his eyes. He knew he'd be trapped in marriage until the children were old enough to understand—an impossible strain to keep such a truce even reasonably peaceful. So much had been said that couldn't be unsaid.

But lessons were learned. He'd found out just how short his tether was. He hadn't really believed Faye would bring such fear to the girls--but she had. Now he knew they'd never be safe unless he stayed. He was sick to death, carrying the weight of guilt for what he'd do to his children if he left, or to Sara if he didn't. He felt so torn. The love he had for his girls had to take first place. Sara would understand. He also realized he had no chance for a life with

Sara--not now, anyway. Giving up her love for him broke his heart. He had let Sara know there'd been a catastrophe the first night of the blowup, scribbling a few words promising to contact her soon as it was safe. But since, all had moved too fast and out of control.

There had been months of letters from Sara, lovingly loyal and supportive, and his letters back--both mixing intellectually stimulating banter with loving, needing, missing each other, looking forward to their Christmas rendezvous and their future. But now Faye had sprung her trap. He had no doubt it was a trap— after all, Faye had waited for the second letter a month after she had stolen the first, pretending not to know.

Why didn't I listen to Sara when she said to get a post office box rather than pick up mail at the War College? And why didn't I file for divorce sooner. It's my fault. I hesitated out of anxiety for the girls, and Faye acted first. I realize now she has known the whole time, waiting for her chance to entrap me.

Neil felt sure Sara would understand that he must give in for now, to save the children further damage. He'd been waiting until he knew something for sure. Now he knew! *I'll write Sara as soon as I can explain,* he thought, *when I can figure out myself how serious this setback is and find a way out of this mess. This is the hardest decision I've ever had to make. Why didn't I call Sara immediately? She should have been the first to know. Was I in denial—hoping for a miracle?*

His mind jumped from the girls, to Faye, to Sara, and back again. He knew Faye's divorce suit would come with the implied, off-the-wall threat she'd made that he had molested the girls—a sure-fire reason he would lose his children, and his career, if he didn't go along with her demands.

Was I procrastinating--waiting for Faye to agree we should part because that was easiest? Neil realized he'd gone through the motions of duty for years, allowing Faye her fantasy of the "perfect marriage," perhaps out of his own embarrassment that he had made such a youthful mistake. No one would believe, now, that he'd had grounds for divorce years ago. Faye could make it look to a judge as though the marriage had only begun to founder with his love affair. He cursed himself for not confronting facts years ago. He should have told everyone he knew instead of covering up for his faulty marriage. He also cursed himself for seeing no way out now.

He shivered in spite of the fire in the fireplace, suddenly aware that the primitive little cabin in the woods was warmer than this sterile house in Carlisle Barracks with its crystal chandeliers and vases. He'd not noticed before how the warm smile and touch of someone who loved him could set the tone for a home. *This house will never be a home.*

Neil found it ironic that Faye's discovery of the letters, and earlier, the "Charlie" bottle, had alerted her to his love affair, yet she still refused to face the fact that her profane anger might have given him reason for leaving. She was no closer to seeing that she had helped cause the marriage failure--still denying, and therefore, still unwilling to help correct the problems. They would be living in an armed camp for a lifetime.

"What am I to do now?" He asked the question of himself—God--anybody who would listen. He had loved Sara so much, he had risked everything, thrown it all to the winds, and he had lost her. He wished Sara were here. They did their best problem solving together, as a team. But he could receive no more letters from Sara, nor could he risk writing to her, with Faye watching his every move—for now.

It hurt to think what this abrupt trauma might do to Sara. Instead, he rationalized to himself that Sara was well set, had a good job, friends, and a nice apartment. *And she's tough. She'll be okay, he thought. But he also remembered his promises—the feel of her face in his hands, her trusting eyes when he'd kissed her goodbye. God, what have I done?* He pushed the thought away. He dared not contact her until this mess was over. If he waited awhile, a divorce judge might be more understanding so that he would at least not lose his children, even if he lost his career.

Neil noticed a movement from the corner of his eye and turned to see Katy leaning against the door, watching him. He motioned to her, and she came to join him.

"Are you okay, Katy?" He could see concern in her eyes.

"I guess so, Dad. I wish Mom weren't so mad, and you weren't so sad. The whole house feels cold and empty, doesn't it?"

"I'm afraid it may be like this for awhile, Katy. I've certainly not been successful in trying to keep things peaceful. Any suggestions for your old dad?"

Katy hugged him. "Just promise me that no matter how bad it gets, you won't leave Micki and I alone with her."

"I'll never leave you two behind. I'll work out something."

The young girl stayed close, quiet for a moment. "Dad, I don't know how you can stay, when Mom yelled at you like that. She was totally crazy, and you didn't even fight back. Both Micki and I were scared she would kill you or something."

Neil tried to laugh off that perception, for his daughter's sake. *I never fought back, hoping to keep the peace, but peace wasn't possible anyway. Perhaps I should have fought back. Open confrontation might have worked better than appeasement. It did on the battlefield. But Katy will have a lifetime she'll need to trust her mother.* So he answered with a forced smile, "Hey, remember me? I'm the old warrior. Let me do the worrying, okay?" *Why couldn't Faye leave the children out of their personal conflict?* He hugged Katy the way he'd comforted her as a child. *Would it ever again be as easy to comfort his little girl as it had been then?*

"Okay, Dad, I'll leave it up to you." Katy shifted gears, as only children can do. "Are we still spending Christmas with Sara?"

Neil realized then, that his daughter had not understood this latest catastrophic blow-up, and he resolved to keep it that way. "I'm afraid not, Katy. I can't leave Micki alone. We'll need to be careful not to anger Mom for a while. She'll get over it, eventually, and she'll pretend everything is all right. She always does."

"But it's not *really* all right, is it, Dad? It's hard for you to stay here and pretend. I wouldn't be able to. You're much stronger than me." She hugged her father and hurried off to her homework.

Neil rubbed his eyes. *It's best you don't know the half of it, Katy. I'm going to need to be stronger than I've ever been.* Having enjoyed the warmth Sara brought into his life, it would be all the more painful to abandon their plans. He tried to comfort himself that he had at least been loved for a little while.

The disconsolate man sat down at his desk in the den and listed his reasons to either divorce or stay married on a notepad, hoping a list of pros and cons would help him accept what seemed inevitable. In five minutes, he had a long list of reasons to divorce, regardless of the consequences, running down the right side of the paper. Faye's threats, accusations, profanity, fearful outbursts of temper at the girls and himself, endless arguments, constant manipulation of his life, total rejection, his loneliness, the need for intellectual companionship, the need to be loved, Sara, Sara, Sara.

On the left side as reasons to stay, were only two—to protect the girls from Faye's anger so they'd have a chance to grow up more or less normally, and to stay with a career in the Army long enough to make a difference. *There's that old "duty, honor, country" again that Sara always said ran in my veins.* The left list of two items weighed on him most heavily—especially the safety of his little girls. He'd have to spend more years with Faye, the woman who had emasculated him. They'd ruined each other's lives so long ago. He could see nothing he could do about it now.

I told Sara only until Christmas. Those were my words to her-- and now I've gone back on my word to the only person who ever loved me. Yet there's no choice except to keep my girls and carry on this obscene pretense to keep Faye peaceful at any cost.

Now he knew that the "cost" was losing Sara. Sara believed in him. But the trauma of Faye's threats had paralyzed him at this critical phase of his career. *I'm not ready to give up my girls or my career. I must get back to a safe place before I can do anything else. That's my only practical course, at least for now.*

As twilight gathered, the room drifted into gloomy darkness, Neil didn't bother turning on the light. His thoughts ran rampant as he folded his list and stuffed it in his desk drawer. *Sara, my love, it is you and I who must sacrifice now. Like Tess of our poem, we are the ones to take the bullet. There you are, on another continent. God help me, Love, but you're not here, so, for now, I must let you go. You'll have to go your way, and I'll go mine.* But he wondered if they could promise never to see each other again, as though the flick of a switch could end all they'd given each other. *In this crisis, the little girls must come first. What can I do for myself, or for you, my love? Probably nothing. But it's not all about us, is it? I have only one choice for now.*

His whole life had fallen apart. *Sara trustingly left it all in my hands. In that way, she is as innocent and loving as Micki. I can't bear to think about that soft look in her eyes—the touch of her fingers—the warmth of her smile.*

Neil moved to where he had hidden the rest of Sara's letters. He couldn't take the chance of Faye finding them, too. He had relished the encouragement and confidence they gave him, but now, he threw the letters, one by one, into the fireplace. As the last letter curled into the smoke and flame, he leaned his head against the brick and whispered, "Forgive me, Love." He wanted to believe that even if he could never contact her again, Sara would be all right. She'd be strong. He accepted this deception, to save himself.

The War College was too demanding and competitive during the day—there was no time to think. But now he lay on the den's couch and thought of holding Sara close. In his mind, they once again walked along the Danube in the rain, watched the stars, and laughed at their near disaster at the Czech Border. He chuckled to himself. *Only* Sara could have brought him through such a fiasco. She was the life's companion he needed. He pictured their making love tenderly on a hill overlooking the Rhine and chasing each other, laughing, on a balmy night in Gettysburg. He deliberately convinced himself Sara would be all right and could go on without him.

Remembering their warm companionship, and pretending he could feel her body curled up right there beside him, he finally fell into a troubled sleep.

28

"Sara. You didn't tell me you were pregnant."

Casey moved to Sara's bedside in the German hospital at the first flutter of her dark eyelashes. He quietly took her hand to keep her from struggling with the oxygen tubes. In answer to her weak, vacant look, he added, "The doctor told me you were four months along. He thought I was your husband, but I didn't correct him. There are some internal injuries. You've been unconscious awhile from hitting your head. Why didn't you tell me?"

As reality returned, Sara curled her hands protectively around her abdomen and asked in alarm, "He didn't say I'd lost the baby, did he?"

"No, but he said the fetus is distressed. You may lose him."

"Him? A boy?" Unconsciously, she smoothed the sheets across her body, as though she could touch the child to send a message. "I'm sorry, Casey. I didn't even tell Neil, though I thought he might have suspected. I didn't want to put any extra pressure on him. I planned to surprise him when he came for Christmas, but now he won't be coming." Any control she was struggling to maintain dissolved into wrenching sobs.

Casey waited quietly to comfort his friend, alarmed by her pale countenance. "You scared me to death. How did you crash into that heavy table, anyway?"

"I don't know. The room was spinning. I tried to grab onto something? Did I break it?"

"No, but you tipped it over onto yourself. What upset you so? You were fine…."

Sara looked around in alarm. "Her words…the letter…where are the letters?"

Casey pulled the wadded up bunch of letters from his pocket. "One was open. I picked them up so no one would see. I figured they might be private."

"You might as well read it, Casey. Please give me the others." Sara opened the last of Neil's letters first--a thin sheet of paper, then bowed her head as she hugged it to her breast.

Casey unfolded Faye's letter. The only sounds were Sara's soft moans and the wheezing of the oxygen machine. Finally, he said, "God, Sara. Do you think Neil knew she was writing you a letter like this? She says she wrote it with his approval. It's filth! She says she'll see Neil in Hell and you should die?

"I'm sure he wouldn't have seen her letter. He knows these are lies, and I know he wouldn't let her write such garbage to hurt me." *But would he have been able to stop her?* Sara's breathing was shallow and labored, and tears ran down her cheeks.

Casey dabbed at them with tissues from her bedside table. "Sara, if you don't think this letter is his doing, you need to get on the next plane and help him through this mess--as soon as you can safely travel, I mean. What if he really can't come to marry you? What if you're left alone and unmarried with a child to raise?"

In answer to the surprise and anxiety in her eyes, he added, "Look, Sara. We're friends, and I care about you too. I'd gladly marry you to give this little boy a name, in case Neil can't do it. I don't want you or the baby to suffer. No one would ever know."

"You're so good, Casey, and I appreciate the offer, but I don't know from these letters what to think. I trust Neil to take care of us, as soon as he can take care of Katy and Micki too. I just can't lose his baby!" Her voice broke. "Neil must feel so trapped right now." She started sobbing again.

Casey held her hand and patted it clumsily. "It amazes me you're worried about him, while you're the one lying in a hospital bed." His brow creased with wrinkles. "Okay, Sara, we'll wait until he tells you what to do, then. For now, just hang tight. He'll call soon. He knows you'll need his emotional support. So you just concentrate on getting well."

"Faye says she has our letters," she gasped. "I begged him to get a post office box, but he was so sure he could control…."

"Worrying won't help you get well, Sara. Try to breathe slowly and stop crying."

Sara vacillated between confusion and anxiety. "Neil loves me, Casey. He's said so a million times. He wouldn't lie to me.

But, if he got the same kind of threats she made in this letter, I don't know if he can stand up to Faye or not. He's rarely been able to before. I've been so afraid something like this would happen."

Sara's plaintive eyes and tear-stained face searched her friend's for some sign of consolation. She found none. "If Neil can't write or call me, how will I know what harm Faye's done him already? Why didn't he tell me more so I'd know what to do?"

Neil's note had been stunned, confused, disjointed, as though he hadn't known what to do or where to turn. His handwriting was scribbled—strained, or perhaps rushed. After Casey left, Sara read the words over again until they were memorized, searching for some clue as to what Neil might want her to do. "Darling: Katy and I won't be coming to Germany. Faye filed for divorce. We must not communicate for a while. I will be in touch as soon as it's safe. Love you, Neil." That's all the note had said. It didn't answer any of her painful questions.

Of course, she could not avoid reading Faye's letter again and again as well. Casey was right. Sara couldn't imagine anyone using such filthy language. Faye had called both Neil and Sara every name imaginable, topped by a strange assessment that Sara was "an oversexed nothing," whatever that meant. Faye said she'd already sent copies of her purloined letters to Sara's principal and to the Department of Defense.

It also reiterated Faye's statement that if she didn't pin the stars on Neil, she would "…make damned sure he never got them." Neil's career might be finished. "He'll rot in Hell," Faye had said.

I knew she would be angry, thought Sara, *but the total lack of reason in this letter is frightening. Anyone would be angry to find out their husband loved someone else. But Faye must have known about this for some time if she took at least two letters as she said. And she doesn't love Neil--doesn't even want him around. If she had loved him, he would never have found me. What would be her advantage to wait this long to confront the problem?*

Suddenly Sara knew. Faye had waited to get Neil into the most vulnerable place—War College, on the colonel's list, alone, and far away from her love—so he couldn't protect himself from blackmail. *She knew all along!*

Sara cried for the children she'd come to love. Faye demanded she never again write to Katy or Micki, which meant Sara couldn't mail the letters she'd written in response to theirs, and the children would never know why. Faye wrote, "I told the girls you only pretended to like them to seduce their father. They don't want to hear from you." Faye also said she'd see that the girls "…didn't make it to their father," if he fought for custody. *My God, is that meant as a threat?* There was, of course, the demand that Sara not contact Neil. The PS said, "Neil approved this letter. He never wants to hear from you again. His duty is to me. And don't think Neil ever loved you. He never did, and he never will."

Sara wanted desperately to dispute the letter, point by point. Obviously Faye didn't see her own role in the collapse of her marriage. Everything for her was always someone else's fault—usually Neil's. But, if Sara answered the letter, Faye would have further "proof" of Neil's affair to use against him in court.

She had faith that Neil would straighten out the untrue tales told to the girls. But then, she didn't know for sure what had happened. *What if he had simply given in without a fight?*

If Faye had actually sued for divorce, she must have done it first. Sara felt sure this letter could be used to prove Faye's unfit character as a mother in the divorce court, since no sane person could write such a letter. But since she couldn't contact Neil, how could she get the letter to him?

Sara had no idea if Faye had completed her threats and Neil's career was already destroyed, or if she'd actually told the girls such lies, or if she'd sued for divorce at all. What if the whole letter was a bluff to make her desert Neil? The shock and fear were too much for Sara. It seemed the end of everything she and Neil had hoped for. She lay back on the pillow and sobbed until her throat ached. *Neil, please call and tell me what to do now.*

The doctor prescribed bed rest to try to save the child, and

Sara wore loose sweaters so friends couldn't tell. Casey spread a protective rumor that Sara needed more time off work to recuperate from her accident. Even as Sara fought desperately to save their son, she couldn't imagine why Neil had not called to calm her fears.

In mid December, Sara felt fluttering again that indicated the baby was still alive, and she decided that he would carry his father's name proudly. She prayed he would be as physically strong as his father. She began wondering how Lisa, Lynette, Katy and Micki would like having a brother with such a large age difference. But she felt sure she and Neil together could tell them in such a way that they would like the idea of a new baby, provided they could be together at all. But with no news, and so much to fear, she dropped into a terrible depression.

By late December, Sara was hemorrhaging. Casey again drove her to the German hospital. The baby was dead, and doctors removed his tiny body. Sara didn't want to go on, and nothing Casey could say seemed to penetrate her uncharacteristic silence. Still, there had been no word from Neil. Sara could not understand why he had not written or called. She mourned their son, alone.

The ski trip a week later was a must, according to Casey. "I know you're weak, Sara, but you need to be with your friends right now. Too much has happened in these last weeks, and you mustn't be alone until this mess is resolved." She was reluctant, but she allowed herself to be persuaded to tag along.

Sara only watched the first day. Saturday night, she and Casey sat in the lounge after dinner, waiting for the rest of their ski group to come down for a Christmas party at their Innsbruck hotel.

"It's too painful to pretend everything is all right, Casey. I can't keep smiling, yet if I stop for a moment, someone tells me, 'You're not yourself. What's the matter?' Neil used to say the same thing happened to him when he walked into his office after a fight with Faye. Secrets are so painful. I have to act normally in my classroom, at the Officers' Club, with our friends, so I can only fall apart with you. I can't share my grief over having lost Neil's baby. I can't tell anyone that the poor little one even existed."

"Sara, you know the miscarriage wasn't your fault. Between Faye's shocking letter, your subsequent collision with the table, and such uncertainty with Neil's not calling to reassure you, your whole system has collapsed in response. But you're going to be all right. Stop blaming yourself."

"I know Neil wanted a boy, another child, and here we had a boy, and now he's gone. I should have been stronger."

Casey was exasperated. "How could you have been stronger without any support? Stop defending him!"

"Casey, I don't know what his situation is. She may be watching him constantly. It's the uncertainty that's killing me. I'm sure he's doing the best he can with a disastrous situation."

"It's hard for me to believe he can't send you a message or, if she really filed for divorce already, he may be alone by now and he could call. Sara, he's been spineless, yet you keep defending him. You haven't heard anything from him since that first note five weeks ago, have you?"

"No." Sara looked down at her shaking hands. "I can't understand his silence either, but I must keep faith that he's trying. If *I* give up on him, he'll have *no one*, and that was always his biggest fear, that no one had ever loved him." Sara was lost in thought for a moment, hearing Neil's words echo in her mind.

"Sara, I told you that if his emotional life got in the way of his professional life, he'd have to sacrifice his emotional life since he never even *had* one before he found you. He'll hurry right back to his status quo just to keep the peace. You must accept that he's already done that in order to protect himself."

"He wouldn't just drop me into this abyss without even telling me I'm the one he's had to sacrifice. He couldn't just shut off his feelings after all we've gone through together, could he?" Sara was beginning to realize that everyone did not see Neil in the same way she saw him, yet none knew him as she did either. Sobs shook her whole body, and she couldn't speak.

The other Wild Bunch skiers started entering the party room. Sara quickly mopped her eyes and shrugged at Casey, knowing her friend would help her keep her painful secrets.

The Christmas party lasted until midnight, but Sara couldn't hang on that long. She gave each of the Wild Bunch skiers a huge popcorn ball wrapped in cellophane and tied with a bow. She had made dozens the night before to bring along on the trip for her friends. It had kept her too busy to take another bottle of pain pills like she'd unsuccessfully tried three days before. To her amazement, all the pills had done was make her even more hyperactive than usual. She had found herself cleaning her apartment in a frenzy of compulsive activity, even down to washing bedsprings. Now, as she bid her friends good night and Merry Christmas, she dragged up the stairs to her room.

Perhaps Casey's right. Neil has already scampered back home, and Faye has already won. If that's so, he should have told me. Doesn't he know that I need him in order to go on? If I weren't around, his life would be easier. Sara was not rational--only wrenchingly, achingly sad.

Alone, she sorted out her options. Continue waiting? For how long? Go to him? It might make things worse. He had apparently let her down. *But I let him down, too. I lost his baby. If I were out of the way, Faye might be kinder to him and the girls. Her letter said I should just die. She's probably right!*

Sara examined the stall shower and located the electrical outlets. Interestingly enough, the hair dryer would reach into the shower. *That would be a quick and easy way, wouldn't it, and it would look like an accident, so my children wouldn't know.*

She removed her shoes and started to undress, then stopped, her natural modesty erecting a barrier. She didn't want anyone finding her naked. The incongruity of someone dead of "accidental" electrocution in a shower with her clothes on didn't penetrate her mindless pain. All she could think of was not being in Neil's way as he fought to protect his career duty and his girls. Nothing else mattered. It didn't enter her mind that perhaps Neil had already solved his problem, and she was not even the deciding factor. *After all, he promised I'd be a part of his life forever.*

Sara stepped into the shower, clothes, hairdryer, and all. The hot water poured over her shoulders and she remembered sharing the warm shower during their nights at Neil's cabin. She had never felt shy with Neil. In fact, she had felt quite natural with him. She could almost feel his hands on her, touching her with the tenderness he had learned from her.

She switched on the hair dryer.

There was a flash like lightning, a crash, and all went dark. *Was this death*, she thought--*just darkness?* She moved her foot and felt sharp glass shards. *What happened?* She slid down in the shower stall. Glass spread around her on the floor. Her mind wandered—nothing had continuity, nothing made sense.

She became aware of shouts and running feet in the corridors. "Where's the fuse box," someone yelled. "Are the lights out on the second floor too?" Someone pounded on her door. "Sara, Sara. Are you okay in there?" She recognized Casey's and Michael's voices calling her. Casey burst through the door and called out, "Sara, where are you?"

Any attempt at secrecy was lost. "I'm in here, she called out, "on the floor in the shower." When Casey stepped into the room, she warned him, "Be careful. I think the light from the wall exploded all over the floor. Don't cut yourself."

Casey yelled at Michael to bring a flashlight. Its beam fell on Sara. "I guess my hair dryer must have short-circuited something," she said, hoping that sounded plausible.

Carefully, Casey and Michael lifted Sara to her feet and Casey threw her over his shoulder to carry her into the bedroom. Her feet dripped blood. He wrapped them with a towel, patiently picking glass shards from her skin. "It's okay here, Mike. You go ahead with the flashlight to help the others. I'll take care of Sara."

Casey sat beside her on the bed and said, "Well?"

"Well, what?" She turned her head away.

"Since when do you use a hair dryer in the shower with running water?"

"I don't know, Casey." Sara buried her head in her hands

and sobbed. "I'm so sorry. I didn't realize it would blow the fuses. Look at all the trouble I caused everyone."

"Why would you do such a thing, Sara? He's not worth it!"

The innkeeper and his wife came rushing into the room. "I'm so sorry," cried the man. "Something must have been bad with the wiring. It's such an old house. Are you hurt?"

Sara quickly told the elderly couple she was all right. "I'll be glad to pay for the damages I caused with such a stupid mistake," she offered.

"Oh, heavens, no. The wiring is very old and obviously needs replacing. Our maid is bringing kerosene lamps for everyone tonight, and we'll get the wiring and lights fixed in the morning." Already the woman was sweeping up glass in the bathroom by the flickering light of a lantern. Sara didn't know what to say except to apologize all over again for her "clumsiness."

After the old couple left the room, Sara had to face Casey. Even in the lamplight, she could see worry etched in lines on his face. "I'm sorry, " she said meekly.

"I'm not leaving you, Sara, so don't even consider it. We can sit here and talk, or take the lantern downstairs to the dining room, but you're not getting another chance."

"I'll be okay, Casey. It was a stupid idea. All I did was mess up others. It's weird to short-circuit the whole building, when I only wanted to short-circuit myself, isn't it?"

"I'm glad you realize that! Now go in there and put on some dry pajamas. I'll sit in this chair until you fall asleep.

And that is the way it had happened. Sara woke to his heavy knock on her door in the morning. "Time to ski."

"But I think…. Maybe I'm not strong enough yet…."

"You're going with us--period!" he said, as he pointed at the door for her to get dressed and come to breakfast. "And keep those bandages on your feet." When she still didn't move, he added, "Do I have to wait here, or can you get your ski clothes on and get yourself down to breakfast without surveillance?"

She nodded, and Casey withdrew.

What an idiot I am, she thought. But her despair was only

that she had failed, not that she felt any less likely to try again. She still felt the same aching void--nothing was left.

Sara was distracted—unable to concentrate as she tried skiing again after so long. While standing at the top of a slope with a young lieutenant ski buddy as they waited for others to catch up, her mind wandered again to Faye's evil letter. "You should die," it had said. Without even realizing it, Sara began sliding backwards. Rusty yelled a warning, but she didn't have enough strength to correct her position before the fall. Her right knee crunched as she fell over the edge in a straddled position.

A miserable bus trip home, a more miserable cast at the hospital, and Sara was sidelined for several weeks with a torn ligament in her right knee that wouldn't seem to heal. Life was untenable. A fellow teacher, Ellen, drove her to school each day, though she had to teach sitting down. She had already missed too much work. Sara's spirits sank even lower. Adding to her searing emotional pain, she now was in constant physical pain as well.

The following week, their chaplain, Leo, held an open house for church members. Ellen had insisted Sara go, crutches and all. "I'm not leaving you here alone when there's a good party, Sara," she said. You've been too quiet lately. This isn't like you. You're the one who normally keeps the rest of us upbeat."

At the party, Sara wandered from room to room on crutches, awkwardly, realizing how painful it was to have to keep secrets from friends when she felt like crying and everyone else was laughing. Finally, she could not stand the hilarity any more and went out into the entry hall.

Chaplain Stewart followed her. "Sara. You've not been yourself. I was hoping you'd come in to talk to me."

Sara shook her head, battling back the depressed tears constantly close to the surface. "I'm fine, Leo. Just tired."

"You're not fine, Sara, and I know why. It's Neil, isn't it?"

Sara looked up, startled. "Why would you say that?" But

her reaction confirmed his statement. Her tears exploded. Leo rushed her into his den and closed the door.

"Sara, I've known about you two for almost a year. I know you were at Graf. I was working part time at the little chapel across the road. I saw your Mustang at his cabin at least twice a week, and gray mud on your car when you returned. And though I know he left to drive out there on Sunday nights, he never arrived until morning, so I assumed he had to be with you.

"Why didn't you say anything? We were so careful. We thought no one knew."

"Sara, I wouldn't have interfered. I've known Neil for years, and he's been happier these last months than I've ever seen him. He's become a whole new person, gaining a sense of humor and delight in life. He was an unhappy, warmth-starved man before. You two are good for each other. Of course, saying that now is a large departure from the advice I gave him years ago."

She tried to stifle her tears to listen. "What do you mean?"

"I advised those two to have another baby to cement their marriage. I can only say in my defense that I was out of my mind. They should never have been married in the first place. Micki was the child that was supposed to glue their marriage together for my mistaken conventional reasons. But the baling wire and bubble gum didn't work. You could shine up the surface all you wished-- the whole thing was phony underneath. I've kicked myself a hundred times since. I'm afraid I believed Faye's statements that it was a temporary problem between them back then. Later, I realized it was much more complicated, and not temporary at all."

Trying to stifle sobs resulted in Sara's ragged gasps for air.

"I've watched you wander around in a fog for weeks," Leo continued, "and I know something must have gone terribly wrong. I thought you'd be in Carlisle with him by now. What happened?"

"I don't really know, Leo." They sat on the weathered leather couch in the library, while Sara explained Neil's confusing letter and Faye's horrible one, followed by the total lack of contact. She did not mention her miscarriage or the two suicide attempts.

When she finished, Leo said flatly, "He would have to be a

totally irrational fool to throw away the woman who loved him to go back to the one who hated him, so I'm assuming he's fighting back, Sara. But you need to know for sure what's happening. You can't go on like this. Either you call Neil, or I will! You know he can't function under Faye's manipulation--not alone. She has always been able to make him cave in. She'll hold the girls and his career over his head to win. You can't let her do that. It's not fair to anyone. He's a good officer, and he'll need you there."

"But I talked with a lawyer friend about this situation, and he said if I were on U.S. soil, Faye might subpoena me and have even more proof in court to use against Neil. He could be court marshaled. And she can get violent when she's angry. I'm afraid of what she'll do to Neil. I don't know what to do."

"Sara, it may be worth that chance. Faye will crucify him, and he'll waste his life trying to get out of a stifling marriage, while you waste your life waiting for him." Leo paused for a moment, thinking. "Of course, you must remember that he's an ambitious man. The military has been good to him, and he feels a debt to repay. He has a bright future, *if* he can stay in. It's hard for a military man to know where his duty lies, but when he's forced to a choice, he'll usually decide to stay in the Army. It may be too much for him to risk. I'm only concerned about you now, and you're fading away before my eyes out of your fear and concern for him. This has to end! We must think about what you need for a change. Call him, Sara." Leo picked up the phone and held it out.

"Don't you see, Leo, I might make things worse. He said in that cryptic letter that he'd contact me as soon as it was safe. It must not be safe for him yet, or he would have called by now."

"I'm only concerned about what's safe for you, Sara. I see before me a 'died in the wool optimist' coming apart with grief. That shouldn't be—an impossible contradiction. Things can't get any worse. You're dying in front of my eyes. If Faye really intended to sacrifice Neil's career or get a divorce herself, she would already have done so." Leo smoothed his thinning hair by running his hand over his head in frustration. "Or perhaps he's not the man you and I thought him to be. Perhaps he's incapable of understanding how much you love him, and what trouble you're in right now. We won't know unless you talk to him."

The chaplain sat back and folded his hands. "Knowing Faye as we do, she will do what protects *her* status and position. She would lose also, if she destroyed Neil's career. I think it's a bluff. The letter she sent you might help him in court. That's why you need to get on the next plane to the States, take it to him, and help him stand up to her threats."

"I don't know what to do, Leo. If I go, he may lose the girls and his career because she would pull out all the stops to hurt him. If I don't go, I could lose him because he'll not be able to fight alone and he doesn't know the situation here."

"Will you at least call him and see if he's still in trouble, so you can get some rest?"

"All right--later tonight. Not now, with all these people in the house."

"And you'll come to the chapel tomorrow and talk to me about the conflict you're carrying around like a ball and chain?"

"Yes, Leo. I keep trying to be as strong as Neil thinks I am, but I know I really can't be. It's almost a relief that you know. It's so hard to keep it all in. Casey is the only one who knows."

The chaplain put an arm around Sara as he escorted her back to the party. "And I'll be here for you while we find out what's happening, so you mustn't worry any more. Let's get back out there and dance with the crowd."

Eyeing her cast and crutches, he laughed and added, "Well, at least you can watch Lois and me dance."

She dabbed at her eyes with a handkerchief.

"They'll never be able to tell you were crying, I promise."

They rejoined the crowd of partiers, while Sara fought to keep her face from showing her inner desperation.

29

Casey placed the call for Sara later that night. Germany and Pennsylvania were several hours apart, so Saturday night in Germany was daytime Sunday for Neil. Casey asked to speak to Lt. Colonel Sedgwick and, surprisingly, Faye called Neil to the phone. Sara took the phone from Casey with shaking hands.

Neil was breathless when he heard her voice. "Wow, I'm *so* glad you called. What a marvelous surprise! You'll never know how much I've needed to talk to you."

Sara could hear the joy in his greeting, but he sounded very normal—not at all like someone under threat of disaster. And why should Faye still be there if she had already filed for divorce?

"I've been terribly worried about you, Neil. Are you and the girls all right?"

"Yes, more or less. Things have been horrendous, as you can imagine, terrible scenes and threats, but they are now settling back down, somewhat."

"So what does that mean?"

"Things are back to the usual armed truce, and I'll be finishing up the War College soon. I should still be on the Colonel's List, and career-wise, I'm on track. How about you?"

"The letter I got from her said she was going to the Commandant, and that she was filing for divorce."

"It didn't happen. I didn't know she had written to you. I'm sorry about that. I can imagine that it was as ugly as the threats made here to me. I had to make concessions, Sara, but things are more or less back to our normal unhappy existence now, until the next conflagration."

"Was your concession not communicating with me?" Her voice trembled.

"Only for the time being, Sara. When the girls are safe, I'm out of here! I'll be able to write you this week while I'm on temporary duty to New York. I'll tell you everything then, Dear. I couldn't write with her here."

"Are you being watched that closely?"

"Pretty much, and it's not easy to talk right now, with her in the next room. In case we have to cut this off abruptly...."

"Should I not have called? Chaplain Stewart said if I didn't, he would. I've been a bit distressed and needed to know if you and the girls were all right...."

"No, we're okay for now, and it's so good to hear from you. Every call I make outward is monitored, but one coming in may be all right. I'm being cautious for now--walking on eggs."

"Then she believes I'm out of your life." Sara trembled. "Am I?"

"No, of course not! I can't say that more emphatically. This lack of communication between you and me is purely temporary."

"Temporary for how long? Until your colonel's promotion comes through?" Sara tried to keep the pain out of her voice, but her tears ran down her face unchecked.

"It's not *all* about that, Sara, but of course, that's part of it. The girls were in deep trouble, but I'm hoping that's calmed down now. You were on another continent, and I had to keep the peace. I needed you here, Darling."

"If you had told me you needed me, I'd have been on the next plane, Neil. You said to wait until you could write--and then you didn't."

"Sara, if you knew what has been happening here. I'm so sorry I let you down, but you were stronger than the girls and...."

"So sacrificing me was the price you paid to keep the peace? I wasn't there, so I was expendable? Is that what you're telling me?" She was sobbing.

"No, Sara, no!" He had lowered his voice to a whisper. "It's not like that at all. I had to make the most horrendous choice of my life. I'll explain it in the letter. Trust me, darling, please."

"Won't you please get a post office box now, so we can at least communicate safely? It's already too late for much of the information we needed to exchange, but I need to know what's happening and what you want me to do--what is safe for you...."

"Please, just keep believing in me...I'm trying...I'm

working things out. Once things are calm and less threatening I can start again."

"Start *what* again, Neil? I've lost everything here, and I don't know what to do now. It all has to be your decision, but I need to know."

"Please don't give up on me, Darling. I'll explain everything in the letter...."

Sara heard the click of a phone. She found herself whispering into an echoing void, "I do love you, you know." Then she heard another click, and the line went dead.

She immediately erupted into gut-wrenching sobs as Casey pried the phone from her hand, replaced it on its cradle and handed her the box of tissues.

"What happened, Sara? Tell me what happened." Casey's worried voice penetrated her fearful crying and she fought to stop the painful closing of her throat.

"I'm not sure." Sara gasped and choked. "I think Faye may have been listening on an extension, because we were cut off in mid-sentence. Oh, Casey. Calling Neil may have gotten him into even worse trouble."

"But they're still together!" Casey's voice was incredulous. "And you're worried about *his* safety! What about yours?"

"I suppose nothing will happen to me, Casey, at least at work. I already took Faye's letter to my principal so she would know ahead of time if any mail came with accusations against me. She said not to worry—that she wouldn't allow such a maniac to criticize me or hurt my career. But *his* whole career is on the line."

Sara was vaguely aware she was babbling inanely, yet she couldn't seem to stop the rambling or slow the speed. *Please God. Something must make sense to me soon!* "The principal said all she cared about was my work with children—my private life was my own. Why didn't Neil do the same thing—just go talk with the commandant himself? Bur perhaps he felt too threatened to think of it. Some officers have divorced and still gone on to promotion, but that was only an early, quiet, agreed-on divorce, not a violent one for adultery. Faye's so vindictive that Neil would lose it all."

She couldn't stop words just tumbling out at random. *What is happening to me?* "And I know Neil worries about the girls. Katy was already talking about never marrying because she doesn't see marriage as a loving and happy place to be. If he goes back to an unhappy marriage, he'll simply confirm Katy's single status, because she'll see unhappiness in marriage as inevitable...."

Casey grabbed Sara's shoulders and shook her to stop her rush of words. "Stop it, Sara! I'm not talking about the girls. Sara, listen to me! I don't even care about Neil's job. I'm talking about your emotional safety. Your life!"

"But I *do* care about his job! He's destined for more. He loves the Army. He has a duty he can't avoid, ever...ever...."

Sara's sobs were out of hand--near hysteria. Casey shook her again and shouted, "Sara, please!"

"Oh, Casey, I tried to do just what he asked of me, to love him because no one else ever had. Now, it's all falling around my ears anyway. He can't protect both the girls and me. He still thinks we can be together later. I'm afraid it will never happen.

"Sara, I can't understand why you still care about him, when he's let you suffer, not knowing, yet here he was safe the whole time. You've always had the problem of putting the needs of others in front of your own. Neil *knows* that. He should have known you'd be more worried about his situation than your own and contacted you somehow to tell you."

Sara could not respond.

"So, if I'm getting all this correctly, Neil and Faye are back together again, the girls are with them, and his career is intact. So where do *you* fit in, Sara?"

"I don't know, Casey. I guess I don't! He says he's there temporarily and we can still—but how can he get free and keep his duty to the Army? I've been so stupid and naive. Neil told me he needed me, and I've believed him, and I've loved him because he needed love so much. I can't just turn off all that love now. This hurts so deep inside...physical pain, Casey. What am I to do?"

Her voice came in sobbing gasps. "I'm beginning to understand why Gary worried about what would become of me if he died first. He said my heart went to those who needed me, and while he could protect me, perhaps no one else ever would." Sara buried her face in her hands. Casey could barely hear her choked voice. "I thought it was impossible that I could ever lose him. And now look at me. Gary's dead, Neil's gone, and I obviously didn't know how to protect myself at all." The sobs were uncontrollable.

Casey could only sit and wait. Finally, after many minutes, Sara took a ragged breath and grew unnaturally calm. "You know, Casey. Faye was right. I really don't deserve a life. But I'm really tired, so I'll say good night. Thank you for standing by me."

"Are you sure you're all right now?" The more he asked, the more Sara simply nodded and smiled. She could see his reluctance, but finally, Casey, her last link to reality, left her alone.

All day Sunday Sara hobbled aimlessly on her crutches and watched the walls, never answering her phone. Day after day, it hadn't seemed worth getting up in the morning. Depression engulfed her in long sweeps at unexpected moments, spoiling even a reasonably good day. In her innermost soul, she knew Faye could not touch the companionship she and Neil had felt for each other. But Neil seemed to think he had to pay the price for it, anyway.

Much later, after midnight, Sara needed to teach the next day, yet she spent more time fighting tears. *I can't make it alone again. Neil and Gary both gone...nothing I could do for either. Can't stand any more of this fatigue. I must get some sleep no matter what. Maybe something will change in the morning.*

Only shivers and sobs came, instead of the needed sleep.

She picked up a book she'd been reading for Book Club. Sylvia Plath's The Bell Jar was probably not the best choice for a depressed person, but it was the club's pick, and she'd been wading through it. A sudden insight made it seem quite logical. If one had no one to live for, and didn't know where to go next, and was not needed by anyone—certainly Neil did not need her now-- good old Sylvia Plath knew how to check out the painless and easy way—much easier than electrical hi-jinks anyway.

Sara slithered her bathing suit over the cast on her leg and pulled it up. She wouldn't have to worry about being found naked. She couldn't get Faye's statement out of her mind. "You should die." Neil had taken Faye back--nothing else mattered anymore.

She rummaged through her kitchen's junk drawer to find razor blades she kept for cutting bulletin board letters. Something was caught. She jerked the drawer, and out flew a package of Lucky Strikes. She was surprised, remembering that she used to keep an extra pack for her old friend Skip, because often, when he came out for a walk, he had worked late and had already run out. Since German stores weren't open at night, and he chain smoked like a chimney, it was easier to keep a pack on hand so they could walk in peace without his nervous fidgets. She hadn't thought of Skip's midnight walks for a long time, and briefly wondered how he was doing with his alcoholic wife and his little boy in California.

She set aside the cigarettes and found the razor blades.

With some quiet music playing on her tape cassette, and a bathtub full of hot water--*Sylvia said it had to be hot*--Sara poured in some bubble bath. *What the heck...use it all...what does it matter now?* She emptied the bottle, laid the razor blades on the side of the tub, and climbed in. It was an awkward act, since she had to prop her cast up on the side of the tub to keep it from getting wet, though why that should have mattered, she wasn't sure. Sylvia was right. With everything hurting, and with no further purpose to her life, what did it all matter? Her mind drifted away to happier days, with Gary, with her children, with Neil. Nothing seemed worth any more pain. She felt alone and unneeded. Her whole body and soul simply demanded rest.

As she reached for the razor blades, there was a knock at the door. At first, she ignored it, since it was at least two in the morning, and she was expecting no one. But the knock came again, harder, more insistent. She remembered that the young girl in the apartment across the hall was overdue with her first baby, and her husband was out on alert at the Border. *What if she had gone into labor and needed help?*

Awkwardly, Sara managed to slide her cast over the side of the tub, roll out to the floor, and pull on her robe, though bubbles crept out of its collar. Hobbling on her crutches, a wide swath of dripping water followed her through the entry hall.

She opened the door and there, curling his tall, lanky frame against its jam, was Skip!

In her surprise, Sara could only mumble, stretching one arm toward the kitchen, "I...I just found your cigarettes in the kitchen drawer."

His grin erupted into laughter. "Are you going to invite me in, or do you want me to smoke them out here in the hall?"

Sara sighed, looking to the heavens in frustration. But out loud, she said, "Of course, Skip. How nice to see you. Come on in. Sorry, I'm drippy at the moment, but I was in the bathtub. Let me go get some dry clothes on, and I'll be right back. Please, sit down in the kitchen--and have one of your cigarettes."

She hobbled back to the bathtub, let out the water, peeled out of the wet bathing suit, and dried herself off. After donning a warm running suit, she examined the razor blades. Finally, she sighed, and tossed them into the wastebasket. *Okay, I give up, God. You just aren't going to let me get away with this, are You? Three tries--three ridiculous and impossible interruptions. Whatever it is You still intend for me to do--wherever You think I'll be needed, please let me see Your plan, so we can get on with it.*

Skip sat at the kitchen table while Sara fixed some hot chocolate, and he carried it to the living room sofa as she hobbled along behind him. They chatted amiably about her cast and the ridiculous injury that caused it, his home in California, his little boy, and his new job. Finally, she just had to ask, "Skip, what made you come here tonight, of all nights?"

Skip looked a bit sheepish as he hunched his shoulders over the coffee table. "This is going to sound pretty dumb. I think you knew I never got another command after they found out about Helga's drinking problem, so I left the Army and began working for a civilian contractor. I came to Germany on business--a meeting tomorrow at 1000 hours in Nürnberg. I tried to call you from Frankfurt, but you weren't home."

"I was sort of avoiding the phone--sorry about that."

"Well, I gave up on seeing you because I knew a hotel room was waiting for me in Nürnberg, and I was running quite late after the charter plane landed. But as I drove down the *Autobahn* and started past your exit, I found I just couldn't go by without turning off and coming to check on you. Something nagged me into thinking you needed...I don't know...just *something*...a friend?

"Anyway, I was cursing myself all the way up the road figuring you'd think I was crazy coming at this hour, that you'd be angry with me for bothering you, yet I couldn't turn back." He paused, scrutinizing her eyes. "This feeling that I *needed* to come just wouldn't go away--and here I am."

"That's about as crazy as your cigarettes popping out of my kitchen drawer, tonight of all nights, making me think of you. Maybe we were just on the same wavelength for a few moments, and you 'got my message.' Anyway, whatever brought you to my doorstep once again, I'm glad you came--really."

They laughed and talked. Sara was surprised she could still laugh about anything, but she found that she could. It was an odd revelation, since it seemed like an eternity since she had last heard her own laughter. Her gloomy feelings lifted a little as she listened to Skip describe his full-time housekeeper.

"She's a grandmotherly lady who runs both Helga and Stefan around like a sheepdog herding her flock. She keeps them out of trouble while I'm at work. Heck, she even runs me around when I'm at home."

They both chuckled at the thought of a little five-foot matron ordering a seven-foot giant around the house.

"Has it helped to have her in the house, though?"

"Yes, it has. She loves Stefan and takes care of Helga. That leaves me free to earn a living for all of us, though I'll admit I'm sublimating my own desire for something more from a marriage than mere existence. Life gets complicated, doesn't it?" He looked pensive for a moment, then asked? "And what's complicating your life these days? I see some heavy sadness in your eyes."

"Same thing, I suppose, Skip. Love—the need for it, the fear of accepting it—or of not accepting it when it happens to come along—the pain it can bring. Do you think all our concerns about it make it seem more important than it really is? Some people seem to manage to live their lives without it, assuring themselves that there's no *need* for love in their lives."

She cupped her hands together in her lap as though catching some invisible cascade, and sighed. "I've finally fallen in love again, Skip, and now I feel this burning necessity to make only one certain person happy--to feel needed again. And I'm afraid it's not ever going to happen. There must be a message in there somewhere, but it escapes me at the moment."

"I know what you mean. I've sublimated all my feelings into seeing that Stefan is raised safely. I couldn't leave him behind. Of course, the pain of missing something important is still hovering in the background of my life."

"Do you suppose it ever goes away? The pain, I mean?"

"I hope so. I'll let you know if I recover some day." He smiled and took her hand. "Sara. I know you would never mean to hurt anyone. Somehow whatever is hurting you now will pass. If this person knows how much you love him, he's a fool not to run right back here to your door."

She smiled. "Absolutely, *if* he knew. We can't talk together right now. I'm having trouble accepting the results of that lack of communication. I don't know what it means. I think he may have given up our dreams, and I know he can't leave his children behind either. I wouldn't want him to." She looked at Skip, shaking her head in wonder. "And I just realized with your arrival tonight that I've not been thinking rationally for some time, either."

"Not knowing is the hardest, isn't it? Remember that you are a worthwhile person in your own right, Sara, whether this guy has the good sense to make wise choices or not." Skip put his hand under her chin to make her look at him. "Understood?"

She nodded, tears trembling on the edges of her eyes. "Understood, Skip. Thank you."

Maybe I've just understood more than you'll ever know,

Skip, she thought. *You saved my neck this time, and now, I think, just maybe, I've turned a corner. I guess God still has plans for me or I wouldn't have been such a failure at doing myself in. Besides, now that I think of it, dying really wouldn't help anyone, not even Neil. After all, it was Faye's idea that I didn't deserve to live—that I should just die. Why on earth should I allow myself to be so influenced by her as to let depression take over completely? How foolish to give in to Faye's wishes, of all people. She's trying to use us all, and I very nearly let her do it. That's dumb, Sara...get your head together!*

During her thoughtful silence, jet lag began to catch up with Skip. Sara noticed him nodding. She rose and got a blanket, playfully pushing him over on the couch to a prone position, even though his feet hung off the end of the couch. She put a sofa pillow under his head and wrapped the blanket around him.

"I'm sorry," he mumbled, yawning. "Guess I was more tired than I thought."

"It's late, and you couldn't drive to Nürnberg safely now. Get some sleep and I'll make sure you get to the meeting on time."

"Sara?" His voice was softer and slower.

"What, Skip?"

"Was I right in coming? I wasn't wrong about your being in trouble? You *did* need help, didn't you?"

"Yes, I did. I'm grateful you came to the rescue. Thank you, my friend. I think I'll be okay now. But you need rest." She kissed him on the forehead and headed for her own room, shaking her head at what an extraordinary evening it had been.

Sara woke early, as always, and prepared for school. Skip was still asleep on the living room couch. He looked so peaceful, she didn't want to wake him. She set her alarm clock by his side so he'd wake, eat the hard-boiled eggs, toast, and coffee she left for him in the kitchen, and still make it to Nürnberg on time.

She went to school and somehow completed her day in

better spirits. Her students were lively and, for a change, she noticed and relished each thing they did. *Where has my mind been that I've missed the joy I normally feel in teaching?*

She felt ready to wait for whatever life held. She knew she and Neil loved each other and would always be best friends. That knowledge would have to be enough to hold her steady until they could at least talk things over. He said it would just take more time, and she had the time to give him now—since she had vowed to stay alive to see what happened next.

She laughed at herself. *It's just too impossible to kill myself anyway, with everything and everyone popping in to stop me.* It felt good to laugh about what had almost been a fatal decision.

On her way home, she puzzled over what mysterious force had brought an old friend to her just in the nick of time. *God, do You send angels in seven-foot sizes?* Smiling, she pictured gangly Skip with wings. She mounted the steps carefully, on her crutches, wondering if perhaps she had imagined the whole late night visit and had just somehow come to her senses on her own. But when she entered her apartment, the "apparition" was, of course, gone, but *every* ashtray in the apartment was full! *Thank you, Skip.*

He'd be flying back to California to his own personal brand of loneliness. She wished him courage to get through. She knew she needed courage, too.

Eventually, days dawned warmer. The chill inside her heart seemed to dissipate as Sara watched rabbits coming out of their burrows and jays sitting on her windowsill. She noticed nature again, and she hoped the remaining numbness would wear off soon. Perhaps the depression that had completely paralyzed and immobilized her life was lifting. She would simply have to trust that she would understand what God's plan for her was someday.

30

June 1983—over two years later   Sara sat at her
dressing table, gazing absently into the mirror at the reflection of
her luggage on the bed, already packed for her summer trip to the
States. It was much more difficult to look at her own reflection.
Three years of waiting and, in spite of a busy, active life and many
friends, she was lonely. It showed in her eyes.

Idly, she picked up the stacks of letters from Neil that kept
her hoping. They were all loving and newsy--still asking for more
time to resolve his difficult situation. But could it *ever* be resolved
with his military duties expanding? Was being together possible?

Yes, she still loved him, and she knew he loved her. But
she missed his closeness—being able to reach out and touch him
on an everyday basis. It had been a long time now that they could
not be together where they both felt they belonged. Touching had
always been their special language, something warm between the
two of them. And now….and now…they were still an ocean apart,
and could see each other only rarely, for a day or two at a time
when she went home for summer vacation. Their relationship had
become a long distance one, waiting for Neil to get his life
straightened out. They relied heavily on almost daily letters and an
occasional phone call to sustain and support each other.

Sara laughed with a trace of bitterness. *Faye couldn't even
call me "the other woman" in Neil's life. We see each other so
seldom, yet I know she still dangles me over his head.* Sara
couldn't avoid feeling that perhaps she should give up on love
entirely. Perhaps she was never meant to have it again.

She struggled to think of something else. The letters lay in
her lap and, distracted, she looked through a few of them. She
picked up one letter that made her laugh. She particularly enjoyed
it when Neil tried to give her a "lesson" of some type.

March 1983 – Washington DC
"Dearest Sara: You always say it is hard for you to

write a short letter. Let the old pro give you a demonstration. Here goes:
1) I am: physically fit, lonely, handsome, tired, overworked, slightly sick (VietNam Agent Orange again)
2) I love: little girls, warm puppies, Washington Redskins, German beer, old Alpine Inns with attics, skiing, battlefields (especially at night), walking in the rain, good conversation, good books, Rhine River castles, handball, affection, good wine, Boston Celtics, classical art, white fuzzy rugs
3) I hate: fat, gray hair, sloth, bigotry, gossip, profanity, Dallas Cowboys, humidity, good-byes, romance novels, politicians, American beer, rock music, broken promises, lost romance, empty wine bottles
4) Children: fine. #1 on swim team and at Asoteague summers, #2 doing well, some illness, believe Vietnam A.O. also. Starting to hope she and I were not killed in VN and didn't know it.
5) Promotion possibilities: good--you were right (did I tell you that before?)
6) Future events: I will be at the office phone, waiting for your call.
There darling, all the news in only a few lines. Of course, it helps to keep a letter short when I haven't much to say, except I need your companionship, miss you, and love your letters, long or short. Love, N"

The letter brought a smile to her lips, until she remembered that the Agent Orange condition had cropped up a few times over the years, and she had a chill thinking it might presage some early onset of disease. But then his War College physical had only hinted at it and promised him a long life. She shuffled through the letters looking for that one. Finding it, she read again:

February 1981
"My Dear: You asked about the results of my intense top to toe physicals for the War College doctors. I

think they want to know if all of us are healthy enough for them to invest in our education to be generals. Will we live long enough to be 'cost-effective?' The psychological part claimed I had more than normal ambition. I know you will laugh at that. Physically, they practically named me Superman--say I will live until 84. Will you grow tired of me by then? Agent Orange was the only unknown quantity, but several others had been exposed as well. Good night, my only love, Neil"

Yes, she had worried with increasing concern about his health. The newspapers were filled with stories of cancer attributed to Agent Orange. Was it something about which he should be more concerned or watchful?

She picked up another letter that had made her cry at first--and laugh when she got his return answer, but it had explained a lot. During one of Neil's early attempts to leave home, Faye had called in the "big guns," Neil's father, whom he had spent a lifetime trying to please with little success. His dad's fire and brimstone admonishments for him to renounce his "sin" and perform his lifetime "duty" to his angry wife caused him to write Sara how he must "atone for his sins by polishing up the halo of honor and integrity."

Sara had been hurt and angry to be labeled Neil's "sin" when all she had done was to love him after Faye had thrown his love away and threatened to run him through with a knife. She heartily resented his saying he had been "hedonistic" to fall in love and had forgotten his duty to Faye--and suddenly Faye was the one his father felt should be the recipient of this "halleluiah chorus."

However, when she wrote a letter that was rare for her, filled with anger and pain, she reminded him that they had prayed together many times for guidance and had felt God had brought them together for a reason in their darkest hours. She had asked him where he had gotten "...such holier than thou, pompous, pig-headed, and sanctimonious, Jonathan Edwards style ideas." She had added,

"And if you are ascribing hedonistic motives to our love, I'm offended. We both know we never intended to fall in love. Had we been 'hedonistic,' we could have simply run away together and never looked back-- ridden roughshod over Faye, the girls, convention, and our responsibilities. We chose instead to try to work within the legal system to save the girls pain, and we've waited years to save Faye's pride and the Army's control. Our promises to each other were voluntary, never extracted by 'threat' as she has demanded of you."

Neil had quickly written, confessing his father's influence.

May 1981
"Darling: I'm so sorry I wrote that ridiculous letter. I haven't felt so helpless and sinful since the teacher whacked my knuckles with a ruler for pulling Mary Jane's hair in the third grade.

I got the lecture of a lifetime...all about my duty to 'the woman God gave me.' I couldn't make him understand that I felt God had given me you--that Faye wasn't from God—she was my own dumb fault, a mistake of my youth. I was called into question for my 'hedonistic actions' in allowing myself to love anyone else. My Dad's answer to my plea to at last be happy with you was, 'It doesn't matter if you are happy or unhappy. God expects you to do your duty and raise your children with Faye. You have no right to love. Love is only an illusion. It is duty that rules man's life in God's eyes.'

Dad was in fine form, and I couldn't worm myself away from those piercing eyes of his-- demanding my solemn promise that I would never see you again, and that I would 'stay with my duty as long as I live.' It was terrible, because I love my dad, and he made me feel I was letting him down personally--as though his judgment and God's were one and the same. His is a God without pity or solace apparently--

not our loving God who seemed to know our needs
and who brought us together. Forgive me, my love."

In response to his explanation, Sara had understood where Neil's hurtful and uncharacteristic words had come from. In his father's presence he was once again the "fat, dumb, and ugly" little kid who desperately wanted to please the harsh old farmer. It didn't matter that he was now a Colonel and a respected engineer. It didn't matter that he had financially supported his parents and put his siblings through college. It was still "Little Neil" facing his beloved father who could find nothing in his life he had done *right*.

The letter continued:

"I'm a grown man, and supposedly I've done some
things right with my life, yet in the presence of my
Dad, I still feel the pain of his disapproval. I always
seem to have a problem standing up for myself, don't I
darling? I need your strength to prop me up whenever
I stop believing in myself.

I never should have written you that letter. You
are absolutely right that I was pig headed,
sanctimonious, all of those things, plus I should add to
your list spineless and cowardly, especially where my
father is concerned. I'd rather face death by a
thousand Viet Cong. I just cannot bring myself to hurt
him by telling him to go jump into his lake of fire and
brimstone. Perhaps some day he will understand me
better, hopefully before we both die."

Sara smiled thinking how she had hurled those words at Neil in anger--something she never had done before, but the words had brought him to understand that he would have to stand up to others, not only as he did in the Army, but in his private life as well. They had resolved the issue between them and had continued sharing their messages of hope that one day they could be together.

She looked in the mirror and didn't feel as hopeful now.

Of course, there were dozens of letters of an intellectual nature too--the ones where he had offered book lists for their shared reading and debate, critiqued each others' writing and speeches, or one strange letter where he had asked her to write a former classmate of his. She had done so, and received this reply:

> *September, 1982 – Ft. Monroe*
> *"Darling, I'm eternally grateful for the letter you helped me write to George Finn. When I got the letter he sent to all our West Point classmates trying to recruit them to boycott the Pentagon for his anti-war causes and become "activists for peace," I was so angry I just couldn't seem to find the words to answer him. I'm so glad you could. You instinctively knew exactly what I was trying to say, and you turned my words into a more forceful yet more tactful argument than I could have done. I received kudos from class members. George has never responded, but he has not sent any more anti-war pitches to his West Point classmates either.*
> *As always, I count on you when I am in need of comfort. Thank you for always being there. Your loving words keep me going when my mind tells me I cannot go on. Love always, Neil"*

Yes, intellectually, they still relied on each other, and that wasn't a bad thing, she thought. They kept each other's minds active and stayed involved in each other's lives through their speeches and writing. It was at least something--but perhaps not enough for a lifetime.

Her fingers touched one letter with a photo of him running in a race. She grinned as she read the caption he had written underneath:

> *"Enclosed for laughs is a picture of a friend of mine. Good old Walter Mitty, entering the Coliseum to win the Olympic Marathon. Actually it is in Williamsburg…"*

There had been many loving words that she had needed to carry her through the lonely wait. She removed a couple of well-worn missives from their envelopes to read yet again for courage.

> *July 1982 Washington DC*
> *" My love: You restore my soul. Seeing you on your way west made everything seem possible, and I feel 10 feet tall. Whenever I look in your eyes and am confronted with your gentleness and loyalty, I feel a stab of pain that you deserve so much more in life than I've been able to give you. What am I to do? I need you in my life. Love, N"*

> *August 1982 The Pentagon*
> *"We do not handle good byes well, do we, Love? I don't want us to have any more goodbyes.*
> *Darling, I want you to know that over our time together, you have helped me to see life as richer and more enjoyable. What comes to mind is everything from our collaboration of the minds, sharing poetry, literature, history, and our stimulating debates, and learning to laugh again, to our lovely winter walks in the countryside, and rainy days hand in hand. You have given me a loving intimacy that I yearned for so very much, but had never known--all wonderful.*
> *The softer side of me came out. You said it had always been there, buried, but I know it would never have emerged without you. All we've had together are things that I had never enjoyed before. With you, I've come to realize that a wonderful part of life was out there and I'd been missing it. It was a new world. I feel bad that things have become so complex now. We dreamed of more, sooner, rather than later. I must see the girls safely through before I can get my freedom, dear. You and I have agreed on that, since we both know they could not handle being in the total custody of Faye's anger and humiliation. And we both love them. Good night, my only love, N"*

As always, his loving words brought tears. Sara wiped her eyes, wondering how it could presage anything good for a lifetime, when loneliness for Neil always made her cry.

She knew and understood his concern for the girls, but the Army was a big concern as well. He wrote in early 1983:

"Faye's game is manipulation. I guess all these years I didn't understand that, for her, it's all a game—one where she holds all the game pieces so I can't seem to ever win. I wish I worked for Kodak. If I did, a divorce, or a scandal, or whatever, would be no one's business but my own. But I'm a soldier, my love, for better or worse, and I must resolve to somehow see the girls and the Army through. I owe the Army my allegiance for educating me and giving me a career I love when, otherwise, I would never have had that opportunity. You know me so well, Dear. She claims that I always start the arguments. I don't even know any more, I'm so frustrated. Perhaps I do. Love, Neil "

Sara's own melancholy and frustration had pierced through their correspondence as well:

"By the way, I miss you too, Love. I manage to stay as busy as I can with ski trips, school events, volleyball games, and the usual friends, but it is never the same as having you with me. I miss just yakking over hot chocolate in my warm kitchen, and don't even get me started on how much I miss lying on the fuzzy rug watching the candlelight change patterns on the ceiling, and listening to good music, and, and, and....I don't need to say it...you already know. Memories! I will persevere...you too...we'll survive all this somehow, and still be friends...Love you, Sara"

Sara knew Neil could not leave his girls. Neither could he withstand the loss of the career he loved when Faye kept brandishing her twin threats of adultery court marshal and possible child abuse charges. Though logic said that sooner or later Faye would tire of the game and let him go, it was becoming apparent that he could never win, and Faye did not intend to be logical.

Sara was also concerned by Neil's constant references to her moving back to the States. She couldn't go back to live there as his lady friend in the shadows. It wasn't her style, nor his either. But he had never yet found the right moment to gain his freedom. He couched his requests in patriotic terms, such as, "Why do you like Europe so much? America is the place for you. Come home."

Why didn't he understand that she was not a continent away from him by choice? She needed to work. Sara dismissed a cold shiver in her spine, fully aware that he might never be able to make a legal place in his military life for her. There might always be something to keep him in Faye's little box.

I need to finally ask him what his long-range plan really is. Does he even have one, or are we simply bouncing along in limbo, waiting for the impossible? She feared her original estimate of ten years, which Neil had so vehemently denied, could be more accurate than his assessment of two months--the two months that had turned into years. She had been living her life "on hold" for a very long time, and it hurt.

How much longer could she wait for Neil before she became the clichéd old maid schoolteacher, bitter and isolated? How long could Neil keep fighting for an independence from Faye that would never come?

Sara heard Casey's knock at the door, right on time to drive her to the airport in Frankfurt. She quickly shoved the stacks of letters into her vanity drawer and rose to go meet her friend.

Casey was particularly somber on the drive, with his pending departure for another assignment only four months away. He had extended his career moves twice to remain in Germany by transferring from unit to unit rather than taking a Stateside assignment. But now his time really was running out, and he seemed to Sara not to be very happy about his transfer, even though it would bring a promotion.

Finally he broke his silence. "Will you see him this time?"

"Yes. He's picking me up at Dulles Airport."

"Do you think you'll finally decide what you want to do?"

"Casey, we both know there's no solution until he can find one. But, I'll admit I'm tired and depressed and lonely, and I'm aware that I might be spending the rest of my life waiting for him to gain freedom I don't know if he even wants anymore. We're both tired, and every month spent apart only seems to get him deeper into his rut, which is still protecting the status quo."

"You know, don't you, that my offer is still good. You could go with me, and we could at least keep each other company."

"That's sweet of you, Casey." Sara looked away out the window at the cars speeding by on the *Autobahn.* "You've helped me through all my sorrows and pitfalls. I can't even imagine why you would want me around. But I can't seem to make my love for Neil vanish simply because I'm being hurt by it."

"You need protection--solace--a safe place to rest from these grinding cycles of hope and pain. You need out of the squirrel cage, Sara. I can offer you that safe place, and I won't let anyone hurt you ever again."

"But, you know…you know I don't…"

"I'm not expecting some heart-popping, adolescent love, Sara. I know you don't have that to give, and I probably don't either. But we're good friends. There are lots of things we like to do together. Heck, I'd be content with just a good partner at playing cards. I'm not expecting anything from you--just to be good buddies like we've always been. I think we could have a comfortable relationship for the rest of our lives. We get along well. We could just continue on, taking care of each other as we grow older, and we could put residual pain behind us."

"I've waited a long time for Neil…."

"And I've waited a long time for you…."

"I never knew that." Sara looked sideways at Casey's profile, his hands firmly on the steering wheel. "I've relied on you so, I would never have meant to hurt you."

"I realize that, Sara. But I simply hoped one day, if I waited around long enough, you'd come to your senses and accept that it was never going to happen the way you and Neil wanted it to, and you'd both give up on each other." He laughed. "I suppose I wanted you as a friend too much to risk losing our friendship by asking you to care about me and having you say no."

Sara was flustered, surprised. She couldn't quite manage to see Casey in this new light so suddenly. "Case, I've always cared about you tremendously...I just never thought...I never realized...Gosh, Case...I can't even stop stuttering and think of something to say...."

"Don't say anything, Sara. Just keep it in mind and think about it later. It could be some sort of companionate marriage, just so each of us had someone around that we genuinely like, so neither of us had to be lonely. I just can't imagine not having you around, and I want to keep you safe--that's all."

Sara had tears in her eyes as she touched Casey's arm. "Case, I just don't think I could love you the way you deserve. You've been so loyal and such a good friend to everyone. I wouldn't want to take you out of the running for some lovely lady who would be *so* lucky to find someone as kind as you."

He chuckled. "Haven't been looking for any lovely ladies for several years now, Sara. Don't think I'm going to find any if I'm not looking, right?"

"But you could. Casey, you don't want me...I'm a mess."

"That's not the way I see it. I've always thought that all women should take 'Sara lessons' so there would be enough of you for every man. You're the compassionate heart, the one to whom all can come with their troubles. You could have had any of us you wanted--you just chose one who should have taken better care of you--that's all. I know I can take better care of you--at least I would always be there so neither of us would have to be lonely or regretful."

Sara looked away, wondering what she could say to such an offer. Of course, Casey was right about part of it. She *was* tired of hurting. Rest and safety sounded good after wanting so long what she might never have. But she could never love Casey in the way she loved Neil. They were loving friends, and that was all. It wouldn't be fair to him.

As though reading her mind, Casey said, "I know you don't love me in the same way, Sara, and maybe you never will. Though, I've come to believe we can love many people, just in different ways. You loved Gary in a different way from Neil, didn't you?"

When he looked at her, she could only nod.

"Then maybe you'll love me in yet another way. That's okay. I'll take my chances. Wait until after you've seen him. See what he has to say this time, and how you feel afterward. Perhaps you'll be tired of it all and will take me up on a life together. You don't have to tell me until you get back—in fact I don't want you to answer until after you've seen him. I guess I'm hoping that maybe—just maybe—you'll come on back home to me. Either way, I'll understand, and I'll still want us to be friends."

He pulled up to the curbside check in, and a porter took Sara's bags. There were only minutes before she would board her flight and she had not words--only tears welling up in her eyes. Quickly, she hugged Casey good-bye and ran into the building, anxious to get on the plane and escape from any further conflicting thoughts and painful decisions.

As the plane flew across the Atlantic, Sara gradually began to lose her blue outlook, in anticipation that she would soon be with Neil. But the nagging thought wouldn't go away completely. *How long can Neil and I keep living on hope alone?*

And why on earth did Casey, a friend I've relied on, hit me with this shocker at this point in my life?

31

Neil met her a few hours later at Dulles International Airport. He'd come straight from the Pentagon, still in his dress green colonel's uniform.

He held her tightly, breathing in her scent and absorbing her warmth. She regaled him with light-hearted stories of her latest travels on their way to dinner, and they shared news over Kung Pao Chicken and fried rice. As always, they were filled with communicating and touching, as comfortably as though they'd never been apart. He couldn't stop smiling.

"God, it's hard to have so little time together to catch up with everything at once," he said. "I want so much more of you."

"I know, darling," she said. "Whenever we meet, it's always like this, isn't it? We keep hoping *this* year will be our year to have no more goodbyes." Her smile warmed him, though he sensed that she wore it only for him, not for herself. She seemed sad, somehow, and it worried him.

The Chinese restaurant was almost empty at this late hour, and even the ivy entwined up the latticed walls looked tired, but they had the privacy to talk honestly together.

Neil took her hands and looked in her eyes. "Sara, I can't tell you how much I've missed you. Why won't you decide the good old U.S.A. is worth coming home to stay?"

"We've talked about that, Darling. Even if I got my teaching credentials cleared for DC, you'd soon be off to another assignment. And if I gave up teaching and came back to the States, where would I live? Alone? Where would I work—some 7/11 with no insurance and no retirement? We've both about reached the top of our careers, but you know I'd give mine up in a heartbeat and come to you, *if* we could marry, raise the girls, and be together."

He could feel her searching his face.

"But it still doesn't look like that's possible, does it?"

The question hung between them.

Finally, he answered. "We could still be together, Love--

sort of like we did before in Germany when you came to Grafenwohr and I came to your apartment. We could still live nearby, spend our free time together …" He held her hand tightly, anxious lest she pull it away. "I need you with me, darling. You lift my spirits and we broaden each other's minds…we…"

"Could we spend a Christmas Eve with the girls and help them trim the tree? Could I come to your Change of Command Ceremony? Could I attend Hail and Farewell parties with you and be there for Katy's graduation? Could I fix your favorite dinner and you'd pour my favorite wine for a party of our friends, or even go out publicly with friends? Could we take family vacations together and teach the girls to drive? Would you give my Lisa away at her wedding next spring? Could I someday make Katy's wedding dress? In years to come, would you be the one to play with our grandchildren, and could we take the kids to Disneyland together. Could we…" Her voice broke into a flood of tears.

"Stop, Darling" He put his head in his hands. "I'm only now beginning to see how I've changed your life. I've isolated you by keeping your life and your love all for myself, haven't I?"

She reached out and caressed his cheek. "I love you with my whole heart, and I could never regret loving you—I'll never even be able to stop. It's been a good thing--for both of us--a gift from God who knew we needed each other." She took a deep breath, gulped back her tears, and looked into his eyes.

"But yes, I need to be honest. There have been painful times too. And if you can never get your freedom, I'd always be on the periphery of your life, on the outside looking in, spending all my holidays alone, even if I were in the U.S.A., even if I lived just down the street. That kind of relationship was *never* our dream."

"My dream is to have you with me for always."

"But you've not been able to make a place for me in your life, Darling." She continued, "I need to tell you something now, that I've kept secret for a long time. Neil looked up.

"Do you remember when I called you at Carlisle in early 1981, and I said Faye wrote me a letter before Christmas?"

"That was a long time ago. I remember being worried

because you sounded emotional and hysterical. You knew I was trying to manage the crisis, but I just couldn't get it under control. I'm still sorry I let you down. I've tried to make up for that since."

"Some things were a permanent loss, Darling. I've not told you because I didn't want to make the dilemma you were facing any worse. When Faye's letter came, and you waited so long to write, my whole world fell apart. I never needed your support and reassurance so much. I know you were confused, beset by lawyers, threatened by career loss, and afraid for your children. I worried about those things too. But I needed you, and I lost an important part of my life--of our lives."

She obviously was having difficulty going on. Neil reached out to stroke her hair. "I'm sorry I wasn't there, Love."

"I never told you that I had a miscarriage during that time. Believe me, I had reason to sound hysterical."

Neil gasped, "My God, Sara…."

"After Faye's letter—a horrible one--I tried so hard to save our baby boy, Neil, but I couldn't. I couldn't work for weeks." Sara dropped her head, not sure what his reaction would be.

"My God, I never knew. Why didn't you tell me you were pregnant? I never knew…a son…Sara, I would have…"

"I thought you might've guessed from the 'missing object' we joked about in Gettysburg. Our baby was to be my surprise when you and Katy came for Christmas. You never came."

"Darling, I can't get over this news. You know I would have wanted our baby. I had no idea…."

"I guess that's my point, Darling. How could I have told you when my last message from you was to wait for contact until it was safe? You never called, so I suppose you never felt it safe. I needed you, and our baby couldn't wait."

"I would have found a way to come, Sara! I'm so sorry I didn't know. I wish you had written me?" He held her hands in silence as a lump formed in his throat. "Oh, my dearest…."

"You had no safe place to receive mail. And knowing would have only made your choices more difficult. There would have been no way you could have come to save me. You were saving yourself and the girls. Neither our baby nor I had a chance, Neil, with Faye's threats, with your career on the line...." Sara wiped away tears with her hand.

The waiter kept watching them as though he should provide some service, yet he seemed reluctant to come to the table.

"You had enough to worry about at that moment. And," she looked up at the ceiling to stem the flow of tears, "you had already decided to stay with Faye. I just was the last to know about it."

"No, darling, I made my choice to *leave* Faye, as soon as I could ensure she would do no more harm to all of us."

"It amounted to the same thing, didn't it? And has that point ever been reached? We're both still lonely for each other."

Neil stared into her eyes a long quiet time. "I don't know what to say. My love for you is greater than my heart can hold, yet I wasn't able to spare you pain. It wasn't fair, was it?"

"I guess not. Maybe I couldn't have carried the baby to full term anyway, with so much worry. It's just that Faye's hateful letter killed our child." She sobbed with all the repressed grief she'd hidden years before. "I'm still sad for losing our baby boy."

Neil moved to her side immediately and held her to him, dragging his chair around so he could sit beside her. "My God, Darling, we could have had a child, a little boy! It's excruciating for me to take in. It's so long after the fact, and yet it feels as painful as though it just happened."

"With the loneliness, the crying myself to sleep at night--I felt we had let each other down somehow, and I couldn't even tell you what I was feeling. All I could say was, 'Yes I understand--yes, I'll wait for you--yes I'm fine.' I *wasn't* fine, Darling. I tried to be dead, and I wasn't even able to do *that* successfully."

"Not because you were carrying our child...no...."

"No, of course not." She laid her head against his chest. "Because I wanted our baby and I couldn't save it alone, without you. When I opened Faye's letter, I knew my life was over. She said I should be dead, and I very nearly let her have her way— because... Oh, Darling, I don't know why. You thought I was hysterical, but you'd already taken her back, and I didn't know then about the threats and that you felt you had no choice, or that you thought it was temporary. Without communication, I feared you thought our love was a mistake and maybe you would have thought our child was a mistake too." He could feel her shivering in his arms. "Neil, you believed I was strong, but I really wasn't, not strong enough to do it alone."

He pulled her head again to his chest. "Sara, our love was never a mistake. Our child wouldn't have been a mistake either. And I'm horrified that you would even consider taking your own life. You have so much to give. You know I love you and need you so. You're the best thing that ever happened to me. I was a fool who could fight on a battlefront, but was ineffective on the home front." He lifted her head to look into her eyes. "I'm so sorry, my love, that I couldn't handle it all better than I did. I needed you with me, and you needed me and I wasn't there. We should have never been apart. I don't want to be apart any more."

He held her closely, knowing there was no way he could assuage her pain, or his own. "These three years, we've shared smiles and you've been upbeat and never said a word. You've kept me believing you were all right to protect me, haven't you? We've laughed together, yet the pain you were carrying…. My darling, this will hurt forever. I'm still taking it in."

Neil simply held Sara silently for a long time.

The waiter turned away and went about polishing glasses at the bar, his back to them, trying to give them privacy.

"You needed smiles to 'prop you up,' as you always say. I promised I'd love you as long as you needed me, and I would never allow myself to put extra pressure on you, but now, I just can't pretend I'm okay any more. I'm so tired of holding it in."

"You've always protected me. I just never knew or thought about the price you were paying to do so. I was a selfish fool."

"I had to tell you now because I didn't want to discuss our future with any secrets left between us. It's behind us now. Our baby died, I grieved alone, I eventually survived the depression, and I didn't wind up killing myself, so we're at a new phase. Let's look at our options *now*, Love." She tried to smile at him.

He responded with a rueful shake of his head. "I feel pretty hopeless, my Love. I've tried everything I know. Her threats are always the same, and I'm exhausted from the tension. It's a continuous battle. Every day is a crisis all over again."

"A military man doesn't have many options if his marriage is rocky. It would've been simpler had you worked in a steel mill. A divorce or scandal there wouldn't have been a problem. But you have that 'duty, honor, country' of the military written on your soul, Love, so there's no option for us to consider except how we can help you stay in the Army and do your job."

"Right now, I'm wondering why I *didn't* take a job with that steel mill years ago. It would have been easier for us."

"Because you are a military officer through and through, my dear. Another career was never a consideration for you. A military officer with a leaky marriage has three options."

Neil couldn't help but smile at her analytical approach to all problem solving. It was one of the things he loved about her. "And what are those, my love?"

He can get a divorce, but probably never get another promotion, if the divorce is very visible. Faye still holds infidelity and the threat of child abuse over your head—your divorce would be *very* public. Look at the folks we know--our friend Lex, Ken Warner, Ed Jones…it never mattered whether the divorce was their fault or their wives.' Lex's wife even ran off with another man, but that didn't matter. Those three never made General, did they?"

Neil shook his head. "All those men were good officers and should have been promoted."

"Choice number two," she continued. "The officer can have an affair and spend his time with the woman he actually loves 'on the side,' as you suggested, should I come to the States to stay nearby for you. Not only would I not want to be 'the other woman' the rest of my life, but also, there would always be the threat of a scandal ruining your career anyway. If I were here, and we were together as much as we want to be, sooner or later, someone would see us, and she would take your career down in an adultery scandal. I love you too much to allow that to happen."

"The Army says it doesn't happen in these modern days."

"But we know better, don't we, Love? Look at the most recent example--a four star general cashiered only days before his retirement. They said it was because he disobeyed a direct order. But if you received a direct order to stop seeing me forever, would you do that to save your career? Look at us! We've more or less been trying to live by that kind of direct order from Faye for over three years, yet we haven't been able to stay apart."

She took a deep breath and moved on. "That general had been in love with the woman for many years, and his marriage had been a sham since he was a battalion commander--his wife knew, yet the scandal caused the Army to court marshal him for adultery anyway." She cradled her forehead in her fingers. "Something like that would not only ruin your career, Darling, but also hurt the way your girls see you as well." She paused, with eyes glistening. "And I'd *still* be in the shadows the rest of my life, alone.

"Then there is the third option, and most military men seem to take that path, as the course of least resistance."

"What's that, my love?"

"Exactly what you've been doing these last years, Neil." She looked straight into his eyes. "You went back to a wife with whom you had nothing in common, begged forgiveness, smiled for the world, kept your arguments under wraps, and went on with your career and your life, right through the latest promotion to colonel. It's the easiest for most men--and the result is that they make rank and play out the 'fairy tale' until he can retire with full honors, and then, maybe, if they are not too fully entrenched in the status quo, they get the divorce they've needed for years."

Neil watched anxiously as tears rolled down her face.

"A long time to wait, and I doubt you are any closer to being free now than you were years ago, are you, my dear?"

He choked back his own painful feelings and knew he had to answer as honestly as he could. The only love of his life was searching for his honesty, here and now. "My dear, you know how I've tried, and you know I need a little more time. It's been so hard to persuade Faye to do it quietly. Every time I try to talk about it with her, it becomes a shouting match, and she still holds my career and my children in her hands."

"And it looks like she probably always will, my love. I understand your concerns, and the dangers of confrontation, but these years have been hard ones for me, too. You've at least had the children to keep you going."

I'm going to lose her, aren't I, God? No, please no.

She finally asked the question Neil was afraid to hear. "I'd really like to know, now, if this is ever going to happen for us, or have we been deluding ourselves all this time?"

Neil looked down at the napkin in his lap, then steeled his will and wrapped his arms around the woman he loved, holding her head close against his chest and running his fingers through her hair. His own tears flowed freely now. "I've almost given up, my love. Meeting like this whenever you can come to me may be all we'll ever have. If I'm honest, and I guess honesty is what you want right now, I fear I'm never going to be free in this lifetime."

"You're sure?" She looked up at his face. "God help me, I'd wait for you forever, if I thought there was any chance."

"I've tried all I dare, my love. The problems in gaining my freedom just don't go away. They seem to get more complicated the harder I try. The girls need me to balance Faye's anger, so they don't have to bear it all. She takes most of her venom out on me now, and if I were not there…. " The words died in his throat.

"I must at least see them through college, and even then, Faye has threatened my career and my life, should I leave her. If she killed me, it would be no great loss. But I owe the Army so much--my duty to the Army--and I'd like the chance to finish the job I've started. The aching truth is that I've wanted you by my side through the triumphs because you've been the only one who believed in me during the difficult times."

Neil looked away at the waiter lurking at the bar in an uneasy need to stand by.

Then he wiped his eyes. "But, my love, she holds all the reins with the children, with my career, with my reputation and yours. I've ruined your life and my own. I've thought so long that I could fix it all, and I'm afraid my wishes and good intentions never mattered. I've prayed and hoped, but I've about given up on our chance to be together in marriage, though I'm hoping we can still continue on, if you'll move here just to be with me. I need you so. He searched her eyes for an answer to that suggestion.

She shook her head sadly. "Only if I'm a part of your life, Darling. If you won't ever be free to make that life for us then, for the children's sake, and ours, we need to make this the last time we meet like this. We must stop hoping, my love! It tears me to pieces to hope so longingly for something I'll never have, and I know it does the same to you."

Neil started to protest, but she put her fingers softly to his lips. "Please listen while I'm still capable of being rational, Love. Neither of us can keep on like this forever. There's too much tension for both of us--too much danger of discovery for you--too much exhausting pain for us to wait and wait and still have to say good bye each time."

She took a deep breath, obviously in distress. "Darling, we've both known our being together was against all odds, given your situation. You asked me to love you, to give life back to you, and I've loved you with all the faith I have--and we've been good for each other, haven't we?"

He could only nod, mutely, aware of a sharp pain tearing at his side and his throat.

"You need to do your duty, go off to be a general, and stay with your children. I need to somehow make a life for myself so I don't spend the rest of it waiting and longing for you, alone. We can't go on forever 'giving each other more time.'" Her voice shattered over the words. "We're getting older, and we've sort of run out of time, haven't we, Darling?"

"I don't want to lose you, Sara. I can't go on…."

"You'll never lose me, Neil. We promised we'd be friends forever, and that each of us would always come when the other needed us, didn't we?" She smiled a pained smile he couldn't return. He felt the lump in his throat.

"If you ever need me, darling, I'll be there," she said

quietly. She looked down at their joined hands then raised her eyes to meet Neil's.

"What will you do, my love?" he asked quietly.

"I really don't know, Darling. I've loved you and waited for you so long—and I'm grieving now, trying to accept in my heart that we can't go on together. This grief tears at my insides. I can't even consider ever loving someone else like I love you." She choked on the words and had to stop a moment.

"Sara, you know I've loved only you…I can't bear this…."

"You have your girls to protect, darling, and you have your duty to the Army. There's apparently not going to be a time when you can protect me too." She smiled, ruefully. "I *have* had a surprising offer, though. Perhaps you'll laugh."

Neil looked curiously in her eyes. "What, darling?"

"Casey asked me to marry him. He's such a nice guy. He's stood by me through all these heartaches and painful years. He thinks we could make a decent life together."

"Do you love him? Have you…."

"No, darling. I haven't made love to him--I couldn't, loving you the way I do. It's never even come up. His proposal was a complete surprise. I never knew he thought of me in that way, and I certainly never thought…I suppose I love him in a special way, as a trusted friend. We have much in common--skiing and traveling. Neither of us likes doing those things alone. He thinks we can simply create a life for each other. The couples' world is not welcoming to those who are alone, so he feels it might be easier and safer for us to team up to face middle age and old age--the old age I dreamed of spending with you. It now seems impossible that you and I will ever get there.

"I look in the mirror and see my life slipping away while I'm waiting for you to get free--and now you tell me it's never going to happen. I wanted to grow old with you. But we've been living only for our next letter or our next yearly rendezvous. How long can we continue doing that? I think I only realized how alone I was recently over a silly hurt finger."

"What does that…."

"Bear with me a moment Darling. You'll see what I mean. I slammed my finger in the car door in April. I had to drop the groceries so I could open the car door with my free hand. I picked up the sticky, broken mess one-handed. My finger throbbed as I kept it in ice--every night more painful. A blood clot formed under my fingernail. Finally, I drove myself to the hospital and the doctor drilled a hole through my nail to let the blood spurt out to relieve the pressure. The doctor asked if I had someone to drive me home because I was so shaky. I didn't. When I got home and looked in the mirror, I realized that I'm so alone, waiting for you, Darling, and I'm so lonely. It was such a silly little episode, one I normally would have laughed over, but it made me realize that you would never again be there to help me if I needed you to fill the ice bag, hold me when I hurt, or kiss away the pain. And you aren't ever going to be there, are you, Love?" Her eyes were brimming again.

Neil couldn't speak for a moment, thinking how his love for Sara had set her up for loneliness. "I see what you mean. I can't be there when you need me. I wasn't even there when you needed me most...our little boy...that will haunt me forever."

"Or when you needed me, darling." When you've written about feeling sick--this Agent Orange thing that scares me so--I remembered how comforted you always were when I held you in my arms at night, cuddling your back to keep you warm, or massaging your neck until your headache eased. I can't even be there to make things better for you when you need me. That hurts so much." She reached out to caress his temple. "All I ever wanted in my life was to make you happy and make you feel loved   to make up for all you'd missed. I guess it was just meant to be for a little while. Perhaps it was too much to ask."

Neil pulled her against him tightly, as though he could restore her lightheartedness of years ago merely by wishing things were different. He could see that her lively bubbly nature was subdued, perhaps gone. *Please, God, I don't want this to be happening. I botched the job, and now I'm losing my companion--I love her so completely.*

Words wouldn't come. When he tried to speak, Sara put her

fingertips softly to his chest, caressing him as she spoke.

"I need you with all my heart, Darling, and I love you beyond belief, but I am so tired, and it has been so hard to recover yet again from the pain of losing. I hoped I'd never have to face that kind of grief again. I need sanctuary and rest, now, Neil. You're back where you feel you need to be--with the girls--with the Army. I have no one to go back to…I'm so lonely for you."

"What did you tell him…about me, I mean?"

"Casey? I told him that I would always be in love with you, but we might never be able to make it work. He understood, as he always has. He felt I should come to the U.S.A. this time, see you, and talk it over. He wanted me to see if there would ever be any hope that you and I could be together. Then, I'd make a decision when I returned. He said he'd abide by my decision."

"He's a good man."

"He is. Actually, I think you two could be real friends."

"But you could still tell him 'no?'"

"I could, and I will immediately, if you can tell me that you see any light at the end of this tunnel for us to ever be together. But do you see any? Perhaps we've both been kidding ourselves that Faye would ever let you go, in one piece, that is, with your career and custody intact. And I'm not sure you want me to be alone forever, growing older, still waiting for you."

Her face was anguished. It hurt him to see her pain, knowing it was his inability to act decisively that had caused it.

She sighed. "I'm tired, Darling. I need somewhere to rest."

"I'm so sorry I've caused you such hurt, Love. I see that it wouldn't be fair for me to keep holding on to the dream when it leaves you hanging in limbo. At least, with a good friend like Casey, I know you'd be safe. He would be good to you."

Neil held her close. "I don't know why I could never get control over this dilemma. I guess I was married to the Army as well as irretrievably bound by Faye's threats. And I just couldn't leave my girls. My hardest decisions were always about my anxiety for the girls."

"I love them, too, darling. This sacrifice is for them. I think their lives will settle down and be more secure when you're no longer constantly fighting to find a way out of their home. And with no adultery charges to hold over your head, perhaps Faye will stop threatening your career. You and she can simply ignore each other and that might be more peaceful for you both. But the girls need you in their lives to protect them, darling. Our lives don't matter so much--theirs do." She sighed. "At least you'll be there to love them--for both of us. Maybe someday you can explain that I loved them, too, and that I didn't leave them on purpose, do you think? This must be our safest decision for their future."

"Sara, you've made me happier than I've ever known I could be, than I've ever had a right to be. And you've waited for me patiently all this time. I want you to have a life, even if it's not meant to be with me. It's just hard to accept that you won't be mine. You're such an intrinsic part of my heart and my mind." His tears came once again, and the waiter moved into the kitchen.

Sara ran her hands over his face, touching it softly and putting her cheek against his wet one. He could feel their tears melding together.

"Neil, Darling, I've belonged totally to you ever since St. Veit, and it's been the best time of our lives, hasn't it?" She pulled back to look into his eyes.

He nodded, slowly.

"We've loved truly, Darling. You once told me that loving truly, even if it's lost, is a rare thing--a *complete* life."

"Loving and winning would have been better." He caressed her face, her neck, tenderly trying to memorize the feel of her skin.

"We didn't win, my love. She did." Sara laid her slender hand over his big one.

"It's all my fault, Sara. We loved each other enough to throw everything to the winds, and I hesitated—panicked--at a crucial moment. I lost it all. A decision I'll regret the rest of my life. You've been everything to me, but I can't bear for you to be lonely, either. I wanted you to be my wife, so we could be together forever. It seems we have no chance for that dream now."

"Then perhaps I'll agree to consider Casey's offer when I

go back, if that's to be the joint decision between you and me. At least, you'll know I'll be safe and taken care of. He's a wonderful person, and he cares about me. Neither he nor I want to be lonely for a lifetime. I can make a good life for him too. I'd never hurt him. We're trusting friends. Of course, that's unless you see some other possibility for *us*, my dear, but I don't think you do."

Neil reluctantly bowed his head and slowly shook it, devoutly wishing he didn't need to do so.

Sara tried to chuckle through the tears. "You know this is the weirdest situation, isn't it? I'm actually asking the man I love whether I should marry my friend—for permission to do so." Then the tears became a flood, and she covered her face with her hands.

Neil rose quickly from the table and pulled her out of her chair. He took her in his arms and said gruffly, "Let's get out of here." He threw a sum of money on the table and walked Sara out past the waiter who uncertainly offered fortune cookies.

At their hotel room, they sat together on the edge of the bed while he soothed her spirit and caressed her face. "Seeing you and getting your letters has been all that has kept me going. What will I do without you?" *I can't let her go. All I can do is hold her.* The eternal lump in his throat just wouldn't let him speak further.

"It's going to be all right, Neil. It's been good between us-- our bond will always be strong. We both understand the need to sacrifice our love now--for the girls, for your career."

He was still silently struggling.

"Darling, your dream was always to make a difference for the Army, and you're doing that. We both know she could ruin it all. For you to get tossed out now, when the next step is to be a general where you can truly make that difference--it wouldn't be fair to you, nor to our country." She patted him on the cheek and added, "After all we've been through, and the sacrifices we're making now in giving up the dream, you'd better be the best dad gum general our country has ever seen!"

"You know I'll always love you, don't you?"

"I know. I'll never change either. If this must be our last night together, we'll make it one to remember, won't we, Love?"

"I still see the loyal love for me in your eyes. You can't deny that--no matter what happens." With great tenderness, Neil took her in his arms, and they lay back on the bed holding each other gently until the tears morphed into a feeling of desperation to love each other one last time, that they might memorize the feel of each other's bodies and hold on to their devotion forever.

Hours went by, until they again lay quietly, her head nestled in the "soft spot" on his shoulder and his arms wrapped around her, their legs entwined.

Neil was intensely aware of her body quivering against his. He buried his face in her neck, her dark hair lying over the pillow, and they both cried. "How am I to give you up?"

He choked on the words and had to gather himself together to continue.

Sara waited quietly, while softly stroking his shoulders and chest in the way she knew comforted him.

"We must still have at least our intellectual partnership," he said—"our news, our readings, our debates--because I can't do without your belief in me. You must keep writing to keep up my resolve, my confidence. If I'm ever to make that difference for the Army, you're the only one who ever has believed I could…that I would…."

She nuzzled his ear and rolled over on top of his body so they were nose to nose, toes to toes. She knew it always made him laugh…both of them together…as always.

"You said you know now that you'll never be free in *this* lifetime?" She tried valiantly to smile. "Can we make a date for the *next* lifetime, and you can tell me about how it will be?"

He pulled his face into the smile he knew she needed from him now. "We'll go walking hand in hand along the beach in Maine, my love, and I'll point out the stars to you and we'll watch the sea birds together. I know you don't believe it now, but I'll be there waiting for you, I promise…in our next lifetime…."

32

1994—eleven years later   The young woman
in a Captain's uniform smiled as she saw Sara, and ran across the
cafe for a hug. Sara motioned to a nearby table and they sat to talk.

"You haven't changed, Sara. I would have recognized you
any place," said Katy. "I'm so glad you called me. I've been afraid
all these years that I'd never see you again, and right out of the
blue, you called me--a marvelous surprise. I'm almost ready to go
home to the States for my discharge from the Army, so we might
have missed each other."

"And you're still as bubbly as ever. You look great in
uniform. How is Micki?"

"She's almost finished with her engineering degree and
wants to work overseas. She's done well. I'm in engineering
research too, but I'll probably stay in the States after this
assignment in Germany. I've been away from tacos long enough."

Several minutes passed in excited updates on their lives and
much laughter. Katy was delighted, as though the two hadn't been
out of touch for years. Within minutes she was discussing complex
issues with Sara as comfortably as she had at age fourteen.

"Sara, I'm so angry with my dad." Her face darkened.

"But you two have always been so close."

"I know." There were tears at the corners of her eyes as she
shook her head sadly. "But I can't figure what's going through his
head right now. He must be in mid-life crisis or something. He
waited all this time until he was retiring from the Army and then
he suddenly moved out of my mother's house the same week.
Mom told me how he waited until she was old and helpless, after
she supported him in his career all those years so he'd make
General. Then he retired and walked out on her. She was shocked."

Sara wondered how best to erase this misperception.

"Katy, perhaps I need to tell you something you may not
remember about your parents. There was nothing 'sudden' about

this. And there's nothing 'old and helpless' about your mom, either. She's quite healthy—much more so than your dad."

Sara couldn't help a twinge inside at the thought of Faye's ever being helpless, but she kept her exterior expression calm for Katy's sake. "This event wasn't sudden at all, Katy. Your dad had wanted a divorce since you were a baby, and he had asked for it again and again over many years. Your mom never liked his Army career. He made general on his *own* merit—his *own* dedication to duty--*no one* helped him. And his desire for a divorce wasn't anything new to your mother. She knew a long time ago."

Katy's smoothed the skirt of her dress green uniform with her hands in her lap. "She keeps saying it was all a surprise, and she never knew there was any problem at all. Are you sure?"

"They tried counseling many times, when you were a little girl. Micki was their attempt to try to salvage the marriage. Another child didn't make it any easier because they still had nothing in common. I'm sure they both tried."

The waiter stood at their side as they ordered a light lunch. When alone, Katy asked, "If she knew, why didn't they do it sooner? It's a little late in their fifties."

Sara laughed. "Fifty is not so old, my dear, and it shouldn't be that surprising to you. You may remember that at 14, you were the one who said your mom and dad were like green chips and blue chips and should never have been in the same game."

That quieted Katy for a moment. Sara could see the young woman thinking it through.

Finally, Katy said, "I had forgotten about that. I wonder why I had forgotten that. I guess Mom has told me so many stories since, and I've not lived at home since I went away to college and then was commissioned in the Army. Why did Dad wait so long? Why didn't he leave then? It would have been easier to make a break when they were both younger and could start over."

Sara had no time to respond before Katy thought out the sequence of long-gone events.

"Now that I think about it, though, they fought a lot. I sort of remember that sometimes Mom scared me with her screaming. I guess I thought that was normal. She seemed angry all the time when I was little. She actually took us to New York once, and I didn't want to stay with her. I wonder how I forgot about all that turmoil. Is it repression or something?"

"Perhaps, Katy. We all have a tendency to forget the unpleasant things in our lives. Your dad wanted to go a long time ago, many years before I met you both. He wanted someone to love him, when your mom often said she…just…didn't. But he couldn't leave the two of you. He stayed all those years for you and Micki, because he felt you needed him. Your parents lived under the same roof, perhaps with less friction after he decided he would have to stay, maybe because they avoided each other and tended to their own interests. It may have seemed as though they got along better, and you simply forgot about the terrible arguments of long ago. There was a lot you didn't know."

"I'm still surprised I didn't remember that." Katy tried to focus on the past. "It's more clear to me now. I'm remembering a lot more. I thought then that my mom hated him—and sometimes me, too. Why would my mom keep telling us she was surprised by his wanting to leave *now*, when she knew all those years?" She picked at her lunch, puzzled.

"I can't answer that, Katy. You might ask your father."

"I'm not talking to him now. Micki and I haven't spoken to him or returned phone calls since this came up. Neither of us wants to encourage him to leave our mother." She paused a moment, wrinkling her nose and scrunching her eyes in thought. "You think that's a mistake, don't you?"

"I think it is, Katy. You know your father loves you and Micki. Why else would he have stayed all those years? It wasn't just to make general, you know."

"I hadn't thought of it that way. You're right. Mom rarely did anything with us. It was always Dad who took Micki and I places, and helped us with everything. I know he loved us."

There was a long pause as Katy mulled over the idea. Then she smiled and said, "We've been talking about them. What about you? Why did you disappear out of my life so suddenly? You talked me through much of my teen-aged angst. I've missed you."

"It wasn't by choice, Katy. I loved you and Micki very much, and I've missed you too. It's been a long time." She paused, wondering how she should answer. *The truth is usually better*, she thought. "I made the mistake of falling in love with your father, and it was just too painful to be nearby."

Katy didn't seem shocked. Rather she had the look of putting two and two together and at last getting four. Then her face bloomed in a slow smile. "Now that I'm thinking about that time, he was in love with you too, wasn't he? At least I remember how happy he was when you went along with us downtown, or when I got to go skiing with you two. You laughed and talked so easily."

"Then this doesn't surprise you so much? He'd been alone for a very long time when I met him, Katy. And they had already decided to separate. I feared you might hate me."

She smiled. "How could I hate you, Sara? Apparently, you understood my dad like you always understood me. We both needed you."

"In all honesty, I must tell you that our love wasn't intentional. It was just a very lonely and unhappy time in both our lives. We sort of grew together, Katy, and we dreamed of creating a calm and loving home for you girls. But it wasn't meant to be."

Katy cocked her head to one side and asked, "Why didn't he just leave? Why didn't you go with him?"

"We finally decided he had to stay with you and complete his duty to the Army. He couldn't leave you girls there alone all those years until you could be grown up and on your own."

"He passed up his chance to be happy--and so did you--for us?"

"You were the main consideration, my dear. We both loved you and Micki too much to put you through a separation from him. He needed to stay and protect you, and he couldn't ever have gotten custody."

"Why not? I'd have gone with him any place then. So would Micki."

"You'd have to ask your mother that, Katy. It's not for me

to say. The point is that he waited for you girls to grow up, and to complete his duty to the Army, before he moved out. He's never been good at dealing with anger, so he avoided any issues or friction as much as he could at home with your mom. Try to understand that now he just wants some peace as he grows older."

"Will you go to be with him once he's divorced?"

Sara's smiled sadly as she shook her head. "It's too late for that now, my dear. We had to decide many years ago that continually hoping for something we could never have was too painful for both of us. Since it seemed impossible that he would ever be free, I finally married a dear friend. Your dad encouraged me not to be alone forever. I couldn't ever hurt this person now when he's stood by me. Call it a matter of bad timing."

Sara brightened. "But, your dad and I are still best friends, Katy. We always promised we'd be there for each other in any crisis. I guess this is one of those crisis points. He's devastated that you and Micki don't understand his decision to move out. And neither of you is communicating with him so he can even explain his decision. The blues have hit him painfully hard. When I received his letter, he sounded so sad, I felt I had to talk to you."

"Mom says, 'I'll never give him a divorce so he can go off and marry some young wife.' You know how she always talks. Maybe she's just angry that he even asked again after so long."

"Perhaps they'll only separate, Katy. He just needs some peace from the fights, now that you girls are gone and don't need him in the house. He's growing older and needs more quiet."

"Yes, now I remember it all. I knew about the lack of peace and quiet. Perhaps he does need a little of that now. But, obviously you two have been in touch all these years or you wouldn't have known where to find me now."

"Yes, we've corresponded over the years, supported each other's goals, and discussed books. I loved you girls too, you know, and it was a terrible loss for me not to be allowed to contact you. Your dad kept me up to date--sent photos of your graduation and of Micki's first real horse."

Katy laughed. "I remember that horse! You'd have thought

she was a princess riding around."

"When you excelled on swim team, when Micki learned to drive and you learned tennis, when you went off to the university, some of Micki's writings…."

"Which ones? She writes a lot."

"A tone poem about walking on the coast in Maine was my favorite."

"Mine too. You loved us all those years? It must have been difficult. I never knew."

Sara chuckled. "There was a time when your dad and I thought you *did* know. We came very close to telling you."

"I'll bet I know." She laughed out loud. "Was that when we all skied together several times and I walked between you? I remember that I kept trying to get you to hold hands. We had such fun together. He was much happier then, and so was I. You know, it was my dream to have you both as my best friends forever."

"Ours too, Katy. It just couldn't be--not once we realized a divorce would have separated you from your dad. Neither of us believed your lives would have turned out as successfully if he hadn't been there to balance…the influences."

"And you agreed?"

"It was a joint decision. It hurt, of course, and we tried to work it out for awhile--we couldn't. We both knew we couldn't let you girls pay the price for our feelings. I also knew he needed to go on to be a general, too, and he wouldn't have made it with a messy divorce on his record." Sara smiled with mischief. "After all, didn't you enjoy having the handsome and respected General Sedgwick make your last parachute jump with you? He wanted to do that very much, though 'blooding' you, that old tradition of hitting on your jump wings to draw blood was, he said, one of the hardest things he had ever done--to hurt his 'little girl.'"

Katy laughed. "He hesitated so long I thought he couldn't do it, and I practically threatened him, whispering under my breath, "Do it! Just hit the wings and do it!" I was already hurting from breaking my leg on the previous jump and I just wanted him to hit my chest with his fist and the pin and get it over with so I could go to the hospital before I lost my balance and fell down."

Sara grinned. "I can imagine. He was so proud of you for making that last jump, injured leg and all, just to graduate with your unit. He felt you had the dedication to make a fine officer."

"I'm glad he was able to tell you about his triumphs and frustrations for all this time. It probably helped him get through." She smiled sadly. "I wish…."

"So do I, Katy, but I don't think we ever had a chance. Convention always wins, and we were both far too conventional to exist outside the rules. But our friendship has helped us both. I hope you understand better now and will accept his decision. He loves you girls beyond all else. Please don't turn on him now. He'll need you all the more in the future--you know that--especially with his cancer returning."

"You knew about that too?" Katy smiled. "He tried to keep it a secret. I think he's on radiation now."

"A lot of emotional pain came with it, Katy. That's all I can tell you. Actually, there's a lot he never told you or wanted you to know. I hope it doesn't hurt for me to be candid with you now that you're an adult. Perhaps you'll understand his feelings."

"I do, Sara." Katy smiled, taking Sara's hand across the table. "And what will you do now?"

"Continue to be his long distance friend, and yours too, I hope, now that we've found each other again."

"I know Mom would be angry if she found out we were friends again, but we can keep in touch, and I'll let you know what is happening with Micki and me."

"Your mom loves you too, Katy. And I'll be happy to hear from you or see you whenever you feel comfortable with it. You're always welcome wherever I happen to be…in whatever home I have."

"I'll remember that, Sara. I'm really grateful you called me today. Micki and I apparently jumped to conclusions and only listened to one side of a very complex story. Now, I understand. Thank you for being so honest. It must have been difficult for you to call me and to see me today. You did it out of loyalty to Dad, didn't you?"

"And out of loyalty to you and Micki. You girls need to understand your father as well as your mother. You mustn't take sides, Katy, because they both love you." He feels very isolated right now without you. You girls are his whole life. All decisions he ever made, good or bad, were to protect you."

Katy was silent for a moment. "You know, I had intended to go straight to my mom's on terminal leave from the Army, but now, I'm going to call Dad tonight and tell him I'm coming to see him first. I've missed him terribly." She grinned, happily. "We have some fences to mend, don't we?"

"I think so."

As they rose to leave, Katy took Sara's arm and said, "Thank you so much. I didn't realize all that he--that both of you, gave up for us. Telling me must have been painful for you, but I needed to know. And I *do* understand."

"Don't ever desert him, Katy, please. It would kill him after everything…. He loves you so much. I can't bear for him to be so unhappy without you." Tears welled up in Sara's eyes and they were already rolling unabashed down Katy's cheeks.

"I promise--not ever, Sara."

With a tearful hug, Katy was gone."

34

2005 – Maine   The hour grew late, the wind chilly, and the two were still talking quietly together, each sure there was far too much to catch up on to ever stop sharing.

"And so here we are, Love, just like old times, but with many years and painful changes in our lives."

"Not really so many changes."

"I know." He hugged her. "I can still see myself in your eyes—a revelation. Your eyes never lie. Are you all right with everything?"

"I think so. It's been a good life, and I've been safe from further pain. We've traveled, skied, lived comfortably without friction--better than I thought it might be. Casey and I are comfortable old friends and we love each other in a special way. He's been good to my girls, and to me." She paused. "And you?"

"I've survived. These years I've been retired and living alone, it's no longer a crisis. It's peaceful, at least. And my girls visit."

"Too bad you hadn't been closer to retirement 20 years ago. But you've done well, Neil. You made that difference for the Army. It was what you always dreamed."

"You know, it's strange, the changes in Grafenwohr that I worried so much about in 1980 are probably obsolete since 9/11. What a horrible tragedy and, like so many others, I lost friends at both the Pentagon and at our favorite building, the World Trade Center. As I watched it fall, my heart stopped." He sighed. "Terrorism tactics won't necessarily be stopped by the training ranges we built back then. It's a new kind of war, and someone will need to come along with new solutions." He smiled. "We're obsolete now, aren't we, Love? But I'm content that there are fine young men and women ready to carry on the Army's duty."

"You made a good and respected general--much to be proud of. I've heard nothing but good things about you."

He laughed softly. "I *had* to. You practically threatened me if I

302 M. J. Brett

didn't, though I admit it hurt me to hear you say I needed to 'go off and be a general.' I thought about those words that night, and almost daily since. You knew that wasn't all of it…the girls…."

Sara touched her finger lightly to his lips. "I knew that, but it was the only way to help you walk away, and for me to walk away as well. I meant it in a positive way. You really *did* need to be a general and make that difference, for us. Otherwise, it would all have been for nothing."

They talked of their shared intellectual friendship, and Neil congratulated Sara on her think tank papers and her latest book. "You outdid yourself--some of the best things you've ever written."

"I enjoy your writing, too. Our E:mails hum, don't they?"

They sat quietly, barely touching. Their companionable silence was a type of communication, too. Neil said, "When I think of all the times we've come to rescue each other over the years, I want to thank you. You've been there at the crisis points--especially now."

She smiled at him. "I promised you, didn't I? And I always keep promises. I guess there *were* quite a few times we rode to the rescue on the shiny white horse, weren't there? Let's see, there was my trip to Boston while you were taking an advanced degree, and you sounded so depressed."

Neil chuckled. "You always did worry about my frame of mind whenever I lost confidence. Then there was the time we got lost on the NY subway, and I missed my ferry back to Governor's Island and had to sleep in the Coast Guard Station. And don't forget when you got hurt badly at skiing, and I came to Germany to see that you were getting good care from Casey. I needn't have worried. He loves you too."

" It did my heart good to see you get off that train straight from a NATO meeting in your general's uniform, every inch the leader. I've been so proud of you. We've done okay, haven't we? We've never let this beat us. We've kept smiling."

Neil kissed the palm of her hand by way of answer.

The simple and long-remembered gesture brought a wave of nostalgia, and she fought to regain composure. *He mustn't die…I can't give him up again.*

Their eyes locked, and he knew that she knew. He rescued the moment. "How about that quick visit to go skiing in Germany with both of you?" he said much too jovially. That was fun going again to a Christmas market downtown and sharing *Gluhwein* and *Lebkuchen*--seemed like old times, and we all laughed lots. I could see that Casey was good to you. I needed so much to know that."

"I worried about you when you finally felt it was safe to leave Faye again in the 90's. Katy, was really angry with you."

"Of all the times you've rescued me, that one was the most important. That hurt so badly. I didn't know how to make the girls understand." He brought Sara's hand to his cheek. "I never asked what you said to Katy to change her view that I was 'rat of the year' for leaving her mother 'suddenly, in her old age.' Faye gave her an earful, and she believed it all. Katy wouldn't even talk to me."

"I only told her the truth, that this wasn't sudden at all--that both you and her mom had known for years that you were incompatible, and you had stayed as long as you could. I even reminded her she had known for herself at fourteen that you were unhappy. She remembered then, even though Faye had complained mightily to her ever since, and accused you of all sorts of things."

"Did she ask?"

"She asked, and I told her the truth--that we had been in love but that there was no way we could be together and still protect her and Micki--that you had stayed all those years just to see them through to adulthood. She finally understood and was sympathetic to the sacrifices we've endured. We shed a few tears over it, and she promised she'd come see you and make up--that you two needed each other."

"Believe me, it was a blessing that you talked to her. We've been comfortable together ever since. I don't know what I would have done if the girls hadn't finally understood why I needed to leave. After everything you and I gave up...."

"I know. I felt Katy would understand if someone just told her the truth. I don't know if she ever told Micki, but at least they've tolerated the separation well since then."

"Isn't it ironic--Faye still tells her lawyer she needs more money, when I'm paying her under the separation agreement more than she can possibly spend. She's dyed her hair, lost weight, and bought a new wardrobe--finally. I didn't recognize her. It just wasn't worth any more court battles or verbal tirades to pursue the divorce. Let her keep her precious 'Mrs. General' title as long as she keeps away from me. We never see each other. Since it's too late for me to have you with me now, anyway, a separation is okay. At least I don't have to listen to her anger."

"Katy writes me that she '…goes to visit her father and then her mother,' as though that's quite normal. She thinks the separation was a good idea, for both of you. She almost sees it as funny now, that you two played that game so long."

"Our New York visit wasn't funny though my dear, was it? I never needed you more."

" I would have had to come, that time, whatever the risk. I was terrified when you wrote me you had cancer, when you spoke of the 'beast' you felt was inside where you couldn't control it." She chuckled. "You always did keep trying to be in control. Cancer doesn't cooperate with that idea any more than Faye ever did."

"You could always tell when I was feeling insecure."

"Of course, I had to laugh at your loss of 'pride' when you thought you were having a nice 'private' prostate operation, only to awake and find your vital signs being broadcast to military units around the world during Desert Storm." She smiled as he shook his head. "I think you saw the disadvantages of a general officer being considered an 'asset' by the Army. They *all* had to be informed of your availability and condition, right down to how much urine your body was producing. It would have been funny, had you not felt so uncomfortable with the loss of privacy. Under the microscope once again, weren't you?" She squeezed his hand to let him know her understanding of his embarrassment.

"Of course, that wasn't the worst of it. After surgery, when we knew they hadn't been able to get it all, Faye kept telling me that 'now I was no longer a man--that I would never be able to satisfy *any* woman,' not that she had ever cared. I knew she meant you, like you might just turn up again out of the blue. She knew there was never anyone else in my life. I needed you--for moral and emotional support. I felt all hope for life had ended."

"I was on the next plane when you wrote that she had gone behind your back to suggest your surgeon castrate you--that was the last straw! She had no right—you were fighting for your life. I had to come. It seemed as though you accepted her words as truth and believed her put-downs, instead of knowing your own self worth. That was a problem between you two. I didn't want you accepting her views on that topic. I knew she was wrong."

Neil took Sara's face in his hands and smiled. "My dear, I knew as soon as you walked off the plane that Faye was wrong. Just seeing your smile turned me on until I wanted to make love to you right there in the airport, and I wasn't even recuperated yet."

Sara chuckled, low and warmly. "I could tell that. We just needed time together to talk about positions or methods that would still work for you after such devastating surgery. I did the research. You knew I'd come, so you wouldn't give up on yourself, or on loving again someday, in case you might ever have been free."

"And Casey?"

"He knew, and he had no qualms about my going. He understood that I couldn't ignore that letter. He knows I love him in a different way, and that I would never betray him, but I could never have turned my back on you, either." She sighed. "He once told me that he thought it was possible to care for different people in different ways. Over the years, I've decided he was right."

"Does he mind us talking out here the whole night?"

"Not at all. He's reading, or maybe he's in bed by now. He knows we have a lot of catching up to do---that you needed me to come help you through this episode. He cares about you, too, you know. He and I understand each other. We're *both* worried."

Neil nodded. Then he smiled and said, "I'd really like it better if he thought I might need to be shot or something. You know, like the joke about how a guy wanted to die, '...being shot by a jealous husband at age ninety.'" He looked out at the bay, now dark and shiny in the starlight. "At least that would be quick and painless, wouldn't it, and a great story for my West Point classmates to spread?"

"Not a chance, my dear…merely wishful thinking." She smiled brightly and squeezed his hand, knowing that Neil was understandably wondering about how the end would *really* come.

He changed the subject. "We've always had just plain fun together, and it's reassuring to me that our companionship never ends. You know, it was never just about making love between us, though that was always lovely, too, in the good old days." He grinned with mischief, for a moment, just like the old Neil.

"But, we've had so much more together. Your being beside me through both the good and the bad has mattered so much." He put his free hand over hers to close it in. "Of course, we talk our heads off, as usual. We never could stop talking, could we?"

She nodded, thinking about how important communication had been between them.

"It's been too long a time apart before this," he added.

"I was scared this time, Neil, with your heart on top of your cancer coming back yet again. When we were conversing on E-mail that day, I knew something was wrong when you complained of dizziness and pressure, saying it was 'probably only your imagination.' I felt sure it wasn't. You've never been 'imaginative,' my dear. It was two weeks before I knew what had happened. It was another of those 'wait until you are safe' things-- *déjà vu*--only this time with the danger of a multiple bypass."

"I've been aware lately that too many things are going wrong with my body. I guess I suspected years ago that those Agent Orange episodes weren't going away."

"You'll get on top of them again. Why, in '98, when cancer came back the third time, you wrote me, 'Don't you worry. I'll kick this beast again with chemo.' Optimism will win out *this* time too, my dear—it must!" She fought not to cry.

"You always could read between the lines and know what I was thinking. You knew I was scared then, even though I tried to sound upbeat. But this time--God, Sara, this is the fourth time now, and metastasizing into the bones is pretty ominous…." His voice trailed off, and they listened to the waves lapping against the shore in the darkness, clutching their fingers together.

Neil sighed. "Maybe I'll find my Valhalla yet. You know, I still like to remember that snowy day with you beside me, exploring together. I keep that thought close to me to get through, because this time, I don't know who will win—the beast or me."

"I knew you'd need to talk about it, Darling. I'm here, and you know I'm praying and believing *you* will win."

"You've always believed in me too much, Sara--my biggest fan and cheering section. It's sad that I let you down again and again over the years--my life's greatest regret. I fear you may believe in me too much this time. Please don't be disappointed in me, my love, if I can't win this battle. I'm trying, but...."

"I could never be disappointed in you, Neil."

They talked late into the night, holding hands and sharing hugs for mutual support when either felt pain or doubt.

"Do you ever think about it, that our little boy would be in college by now?"

"Pretty often, actually, wondering how I might have helped you more. It still bothers me that I couldn't spare you—that I didn't even know you were in trouble."

They held each other quietly, remembering this additional painful sadness in their emotional lives together.

He finally spoke again. "And now, again, we don't know how this adventure will turn out, do we, Love?"

"Whatever happens, we'll be with you, whenever you say."

He chuckled. "You can do one thing for me. When they put me away, I want you standing by to say something funny that will make me sit up in my casket and laugh at the solemnity of the whole damned thing. I'd love to see Faye's face when she realizes she took me to the cleaners and ruined my life, but you and I are still friends, that our devotion never ended, in spite of her hatred and threats. And we'll be able to laugh about it all. You can bet she'll be there to crow over my demise--and her half of the inheritance."

Sara smiled quietly, knowing it was time to hide her breaking heart. "I guess I know quite a few stories that will make you laugh, under *any* circumstances. For starters, I seem to remember a ski bus delivering an injured member of the Wild Bunch to the Nurnberg Military Hospital with her broken leg, singing bawdy songs all the way to entertain her. You took care of a sticky situation when the officer in charge thought it 'highly irregular' and didn't want to admit her to emergency surgery in the middle of the night. That's the only time I've ever seen you pull rank. You drew yourself up to your full height, hiccupped loudly, and announced, 'I'm Lt. Col. Sedgewick, Captain. Take her in to surgery—*now*--or I'll lead this whole busload of drunks in singing at the top of their lungs until you do. If we wake the rest of the hospital, your commander should be *very* pleased.' The poor man moved pretty fast. It was the talk of the Post for weeks."

Neil roared with laughter, until pain overtook him and he doubled over, grabbing Sara's hand as she kept him from falling.

"I'll assume that obligation of a story for you," she said quietly, holding him close. "Just be sure you don't make it too soon, and remember that date of ours in the *next* lifetime, okay?"

When he got his breath, he said, "Actually, we're almost living it here, aren't we? We've walked on the beach as much as my hip joints will stand, we've kissed goodbye, and we've held each other to watch the stars. Have we missed anything, Love?"

"I would never have missed any part of it for all the world, Neil--the joy *and* the pain. It's been a marvelous journey together, one we both know will never end. We'll still have that *next* lifetime, my dearest love."

She touched his face with her fingers, her hands now older and more wrinkled, but her touch still soothed his worst fears.

"When I think of all the people who have missed devotion and loyalty to another human being--the gift of it," he said quietly, pulling her hand to his lips and kissing her palm one last time. "We've at least had that, no matter what happens…or how soon…

Epilog

The general officer corps is a close knit club and the General Officer Management Office (GOMO) sends out a formal notice every time an officer turns in his mess kit and is honorably discharged from the ranks of the living:

"It is with deep regret that we inform you of the death of Brigadier General Neil Sedgwick--retired. He passed away in September. A graduate of West Point and a veteran of Vietnam, he retired after 30 years of distinguished service to the nation as an officer of engineers. He was 65 years old at the time of his death. General Sedgwick is survived by his wife and two daughters. Funeral services will be held at Fort Myer with internment at Arlington National Cemetery.

It was a crisp fall day at Fort Myer, Virginia. Across the Potomac River in the distance stretched the Washington Mall with the Lincoln Memorial, the Washington Monument, and the Capitol, almost in line.

The Caisson Platoon had been at work for over three hours. The horses were fed, washed and groomed until their coats glistened like satin. The soldiers assigned to the funeral detail polished their leather--knee-high boots, saddles and harnesses. Brass buttons and buckles gleamed. They rolled the horse drawn caisson out of the barn and ensured that it looked as shiny as the day it had been delivered to the Army nearly 150 years ago.

The enlisted men harnessed six horses to the caisson and saddled two additional horses. One awaited the commander of the funeral detail--the other was outfitted with a pair of riding boots in the stirrups facing to the rear. This was the traditional "riderless horse" to follow the caisson in honor of the deceased general.

The horses of the Army's ceremonial unit were handsome

animals, and the soldiers were resplendent in their Army blue uniforms with a gold stripe down their trousers. The chinstraps of hats were cinched tightly in place.

The lieutenant in charge approached and was formally saluted by the sergeant. "Sir, the funeral detail is prepared."

Lieutenant Krstulovich ordered, "Mount up!" Four men mounted horses harnessed to the caisson. Another took the bridle of the riderless horse and led him into position behind the caisson. The lieutenant maneuvered his mount into lead position. He turned to face the detail and reached a white glove-covered hand into the side pocket of his uniform to withdraw a small piece of paper. Reading from it, he announced, "Today's funeral is in honor of Brigadier General Neil Sedgwick." He then turned his mount and led the procession out of the stable area onto Jackson Avenue, toward the Fort Myer Post Chapel.

It is a familiar scene at Fort Myer. Almost every day a fallen warrior is remembered and honored by his family and friends and interred in the adjacent Arlington National Cemetery. The cemetery, most of it occupying land seized by the government from the estate of the family of Robert E. Lee during the Civil War, is the burial ground for many of our Nation's military. The funeral detail had conducted these ceremonial duties many times, and every soldier was proud to play his part. Fort Myer, one of the oldest Posts in the Army, was proud of its role also. As the horses clomped along the pavement, cars reverently pulled to curbs and stopped to yield way. Pedestrians along the sidewalks stopped and stood silent as they passed.

The procession came to a halt directly in front of the Old Post Chapel. Lt. Krstulovich ordered his men to dismount and move quickly to hold the horses.

Neil's funeral continued inside. Someone delivered a eulogy and words like "dedicated," "patriotic" and "hard-working" were heard through the open doorway, punctuated at times with soft laughter when some old friend told a "Neil story."

In due time, the service concluded, and the congregation joined together to sing Julia Ward Howe's "Battle Hymn of the

Republic." Chaplain Williamson, the Fort Myer Post Chaplain delivered the benediction as he had done so many times before.

Neil's funeral was over. Attendees streamed outside and stood in two groups on either side of the walkway making room for the pallbearers and casket. Nearly the last to exit were Faye and her daughters, one on each side. Faye was dressed in a long black dress. A widow's veil covered her face. She was making a great show of crying and wiping her eyes frequently under the veil. Sara stood quietly in the cortege on Casey's arm, wondering whether Faye's tears were genuine regret or false posturing.

Both Katy and Micki had acknowledged Sara's presence with a shy wave of their hands, but Sara didn't want to intrude on their sorrow. She only smiled back softly and nodded. Faye was unaware of her presence and would not have recognized her after so many years, anyway. Silently, Sara prayed, *please Dear God, after so much suffering at the end, please let Neil find his Valhalla wrapped in Your loving care.* She bit her lip to keep from crying out at the stabbing pain in her chest. *He tried to comfort me on the phone by saying it had been a complete life, and he was ready, but I wasn't....* She looked up at trees nearby to try to control tears.

Slowly, reverently, the pallbearers and flag draped casket emerged from the double doors of the chapel and made their way to the caisson. The pallbearers, all of whom were Neil's' fellow officers, lifted their burden chest high and slid it onto the platform. The soldiers secured the casket in place, and firmly anchored the nation's flag of red, white and blue to the casket so that the breeze would not catch it. Lt. Krstulovich again gave the order for his men to mount. The funeral procession—soldiers, caisson, riderless horse, with mourners in trail, left the chapel behind and entered Arlington National Cemetery through the nearby gate in the stone wall that separated it from Fort Myer.

It took over twenty minutes for the procession moving at the pace of the dignified horse's walk to reach section J well down the hill where the cemetery flattened as the terrain approached the Potomac. Neil's grave was sited across from the Pentagon and offered a scenic view of the nation's capitol in the distance.

When the procession arrived, Faye, "Mrs. General" to the end, nodding to other generals assembled on either side, was escorted with her daughters to graveside and seated on folding chairs. The remainder of the procession left the roadway and moved to stand nearby. When all were in place, the soldiers and pallbearers moved the casket of the general to his grave. Chaplain Williamson delivered a short prayer.

Micki sobbed as Katy tried to comfort her sister through her own tears. The honor guard fired an eleven-gun salute. A bugler from the Army Band, affectionately nicknamed "Pershing's Own" after the Army general who had first established the band, stood under a nearby tree. He lifted his instrument and played "Taps." As the haunting notes of the familiar dirge echoed across the thousands of gravestones in the cemetery, the flag was removed and the casket of this respected soldier was lowered into his grave. "Taps" always brings tears to a military person's eyes. It is a last "good-night" and signifies the end of life for a warrior.

Sara watched with sadness as Katy and Micki held hands until the last notes died away leaving only the echo behind. Suddenly feeling as though she would fall, Sara leaned on Casey for support. He tightened his hand around hers. She could only think of the last message on her answering machine when she got home from an errand saying incoherently, "I'm trying to find you, but the branches are blowing against the windows, and I can't find you...I'm sorry, my Love. I can't hold on...." The line had gone dead. *Of all days for me to be gone...I'll never forgive myself.* She couldn't stop her tears. Casey handed her a handkerchief and put his arm around her shoulders, tightly holding her steady.

The soldiers expertly folded the flag into thirds along its length and then into small triangles. The binding along the edge was tucked in so that only white stars on the blue background showed. The sergeant accepted the flag, turned to Lieutenant Krstulovich, placed it reverently into his outstretched hands, stood back and saluted.

The young lieutenant turned slowly and moved in front of Faye. Bending to where Faye was seated, in a low voice he said,

"Mrs. Sedgwick, on behalf of a grateful nation, I present this flag to you for the service of your husband to the United States of America." He stood upright, took one step back and saluted.

Faye stood and acknowledged condolences from several of Neil's fellow officers and their wives who shook hands and spoke kind words to her and to Katy and Micki. She said little--only nodded regally until the last of them moved away from the grave toward their cars on the roadway.

Suddenly, Faye firmly planted her feet and hurled the flag into the open grave. There was a collective gasp from those few remaining witnesses to this sacrilege.

Defiantly, Faye shouted, "There, you son of a bitch! I told you I'd live to see you into your grave! Damn you forever!" She turned and strode away toward the family limo, dragging Micki with a firm grip on the young woman's arm.

The minister, the funeral detail, a few last mourners and Sara and Neil, who had waited to speak to Katy and Micki alone, were aghast. Hushed voices tried to make sense of this unexpected and disrespectful act. All of them military, they couldn't witness such a thing without intense and personal shock, both for their friend, and for their flag so dishonored on hallowed ground.

Above their voices, Katy screamed, "Mother!" Her cry was a shriek of pain.

The sergeant moved towards the flag to retrieve it. He stopped when Lieutenant Krstulovich held up his hand and ordered calmly, "Leave our country's flag with the general. He will honor it in death as he has in life. Fill in the grave."

Sara moved quickly toward Katy as the young woman turned an anguished face to find her. Katy sobbed uncontrollably on her shoulder as Sara wrapped both arms around her in comfort.

When Faye entered her limousine by the curb, Micki broke away from the angry woman and raced back to her sister and Sara to be included in the embrace. Faye's limousine drove away.

Sara stood at the graveside with one arm around each sobbing young woman and watched tearfully as the grave filled. Neil was, indeed, wrapped in the flag of his nation, with duty, honor, and country to comfort him. He would find his Valhalla in Heaven, much as they had found Valhalla on earth, the haven for dutiful warriors, one snowy day long years ago.

The last graveside mourners dispersed amid a hushed murmur of astonishment that Faye had so dishonored her late husband.

Even through her tears, Sara slowly became aware of a warm glow--a decided feeling of contentment, as though she could feel Neil's presence, laughing at this final irony. She understood at last, who needed her after all.

She murmured to the young women in her arms, "We grieve for those who've given us most joy, my dears, and your father has given us all great joy." As Katy and Micki turned their faces to hear, she whispered, "I can almost hear your father's last words ringing in my ears. At the time, I didn't know completely what he meant, but now I do. He said, 'True devotion never ends, in this world or the next.'

Katy leaned against Sara and reached out for Casey's hand. "I understand, Sara. He's here with us still, isn't he?"

"He always will be in our hearts."

The man she had loved for so long, who had brought her so much happiness and so much heartbreak, was at eternal rest. Here in her arms, Sara held his most precious legacy. She gave each a hug, as Casey embraced them all--in his own way, as always, protecting those entrusted to his care. They turned to walk slowly away together.

> *"And when our work is done,*
> *Our course on Earth is run,*
> *May it be said, "Well done:*
> *Be thou at peace."*

(Taken from West Point's tribute to fallen warriors)

About the Author

M. J. Brett (a.k.a. Margaret Brettschneider) always loved reading and telling stories, from her three-year-old imaginary sagas told to a farm cat (the only one who would listen) to the classics. But writing was on hold until she retired from teaching. Everyone knows teachers have little time for their own pursuits.

Twenty-one years teaching literature and journalism on U.S. military bases in Germany and marrying an Army pilot triggered her interest in the unique challenges of our nation's military families. From both single life and that of officer's lady, Ms Brett has seen all sides of the marital enigma.

Watching five friends whose marriages fell apart under the stress of command, Ms Brett began to wonder what characteristics in a military marriage enabled it to succeed and what caused it to fail. Were military people that much different from civilians? Did a wife who believed in fairy tales become disillusioned and turn to alcohol or violence? Did an officer find he had more difficult decisions on the home front than in battle? Could couples be driven apart by coldness or lack of spontaneity? What were realistic expectations in families torn by war and the threat of war? Could an officer's career suffer through efficiency ratings that reflected his private life as much as his command decisions? These interesting psychological questions, plus the unending variety of emotion and error inherent in *all* human relationships, prompted this novel of an unconventional love, *Between Duty and Devotion.*

This is Ms Brett's third novel. Her first, *Mutti's War,* tells of a mother forced to smuggle her children across Europe during WWII. It won the prestigious Paul Gillette Award for Historical Fiction in 2003.

Shadows on an Iron Curtain tells of life on the Cold War Border delineated by both communist intrigue and the unique camaraderie of those soldiers who defended against it.

Ms Brett and her husband retired from their overseas military lifestyle in 1995 to enjoy life in Colorado Springs.

Letters from readers on M.J. Brett's other novels: *Mutti's War* and *Shadows on an Iron Curtain*

Ms. Brett:

I had to let you know how much my colleagues at the Red Cross loved *Mutti's War*. Once started, none of us could lay it down. You are batting 1,000 here in Alexandria. Thank you for such a great book!!! Christa L.

Dear M.J.Brett:

This book needs to be in everyone's hands. I was particularly intrigued with the view of World War II from inside the enemy's camp, and the strength Mutti gained as she fought not only her own government, but her discoveries as well. How she had the strength to make her decisions, yet keep them secret, I'll never know. There was a will of steel under that cloak of daintiness.   Elaine P.

Dear M.J. Brett:

When will your next book be ready? Please reserve one for us! Is there anything we can do to help you to write faster?   Cathie and Bob D.

M.J. Brett: *Shadows* is a great read. It seems, now, that all anyone remembers of the Cold War is the Berlin Wall--never our more dangerous and secret Border. I especially liked your portrayal of our aircraft being "painted." My kids never understood the term when I tried to tell them what it was like guarding the communist Border. Now they know. Thank you. Please do another book soon.   Jake S.

Dear M.J. Brett,

Having been an Army pilot flying the communist Border, I can only say, "Bravo" for your portrayal of the dangers we faced in your book, *Shadows on an Iron Curtain.* I've found no one else who ever told our story or understood the frustrations as well. At last, someone who knows what NOE means! Others should understand that the Cold War was not as "Cold" as most Americans thought at the time. Thank you for "getting it right."   Frank M.